The Fake Out

THE VANCOUVER STORM SERIES

STEPHANIE ARCHER

For Helen Camisa, who believes everyone deserves to move and feel good in their body

ISBN: 978-1-7382088-1-4

Editing: Happily Ever Author

Proofreading: VB Edits

Cover design: Echo Grayce at Wildheart

Cover illustration: Chloe Friedlein

CONTENT WARNING

Some details of the professional hockey world have been adjusted for your reading enjoyment.

To check content warnings for this book, scan the QR code below or visit www.stephaniearcherauthor.com/content-warnings

CHAPTER 1

RORY

BLOOD POUNDS in my ears as I skate toward the net during my first game with the Vancouver Storm. We're tied in overtime, and there's a crescendo of noise from the crowd as I rear back and slapshot the puck at the net.

It pings off the crossbar, and the Vancouver fans let out a collective groan of disappointment.

Stars score goals. My dad, Canadian hockey legend Rick Miller, has said it so many times over the years, and it's what I chant to myself as I snag the puck out of the mess of players and skate backward until I'm open.

The whistle blows, the game stops, and I look over to the pretty girl who's been catching my attention all night.

Hazel Hartley, one of the team physiotherapists—stunning and sharp-tongued, with long, dark lashes, a plush mouth the perfect shade of pink, and the most striking blue-gray eyes I've ever seen—sitting behind the net with her sister, Pippa, looking like she'd rather be anywhere else.

Hazel Hartley, my high school tutor who had a boyfriend, who can't stand me and doesn't date hockey players anymore. Despite Pippa wearing a Storm jersey with the name of her fiancé, goaltender Jamie Streicher, on the back, and despite

Hartley working for the team, I haven't seen her in a jersey since high school. Tonight, my gaze catches on her chestnut hair pulled up in a ponytail, her pale purple puffer jacket. I bet she's wearing the black leggings that always make her ass look incredible.

I wink at her; she rolls her eyes.

I grin; she pretends to yawn.

Something electric and addictive floods my veins at our back-and-forth. It's always been like this with us, ever since high school.

The players line up for a face-off and I pull my attention back to the game. Around the arena, the fans are getting anxious, desperate for a win. The whistle blows and I'm off, hustling the puck toward the goalie again.

"Let's go, Miller," Coach Ward calls from the bench.

Determination fires through me. Tate Ward wanted the top scorer in the league, so I need to show him what he paid for. I've idolized him since he was a player.

Playing for him this season will fix whatever's gone wrong in my head. It has to.

Hayden Owens, a Vancouver defenseman, is open. He has a clear shot on net, but stars score goals, and I'm not here to pass the puck.

I snap the puck toward the goalie; it hits the back of the net, and the arena explodes with noise at my game-winning goal. The goal horn bellows, the arena lights flash, and the rest of the Vancouver team surrounds me. Over at the bench, guys are cheering. Even quiet and serious Coach Ward is clapping. I wait for the consuming, proud feeling in my chest that this moment should bring.

Nothing. Fans rattle the glass and the team surrounds me, but I experience blank, silent emptiness.

Shit.

I used to care. Scoring goals used to make me feel on top of the world, like nothing could touch me. Now, I feel flat, like I'm checking a box. Playing professional hockey, being the best in the league, used to be my dream, but these days, it feels like a job.

Coming to Vancouver to play for Ward, to play with goaltender Jamie Streicher, my best friend—these things were supposed to change that.

"Look alive, Miller." Owens grabs me by the shoulders and tries to put me in a headlock. "You just won the game."

I laugh and shove him off, shove away all the weird thoughts as we skate past the net to the bench. When we pass Hazel, I give her the cocky, smug grin I know pisses her off.

Fans watch as I tap my stick against the glass and she lifts her gaze to meet mine, arching an eyebrow as if to say, *what, asshole?*

Do you want an autograph? I mouth, making the signing motion in the air.

I watch her lips curve into a cool smile. *You wish,* she mouths back at me as she stands.

My chest expands with a tight, excited feeling. No one talks to me like Hartley does. I've always liked that about her.

And these days, sparring with her? It's the only time I actually feel something.

Beside her, Pippa grins at me, waving. "Nice goal, Rory," she calls over the glass.

Owens pounds on the glass, waving at her, and she laughs, eyes lighting up as Streicher, her fiancé, skates up to greet her with a quiet smile.

Something tugs around my heart as I watch Pippa blow a kiss to him. Behind her, Hartley's already halfway up the stairs that lead out of the arena, ponytail bouncing with each step.

She *is* wearing the leggings, and her ass *does* look incredible.

"I think Hartley likes me," I say to the guys over the arena music, keeping my eyes on her retreating form.

Owens laughs, and even surly Streicher snorts.

"Not a fucking chance, bud," Owens crows, slapping me on the back as we skate off the ice.

My competitive, determined instincts roar to life, honed by years of hockey and training. I thrive on a challenge, and I hate losing.

Hartley not giving me the time of day sticks in my mind like a thorn. I like her, but I don't know how to make something happen with her. I think, deep down, she likes me, too.

Hockey is everything, my dad always says. *Hockey comes first.*

Getting hung up on a girl is a dangerous game, but I can't seem to forget about Hazel Hartley.

"Miller," Coach Ward calls as I head down the corridor to the dressing room. "Stop by my office after postgame press."

I nod and make my way to the showers, head still filled with thoughts of Hazel.

———

After my sit-down with Ward, I return to the dressing room, thoughts whirring. Streicher's in there still, gathering up his stuff.

"Good game tonight," he says with a nod.

I bite the inside of my cheek as the weird thoughts about feeling empty and the wins not being as sweet anymore threaten to spill out. Streicher and I have played hockey together since we were five years old, and I trust him more than anyone, but after what Ward said upstairs, I know I need to keep it to myself.

"Are you meeting Pippa?" I ask instead as we haul our bags up and head out.

She usually waits for him in the team's private box upstairs with the other partners and family. Maybe her sister's with her.

"She went straight home. She didn't want to be out late tonight because of the engagement party."

"Right." It's tomorrow night at a restaurant in Gastown, near their apartment.

We head down the concourse, nodding good night to the arena staff.

"What did Ward want?"

Anxiety spikes in my gut. "He offered me captain."

Streicher's eyes meet mine, flaring with the same surprise I felt. "Really?"

"Ward knows talent when he sees it." I give him my cockiest, most winning smile, but my chest is still tight with uncertainty.

Clean up your act this season. Earn your spot, Miller, Ward said. *Be the captain this team needs.*

Last year when I played for Calgary, and before we patched things up, I started a fight on the ice with Streicher. During another game, I got pissed off at the fans and flipped them the middle finger, earning myself a penalty and a spot on the sports highlights for the rest of the week. Tonight, when the goal horn blared and the rest of the team was congratulating me, I didn't care.

None of these things are in line with a good captain. I'm not the leader type. I'm the asshole. The superstar. The guy everyone loves to hate.

"You going to do it?" he asks.

"I have to." My throat feels thick. "I'm on a one-year contract."

When he started with the team last season, Ward traded for a handful of free agents, signing them for short terms, citing to the press that he wasn't just acquiring players, he was creating a team. At the end of the season, about half of those guys were traded.

"If I want to stay in Vancouver," I add, "I need to keep Ward happy." I rake my hand through my hair. "And Ward's the only guy I want to play for."

A decade ago, Tate Ward was one of the most promising players in the history of professional hockey—until he blew out his knee and ended his career. His posters were all over my bedroom wall. Besides me, he's the only other guy to have beaten my dad's stats.

"Ward's different," I tell Jamie.

Every coach I've played for, including my dad when he took over the peewee team Streicher and I played for, used aggression and intimidation to motivate players. Ward doesn't yell. He barely fucking talked during this week's practices. He explained the plays and watched. Once in a while, he'd bring a player over to the side and give them quiet notes.

I've always been a sucker for fatherly approval, and I want to make Ward proud.

Jamie makes an acknowledging noise in his throat as we reach the elevators to the parking garage.

"And, uh, now that you and I are good again," I hit the elevator call button, "I like playing on the same team."

We don't talk about what happened—the seven-year stretch where Streicher and I didn't talk because I was stupid enough to listen to my dear old dad's advice. *Don't be friends with guys on the opposing team,* he said when we were drafted.

Rick Miller's never been an expert on any type of relationship, but it took me a while to figure that out.

We listen to the sounds of the elevator changing floors, and Streicher nods. "I'm happy you're here, too, man. So is Pippa." The corner of his mouth twitches, the grumpy fucker's version of a full-blown smile, and something eases inside me.

Maybe this captain thing is the kick in the ass I need. Maybe this is what finally fixes whatever's broken in my head. A new challenge.

"I thought you just took the trade so you could bug Hartley all year," he adds.

I crook a playful grin at him, thinking about the way she yawned tonight. What a fucking brat. "Maybe a little."

I think about playing for another team and not having someone to tease, and I get that flat, uninspired feeling I had after I scored the goal tonight.

"I can see it. You being captain." He hits the button on the elevator panel again, impatient.

I know I'm not the right guy, but it lit that flare of competition and challenge in my blood again. I have to try.

Our phones both chirp.

"That'll be the announcement," I tell him as he pulls his phone out.

"Yep." He scrolls, reading the email. "Rory Miller, new captain of the Vancouver Storm."

The elevator finally arrives and we step in, Streicher still reading as I hit the button to bring us to the parking garage.

"There's a new trade," he mutters.

"Who is it?" Between the juniors and our years in the league, we've played with or against almost everyone.

"Connor McKinnon."

I freeze, gaze snapping to Streicher's as a bad feeling moves through my gut. "That's—"

"Yep." He glares at his phone, rereading. "Hazel's ex."

My shoulders tense. I fucking hate that prick.

Yes, I'm a cocky, antagonistic asshole who needs to be the center of attention. But McKinnon? McKinnon is fucking *scum*. He went to our high school. For two years, I watched Hazel make goddamned heart eyes at him while he barely cared. He talked down to her. Dismissed her. On and off the ice, he's aggressive and entitled.

Pippa said they broke up sometime toward the end of Hazel's first year at university. I don't know what happened, but Hazel doesn't date hockey players anymore.

Protective instincts rage through me. I don't want him anywhere near her.

"Who's his physio?" I ask, clearing my throat and trying to keep my voice casual.

Streicher sighs, and I'm already shaking my head.

"Hazel," he says.

Fuck. I need to do something about this.

Tomorrow, at Streicher and Pippa's engagement party, I'll talk to her.

CHAPTER 2
HAZEL

"CONGRATULATIONS," I say into Pippa's hair as we hug at her engagement party the next evening. "I love you and I'm so happy for you two, but if he breaks your heart, I'll photoshop pictures of him in diapers with a dominatrix and release them on the internet."

We pull back and she grins. The intimate restaurant I booked for the event is filled with our family, Vancouver Storm players and their partners, and a few friends from the tour Pippa opened for this summer as a singer-songwriter while she promoted her new album.

"I'm just kidding," I tell her, tugging on a lock of her long, wavy, honey-blond hair.

She laughs. "I know."

Under the soft, dim lighting in the restaurant, she's glowing. Maybe that's what happens to people when they fall head over heels like my sister did. Jamie needed an assistant when he moved to Vancouver; little did he know it would be his high school crush who he'd end up engaged to.

Behind her, Jamie looks on with a small smile, leaning down to give me a big hug.

"I'm not kidding," I whisper, and he snorts.

"Thanks for organizing this." His eyes go to Pippa, who's deep in conversation with our parents and Jamie's mom. "It means a lot to us."

Emotion rises up my throat. "You're welcome. I really am thrilled for you two." I give him a tentative smile. "I know she's everything to you and you'll take care of her, and I'm happy you're going to be my brother-in-law."

He arches an eyebrow, but there's a teasing spark in his eyes. "Even if I'm a hockey player?"

I huff a laugh. At the beginning of their relationship, I made my thoughts on hockey players—that they're treated like gods and feel entitled to whatever and whoever they want—very clear to Pippa. "You're the exception. I wouldn't let just anyone marry my little sister."

That warm, liquid emotion moves up my throat again, stinging my eyes as he gives my shoulder a squeeze.

"Let's get some photos before dinner," my mom says, gesturing at Pippa and Jamie.

"One second." Pippa grabs my hand and starts pulling me away. "I need Hazel to help me with the... something."

"What something?" I ask as she hauls me through the restaurant. "I'll take care of it so you can have fun—"

In the quiet foyer area at the front of the restaurant, away from the guests in the main dining area, she whirls on me. "You've been avoiding me."

"Uh." I scramble for an excuse for not answering her three texts about the team's new trade.

"Connor is on the *team* now, Hazel."

For the tenth time in the last twenty-four hours, my stomach drops through the floor. "I know."

It's all I've fucking thought about. My lying, cheating, manipulative, narcissistic ex is now on the hockey team I work for, and I'm assigned to be his physiotherapist.

All night, I tossed and turned.

"What are we doing about it?" she asks.

I can't quit, because working for the team is an incredible experience, and I actually love my job. The senior physios are knowledgeable and kind, and it's surprisingly rewarding, working with the players. While I'm saving to open my own inclusive fitness studio one day, working for the Storm is a once-in-a-lifetime opportunity. I'd be stupid to walk away.

"Nothing," I tell her, putting on a neutral smile like I don't care. "We're doing nothing."

"He cheated on you."

My stomach clenches, and I think about that party back in university when everyone watched, whispering. What he said to me and how it's stuck with me for years.

"I'm well aware." I keep my voice low and my expression pleasant in case anyone looks over. "Everyone saw that I'm his physio, including him. If we change it now, everyone will know—"

My words hang in the air as I cut myself off. The deeper we get into this, the more erratic my heart beats. Even Pippa doesn't know the full truth.

I don't want him to know he got to me and that I'm still upset about what happened. I don't even like Pippa knowing, even though she's my sister and best friend.

I'm the one who takes care of her, not the other way around.

"I spent two years in high school working ahead so that—" I'm about to dig deep into my insult arsenal, but I'm supposed to be convincing Pippa I'm fine. "So we could go to university together." Connor's a year older than me. I studied my ass off so that we didn't have to be apart. I took summer classes to get ahead.

Her eyes soften, and I hate it. I hate that she feels bad for me.

"I'm not going to run." I straighten up, push my shoulders back, and fake all the tough, strong energy I need right now. "I was here first, and I'm not going anywhere."

Pippa opens her mouth to say something, but I cut her off.

"This is your engagement party. Please, *please* don't make it about me, or I'll plan another one." I tap my finger on my lip, narrowing my eyes. "I'm picturing images of you on tour plastered all over the walls. Jamie would love it."

She snorts. "You're a menace." Her expression turns reluctant as she studies my face. "Are you sure you're okay?"

"One hundred percent fine." I put on a bright smile. From the way she winces, I went too hard, but I give her a gentle push into the restaurant. "Go. Socialize. Flash your big engagement ring around."

She sticks her tongue out at me, and I stick mine out in return before she heads back into the restaurant. Jamie holds his hand out as she approaches, and for a moment, I watch them. His hand resting on her waist, keeping her close. Her soft, affectionate smile as she gazes up at him.

What's it like, I wonder, to be everything to someone? To trust someone like that?

There's a sharp clench around my heart. Girls like Pippa get love like that. Girls like me? We do casual. I sleep with guys once and only once. It's safer that way. No one gets their hopes up and no one gets hurt.

I walk back into the restaurant but bump right into a broad, hard chest. "Sorry—"

Rory Miller tilts his arrogant, amused grin down at me. All the air gets sucked out of the room, and my stomach does that annoying flip-flop fluttery thing.

"There you are, Hartley."

This reaction? It's not my fault. It's his goddamned charisma. I blink up at his crushing deep blue eyes the color of a moody ocean. He's almost a foot taller than me, with dark blond hair that's a little too long. Hockey hair, the guys call it. With his lazy overconfidence, he pulls it off.

Not that I'd ever admit that.

It's his grin that riles me, though. A perpetually amused, flirtatious slant to his lips. It's exactly the way a hockey super-star would smile, like he knows he can have anything.

I hate Rory Miller's stupid fucking arrogant grin. I hate it so much that I think about it all the time.

He steps back, rakes his gaze down my outfit—a dark red midi dress with a sweetheart neckline and a soft, curve-hugging skirt that makes my ass look incredible—and lets out a low whistle.

"You look very pretty tonight," he says.

He gives me that flirty grin again, and nerves flutter through me. I'm calm, cool, and totally disinterested in Rory Miller, and if I tell myself that enough times, it might actually become true.

Heat flushes up my neck and cheeks, and I clear my throat. "Thank you. Excuse me." I move to get around him, but he steps into my path, blocking it.

"Admit it. You wore this dress for me."

"Wow, Miller." My laugh is light. "It sure is crowded in here with that enormous ego of yours."

He gives me a scolding, teasing expression. "Now, Hartley, play along and tell me I look good, too."

My eyes flick over him in his suit. Tailored perfectly to his tall, broad frame, it screams *custom-made* and *expensive*, but it's the rich navy fabric I struggle to look away from. It's the exact shade of his eyes.

"You don't need the ego boost." I should walk away, but

instead, I smack my head in mock-disappointment. "Oh my god. I forgot to reserve a seat for your sex doll."

His grin broadens, and sparks dance in my stomach. He doesn't actually have a sex doll—I don't think—but this is one of my favorite bits.

"I gave her the night off," he says in a low voice, leaning in with a rakish grin and glittering eyes. "She's earned it."

A revolted laugh threatens to slip out, but I hold it down. I will not laugh at Rory Miller's jokes. He's basically a child, and it'll just encourage him.

"Rory." Donna, Jamie's mom, appears with the photographer I hired. "You're here." She gestures at the two of us. "Let's get a photo."

Before I can protest that we're not together, he slips his hand around my waist, pulling me against him. His scent surrounds me—warm, spicy, and woodsy, like sandalwood and cloves. From either the intensely masculine way he smells or the way his body heat warms me, my stomach dips.

"Relax," he murmurs into my ear, giving my waist a squeeze. "You're so tense."

The photographer lines up the focus and I count the seconds until dinner, where I've placed Rory on the opposite end of the table from me.

"Let's go out," he says quietly as the camera clicks.

I snort, even as delight shoots through me. "You're joking. Your sex doll will be so jealous."

His quiet laugh tickles my cheek. "Nah, I'll bring her."

I really do laugh this time, and the flash goes off. Stars burst in my vision.

"Lovely," the photographer says, snapping away. "What a beautiful couple."

I open and close my mouth like a fish. The camera clicks again and I step away from him, putting distance between us.

His hands slip into his pockets as he regards me, gaze dipping down to my neckline, so fast I barely catch it. "Come on, Hartley."

"I don't date hockey players, and I'm pretty sure you don't even know my first name."

His gaze sharpens, his smile turning flirty. "You want me to say your name more, *Hazel?*"

A shiver of something weird rolls down my back. The last thing I need is him pulling out *that* low, seductive voice again. "No."

"Then let's be friends."

The tilt of his mouth and the way his eyes drag over me make me shake my head. He doesn't want to be friends. He loves the chase. A person doesn't get to where he is in his hockey career without being insanely competitive, and me turning him down is like catnip.

With guys like Rory and Connor, it's only a matter of time before they get bored and move on to the next thrill.

"In high school, Miller, you blackmailed me into tutoring you. You used your hot, talented hockey player status to get what you wanted." He spoke to the hockey coach, who spoke to the principal, who spoke to the teachers. "For all of grades eleven and twelve, you used up two of my afternoons per week." I stare him down, ignoring the lock of hair that's fallen into his eyes. "Friends don't do that."

It isn't the whole truth about why I want nothing to do with him, but it's as much as I'll ever admit out loud, especially to him.

There's a pause before his eyebrow arches. "You think I'm hot?"

My face burns. "That's what you got from that?"

He shrugs, baffled. "I made sure you got extra credit out of the tutoring thing."

I scramble for something to say, momentarily tripped up, because I didn't actually know that was his doing. I just thought they were trying to sweeten the deal for me.

I glance around, searching for Pippa, Jamie, Hayden, Alexei, anyone. People are taking their seats for dinner. "I'm going to sit down now."

His hand comes to my arm to stop me. "Hold on." The cocky smirk falls away, leaving something serious and sincere in his eyes. "Did you see the email Ward sent out last night?"

"Yes. You're captain now. Congratulations."

He frowns, shaking his head. "About McKinnon," he says, watching me intently.

"Oh my fucking *god*," I sigh in exasperation. "Do I have a sign on my back that says *Ask me about my shitty ex-boyfriend!* or something? I'm fine. It's fine." I clap my hands together. "Everything is fine."

He crosses his arms over his broad chest. "You said 'fine' too many times there."

I huff a laugh.

He searches my eyes, and my heart jumps into my throat at the concern on his face. He's so close to seeing the truth—that I'm not fine, that I'm freaking the fuck out.

"Do you still have a thing for him?"

I make a choking noise of disbelief, and people glance over. "Absolutely not. I don't want this."

Shame churns in my stomach. Is that what people think? That I've been carrying a torch for Connor for years?

"I'll speak to Ward," he says quietly, so gentle and careful, nothing like his normal arrogant self. "McKinnon can work with one of the other physios. I'll take care of it for you."

If I didn't know him better, I'd read the worry in his eyes as protectiveness. My pulse blips at the thought of Rory Miller hovering over me like Jamie hovers over Pippa, but I catch myself.

He wants what he can't have. It's just another move in a game I don't want to play.

"I don't need your help," I tell him. "I don't need a bodyguard, and I don't want you interfering with my job."

He makes a frustrated noise and runs his hand through his hair. The determination in his eyes makes me feel like he's going to fight me on this, but his Adam's apple bobs and he dips his chin in a nod.

"Okay," he says simply. "I won't interfere."

"Thank you."

For the rest of the night, I'm busy with Pippa, Jamie, and our family, but every time I glance down at the other end of the table, Rory's watching me, still wearing that protective, concerned frown.

"HARTLEY."

Three days later, I'm in the team gym watching her set up for her first physio session with McKinnon.

She sets a weight on the floor, avoiding my eyes.

My trainer walks in the door, and I wave, making a *one moment* motion to him before turning back to Hazel and lowering my voice. "Just wondered if you've reconsidered my offer to go to Ward with you."

Her shoulders tense. "You said you wouldn't interfere."

"I'll back you up. He'll probably listen, even if I'm not there."

She lets out a heavy breath. That soft, plush bottom lip of hers is tucked between her teeth and a frown sits between her eyebrows. She's nervous.

My hands clench at my sides. I've been going round and round in my head, thinking about how her expression tightened when I brought up McKinnon at the engagement party, thinking about the unusual protectiveness that surged through me at the thought of her having to work with him.

"I know you're a tough little cookie, Hartley," I tell her,

crooking a grin at her to disguise the concern and jealousy. "I'm just trying to prevent you from killing the new trade."

She doesn't laugh, and my chest aches. Why won't she let me help?

I take in her pretty ponytail that shows off the back of her neck. The fan of dark lashes around those beautiful blue-gray eyes. The lush curve of her mouth.

"Pass."

So fucking stubborn. If I wasn't so frustrated, I'd think it was endearing.

"He's going to apologize," she says as she places free weights on the floor in front of the mirror.

"Excuse me?" I haven't seen the guy in years, but I know him. Guys like that? They never apologize. My dad's the same way.

She straightens up, meeting my gaze. "He emailed me. He said he wants to talk."

In my head, an alarm blares. "He probably wants to get back together."

"I doubt it," she says, making a face, "and even if he does, that's not happening."

The alarm quiets. That's something, at least.

"He's going to apologize," she continues, "and I'm going to move on."

She's just going to put up with him this year? "He's an asshole."

"So are you."

She's not wrong. I cover the ugly feeling with a cocky grin. "Yeah, but I'm the kind you like."

She's about to bite back a smart retort that I'm sure I'll think about all day, but McKinnon walks in the door, and her demeanor changes. She tenses as he spots her, and a sick, predatory smirk stretches across his face.

I hate this. She's stuck working with him and I can't do anything about it.

"Rory." She turns to me, pleading with her eyes.

My gut drops. We never use first names. Never. Not even back in high school.

"Please," she says, holding my gaze, worry written all over her face. This version of her is so different from the competitive, confident woman I love to tease. "I just want to do my job right now."

McKinnon's walking toward us, but my gaze is locked on her face, searching her eyes. We could solve this so easily if she just let me help. I have the urge to haul her over my shoulder and walk her straight to Ward's office, but she'd probably bite me, and I'd probably like it.

Intrusive thoughts, I think those are called. And I told her I wouldn't interfere, even if I'm right.

"Okay." I suck a deep breath in, and I can feel my teeth gritting.

"There she is."

McKinnon greets her like an old friend, but her shoulders hitch. My protective instincts surge, and I bring myself to full height, wearing my signature smirk.

His attention drifts to me, and his grin sours. I've always been a couple inches taller than him, and it's so primal and stupid, but I get sick satisfaction from it.

"McKinnon." I tip my chin at him.

Hartley may have said no to my help, but my body's beating with possessiveness. I suddenly have an ugly understanding of how Streicher must have felt last year when I was hanging out with Pippa.

His cold gaze meets mine, challenging me. "Miller. Still sniffing around Hazel, huh? Some things never change."

I fucking hate this guy. Something competitive curls in my

stomach, coiling and expanding through me, and my jaw tightens. I look down at Hartley, giving her one last opening to accept my offer.

Her gaze flares with emphasis, and she glances pointedly over to where my trainer waits. "Rory was just leaving for his training session."

Every instinct is shouting at me to stay here, stick by her side in case this asshole says or does something to upset her, but instead, I send my irritating smirk to McKinnon.

I'm going to bodycheck this asshole so hard in practice.

"See you later, Hartley," I say while staring McKinnon down.

During my training session, I'm only half listening, keeping my attention on Hartley and McKinnon on the other side of the gym, watching for conflict, watching her body language to make sure she's okay.

I don't trust that guy for a second.

CHAPTER 4
HAZEL

TO MY EXTREME RELIEF, I'm no longer attracted to Connor McKinnon.

He's always been handsome, but it's in an ugly way, I realize, like a villain from *Game of Thrones*. Standing next to Rory, though, makes everyone less attractive.

My heart beats up into my throat as I run through the physio exercises with him, and I've never been more self-conscious.

If I'm rude to him, I'll seem like the bitter, jaded ex. That's exactly what I am, but I don't want him to know that. My biggest fear is that he'll know he had an effect on me.

If I'm too friendly, he'll think I want to get back together. Another mess I don't want to deal with.

So I'm treating him professionally, like I'd treat any other player, and internally freaking out. He lunges forward, staring at himself in the mirror. He's not even watching his form; he's just staring at his ugly-handsome face.

"Watch your knee," I say as the joint caves in.

He adjusts and goes back to staring at himself with that stupid smirk.

He still hasn't brought up the email he sent me this

morning—*Looking forward to our physio session. There's something I'd like to say.* Maybe he's waiting until our session ends.

He's going to apologize. What else could he want to say? I'm going to get the closure I need to leave the past behind. What he did and said was terrible, but if he feels remorse? That changes things.

In my mind, I hear the words he said to me in the middle of that party while he had his arm around another girl.

I never said we were exclusive. You did.

I'm bored.

Girls like you don't end up with guys like me.

I drag in a deep breath to quell the nausea. It was years ago. I'm not that girl anymore, the one who dissolved into her boyfriend's life.

Glancing over to where Rory's working with his trainer, I meet his eyes. He arches a brow at me as if to say *everything okay?* but I turn away.

Rory doesn't care about anyone but himself, so I don't know why he's so hell-bent on helping. I've watched how easily he can break a girl's heart.

As he completes the exercises, Connor winces and shifts his thigh back and forth, and I get a flash of unwelcome memory of massaging that muscle years ago. He's had groin problems ever since he suffered an injury in our first year at university.

"Do we have time for you to give me a massage?" he asks. "My groin is sore from sitting on a plane all day yesterday."

It takes all my effort not to show my revulsion.

Massage therapy is a normal part of my job. If he were any other player, I wouldn't hesitate. These guys get the crap beat out of them on the ice, and I want to do anything I can to help them feel better and play longer.

This is Connor, though. I don't want to breathe the same

air as him, let alone touch him, but if I treat him differently than other clients, that will mean he's gotten to me.

Just get through this, I tell myself.

"We still have a few minutes. I'll work on it," I tell him, gesturing to one of the tables on the side of the gym for the physios and massage therapists.

He follows me and lies down on the table, rolling up his workout shorts while I pull massage oil out of the cupboard.

He's done this before. So have I. This is a normal thing. It won't be weird.

I apply the oil to my palms, and when I put my hands on him, I try to focus on the way the tight muscles feel under my fingers as I press and glide, but my face is heating.

I've done this for him, years ago. When we used to do this—

Oh god. My skin crawls.

He'd get turned on, and then it would turn into sex.

Ugh. My stomach thrashes with discomfort. I hate every-thing about this, but I also hate how embarrassed I am. This would be a *fantastic* time for him to apologize.

I wonder if the other girls he slept with while we were together did this for him.

Our gazes catch, and my heart lodges in my throat the moment he notices my burning face. A slow smirk slides onto his face, like he's caught me doing something I shouldn't.

"So," he starts, tucking his hands behind his head. "This is a good time to have a quick chat."

My stomach rolls with nerves, but I hold my expression neutral. Under my hands, the muscle is loosening up, thank god. "Go for it."

When he apologizes, I'll be gracious. I won't lord it over him. I just want to move on.

He laughs lightly, glancing down at my hands on his inner

thigh with a conspiratorial grin. "Given our history, can you be professional this season?"

My hands pause. Yeah, he just said that. The sick feeling in my stomach starts simmering, a low boil, and I yank my hands back.

"What?"

He gives me a knowing look, like we're sharing a secret. "Come on. You being my physio this year was a pretty big coincidence, and now this?" He gestures at his inner thigh.

A weird feeling loops through me, pounding harder with every heartbeat. It feels like I'm falling, like the contents of my stomach are in my throat.

He winces. "I just want to make sure it's not going to be weird with us this year."

Oh, Hazel. Wrong again. It's almost laughable how wrong I am about guys.

He's not going to apologize. He thinks I'm *trying to get him back.* After what he did and said, he thinks I'd actually be interested.

To him, I'm the person who walked out of that party crying while everyone whispered about her. I'm the girl who took summer courses so I could follow him to university, like a clueless, lovestruck fool.

I'm *not* that person anymore.

Rage drips into my blood, followed by an intense need to prove him wrong.

"I didn't request to be your physio." My voice sounds weird. Strained.

He arches an eyebrow. "No?" It's clear he doesn't believe me.

"No." Shame squeezes my throat. *Clingy,* I remember him saying about me.

Girls like you don't end up with guys like me. God, even now, the words slice through me.

I want to prove him wrong so, so fucking badly.

Across the gym, Rory watches. He's had one eye on me the entire session. His desire to help earlier pounds in my thoughts.

He lifts a weight, holding my gaze and flexing his biceps and triceps. My pulse stumbles, because even if he is a cocky dickhead, Rory Miller is wildly handsome. I can see why women fall all over him, even if I'll never be one of them.

Wait.

They hate each other, Rory and Connor. They've never gotten along. They're going to be at each other's throats all season. Rory's a better player than Connor, and even though Connor's never admitted it, that's why he doesn't like Rory.

And Connor made it clear that I'd never do better than him.

Rory is the only player on the team whose ego surpasses Connor's. He's smug, arrogant, and competitive as hell, and best of all, he hates Connor almost as much as I do. Like he can hear my thoughts, Rory's mouth tilts into a grin, one eyebrow lifting.

So cocky, so confident.

The back of my scalp tingles as I hold his gaze in the mirror. I'm about to do something very stupid, but I don't care. I'd do anything to get rid of this ashamed, powerless feeling. The desire to spite my ex has me by the throat.

I summon the unflappable bitch-demon deep inside me and give Connor a puzzled smile.

"You know Rory and I are together, right?"

My heart races as I watch his reaction. It might be worth it, watching his expression flip from smug to confused to surprised before he finally looks to Rory and it turns flat-out pissed.

"Really?" Connor asks, glaring at Rory across the gym. "Miller?"

I'm a hurricane of female rage and revenge, and I'm totally fucking doing this.

Rory's trainer says something, but he's not listening; he's just looking between Connor and me.

I give him a flirty, twiddly finger wave. His eyes light up with victory and amusement, and I fight the eye roll as he shoots that grin at Connor.

God, Rory's going to be the worst about this.

"Mhm." I hear the question he asked me moments ago—the one about being professional—and my blood rattles with anger again, but I continue to smile.

Worry flickers in my chest. Rory's unfairly hot, and I've been able to keep my distance until now with sharp barbs and light amusement, but he's going to be all over me, murmuring in my ear and putting his hand on my waist with that intense charm and doing whatever he can to press Connor's buttons.

The soft, vulnerable part of me worries that I'll catch feelings. That I'll fall for him.

My fingertips rub against each other, and when I feel the massage oil on my skin, another serving of molten, furious anger tips into my blood.

Rory's also a spoiled hockey player who's had life handed to him on a silver platter. I'm not going to catch feelings. Connor's a reminder of what would happen if I let that line blur.

With Rory's help, I'm going to make Connor regret what he did.

CHAPTER 5

RORY

"WELL." I take a seat on the bench beside Hartley after McKinnon leaves. "Someone's had a change of heart." I put on a pretty smirk and do a fluttery, feminine finger wave, tucking my hair behind my ear.

Her mouth tightens like she wants to laugh. It's such a nice break from this tense, nervous version of her I've been watching like a hawk for the last hour.

"Is that supposed to be me?"

"I'm guessing McKinnon's apology wasn't what you were expecting."

Any humor in her expression drops. "He said, um." Her nostrils flare, and she takes a deep breath like she's trying to hold back from torching this place.

"What?"

"He made it seem like I asked to be his physio." Her face goes red. "Like I was hung up on him."

I'll kill him. "Really."

A shudder rolls through her, but she shakes it off. "And then the groin stuff."

Oh, I remember. I almost lost it, seeing her discomfort

while she was working on him. Seeing the way he looked at her. Even now, hot jealousy twists in my gut.

Her tongue taps her top lip, and she sneaks a reluctant glance at me. "I told him we were dating."

My thoughts stop before a smile spreads over my face.

"*Really.*"

Well, shit. This day just got a lot better. The smile is ear to ear now as her blush deepens. She's so fucking cute when she's embarrassed like this.

She looks down, fiddling with her fingers. "I, uh. I really wanted to get him back, and he hates you." Her gaze lifts to mine, tentative. "Because you're a better player than him."

"Oh, I know." My heart beats in my chest like a humming-bird. I really, really like this turn of events.

"If you don't want to do it—"

"I'll do it." I beam at her like I'm in a goddamned tooth-paste commercial. "I'll happily do it, Hartley."

Her eyes close and she shakes her head. "I knew you were going to be so smug about this. Okay, we need to set the terms." She wears her thinking face. "We'll date for half a season. Until January first." Her gaze flicks over me, assessing. "Or earlier, if either of you gets traded."

A weight thunks in my gut. It doesn't matter if I'm the captain; if Ward doesn't like what he sees, I'm out.

"January first. Deal."

"You can't mess around with other girls while we're pretending to be together. It'll ruin the illusion."

"Of course not." That's not really an issue these days.

Her eyes narrow. "Why are you agreeing to this so easily?"

I picture us making out while a pissed-off McKinnon watches on, and blood rushes to my dick. My gaze drops to her full mouth. I bet her lips are soft. They look soft.

Alarm rises in her eyes. Shit. She asked a question, and saying that I'm into her is going to send her running.

"Oh." Hazel's expression falls. "I see."

Panic tightens in my gut.

"You want to look good as captain," she says.

"Yes," I rush out, filled with relief. "Exactly."

She hums, thinking. "The fans went nuts last year when Jamie and Pippa started dating."

Clean up your act this year, Ward said in his office.

A hockey player with a nice hometown girl on his arm is the fastest way to clean up a reputation.

I wouldn't exactly call Hartley *nice*, but she's well-liked by the players and organization. Ward wants a responsible guy, and Hartley's my ticket.

"I'll play your devoted boyfriend and do everything I can to piss McKinnon off," I tell her, "if you help me look like the captain the team needs. Ward wants a guy with a squeaky-clean image. You're great at your job and everyone likes you."

Her lips part in surprise. "Thanks."

"It's the truth."

I shrug, clearing my throat. We tease each other, but we don't compliment each other like that. I'm not sure why it slipped out.

"I'll need you to go to events and stuff with me. There's a charity event in December and the League Classic game on New Year's Eve."

It's at a local ski resort that doesn't count toward the season, but the teams wear the original hockey sweaters and we play at an outdoor rink. It's a nostalgia thing.

"I'll talk to Ward about us," I add, "but I don't think it'll be an issue." Pippa and Streicher dated last year when Pippa was working for the team.

"Thanks." She plays with the ends of her hair, twiddling

them between her fingers. "I'll go to the game on Friday. Connor's playing, right?"

I nod, and I can see the cogs turning in her head.

"I'll sit with Pippa, and we'll go out with the team after. I'm sure he'll be there. That's when we can—" Our eyes meet, and she seems to lose her train of thought. "Everyone will see us together."

"And you'll wear my jersey." Pride weaves through me at the image.

"Um. No." She makes a face. "I don't wear guys' jerseys."

She wore McKinnon's jersey, but I don't bring that up. "If you want to get to McKinnon, you need to be all in. You'll wear it."

She holds my gaze for a long moment before I get a tiny nod. "And I want to tell Pippa the plan. She won't believe it otherwise."

"You don't think I can be convincing?" I think about how her waist felt under my hand, how fucking incredible her hair smelled. "We should probably talk about boundaries, in case I go too far. Agree on a safe word and all that."

Determination and fury flash in her pretty eyes. "I really want to fuck with him." A beat. "You can't go too far."

Jesus *Christ*, Hartley's hot when she's pissed off. I'm half-hard. My eyes drop to her mouth. "No safe word. Got it."

"Miller."

"What?" I'm still staring at her mouth.

"This is fake."

"I know."

"Don't get feelings."

"I won't." I wonder if she'd let me kiss her in front of McKinnon.

She dips her head to catch my gaze. "You need to agree to that without staring at my mouth and drooling."

A laugh slips out of me, and I wink at her. "I wasn't drooling."

She rolls her eyes, but she's smiling. She clears her throat. "Seriously. Don't get feelings, because I won't."

Dangerous. This is so fucking dangerous, playing this game with her. She's going to get to know me and run screaming in the other direction. That's the way it works with guys like my dad and me.

Still, I'm sticking my hand out to shake hers, pulse whooshing in my ears.

"It's just for show." I love how her eyes flare with something interesting as I step into her space. "You don't need to tell me twice."

My hand envelops hers, and my focus narrows to where we touch. Her hand is delicate and soft, fitting right into mine. She's so pretty and mean and perfect, and this is going to fucking ruin me.

"Oh, Hartley." I just give her my signature cocky smile. "This is going to be so, so fun."

PIPPA'S already in her seat when I arrive before the game on Friday night. The arena is filled with excited fans, a sea of gray and blue Storm jerseys, and rock music plays, pumping everyone up. My body's brimming with energy as I make my way to our seats behind the net, holding a pretzel in one hand and a beer in the other.

"Hi." I drop into my seat. "Sorry that took so long. The line at concessions was ridiculous."

A lie. I was stalling, circling the arena three times before finally getting in line.

Without a word, Pippa's gaze goes to my jersey, and her eyebrows lift.

It was sitting on my desk this afternoon inside a gift box. Despite my aversion to wearing a jock's name on me like I'm his property, Rory's right. I have to wear his jersey if we want to sell this.

She's still staring. "You're wearing a jersey."

I take a huge bite of my pretzel, choosing my words. It's going to sound so stupid out loud.

"Hazel." Now she's *really* curious. "Lean forward."

I swallow my bite. "When do you start working on the next album?"

God, I'm such a chicken. Miller's name is practically burning on my back.

"*Hazel.* Whose name is on your back?"

My mouth is dry, and this pretzel tastes like glue. What, am I just going to sit here in this spot until she leaves the stadium?

I move so she can read it. "It's not what it looks like."

She blinks slowly. "Am I missing something?"

The lights in the arena dim, and a roar of cheers rises up as the players hit the ice. As he skates past, Rory winks at me, wearing a lazy, smug grin. Connor's right behind him.

This is it. This is the faking it part. As much as I don't want to do this, I made a deal, and it's on me to play the part as much as it's on Miller.

I give Rory my typical cool smile and wink back. He grins wider and skates off. When Connor does a double take at me sitting here, satisfaction pulses behind my sternum.

Fuck you, Connor.

Pippa sends me confused glances throughout the national anthems, and when we sit, I lower my voice as the players line up for a face-off.

"We're not actually dating." I clasp my hands together. This is going to sound so stupid out loud. My stomach lurches at the sight of Connor on the bench, and it all comes spilling out. I tell Pippa about Connor's email the other morning, how I thought he'd apologize, and then what he actually said.

"What a fucking asshole," she breathes, watching my face, and panic rises in me.

I don't want Pippa to know the effect Connor had on me. She's my little sister, and I've always been the strong one for her. When our parents wanted her to let music be just a hobby, I pushed her to follow her dreams. I'm the one she comes to with questions about life; it's always been like that between us. I take care of her, not the other way around.

I don't want her to know how badly I've been hurt. I don't want her to worry about me.

"Miller and I came to an arrangement." I explain how he wants to look like a better captain to Ward this year and he's more than happy to help me stick it to Connor.

She studies me with narrowed eyes. "You hate Rory. Why do you care if he wants to be captain?"

I open my mouth to protest. After what he did to my friend in high school, I know he's just like every other jock who can have whatever he wants without consequences.

I don't *hate* him, though.

We watch the players scramble for the puck at the other end of the ice. "I care because I made a deal with him. It's only until January, anyway. You can tell Jamie, but please ask him not to say anything."

Pippa's eyes narrow like she doesn't believe me before a teasing smile pulls up on her mouth and she tilts her chin to my jersey. "You wear it well." She wiggles her brows. "Very cute."

"Shut up."

"He got the size right and everything."

"I told you everything so you can be my support person." I give her a pointed look. "Not so you can tease me."

"I *am* your support person." She pulls out her phone and opens her camera app. "But I like to tease you, too. Smile like you would if you were sleeping with Rory Miller."

I laugh at the insanity of it, and she snaps a flurry of pictures. "Oh my god. I would never."

As he skates past, our eyes meet. He grins and mouths *hey* before skating off.

"Oh my god," a woman says behind us. "Was that at me?"

"No," her friend answers. "It was to her."

The back of my neck prickles.

"That's Jamie Streicher's fiancée beside her," the woman whispers, and Pippa grins at me. They have no clue we can hear every word.

"Dad will be thrilled," Pippa adds, peering over to Jamie at the other end of the ice. Next period, he'll be in the net in front of us. "He likes Rory."

I groan. Our dad's a hockey nut. I didn't even think about this element of our arrangement. "If Mom and Dad bring it up, tell them it's not serious."

"You haven't had a boyfriend since Connor." She cuts me a glance. "They're going to get excited."

There's a flurry of activity on the ice in front of us. Rory sinks the puck, and noise erupts in the arena. The fans jump to their feet, cheering as lights flash and the Vancouver players surround Rory. Pippa's hand comes to my elbow and she widens her eyes, pulling me up to standing.

"Clap," she hisses. "Act like you're happy that he scored."

I start clapping awkwardly and Pippa laughs, which makes me laugh.

"I don't want Mom and Dad getting attached to him," I tell her when we sit down. "He has his own parents."

Pippa's frown makes me pause.

"What?" I press.

"Rory needs more good people in his life."

I scoff. "With his ego? He probably grew up eating his after-school snacks off a gold platter." I find him through the glass, speeding up the length of the ice with the puck. "The guy doesn't know the word 'no.' I'm sure he was spoiled rotten as a kid."

Her mouth twists. "He doesn't talk to his mom much, and I don't think his dad's like ours. Have you ever watched Rick Miller on TV?"

I don't watch sports commentary. Rick Miller is a Canadian hockey legend, though. Everyone knows his name.

"Honestly?" She winces. "He's kind of a dick. He's Rory's agent first and his dad second."

An ache pangs through me.

"When I went home last month," she continues, "Dad had framed the ticket from my first concert in Vancouver."

Pippa and I grew up in North Vancouver, and when we moved out of the house, our parents retired and moved to Silver Falls, a tiny ski town in the interior of British Columbia.

My heart squeezes with love. "Ken Hartley is the freaking best."

She nods, wearing a wistful smile. "Yeah. He is."

My eyes find Rory on the ice, and my chest feels tight. Pippa and I have the best dad, and maybe I don't like Rory, but I don't wish a bad dad on him.

"They mentioned a trip out here next month. Let's invite Mom to one of your classes." Pippa wiggles her eyebrows. Outside of physio for the team, I teach yoga, both on Zoom and in-studio. "I think it would be fun."

My stomach sinks as I watch the game. Hayden body-checks a guy from the other team against the boards in front of us. "That's probably not going to happen."

"What if we eased her into it? We don't have to start with a hot class."

The whistle blows as the ref calls a penalty, and people around us shout their disagreement. I exhale a long breath out of my nose, putting my response together for my sister as my stomach tightens in frustration.

"She doesn't feel comfortable in yoga clothes," I explain. "Being in a yoga studio reminds her of how much her body has changed since she used to dance." Our mother was a ballerina in her teens and early twenties. "She won't do it."

I rub my sternum, dragging my palm over the front of my jersey as I think about her.

"How many times did she insult herself when you went home?" I ask. "How many times did she make a negative comment about her body or say she was on a diet?"

Pippa's throat works. "A lot."

"Exactly." We stare at the ice, and I know Pippa's thinking the same thing I am.

We want more for our mom. We want her to love herself. It's why I'm opening my own inclusive fitness studio one day. Everyone deserves to move and feel good in their body. Everyone deserves to love themselves.

The fans roar, and I pull my attention back to the game. Rory nabs the puck, skating away from the mess of players like a bullet. He's on a breakaway toward the net in front of Pippa and me. He's moving so fast his skates barely touch the ice, deft and with complete control. My pulse stumbles at his expression, so powerful and focused, and around me, spectators brace themselves.

I don't see the puck until it's already in.

Noise explodes—fans hollering, music blasting, the horn they blare for every goal sounding—and lights flash around the net.

A strange, proud feeling moves through me as the players gather around Rory, celebrating.

"Admit it," Pippa says over the noise. "That was incredible."

I huff, laughing despite myself. "Don't tell Miller."

The players break apart for another face-off, and when Rory turns, I prepare to roll my eyes at his cocky grin.

His expression is flat, unimpressed, and tired. The emotional kind of tired, the kind that wears you down and makes you feel like things will never get better. He's wearing the same exhaustion I feel after hearing my mom list her flaws, all the reasons her body isn't good enough. A looming sense of dread gathers within me, and I feel a pinch of regret.

Rory Miller is supposed to be a cocky asshole who can have whatever he wants, not a burned-out hockey player with a crappy dad.

Before I can think more about it, the puck drops and Rory snags it. Just as he swings around the net, a player from the other team crosschecks him into the boards, smashing his face and helmet against the glass.

The fans loudly demand a penalty as the ref blows the whistle. Rory winces, rubbing his lip. It's bleeding.

"Shit," I whisper as my stomach knots. "Is he okay?"

Pippa's gaze slides to me. "Why do you care?"

I think about how warm his hand was around mine the other day and the zinging trail of sparks his touch left along my skin.

"I don't." My shoulders lift in a shrug. "I don't want him to get hurt, though."

Her eyes narrow, but her lips curve up. "Interesting."

A knocking noise on the glass has us whipping our heads. Rory waits on the other side, his lip already swelling. I can feel a thousand eyes on us. He points to me, then taps his chin. His eyes glitter with teasing amusement.

"Oh my god." My face burns, and I want to disappear.

"Kiss it better," he says through the glass.

My skin is on fire. "No." I give him a hard look.

"I need it," he insists, still smiling. "And it needs to be you."

I'm sweating under this stupid jersey. My face appears on the Jumbotron. That means it's on TV. Oh god.

"Do it!" someone screams from behind me, and Pippa dissolves into laughter.

"*Kiss him, kiss him,*" the fans behind me start chanting, and my mouth falls open.

This is not happening.

"Hartley," Rory calls with bright eyes, tapping his stick on the glass again. "Everyone's waiting."

He's not dropping this. Behind him, Connor catches my eye, waiting with the other players with a disinterested expression like he doesn't care, but I remember him going off about how much attention Rory got on the ice.

I think about the way he smirked when my hands were on his thigh, and rage bursts inside me, sharp and hot.

I'll kill Rory later, but for now, I lean forward. He tilts his jaw so it's pressed against his side of the glass. People start cheering and catcalling as I lean up on my tiptoes and press my lips to my side of the glass, praying it's clean.

Cheers erupt as Rory clutches his heart. He shoots me a wink before skating away.

So, *so* arrogant.

The Vancouver team glances over at me with a mix of confused and entertained expressions. Hayden's eyes pop out of his head. Connor skates past with a scowl.

That was mortifying, but it worked.

"Everyone knows now," Pippa says, smiling.

The game resumes, but my mind flicks to later, when we're going to meet everyone at the bar.

Rory's a loose cannon. My stomach tumbles with nerves. He's shameless and he'll do anything to win.

The night's just started, and I think I need that safe word after all.

CHAPTER 7

HAZEL

"I *KNEW* IT," Hayden calls as he bursts through the door of
the bar.

Pippa and I are sitting in a booth at the Filthy Flamingo,
waiting for Jamie and Rory. The small, outdated Gastown bar's
entrance is hidden in an alley, with a dirty sign above the door.
From the outside, the place is unassuming, barely noticeable,
but the inside is all warm wood paneling, twinkling string lights
across the ceiling, loud classic rock music, and framed vintage
band posters on the walls. Tacked behind the liquor bottles
lining the back of the bar is a sea of Polaroid pictures of the
regulars. At the back, there's a small stage where Pippa plays
for us sometimes.

Hayden's right in front of me, gloating with a huge smile.
"You and Miller? I knew it."

"You didn't know it." I glance over at the guys who just
walked in. Connor's already at a table with a few of the players.
"No one knew."

No Rory yet. Maybe he's still doing postgame press.

Hayden points at his chest, beaming. With his blond hair,
bright blue eyes, and perpetual smile, Hayden Owens is a
golden retriever in human form. "I knew it," he tells Pippa

across the booth from me. "They have that flirty banter thing going on."

Pippa smiles at me, eyes full of amusement, but I scoff, sipping my drink. "Don't be smug, Owens, or I'll take it out on you in physio."

He just laughs and heads over to the counter to order a drink.

Jamie slides into the booth beside Pippa and gives her a kiss.

"Hi," she says, smiling against his mouth.

"Hi," he murmurs before kissing her again.

I yank my eyes away. A knot forms behind my sternum as they whisper to each other, and I try to wash it away with a swallow of my drink.

They finally pull apart, and Jamie nods at me. "Hazel. Pippa tells me congratulations are in order."

Amusement gleams in his typically serious expression, so I know she already told him everything.

I give him a sarcastic smile. "Don't start."

His gaze moves behind me and the amusement drops. "If he gives you problems," he says in a low voice so just Pippa and I can hear, "let me know."

"I can handle Miller."

"Not Miller." He frowns. "McKinnon. If he does anything, I want to know. I bet Miller does, too."

I'm struck by Jamie's protectiveness. He doesn't even know the full extent of what Connor did—no one does, not even Pippa—but here he is, ready to stick up for me.

Before I can say anything, the door of the bar opens. At the sight of me in his jersey, Rory grins with arrogant male confidence. His gaze is locked on mine as he walks through the bar, the side of his bottom lip swollen and bruised from tonight's hit. A prickle on my neck tells me Connor's watching, along with everyone else. As Rory slides into the booth, into my space, still smiling down at me, I note that his hair is still damp from his shower. His scent surrounds me—clean and sharp.

Hockey players are supposed to stink, but the way Rory smells makes my brain stumble.

"Hi, baby." He leans in and presses a kiss to my temple like it's nothing.

My heart rate shoots up and I'm frozen as his stubble brushes me. I don't think I'm breathing. His hand slides around my waist, pulling me against him on the bench. Across the table, Pippa's eyes are bright and Jamie's wearing that half smile again.

"Hi." My voice sounds strained.

His eyes roam my face, bright and curious, before his gaze dips down to my torso. "I like the way you look in my jersey."

My face heats at his tone. "Don't get used to it." The words are out before I can stop them.

He shakes his head, grinning. "You're wearing it to every game from now on." His hand squeezes my waist, and my abs tense. He's so warm and solid against my arm. "Come on, Hartley, pretend like you like me."

Pippa glances around before she leans in. "Kiss, kiss, kiss," she chants in a whisper.

I glare at her, face going red. "Pippa."

She starts laughing. Even Jamie grins.

"I will kill both of you," I hiss at them, but I'm laughing, even if Rory's hand is still on my waist.

Jamie blanches. "What did I do?"

"You're encouraging her. I can feel it. Just—" I shake my head, flustered. My face is hot. "Be cool." I can't help but smirk at Rory. "This is exactly how I'd act if we *were* dating," I whisper.

His eyes flare. "Yeah?"

"Mhm. I'd be so mean to you."

His gaze drops to my mouth and heat bursts throughout me. He's not going to actually kiss me here, now, right?

I didn't think about the kissing part of this deal. Of course we're going to kiss at some point. Couples kiss.

My stomach wobbles. His eyes warm, resting on me. His hair is curling a little on top, golden highlights among his ash coloring, probably from being in the sun this summer. My gaze trails along his sharp jawline, his stubble, his nose that looks too delicate for such a masculine face.

He really is handsome.

My gaze snags on the purple bruise on his bottom lip and I blink, clearing my head. "Some ice will make that feel better."

"I already feel better." His smile turns lazy.

I make a face at him. "Corny." With his hand still on my waist, I wrench around, searching for Jordan, the bartender and owner. A few tables back, Connor's sitting with some other players, and my stomach drops with anxiety when his eyes meet mine.

He looks away first, and I get another hit of that satisfaction I felt during the game. Rory looks over his shoulder, eyes lingering on Connor's table, but Connor doesn't look back at us.

Rory brings his mouth closer to my ear, and shivers run across my skin from where his lips brush the shell. "Don't look at him. Look at me." His hand slides from my waist up to the back of my neck, warm and solid and strangely calming. "I've got this, okay?"

"Seriously?" Jordan stands at the foot of the table with an incredulous expression. She flattens her palms on the table, and her long, dark hair falls over her shoulder. "Seriously," she repeats, pointing between me and Rory. "You're together?"

I press my mouth into a line to hide the laugh. Jordan's

about my age and detests everything hockey. I'm shocked she allows the group of us to drink in her bar after games.

I just shrug and adopt a guilty expression.

"*Fuck.*" She stalks back to the till, opens it, and pulls out a wad of cash.

"Oh my god," Pippa gasps. "I forgot."

I stiffen. "Forgot what?"

At Hayden's table beside us, Jordan smacks the money down. "Here," she tells him before glancing at me in dismay. "You were supposed to hold out longer."

Hayden looks confused before realization dawns. "Do you have the list?" he asks Alexei Volkov, an older defenseman.

I look between Pippa, Jamie, and Rory. "What's going on?"

Rory winces, but he's smiling. "Hartley, you're not going to like this, but it's important that you know this wasn't my idea."

I have a bad feeling. "Someone tell me right now, please."

Hayden whistles to get the bar's attention. "If you bet against Miller and Hazel getting together this season, it's time to pay up."

CHAPTER 8
HAZEL

EVERYONE PULLS OUT THEIR WALLETS. My jaw drops. My stomach drops. Everything inside me drops because what the actual fuck?

My gaze whips to Rory's, and I widen my eyes in question. "Really?"

"Like I said," he says lightly, "not my idea."

"Eisner, Volkov, Chopra," Hayden reads off his phone, "Jordan, and Streicher, you owe a hundred."

I send Jamie an accusing look, but he has his full attention on his beer, avoiding my eyes.

"Pippa, you, too," Hayden continues.

My mouth falls open in disbelief. "Pippa."

She winces, laughing. "Sorry. If it makes you feel better, I thought you'd hold out until the end of the season."

I shake my head at her while Hayden lists off more bets, but I'm laughing. "Traitor," I say, but there's no bite to my words.

"And finally," Hayden calls, and a hush falls over the bar. "The winner is..." He turns to Rory. "Miller, who has won two thousand bucks."

A round of cheers and laughs rises up, and I stare at him with unfiltered shock.

"Thank you, thank you," he says as people pass him cash. He stands and sets the cash on the bar counter, nodding at Jordan. "Prepayment on anything we break this season."

Everyone laughs, and I shake my head at him as he slides back into the booth. "You bet that we'd get together the first month of the season?"

His expression is pure innocence, eyes sparkling. "I always bet on myself."

"Aww." Hayden jostles me, but I slap him away. "He likes you."

This is so stupid, but I'm smiling. With confidence like Rory's, I don't know why I'm surprised.

He hooks a big arm around my shoulders and pulls me into his chest, and my stomach flutters at the contact. "Get over here, my little fire-breathing dragon."

Pippa chokes on her drink, laughing.

"That is *not* my nickname," I tell him, elbowing him.

Rory just smiles before his hands come to my waist and he lifts me into his lap.

"Really?" I mutter at him over my shoulder, praying that in the bar's dim lighting, he can't see me blushing. God, even sitting in his lap, he's so tall. His thighs are solid and warm under me and I just—

This is a lot. He's all around me. My pulse jolts. This is so much more intense than I thought it would be.

Like he can sense my thoughts, Rory's hand smooths over my back in a comforting motion.

"Play nice, fire-breather."

Another strained laugh lodges itself in my throat, and I *hate* that I like that nickname, but my name catches my attention. Pippa's looking at me with a question in her eyes.

"We're talking about the skating event in December," she explains. "It's for the players and their partners." Her smile turns impish, and I cringe, because I already know where this is going. She looks to Rory. "Hazel can't skate."

"What?" He's baffled. "You work for a hockey team and you can't skate?"

"We don't do physio on the ice."

"You need to know how to skate," he says.

"*You* need to know how to skate. I don't need to balance on knives on a slippery surface. Regular ground with sneakers is fine for me."

"It's because she fell as a kid," Pippa adds.

"Pippa." I stare at her. It's my *shut up now* look. She wiggles her eyebrows. *Make me*, her expression says.

Rory hums a teasing, sympathetic noise and rubs a hand up and down my back. "Poor Hazel. You're scared of skating?"

"I'm not scared." My voice is too high. "I'm not scared," I say again in my regular voice. "I'm busy, and I don't want to get hurt."

"I'll teach you." Connor interrupts, taking a seat at the booth, wearing a stupid smirk. His eyes move over me, sitting in Rory's lap, and there's an edge to his gaze, like he doesn't like what he sees.

Rory tenses, his hands tightening on my waist.

"*I'll* teach you," Rory cuts in, wrapping his arm across my stomach, looking down at me in challenge. It's the competitiveness I see in him on the ice. *Play along*, his eyes say. "I won't let you fall."

My instinct is to fight him, but we're supposed to be pretending and making Connor wildly jealous, so I force a soft smile and gaze up at him like I'm besotted.

"I'd love that," I say softly.

I've never used this voice with a guy in my life, and from the way Rory's eyes spark with laughter, I think he might know that.

"Good." His mouth curves higher like he's won something. "So would I."

Heat rises on my cheeks. Our lips are so close to each other, only inches apart. I glance away first and reach for my drink, taking a sip just to do something with my hands.

"Aren't you two cute." Connor's tone is light, but I can hear the edge under his words. "Wearing your guy's jersey and everything."

My whole body tenses at his perusal, but Rory presses another quick, warm kiss to my temple, and all my thoughts stop.

"I pretty much had to wrestle her into it," he says against me.

This isn't real, because there's no way Rory's brushing his lips against my skin in that sweet, intoxicating way. Where the hell did he learn to act like this?

"But that's okay. I don't mind wrestling with Hazel. In fact," his voice is soft and intimate as he peers down at me, eyes flaring with heat, "I kind of like it."

My body warms, and I remind myself to breathe. I need more oxygen in my brain, because I can't think of a single thing. I'm just staring up at Rory, replaying his words, melting against him.

Connor rubs his jaw. "Wasn't she your tutor in high school?"

"She sure was." One of Rory's hands slides to my thigh. "Lucky me."

The warning bells sound off in my head—where's Connor going with this?—but the large hand rubbing slow, soothing strokes on my thigh distracts me. It's weird how Rory's touch is actually calming me.

Connor's mouth twists with a wry smile. "Were you hitting on my girl back in school? Shame on you, Miller."

When Rory smiles down at me, it feels private, not smug or arrogant but sweet and comforting. It feels like we're on the same team for once. "I didn't hit on her."

I make a face. "You did."

As a joke during one of our tutoring sessions in high school, he flipped to a new page, and it had HAZEL HARTLEY written with hearts all around it.

Rory grins shamelessly. I wonder what memory he's thinking of. "Maybe a little. But mostly I just thought about you."

My pulse trips. He's playing a role here, and he's toying with Connor like a cat with a string, but that sounded so honest.

He's so good at this.

Rory raises one brow. "All I had to do was wait."

He doesn't take his eyes off me, and out of the corner of my eye, Connor shifts, folding his arms over his chest. Rory dips down so his nose is pressed against my neck and inhales deeply. Sparks crack and pop against my skin.

"You smell so good," he murmurs, like Connor isn't even there.

I shiver, and Pippa and I exchange a glance. Her eyes widen, her silent way of saying *he's really taking this faking thing seriously*, and I widen my eyes back at her. *I know.*

"You know what the most interesting part is?" Rory asks. Mischief glitters in his gaze. "Apparently Hartley has had a thing for me for years."

My stomach lodges in my throat, and I feel like both laughing and twisting one of Rory's nipples. He holds my gaze with that provoking, amused smile. "Right, baby?"

I almost gag at being called *baby*, but across the table, Connor's wearing a murderous expression.

Perfect.

"It's true," I tell Rory, giving him a little smile.

"She even liked me when you two were together," Rory tells Connor. "That's what you said, right, Hartley?"

Rory's a master at stirring shit up. I can see Connor's sensitive male pride wounded in his clenched fist, his hard gaze.

I narrow my eyes at Rory, pretending to scold him. "That was our secret."

"I'm going to get another drink." Connor slides out of the booth without another word.

A sense of victory rises in me, and I feel like laughing.

"What did I tell you?" Rory murmurs, and the hairs on the back of my neck rise as his breath tickles my ear. "Trust me."

Our attention is pulled back to the booth, where everyone's in a heated discussion.

"No one wears underwear during yoga," Hayden tells everyone.

Alexei stares at Hayden in horror. "What are you talking about?"

Pippa's giggling so hard she can't breathe. Jamie gives Hayden a baffled look, shaking his head.

Hayden looks around at everyone. "Right?"

Everyone's laughing, shaking their heads at the big, blond defenseman.

"My friend in Pittsburgh told me this. She's a yoga teacher." Hayden frowns, thinking. "Victoria."

"Veronica," Alexei corrects him, shaking his head. "You said her name was Veronica."

My nose wrinkles. Hayden's a lovable goofball with a heart of gold and probably my favorite player on the team, but he has a "friend" in every city. His type skews tall, dark haired, and curvy, and I'm pretty sure by "'friend'" he means "'fuck buddy'."

Hockey players. Even the good ones know they have unlimited options.

Hayden looks to me with a beseeching expression. "Hazel. Come on. People don't wear underwear in your classes, right?"

I burst out laughing. "I don't go around *checking*." Rory chuckles, shaking me, and I'm grinning ear to ear at Hayden. "You're so weird."

The conversation moves on, and I'm trying to listen, but Rory's hand keeps moving on my thigh with firm strokes over my leggings. I'm overheating. My face is warm, and I take a long drink of my beer to cool myself down.

God, I love beer. I love the cold, crisp taste. I love the bubbles, and I even love how filling it is. When I set my drink down, Rory's eyes linger on my mouth as I lick the foam off my lips.

"Yes?" I ask lightly.

"I'm just enjoying watching you enjoy that beer."

Heat blooms between my legs, and I shift on his lap. His hands tighten on my waist like his reflex is to keep me from getting up.

"You don't have to hold me down, you know. I'm not going to float away."

His eyebrows lift, and his gaze pins me in a determined, interested way. "I don't have to hold you down, but what if I want to?"

I huff, face heating at the images playing in my head. His hand on my wrist. His lips against my temple, but with his torso holding me down against the bed as he whispers all the dirty things he's going to do to me.

Wow. Hot. That would be hot.

No. This is Rory. He's a shameless flirt, just like Hayden. The word *monogamy* isn't in his dictionary. I'm not having these thoughts about him.

"So what's this I hear about you not wearing underwear in yoga?"

I hold back the laugh. "Wildly inappropriate, Miller."

"Tell me." His voice is a low murmur in my ear, and shivers run down the back of my neck. "Come on, Hartley. I'm dying to know."

His lips brush the shell of my ear, and I scramble for a sharp barb to toss at him. "Fuck around and find out."

He holds my eyes, the corner of his mouth twitching up, and there's a thrum between my legs that I decide has nothing to do with him.

"Maybe I will."

My eyes drop to his mouth, curved slightly up on one side. He has more stubble than when I saw him the other day, and I'm thinking about what that would feel like against my skin, under my fingers. Between my legs.

I clear my throat and look away. "Good goal tonight."

"Thanks." His tone changes, and when I glance back at him, he's giving me a watered-down version of his lazy smile. The amusement doesn't reach his eyes like when he's teasing me.

If the Rory Miller who calls me a fire-breather and teases me about wearing his jersey is him in full color, this version of him is black and white, flattened, two-dimensional. It's the same emotionally exhausted expression I caught on him during the game.

I don't like it.

I poke him with my elbow. "What's the deal?"

"What do you mean?"

"You won the game. The team is thrilled, but you don't seem happy about it."

He shrugs. "I'm happy."

I'm not convinced, and I have a weird urge to pull him back

to center. For once, I want the arrogant, teasing, smug version of Miller back.

"Hayden's right," I say without a second thought.

Rory offers me a questioning look, and I lean in, inches from his ear. I don't know why I'm doing this.

"About wearing underwear under yoga clothes," I whisper.

His eyes heat, and our gazes hold as his hand slides to my hip, stroking over me to feel for the evidence.

He won't find it tonight. A voice in my head asks what the hell I'm doing, but we're just playing. Nothing's going to happen.

His eyes close. "Fuck. That's so hot."

Satisfaction courses through me and I smile to myself.

On the table, Rory's phone lights up with a text, and his phone background snags my attention.

"Oh my god," Pippa says, laughing and reaching for it, but I get to the phone first, staring in horror at the photo of Rory and me at sixteen and seventeen.

"No," I tell Rory, shaking my head, glancing between him and the photo.

He grins. "Yes."

I cringe. We're in the library after school, books and papers spread out on the table. It's a little grainy, and I'm wearing a small, guarded smile while he beams at me, his arm draped over the back of my chair.

"Where did you get this?"

"The yearbook."

"I haven't seen this picture in years."

Rory transferred to our high school when he was starting grade eleven and sat behind me in Geography, putting tiny pieces of paper in my hair to get me to talk to him.

I had just started dating Connor when this photo was taken.

Sometimes, I wish I could go back in time and warn myself away from him, but then it would have been someone else who hurt me instead.

I set the phone down. "This isn't going to be your background photo."

"Sure it is. It's cute." He tilts the phone to see the picture, and a funny smile twists on his mouth.

"I'll send you another one."

"No." His arms wrap around me again. "I'm keeping it. I like it."

CHAPTER 9
HAZEL

I'M WALKING out of the washroom later when I bump into Connor.

"Oh." The hallway seems to shrink. "Hi."

I keep walking but he clears his throat. "Hazel."

I really don't want to, but I have to work with the guy all year. "What's up?"

"So?" He gives me an expectant look. "This shit Miller's saying about you being into him while we were together?"

It takes every ounce of my energy not to smile in satisfaction. "What about it?"

The innocence in my tone is Oscar-worthy, and I'm queen of the world. From the way his eyes harden, Connor is *seething*. I may not like Rory, but he knows exactly how to piss people off.

Connor's jaw ticks. "Really?"

"Connor, it was years ago. Who cares?"

"Do you ever think about us?" he asks, watching me intently.

These fucking hockey players. They're so competitive.

"No," I lie.

He keeps watching me, and there's a tight, nauseous feeling in my stomach. I pray he doesn't know the truth.

"Hartley." Rory's in front of us, and I relax.

His arm goes around my shoulder, pulling me against him, and without meaning to, I inhale a lungful of his fresh scent.

"Let's go home." He uses a low, seductive voice in my ear. My blood feels slow and thick like honey when he uses that voice. "I'll do that thing you like."

Warmth spreads throughout me, zinging between my legs, as I picture what he could mean by that, if this were real.

I need to get out of the bar, out of Rory's charisma splash zone, and then I can think again. "Yeah. Home. I'm getting sleepy."

His hand slides into mine and he pulls me out of the hallway without another glance at Connor.

After saying our goodbyes to everyone, we step outside, and he whistles. "Did you see his face, Hartley?"

"Yes. God, he was so pissed."

We leave the alley and he walks in the direction of my apartment. "You live in the West End, right?"

How does he know that? "I don't need a bodyguard."

He smiles over his shoulder, slipping his hands into his pockets as I catch up. "In a match between you and the toughest criminals in the city, my money's on you every time. You're a tiny, terrifying dragon."

"I'm not tiny." I'm five foot six.

"I could pick you up and throw you over my shoulder."

"You won't."

His eyebrow lifts in challenge, and I feel that urge to laugh again. "I might."

I glare up at him, but the corner of my mouth is twitching. "Walk me home, then. We're almost there, anyway." My words are casual, cool, and indifferent.

As we walk, he takes a deep breath and lets it out slowly. His gaze is on the sky, at the stars floating in the inky darkness, barely visible with all the city lights.

"You were drinking water all night," I say just to fill the silence.

"Yep."

"Do you not drink?" As his fake girlfriend, I should know these things.

"I drink. Sometimes. Not often. I don't drink much during the season." He rubs the back of his neck. "Alcohol is inflammatory."

"Oh." That makes sense, I guess.

"I'm only worth as much as my body can do for me." He pats his flat stomach. "This eight-pack isn't going to maintain itself."

His words pinch me, right in the chest. They sound like how my mom talks about food.

"One beer isn't going to ruin your perfect physique, Miller. And you don't have an eight-pack."

He meets my teasing gaze with his own, and sparks jump around in my stomach. "You want to see? It sounds like you do. What was that you just said about my body? *Perfect physique?*"

"Shut up." I huff with laughter. "Keep your clothes on."

He chuckles. "I love beer, though. Maybe not as much as you do, but—" His gaze goes far away with a nostalgic, blissed-out expression I immediately want to capture. "I dream about drinking a cold beer in the summer, on a patio with dinner."

He smiles at me, a genuine one without any trace of arrogance. Just pure enjoyment. I don't know what to do with it.

We're in front of my building. "This is me."

As I dig my keys out of my bag, his eyes move with curiosity over the old three-story walk-up.

"Thank you for tonight." I swallow, thinking about Connor

in the hallway. "What you said about me liking you in high school pissed him off. This season would be harder if we weren't doing this, so—" I glance at the sidewalk. "Thanks, Miller."

There's a beat of silence, and when I look up, he's studying me with a soft, gently teasing smile.

"You can call me Rory, you know."

"I know." I smile down at my keys. "Miller's fine."

"Alright, Hartley."

I smile again, and there's something weird in the air between us. It feels a little like we're friends.

Rory tucks his hands into his pockets, watching me. "Invite me up."

I bark out a laugh. So much for friends. "No."

"Come on." He gives me his most seductive smile, and even though my expression says *hell no*, the spot between my legs twinges with anticipation. "I want to see your place."

This back and forth we have going? We'd carry that straight to the bedroom. I imagine pushing Rory down on the bed and him flipping me over, fighting me for dominance.

"No," I say again, laughing at his shamelessness. "What's that smile? Are you trying to seduce me?"

"Is it working?"

"No." *Yes.*

He gazes down at me with a smile less arrogant than usual, less amused. His eyes flick down to my mouth and the smile slides away. Longing and heat flash across his face. For a brief moment, I want him to kiss me.

His eyes drop to my mouth again and determination floods them. My heart pounds. Oh my god. Arousal blooms inside me. I should be freaking out as he steps forward, shoving him back as he enters my space, but I'm not.

The front door opens. Someone walks out, and we jerk,

moving out of the way. I suck a deep breath into my lungs, trying to calm myself.

Rory's going to have his hands all over me for three months, and I can't lose my head every time it happens.

His eyebrows bob once. "We'll be traveling for a week, so I won't see you."

"Okay. Safe travels." I pause in the doorway. "Good night."

"Night, Hartley."

Later, I lie in bed, thinking about his hands on my waist, his mouth against my neck. *Invite me up.* I snort to myself. Never.

He'd be as competitive and determined in bed as he is on the ice, I bet. He'd call me *Hartley* in that low, teasing tone as he dragged his tongue over my skin, watching my reaction.

Never in a million *years* would that happen. Not even once. Because it would be so good, I just know it, and this thing we're doing is fake.

WHILE I SIT on the plane the next day, waiting for the rest of the players to board, I study the photo I posted to my social media. It's the one of me and Hazel at Streicher and Pippa's engagement party—my hand around Hazel's waist, her mouth stretching into a pretty smile from something I said that made her actually laugh, and my eyes are on her.

My feelings for her are so fucking obvious it's not even funny.

My phone buzzes with an incoming call—my dad. My shoulders tighten, but I answer. If I ignore it, he'll keep calling.

"Hey."

"Rory." His tone is all business, as usual. "I sent over the rest of the contracts this morning."

On top of being one of Canada's greatest hockey players, a hall of famer, and a guest commentator on the sports shows, my dad is also my agent. He's always been my agent. He knows the hockey world inside and out, and it was just easiest this way.

"Yep. I saw them."

"Good. I spoke with the dietitian. She's going to make some changes to your macros."

I stare out the window as they load our bags onto the plane. My dad has arranged for the dietician to work with a meal delivery service because getting enough protein is a challenge for me.

"Got it."

"Are you logging everything you're eating?"

"Always."

"No alcohol, no red meat, no sugar, no trans fats," he lists off.

I think about Hazel's expression of bliss as she drank her beer the other night and wonder what it would be like to enjoy food like that.

"I remember."

"Good. If you want to be the best, you need to eat like the best. Food is fuel. Garbage in, garbage out. We need you fast and sharp out there, Rory. You missed that shot in the second period the other night. That could have been yours."

My dad goes on about all the chances I've missed while I half listen. Even if I'm the best in the league, I could be better. Even if I'm the fastest, there's some young guy in the minors just waiting to take my place. If I even look at sugar, the inflammation will slow me down.

"I'm thinking about taking a trip out there," he says—he lives in Toronto with his girlfriend. My shoulders hitch more. He did this last year when I played for Calgary. "Maybe stay a few months."

"A few months?" I frown. "Your girlfriend wouldn't mind?" She has a job there, but I can't remember what. I only met her briefly once last year.

There's a pause on the other end. "We're not together anymore."

Of course. There's something about my dad that makes

women leave. Obsession? Relentless competition? Nothing ever being good enough? I don't want to look too closely, because whatever it is, I've inherited it.

I clear my throat. "Sorry."

"It's fine." Another awkward pause.

Does he want to stay for a few months because he's lonely? Fuck. The thought breaks my heart, and it's on the tip of my tongue to agree, but this year needs to be different.

Ward made me captain, and I want to make him proud without my dad's voice in my ear, in my head, telling me how to be. Hanging with the guys at the bar after games? When my dad's in town, that's not happening.

And spending time with Hazel? He'd never approve.

"It's not a good time," I tell my dad, swallowing past a thick throat. "I, uh. I'm still getting settled into the team."

"You need someone pushing you, Rory."

He's pushed me my entire life, but it's not working anymore. I don't feel the same burning desire to be the best like I used to, because no matter what I do, the goal posts always move. How do I tell him that, though? He'd never understand.

"Now that you're captain, you're a playmaker," he continues. "This is the perfect opportunity to look good."

My gut churns at the idea of choosing plays that benefit me. I make a quick excuse that we're taking off and hang up, and a second later, Streicher drops into the seat beside me.

"Hey, buddy." My mood lightens. "Ready for Columbus?"

Their goaltending is shit, but their offense is strong. He's going to be fielding shots all game.

"I'm ready." He pulls out his phone. His background is a picture of Pippa and Daisy, their dog.

I wonder if Hazel ever wants a dog. She and Pippa take Daisy on walks in the trails around Vancouver all the time.

McKinnon steps onto the plane, and as he passes, his bag shoves against Streicher's shoulder with enough force that a normal person would apologize. Instead, McKinnon just keeps walking.

Streicher's hand tenses and he gives me a sidelong glance. "Heard you're rooming together."

Sometimes, the coaches make guys share hotel rooms on the road. "I asked Ward if I could room with you, but he said no. I don't know whether it's a curse because I have to see his fucking face when I wake up, or a blessing because I get to fuck with him."

Streicher snorts. "He was pissed the other night, seeing you and Hazel."

I smile, remembering his expression at the game after I made Hartley give me a kiss through the glass. My grin drops at the image of her in the hallway. Her shoulders were up to her ears while he loomed over her.

That fucking prick. My mind flicks to what I packed in my bag after I found out McKinnon and I are rooming together, and excitement weaves through me.

I can't wait to fuck with him.

"So, this thing with Hazel," Jamie says.

Anxiety clenches behind my sternum. We're on better terms these days, but I still ditched the guy the second we got drafted. I was still a fucking asshole for all the years between then and now. Images of our fight last year on the ice replay in my head—the wet thud of his fist hitting my cheekbone, the blood dripping from his split lip.

"Don't tell me you're going to give me the old *hurt her and die* thing, Streicher."

The last players file onto the plane, taking their seats. "I know you won't."

An image flits into my head of the four of us—Jamie, Pippa, Hazel, and me. We're at a barbecue, hanging out. Pippa's curled up against Jamie, and Hazel's tucked into my side. I loop my arm around her shoulder, and she smiles up at me.

"Do you know what you're doing?"

"About faking it?" I ask, keeping my voice low, and he nods.

I frown, glancing out the window as an ugly feeling surges in my gut. She thinks it's fake. What if January comes and she still doesn't want anything real? I'm Rick Miller's son, after all. His carbon copy. Women get to know my dad, and soon enough, they're packing their bags.

"Of course," I answer, clearing my throat and shifting in my seat.

That old competitive focus that's been driving me my entire life flows through me. I wasn't lying when I told Hartley that I always bet on myself.

"What happened with them?" I ask him. "Why'd they break up?"

"Pippa says he cheated on her, but she doesn't know details."

I look out the window again, thinking about her, before I unlock my phone and pull up our chat.

I'm serious about teaching you to skate, I text her.

Her response pops up a moment later. *Fuck no. I only said yes because Connor tried and I didn't want to.*

That was the wrong thing to say, because now I want to be the one to teach her even more. My phone buzzes with a text from Streicher. I send him a curious glance but open the link he sent.

Ember Yoga. Spark your love of movement.

"Hartley's online yoga classes?"

He cuts me a side-long look. "Don't tell her I sent you that."

Yoga in an inclusive, encouraging environment. All body types, ages, ethnicities, nationalities, religions, genders, and sexual orientations warmly welcomed.

I know exactly what I'm doing tonight.

CHAPTER 11

RORY

AFTER DINNER, I'm unpacking in the hotel room when McKinnon enters. I pull the framed photo of Hartley out of my bag and set it on the nightstand. It's a zoomed in version of the photo from the engagement party, with me cropped out.

"You don't mind, right?" I ask McKinnon.

His lip curls at the picture, and I fucking *know* he's thinking about the other night at the bar, when I told everyone Hartley liked me while they were together.

"I don't give a shit." He turns away from me, pulling protein powder out of his bag and scooping it into his mixer cup.

"Good." I take a seat at the desk, swiveling back and forth as he mixes his drink.

"Especially," he adds, "because when you fuck up, I'll be here." He glances over his shoulder, wearing his own smug smirk, and mine drops a fraction.

A possessive feeling ricochets through me. "What the fuck does that mean?"

He leans against the counter as he takes a drink. "You think I don't know you've always had a thing for Hartley? She might be having fun with you *now*," he lets the last word linger, "but I had her first." His smile turns cruel and cold, and rage bleeds through me as he shrugs. "Hazel and I aren't done yet."

"McKinnon, this is just sad." My tone is condescending, but my heart pounds with protective anger.

"We'll see."

We stare each other down, but my phone alarm goes off, interrupting. I hit the button to silence it and send him an apologetic look that's clearly fake.

"Now that I know you're pining after my girlfriend, this is going to be awkward." I wake my laptop up, pop my earbuds in, and join the Zoom call.

A moment later, Hartley's face fills my screen.

"Hi," she says into my earbuds, giving me a welcoming smile until it falls abruptly. "*You're* Bert Randy? I knew that name sounded fake."

I chuckle, leaning back in the desk chair, aware that McKinnon is watching over my shoulder. "I miss you, too. Send me more nudes like that one you sent last night."

"Miller," she says, horrified. "I'm working. Go away."

"I'm going to be so good for you, baby." I nudge my laptop so she can see McKinnon behind me. "And I'll keep my shirt on so you don't get distracted."

Understanding passes over her features. "Can he hear me?"

"Nope." I point at the earbuds.

"Good. Don't call me baby." Her nostrils flare, and I smile wider at her irritation. It's like a drug to me. I love playing with her, firing her up. "I get that we need to pretend in front of him, but—oh my god. Is that a photo of me on your nightstand?"

Behind me, McKinnon starts moving around the room, making noise. "You know I miss you like crazy when I'm on the road."

She flattens her palm over her mouth like she's trying to hide a laugh. "Did he see it?"

"Yep." I grin at her, and she snorts.

"Go into the hall if you're going to talk all night," McKinnon says.

Over my shoulder, I give him a disinterested, distracted look and point at my earbuds. "I can't hear you. I'm doing Hartley's yoga class."

"No, you're not," Hartley says in my ear.

I ignore her, shrugging at McKinnon. "You're welcome to join," I lie. He's not fucking welcome. "If you want to work on your flexibility."

"I'm good," he says, scowling as he picks up his phone and wallet.

I swivel my chair back to my laptop, smiling at Hartley as the hotel room door closes behind McKinnon. "That was fun."

The corner of her mouth lifts.

"Admit it."

Her smile lifts higher, and my knee bounces. "Okay. It was fun. Good night."

"I'm staying for the class."

"Miller. This is my job. We fucked with Connor, and now I actually need to teach a class."

Something unpleasant stabs me in the gut. I'm not like McKinnon. I'm not going to make things difficult for her when she's trying to work.

"Hey." My voice turns sincere and coaxing, and I dampen my amusement. "I just want to get a good stretch in, okay? I'm not here to cause problems."

She doesn't seem convinced. "You cause problems whether you're trying or not."

I laugh. "You're not wrong, but I'm going to mute myself. You won't even know I'm here." My brows lift. "Your website says everyone is welcome. You can't kick me out just because I have a perfect physique."

I swear she's blushing. "You're never going to drop that, are you?"

"Nope." She's definitely blushing.

"You can stay on one condition." Her expression turns serious. "These students are not professional athletes. They're normal people. They have normal bodies. My job is to make everyone feel welcome, regardless of what they look like or what their abilities are." She gives me a long look, no trace of irritation or frustration on her face. "I teach bigger bodies, smaller bodies, young people, old people, disabled people... everyone. Everyone deserves to enjoy movement and feel good in their bodies."

An ugly feeling whips through me. Does she really think I'm *such* an asshole that I would make fun of people for not being professional athletes?

"If you make anyone feel uncomfortable," she says, and her voice is firm, "I'll remove you from the class."

I blink at her. "I wouldn't, Hartley. I would never do that."

She looks down, nodding. "Okay. Good."

My eyebrows pinch as I study her. I just found an interesting part of Hartley, and I want to know so much more. And at the same time, I don't like that she felt the need to lay out these rules for me. Treating people with respect is just common sense. I would never—

I think about last year, how Streicher and I fought. How I antagonized people on the ice. How everyone compares me to my dad.

A moment later, six more video squares pop up.

"Oh, *good*, we got new meat!" a woman in her sixties says as soon as she spots me. She has short, spiky platinum blond hair, big eyes, and is sitting on her yoga mat in her living room, bouncing with energy like a kid.

I grin wide. "Hi. I'm Rory."

"I'm Elaine," the woman says, and an orange cat walks by in the background. "That's Archie."

The others introduce themselves: Clarence, a man in his eighties who informs me he just got a new hip; Laura, a quiet, bigger-bodied woman about my age; Vatsi, who looks to be in the later stages of pregnancy; and Hyung, who looks about twenty and appears to be in a dorm room.

"What brings you to the class, Rory?" Clarence asks.

I glance at Hartley's screen, where she's setting up her mat and props. "I'm Hartley's boyfriend."

Elaine gasps in delight. "Hazel, you didn't tell us you had a boyfriend."

"She's overwhelmed by her feelings for me." Amusement dances up and down my spine as Hartley slowly turns to the camera, staring daggers at me. "It's been a while since she's fallen so hard for someone."

Hartley stares at her camera, and I can just *feel* her attention on me, moving over my face.

Elaine raises her hand. "I have a thousand questions."

"You were supposed to mute yourself," Hartley says to me, arching a brow.

I click the mute button and throw my hands up with a grin, signaling that I'll be quiet.

"Let's begin," she says, and I adjust the meeting settings so her video takes up my entire screen. "Take a seat however's comfortable for you."

I move to the floor, tilting my laptop screen so I can see her, watching as she moves into a cross-legged position on her mat.

"Take a few deep, slow breaths through your nose. Expand into your lungs, expand into your stomach, feel the floor or the prop beneath you. If you want, close your eyes."

I suck a few breaths in and out, keeping my eyes on her.

"Find your breathing."

Her voice melts into something smooth and calm. My heart rate slows as I count my breaths, in for five, out for five. Her eyes are closed, her dark hair up in a ponytail with a few pieces loose in the front. She's wearing a t-shirt that says *Don't Touch Me* and navy yoga leggings with constellations all over them.

The deplorable, horny part of me thinks about her telling me she doesn't wear panties under her leggings.

"You get to do this class the way you want," she adds. "You're the boss of your body. Be a good boss and listen to it."

The authoritative yet gentle way she speaks makes me smile.

I scan the background of Hazel's screen. Behind her, a mini fridge sits on top of a counter beside a narrow oven and stove. Her laptop is on the floor so I can't see much except for a pink kettle on the counter. On the left side of the screen, a dark mahogany coffee table has been pushed beside a couch, and on the right, it looks like the edge of her bed.

Jesus. Hartley's place is *tiny*.

"Set an intention," she goes on, eyes still closed. "My intention is to feel good in my body, to quiet my mind, and to get a good stretch in before bed."

In a game, my intention would be to score more goals than everyone else. Impress the coaches. Work until my muscles burn, until my lungs are on fire.

Hartley leads us through the yin poses, and when we move into reclined butterfly, a low groan slips out of me. Thank god I'm muted. The stretch pulls across my tight shoulders and up my inner thighs. The warm, sluggish haze of relaxation flows through me, making my limbs heavy and my thoughts slow.

"Find your breath," she murmurs, and I count in for five, out for five. "Relax your jaw."

I unclamp my molars. She's sprawled out on her back, belly rising and falling with her breathing.

You can relax when you're dead, I hear my dad say. His brutal approach to sports is nothing like this.

"It's okay if your mind wanders," she says, and it feels like she's whispering directly in my ear. A shiver rolls down my spine. "Invite it back. Find your breath."

Finally, we end on our backs, palms facing the ceiling. My body is relaxed, and my mind hums with content stillness as I listen to her soft voice.

"To close today's practice, I want you to think about what makes you feel worthy."

Confusion rises inside me. Worthy. I repeat the word in my head. Worthy of what?

"For me," she says, smiling to herself, "I love hanging out with my sister. Pippa brings out all the best parts of me and I always go home feeling so happy and grateful."

I'm mesmerized. She's so beautiful. I wish I could record this so I could listen to it again and again.

"I love running," she goes on. "Even when I'm huffing and puffing, there's sweat in my eyes, and my face is red like a tomato, I love feeling strong in my body. I love what my body can do for me.

"And lastly, my work makes me feel worthy. I love seeing what the human body can do. We're all capable of incredible things, no matter what type of body we're moving in. I love playing a part in that." She pauses. "Now, your turn. Where do you find your purpose? What makes you smile? What makes you feel loved?"

Worthy. The word flings itself around in my head, searching for a place to land. My purpose is to be the best hockey player possible, and anything less is failure.

What makes you feel loved?

A memory flits into my head. I was eleven, and it was the summer before my mom left. We were walking through the trails near our home in North Vancouver. We stopped at a creek, and she bent down to flick a few droplets of water at me, grinning. Her deep blue eyes, the same as mine, glowed in the forest light. I laughed and flicked the water right back at her.

"*I love you. I hope you know that.*"

A longing ache fills my chest. I haven't heard those words since I was a kid, since she lived with us.

And I was the one who didn't want to live with her. I was the one who wanted to stay with Dad full time because I'm always chasing his approval.

When class is over, there's a chorus of farewells as people sign out.

"Miller," she says. The others have left the virtual meeting room and we're the only ones here. There's something different in her voice as she studies me through the camera. "Are you okay?"

I force a wry smile. "You think I'm so out of shape that I couldn't endure a little stretching, Hartley?"

She doesn't answer right away, and panic spikes inside me that she's not taking my bait.

"I don't think that at all. I just think for someone from the world of macho jocks and push-ups, my class can be jarring."

"Macho jocks and push-ups?" I repeat, starting to smile.

She grins. "I'm not wrong."

"You're not wrong." Her smile makes the tight, ugly feeling in my throat dissipate. "Thanks for letting me join."

She nods. "Good night."

"Good night, Hartley."

She ends the meeting, and I sit there, absentmindedly swiveling.

My dad's approach to discomfort is practice. Practice until you can't anymore. Tackle it head-on. Beat it out of yourself.

Don't run from it; conquer it. Crush it. Be the strongest and the fastest. Anything but the best is failure.

I pull up Hartley's website and sign up for all ten classes in this session.

————

We're walking through the terminal to board our flight home when something sparkly in a shop window catches my eye.

I lean down to study the tiny crystal dragon. It's a pale blue, so cute and chubby like a cartoon, but with red eyes that glow under the lights.

A big smile spreads over my face.

"Miller," Owens calls. "Let's go."

"I'll be right there." I turn back to the dragon and walk into the store.

It's about time I buy Hartley a present.

CHAPTER 12
HAZEL

I'M in my office creating a recovery plan for a player when Rory plunks a tiny crystal dragon in front of me.

He smiles down at me, leaning on the doorframe, eyes warm and soft, and my stomach flutters. "Hartley," he says by way of greeting.

Fuck, he looks good. Today was the toughest practice of the week, but Rory stands tall and his eyes are bright with energy.

I hate how athletic he is. I hate that he truly is one of the best athletes of his generation. I hate it, and yet I can't help but marvel at him.

My eyes go to the sparkly little dragon on my desk. "What's this?"

"You."

My lips part in denial. "It is not."

"Sure, it is. You're my tiny fire-breathing dragon." I glare at him and he nods, pointing at me. "Exactly like that. Red eyes and everything."

A laugh bursts out of me and I pick the stupid thing up, studying it.

It's cute.

"This is dumb," I tell him as warmth spreads through my chest.

"Hey, Hazel?" Hayden appears in the doorway. "Can I grab one of those bands?"

"Right." I rummage through my desk to find an extra band so he can do the physio exercises at home and toss one to him. "Need me to run through the exercises again?"

"Nope. I got them." Hayden's eyes land on the dragon and he grins. "Do you like it? Miller spent three grand on it."

My jaw drops and I turn to Rory. "Three *thousand* dollars?"

He shrugs like it's nothing.

"Miller, that's *way* too much money."

Hayden chuckles. "I told you, he likes you. Later, lovebirds."

As he leaves, Rory gives me a strange look. "You know what I make, right?"

Only Rory would be so up-front about being the highest-paid player in the league.

I blink at the little dragon. "This cost more than my monthly rent. You can't spend that much money on me." I lower my voice. "Especially because..." I give him a *you know* gesture.

He arches an eyebrow, smiling. "Because what?"

"Because I'm not really your girlfriend."

The photo of us from Pippa's engagement party has been making the rounds online, only adding to our credibility because it was taken before we were public about our relationship. In the photo, Rory smiles down at me with a soft look, like he doesn't want to let me go. *He's so gone for her,* one of the comments said.

His gaze sharpens. "But if you were my girlfriend, it would be okay?"

What? His eyes are so deep blue, so spellbinding, and I don't like how out of control and wobbly I feel. I'm at work. I should be in control. I should *always* be in control.

But he joined my yoga class, he told everyone he was my boyfriend, and he seemed to enjoy the class until I asked them to think about what makes them feel loved, and then he looked stricken and lost.

I've been thinking about that all week.

"Don't spend that much money on me."

He hums, narrowing his eyes at me. "That sounds like a challenge."

"It's not." I'm laughing again. "You're unhinged, Miller."

He leans in, bracing his hands on either arm of my chair and bringing his mouth to my ear in that way that makes my pulse jump.

"If you really were my girlfriend, Hartley," he whispers, his breath sending electric currents over my skin, "there's no limit to what I would spend on you, so if we want to sell this? Let me."

I swallow, unsure of what to say.

"I've been thinking about you," he adds, straightening up, and my pulse trips.

"What you do late at night in your hotel room is none of my business, Miller." I give him a cool, disinterested smile despite my stomach doing somersaults.

He's been *thinking* about me? How? In a sexy way? Do I like that?

I think I like that.

My brow arches. "Or in McDonald's bathrooms."

He snorts. "I've never been to McDonald's."

Shock drops the disinterest right off my face. "*What?* Not even when you were a kid? Not even when you're drunk?"

"I don't really get drunk, Hartley."

I stare at him in confusion. "What about the ball pit?"

His chest shakes with laughter, eyes dancing with amusement, and I feel that funny flopping, somersaulty feeling in my stomach again. "The ball pit sounds disgusting."

I give him a *duh* look. "Of course it is, but that doesn't matter when you're six."

"Or drunk." His eyes tease me.

"Or drunk," I agree.

I wonder what he'd be like drunk, or a little tipsy. I bet he'd be silly, handsy, and sweet. Warmth gathers in my chest before I shove it away.

I can't be thinking thoughts like that about him.

I tuck my bottom lip between my teeth, and his eyes drop to my mouth.

"Was there something you wanted?" I ask, face going warm.

He blinks as his eyes refocus. "There's a community skating thing in the arena tonight and Ward is teaching a bunch of kids how to skate."

"Okay. Good for him."

Rory grins, and my stomach dips. His smile lifts even higher, and he's so pretty. He's strong, broad, and so, so tall, and his hair is thick and a little wavy in a way that makes me *itch* to drag my fingers through it, but also, he's pretty.

"And you know I want to look like a responsible, reliable captain."

I know where this is going. "I don't see what this has to do with me."

"Hartley, I'm going to teach you how to skate."

CHAPTER 13

RORY

"BEND YOUR KNEES."

"I'm going to fall."

"You're not going to fall." I hold her waist, guiding her from behind as she skates at a glacial pace, wobbling. "I won't let you."

On every side of us, people skate in a big circle around the community center while music plays. A disco ball scatters dancing lights across Hazel's hair.

"Do you think he saw us?" she asks.

Her hair smells nice. Light and pretty, like vanilla or cookies or something. "Who?"

"Ward."

Right. The whole reason we're here. On the other end of the arena, Ward is in a roped-off section with a bunch of toddlers, teaching them to skate. They're all faster than Hartley.

"He saw me taking photos with people when we arrived."

She makes a noise of acknowledgement and keeps shuffling on the ice.

My eyes drop to her ass. Fucking hell, those yoga leggings. I think about her not wearing panties under her yoga clothes, and arousal tightens in my groin.

I'm a fucking asshole, but I've pictured making her come a thousand times. It would change my whole life, watching her unravel because of me. She's so in control, and making her arch and melt and cry out in pleasure would make my fucking life.

"Miller." My head snaps up, and she's looking at me over her shoulder with a small smirk. "Were you staring at my ass?"

"Yes." I grin. "It's the leggings."

She laughs and shakes her head. "Gross." I let go of her waist, and her eyes widen in fear. "Don't." Her hands come to mine, holding them against her, and my blood beats with pride. "I'm not ready."

She's so cute. "Hartley, you're doing great. I'm going to skate beside you for a bit."

She makes a strangled noise but lets my hands go free, and I move to her side. We're the slowest people on the ice, but she doesn't seem to notice.

Her eyes lift to my face. "You don't need to look so pleased."

I throw my hands up, laughing. "I'm not."

"You're gloating."

"I'm having fun with you."

It's the truth. Hanging out with Hartley like this, I'm relaxed. She looks away, but she's smiling. On her next step forward, her skate slips, and she gasps as she catches herself.

"You got this," I tell her, hovering.

She slips her gloved hand into mine, and my heart jumps into my throat as I stare down at where our hands are joined. Jittery nerves coil in my chest.

"We're supposed to be a couple," she says, not looking at me. "And I don't want to fall."

"I know." My pulse is going nuts.

She's so pretty. Her hair is down around her shoulders. The other day in the shower, I jerked off to thoughts of running my nose along the column of her neck, skimming my hands over her hips to feel whether she was wearing something beneath those leggings.

A shudder rolls through me and I swallow, glancing at her plush mouth. Could I get away with kissing her here? Ward isn't even looking.

She gives me a strange look as we skate. "What?"

My eyes widen. "What?"

"You're being weird."

"No, I'm not."

"Yes, you are." Her head tilts as she studies me, and there's another jump of nerves in my gut. "Oh my god. Are you nervous around me?"

I laugh, looking away. "No."

She loses her balance, and my hands come back to her waist to catch her. "Yes, you are. You're nervous."

A smile creeps up on my mouth. "You're terrifying."

She snorts, and I love the way her lips tilt. "You know I'm not actually a dragon, right?" Her tone is soft and teasing, and it trickles down the back of my neck, warm like honey.

We start skating again, and I slip my hand back into hers. "Why do you teach on Zoom? I thought you taught in a studio."

"Sometimes I do. The studios value seniority, so it's tough to get classes." Her mouth twists. "And it's an accessibility thing, too. It's easier for people to log in online than get to a studio. Elaine likes to travel but wants to keep up her practice. Clarence's elevator is always broken, and with his hip stuff, stairs are hard. Vatsi's about to have a baby, so her life is about to get busy. Hyung likes not having to commute all the way from the university, that's like an hour on the bus each way. And

Laura—" She stops abruptly. I catch a flash of fury in her eyes before it's gone. "Well, Laura hasn't had the greatest experiences with studios. Zoom yoga is the best option for a lot of people."

The fire in her eyes lights me up. "You really love it, don't you?"

"It's my purpose," she answers quickly, effortlessly. "One day, I want to open a fitness studio. We'd offer yoga, Pilates, dance classes, even physio and massage therapy. There's this woman in the States who opened a body-positive studio. It's in New York." Her eyes sparkle. "They have Beyoncé dance classes. It's so cool to see her videos of them all dancing. All ages, all genders, all body types." She shrugs. "I want to create that here."

Something taut plucks in my chest. I should feel that way about hockey, and yet I don't.

Our eyes meet, and her expression stills. "I don't know why I told you that."

I hate that her walls are back up. "I'm glad you did."

I want to stay here forever with her, listening to her talk about the things she loves.

"I assume rooming with Connor went okay," she says.

What he said about waiting for me to fuck up so he can swoop in replays in my head. "It was fine."

If I tell her, it'll just upset her.

"He tried to piss me off, but I gave as good as I got." I wink at her.

"If anyone can get to him, it's you. You're cut from the same cloth."

My brow furrows. She's joking, but she's not joking. "What do you mean?"

"You know." She shrugs. "You guys are the same."

My frown deepens. "No, we're not."

She gives me a derisive look, like *who are you fooling?* and the ugly feeling settles inside me.

"Hartley." My voice is low. "We're not the same."

"You're a hockey player." There's a slice of something honest and angry in her gaze. "You have everything. You don't need to care about other people. Women fall all over you and no one's ever said the word *no* to you."

"I care about other people." The words come out more terse than I mean for them to, and I try to force a teasing smile, but I can't. I hate that she thinks we're the same. "I'm not McKinnon, and I don't like being compared to him. I've never cheated. I'm not like that."

"Maybe you haven't cheated, but I know you." She's wearing this sad expression that breaks my fucking heart, like she's waiting for me to realize what she knows.

I hate that look. My mom wore that look when she left my dad.

"Women are just there for entertainment for you." Her throat works. "We're disposable."

"No." I stop skating, paying zero attention to the people whizzing past us. "What gave you that fucking idea, Hazel?"

She drops my hand. "Ashley," she says, like I should know what she's talking about.

"Ashley who?" Frustration tightens in my body, and I hate that she has this picture of me in her head.

"Ashley Peterson from high school." Off my baffled look, she says, "You took her out and made her feel special and she had this huge crush on you."

I'm shaking my head because I don't even remember this girl. High school was a blur of five a.m. practices, trying to keep up in my classes so I could at least graduate, and endless gym sessions with personal trainers who pushed me to my absolute limit. Getting drafted was all that mattered, and I was never allowed to forget it. Tutoring sessions with Hartley were the one bright spot.

"Blond?" I ask as the vague memory of this Ashley girl filters into my head.

Hartley looks at me with disbelief. "Yes."

I scrub a hand down my face as it starts coming back to me. This Ashley girl and I made out, I think? "Hartley, this was like a decade ago. I don't remember what happened."

She blinks, looking both furious and sad. "I'll remind you. You dumped her the day before the dance."

I dated in high school, but it was always casual. I couldn't handle having a girlfriend. I could barely keep my head above water with school and hockey.

And no one seemed as good as Hartley.

I don't remember asking this Ashley girl to the dance. I give Hazel a *what gives* look. "Okay?"

She exhales a frustrated breath. "I convinced her to go to the dance anyway. We walked in, and you had your tongue down another girl's throat."

The memories hit me. She's right. I did that, and I didn't really care about this Ashley girl's feelings. A kernel of self-loathing hardens in my chest. I'm an asshole, just like Rick Miller.

"She cried in the bathroom. You made her feel like there was something wrong with her. You made her feel small and insignificant and worthless."

The intensity in Hazel's voice cuts through me. There's an undercurrent of emotion to her words that makes my stomach turn.

"Do you know how shitty that is?" she continues with pain in her eyes. "Do you know how"—she points at her head—"damaging and traumatic that is?"

I hear the quiet close of the door as my mom leaves. I hear it again as Lauren, my dad's next girlfriend, leaves a few years later. I hear the aloof way he tells me that he and his next girlfriend are no longer together.

My life is going to mirror his. It already does. I'll be fifty-five and waiting for my current girlfriend to leave me like the others. Shame and frustration wrap around my chest, squeezing like a band.

"Hartley, it was a decade ago. I'm sure she's over it."

Fury rises in her gaze, and I can see her pulse going in her neck. "You sure about that?"

I shrug, brushing it off. Please. Please, can we fucking move on from this conversation? "I would fucking *hope* she's over it by now." The words tumble out of my mouth, fueled by this crushing, cold feeling inside my chest. "How pathetic is that to be moping around a decade later over some guy who didn't even care about you? I doubt she even thinks about me anymore, and if she does, she doesn't have enough going on in her life."

I hear the words, but I can't stop them. Shame has me by the throat, choking me. Hazel looks like she's been slapped, blinking at me with hurt and shock before she lets out a quiet laugh.

"I don't know why I said yes to this. This is exactly who I thought you were."

My stomach sinks.

"I don't know why I thought—" She breaks off, shaking her head as she shuffles away, heading for the entrance to the rink. "We're done."

CHAPTER 14

RORY

I HEAR the end of her sentence a million ways.

I don't know why I thought I could spend time with you.

I don't know why I thought our agreement would ever work.

I don't know why I thought you were different.

It hits me: Hazel's reaction isn't just about her friend. It's about what Connor did to *her*.

I said it didn't matter. That she should be over it by now. I called her pathetic. How fucking thoughtless could I be? No wonder she's done with me.

My dad wouldn't budge. Rick Miller always lets them walk away. He wanted to go after my mom—I still remember his crushed expression when she left—but he didn't.

"Hartley," I call, skating after her. She ignores me as I approach. "I didn't mean it. I'm sorry."

She reaches for the boards, loses her balance, and I'm right there holding her up.

"Don't touch me," she hisses. "I'm mad at you."

"I know." I wait for her to find her balance before I pull back. "You have every right to be mad."

Her jaw is so tight and her eyes flash with all the bad

emotions I never, ever want to see there. She folds her arms over her chest, still glaring at me.

I rake a hand through my hair, pulse going a mile a minute. "I hate that I hurt your friend, so I brushed it off to make myself feel better. I think I thought—" I heave in a breath, watching her face for any reaction, any clue. "I thought that if I made it sound like it wasn't a big deal, I wouldn't feel like this."

"Like what."

"Like a fucking asshole." I search her eyes. "I don't want to hurt people like that. That's what my dad does. I'm sorry I hurt your friend. I was young and stupid, but that's no excuse." She watches me, and I memorize the gray threads in her irises, rimmed in thick, dark lashes. People maneuver around us, but we ignore them.

Understanding, sadness, and pain ebb and flow in her eyes. Hazel's throat works again and her eyebrows pull together before she looks away. "He cheated on me the whole time," she says quietly, staring at the ice.

Streicher told me this already and yet I'm still tensing with protective fury. How dare he fucking hurt her?

"I worked ahead in school so we could go to university together." Her gaze flicks up to mine before looking back down at the ice. "I found out at the end of the first year of university. Everyone knew but me."

Rage pounds through me, gathering power. McKinnon is so fucking stupid, and if it's possible, I hate him even more. My hands make fists so I don't reach for her. No wonder she doesn't take shit from anyone.

She plays with her fingernails. "He said—" She cuts herself off, tapping her top lip with her tongue.

My hands are on her shoulders, and I dip down to meet her eyes. "What did he say?"

She shakes her head.

"Please tell me," I beg.

She shakes her head again. "I just want to forget it."

My teeth clench and that self-hatred pinches my chest again. She doesn't trust me enough to tell me. She thinks I'm like McKinnon.

So maybe I need to fix those things. Maybe, if I want this to be real with Hartley, I need to show her I'm nothing like him or my dad.

"I hate him for what he did to you." Does she know how fast my heart is beating, how tight my chest feels right now? "I don't just hate him for being an asshole; I hate him because he took you for granted. He lied to you and he was careless with you. I don't want to be anything like him."

I can see every shade of blue and gray in her eyes, and I let the mesmerizing colors anchor me, distract me from the looming realization that I've never done this before—this big, sincere apology.

Rick Miller doesn't apologize. It's not a skill he deemed necessary to teach me, and I can't even remember the last time I did it. Last year, when I felt the unsettling urge to make things right with Streicher, we fought it out on the ice.

"I'm sorry," I say again, this time just to hear myself, to know it's real.

I'm not like him.

"Okay." She looks away.

"Okay?" I lean down to catch her gaze. "You forgive me? We're okay?"

She gives me a tiny nod. She doesn't trust me fully, not yet, but the anger is gone from her eyes.

I rub a hand over my hair, letting my pulse return to normal, and give her a tentative look. "Let's keep skating."

She chews her bottom lip. She's about to say no, but I can't leave us on this note. "You're not a quitter," I tell her, mouth tipping up. "And think about how pissed he'll be when he learns that I taught you."

She grins like a little devil. "Okay."

"Congratulations, baby," I tell her as we start skating around the rink again, and her mouth twitches with amusement and irritation. "We just had our first fight."

"Don't call me baby," she says, but I can see her smiling.

CHAPTER 15

RORY

WE'RE STEPPING off the ice half an hour later when a guy in hockey equipment stops in front of me.

"You're Rory Miller."

My smile is easy and friendly. "Hey, man."

He points at the ice with a confused look. "Were you skating out there?"

"I was teaching my girlfriend." I loop my arm around Hazel's shoulders.

It's getting easier and easier to say those words. *My girlfriend.*

"We play pickup out here once a week." He gestures at the ice, where a handful of guys are skating around, talking and warming up. "Do you want to join us?"

I give him an apologetic smile. "Thanks, man, but I've gotta get her home."

The guy shrugs. "Alright, just thought I'd ask."

He steps onto the ice and skates away, and I lead Hazel to a bench so I can unlace her skates.

"Hold on." She puts a hand on my arm, watching the guys skate laps around the rink before her gaze lifts to mine. "You should play."

"Why?"

"Because..." She pauses. There's something sweet in her eyes. Affection, I think. "You had fun tonight, skating with me."

"Yeah." I grin. "With *you*. Not with some middle-aged guy named Steve."

She laughs, and I memorize it. "I'm serious. I think you might have fun out there."

On the ice, they're passing the puck, calling playful jabs at each other. One of them misses a shot and another one laughs, but not in a cruel way. Something strums in my chest.

"I let you teach me to skate," Hazel says. "You owe me."

"Oh, really?" I arch an eyebrow at her.

I think she's trying not to smile, from the way her eyes glow. "Yes. Not everything is a competition," she adds, softer. "Some things are just for fun."

I think about what I decided earlier, how I don't want to be anything like McKinnon. I want to be someone who Hazel's proud to be dating, even if it is pretend.

———

Twenty minutes later, I score another goal to total silence. The back of my neck prickles as Hazel watches from the stands, and I skate with the guys back to center ice for the next face-off.

"What's the score now?" one of the other guys calls to the ref.

"Twelve-zero."

"Jesus fuck," another guy mutters, and my gut tenses. "Miller, you're steamrolling us."

He's joking, but there's an edge to his words. These guys don't play like I'm used to. They're not nearly as competitive and cut-throat, and now there's a downtrodden energy among them. A knot forms behind my sternum. This isn't fun, and I don't know what I'm doing wrong. I'm scoring goals. I'm playing like I always play. I don't know why I thought this would be any different.

My gaze goes to Hazel, watching. A few feet away, Ward surveys the ice with his arms crossed, leaning on the wall with an unreadable expression. Our eyes meet before he turns and leaves.

Fuck. Some fucking captain I am.

"Guys, I need to go," I tell them. "Thanks for letting me play."

The mood lightens immediately, and they all say their goodbyes as I skate away, dropping the stick they lent me on the bench before I head over to Hazel.

"Hey." Her eyes search my face when I approach. "You're done?"

"Yep." That kernel of shame and embarrassment that I felt earlier during our argument lodges in the center of my chest. I kneel and unlace her skates, aware of her gaze on my face.

"Are we still good for the team dinner on Friday?" I ask.

"Oh." She blinks like she forgot. "Yes. We're on."

"Good." I pull her other skate off. The tight, ashamed feelings in my chest fade away the longer I talk with her. "The stylist is going to contact you."

"What are you talking about?"

"You need a dress. It's a black-tie dinner."

I take her socked foot between my palms. She glances at my hands, distracted, and as I press my thumb into the soles, her jaw goes slack.

I grin. She likes that.

"I have a dress," she says, still frowning at my hands rubbing her foot.

"You can't wear an old dress, Hartley." I work the ball of her foot and her eyelids droop. "Remember what I said? If you really were my girlfriend, I'd be spending money left and right on you. That's what Streicher does for Pippa."

I start on the other foot and she makes a noise that's half protest, half sigh of pleasure.

"Um," she says, blinking as I dig my thumb deeper. "Wow."

"Say yes, Hartley." Her eyes are hazy and soft. "Let me get you a pretty dress so you can feel good."

The spot I'm working on must be sore, because when I press into it, her eyes fall closed. "You're not going to make me wear something see-through, right?"

I chuckle. "No. I don't think I could *make* you wear anything." I picture her in something flimsy and transparent, looking hot and painfully fuckable as McKinnon leers, and sharp jealousy twists in my gut. "I like showing you off, Hartley, but no one gets to see your tits but me."

Her eyes open. Is that a *flush* I detect across her cheeks? "You wish."

My blood courses with pride and pleasure at seeing her flustered. I do fucking wish. "I'll set everything up. All you have to do is be there." My expression turns wicked. "And stand still when I make out with you."

She rolls her eyes, and her cheeks are absolutely going pink.

CHAPTER 16
RORY

WHEN I ARRIVE for the team dinner at the old mansion in Shaughnessy, a notoriously wealthy, old-money neighborhood in Vancouver, I notice two things.

The first is that Hartley looks fucking stunning.

I stand in the foyer, slack-jawed and staring at her in her navy-blue gown while my heart races. Hazel Hartley is the most beautiful woman I know. My throat knots as I try to swallow.

Between that crystal dragon she obviously liked but wouldn't admit, the dress, and the envelope tucked in my tux jacket, I'm becoming addicted to spending money on her.

The second thing I notice is that fuckface, McKinnon, circling her like a vulture. He stands two feet away, talking to her while she looks disinterested. His eyes rake over her, lingering on the perfect swell of her cleavage.

He cheated on me the whole time. Everyone knew but me.

My tongue taps my upper lip as jealousy and possessiveness charge through me. Players greet me as I move toward her, but I hardly notice.

Our argument on Wednesday showed me how much I have to lose with her, and I'm not going to give up.

"Hazel." My voice is low. Her eyes widen, either because I'm using her first name or because my hand now rests on her lower back in a way that shows everyone in the room she's mine. "You look beautiful," I tell her, and my heart pounds as I lower my mouth to hers.

She inhales sharply, and for the longest moment of my life, I worry she might push me off, but she melts against me, kissing me back, and in my chest, something locks into place.

CHAPTER 17

HAZEL

RORY MILLER KISSES ME, and the world tilts below my feet. His stubble scrapes my skin, making my breath catch. Kissing him is so different from what I expected.

His mouth is a gentle press against mine, his exhale is soft against my skin, and his fingers trail across my jaw before sinking into my hair. His movements are slow, unhurried. I'd say he was reluctant if it weren't for the way his tongue slips past my lips and lightly strokes me.

The breath whooshes out of my lungs, and I realize I'm gripping the front of his shirt in my fist. His fingers flex for a split second on the back of my hair, and he covers my hand on his chest, flattening it against him. Everything about him is warm, inviting, and comforting.

Nothing makes sense right now, but he smells so good—sandalwood and something clean, like body wash—and the sensation of his stubble brushing my chin is so enjoyable that I stop trying to figure this moment out. The way he smells pulls on a muscle low in my belly.

"Jesus Christ," he mutters to himself against my lips before his tongue glides against mine.

He grips the back of my hair—still gentle, still careful—and pulls. Rory kisses me like he's been thinking about this for a long time, and as sparks shoot over my skin at the feel of his hand in my hair, I make a quiet noise of pleasure against his lips.

He huffs. "Liked that, huh?"

His words rumble against my hand on his chest. I open my mouth to say something smart and sharp, but he strokes back inside, licking into me.

This isn't just a kiss. My head spins with the pleasure of his lips against mine, the way he tastes, the way he feels and smells.

In some dark corner of my mind, I wonder if this is how he'd use his tongue between my legs. The muscles there clench, and I nip his bottom lip. Under my palm, his heart beats fast.

I pull back to look at him, and my stomach flutters as our eyes lock. He looks wildly handsome. It's unfair how his blue eyes pop against the inky black and crisp white of his tux, and it's unfair how he can look so boyishly handsome and yet powerful and masculine at the same time. His hair is in that perfectly messy, just-fucked style that he pulls off so well. The sides are cleaned up like he snuck out to get a haircut this afternoon, and my fingers itch to trace the short hairs, feel the tickle of them under my nails.

Someone clears their throat and I snap back to reality.

Pippa and Jamie stare at us with the same amused expression, and Connor is nowhere to be found. My face heats and I run a finger along my lip line to make sure nothing smeared. Beside me, Rory shifts, breathing hard. Our eyes meet and warmth pulses between my legs at the glazed look in his eyes. We both look away again.

"You look really nice," he says, still not looking at me.

"Thanks." I'm studying a spot on the other side of the room.

There's a beat where we glance at each other again before looking away. He's blushing, I think.

"I'm going to get us drinks," he says, glancing at my dress again before walking away.

His sharp black tux is tailored to fit every inch of his lean, athletic frame. Watching Rory Miller walk away in a tux like *that*, with his broad shoulders and powerful yet graceful movements, is truly a gift. I'm not prepared for how hot he looks, and I know my gaze is lingering too long, but I can't look away.

"Hmm." Pippa's smiling at me, and heat creeps up my neck.

"Don't start." I push my hair behind my shoulders, collecting myself.

Worry swirls through me and I bite my lip. We shouldn't have done that. I liked it too much.

For days, I've replayed our argument, the crushing feeling in my chest as he basically told me I was broken and pathetic, and then his desperate, pained expression as he apologized.

He looked like he'd just die if I didn't forgive him.

I've thought about him lacing up my skates. His gentle patience as he taught me to skate. On the ice, when he looked at my mouth with focus in his eyes, I thought maybe he'd try to kiss me, but he didn't.

That dumb, adorable dragon sits on my dresser, staring back at me as I fall asleep each night.

I glance back at Rory. Our eyes meet, and I look away, taking in the room, the art on the walls, the plush leather furniture, the side tables with antique knickknacks. Near the bar, Ward stands among a group of players, a drink in one hand, listening as Alexei says something. Coaches are supposed to be old, red-faced, and angry, but Ward looks like James Bond in his tux, all handsome and quietly confident.

Rory returns with a drink for me, and I sip it, grateful for something to do with my hands.

"I'm glad you came," he murmurs, and his mouth brushes my ear before he presses a quick kiss to my temple.

A shiver rolls down my back. He's getting more bold with this fake relationship charade, and I wish I could say I'm annoyed by it but... I'm not.

My smile is a bit shy. "Did you think I wouldn't?"

"Well, after the other day..." He glances back to me, rubbing the back of his neck. "I got you something. To say sorry."

"You already said sorry."

"I know." A slight frown creases his forehead as he reaches into his jacket and pulls out an envelope. "I wanted to show you I meant it."

He's wearing that same earnest expression he wore at the rink, like he's in physical pain. A lock of hair has fallen onto his forehead and my gaze lingers on it.

"Open it," he says, tilting his chin at the envelope now in my hand.

I slide out an email confirmation. It's for a weekend at a nearby vacation destination, Harrison Hot Springs—the luxury suite at a *really* nice hotel and two full days at the spa.

"It's for you and Pippa," he says quickly. "You can go whenever you want." He gives me a tight, vulnerable smile that makes my heart ache. "You said spending time with Pippa made you feel worthy."

In my head, the glowing sign that says *Rory Miller is an evil, selfish hockey player* flickers, losing power.

"You're supposed to be an asshole." I keep my tone light and humorous as I stare at the paper, and he huffs a quiet laugh.

That was the guy I signed up for when we agreed to this.

Not *this* Rory. Not the sweet, earnest, honest guy who apologizes like he means it.

I'm starting to think I was wrong. Maybe I don't know Rory Miller at all.

"I wasn't pretending," Rory says quietly, eyes on me.

About... the kiss? I search his deep blue gaze, blue like my dress, and there isn't enough air in here.

"About the dress." Rory's mouth tips into an affectionate smile. "You look beautiful."

Warm, liquid feelings gather inside me, swirling and looping.

"The dress cost more than what I make in a month," I admit, laughing a little.

"How many times do I need to say it?" His voice is low and soft as he smiles down at me, gaze lingering on my hair, my dress, with his trademark cocky, knowing grin. "I'm going to spend money on you."

Longing aches in my chest. It's not the money; it's the gesture. I've always been independent and stubborn. No one takes care of me.

I like it. Rory's smiling down at me like I'm precious to him, and the way he kissed me, hungry and needy and desperate like he couldn't wait a second longer?

I liked all of that, too.

Worry pulls tight in my chest. We've got until January first, and then this is all over, so I'm not going to get used to it.

"Besides," he says, putting his hands in his pockets, "I'm not talking about the dress. I'm talking about you. You're stunning."

"Thank you." My heart gives a heavy thud against the front wall of my ribcage. No one's ever called me beautiful like that, so earnestly. "For everything. For the dress, for this." I hold up the envelope. "I'm starting to think you're secretly nice."

He smiles at me, and I'm fucked, because there's a weird, intense feeling around my heart that I've never felt before.

A glass-tinkling noise rings out and Ward waits as the conversation dies down.

"You have the luckiest sex doll in the world," I whisper to Rory, smiling, and he shakes with laughter.

CHAPTER 18

RORY

"THANK YOU FOR COMING TONIGHT." Ward's eyes glint. "I thought we might start the evening with some healthy competition."

Interest ripples through the party and the players straighten up, listening. Across the room, McKinnon glances at me.

I step closer to Hartley, sliding an arm around her waist.

Fuck. That kiss. It melted my brain, it was so good. I've never had a kiss like that in my life.

"The game is Assassin," Ward continues. "You'll receive a Polaroid of yourself. If another participant knocks you out of the game, you're dead. Hand it over to them."

The energy in the room crackles with excitement as people murmur to each other. Hockey players. We're competitive as hell, even at a stupid game like this. Hazel's eyes gleam with interest as we exchange a look.

"The game starts outside this room." Ward picks up a plastic Nerf gun. With a crack, he shoots a foam pellet at Owens, and a few people chuckle. "These are hidden throughout the mansion. If you get hit, you're dead."

McKinnon shifts on his feet, crossing his arms, glancing at

me again. I think about what he did to Hartley. All the things he said, even the ones she won't admit to me.

"Hartley," I whisper in her ear. "We need to win."

Her eyes flash with determination. "So let's win."

Fuck, that's hot. I grin down at her. I like that look in her eyes.

Ward runs through the rest of the rules, and the camera flashes go off as staff members take photos before handing the Polaroids out.

Pressure expands in my chest, and my muscles start twitching in that excited, anticipating way, like a face-off on the ice. It's like watching the ref hold the puck, every muscle ready to burst into speed as we wait for him to drop it and start the game.

This is better, though, for some reason.

Once we all have our photos, we look to Ward.

"What, you need a whistle?" He shrugs, smiling. "Go."

The room explodes into chaos, and I grab Hazel's hand, pulling her to the hall.

"We have to find one of those Nerf guns," she says as we hurry, putting space between us and the others.

There's a sharp crack in a room behind us, followed by a delirious laugh.

"Let's go to the second floor," I suggest. "We can let them fight it out downstairs. Maybe there are more Nerf guns up there."

We bound up the stairs, and that tight, excited sensation jumps around in my chest like it's trying to get out. I rub a hand over my sternum. This is fun, I realize. This is... *so* fun. More fun than I've had in ages.

Why is this stupid game, where we're running around like kids at a birthday party, more fun than hockey?

I never laugh during hockey the way I am now. I never feel this expanding, crackling feeling through my limbs.

I grab Hazel's hand as we run up the stairs, two at a time, and I'm struck by how strong and fast she is, even as she lags behind me in her heels. Arousal peaks in my blood as our eyes meet, and I shoot her a lazy grin, unable to look away from her pretty blue-gray eyes.

There's another crack, and a foam pellet sails past us, bouncing off a picture frame. McKinnon is running down the hall toward the stairs.

I reach down, scoop her up, and flip her over my shoulder.

"Miller, put me the fuck *down*," she orders as I race up the stairs. "I'm going to barf."

"You're going to trip and hurt yourself in those heels, Hartley. Let's get away from the others and then I'll put you down." I grin as she smacks my thigh. "You weigh nothing. I could probably win this game with you over my shoulder."

"Cocky, arrogant *ass*." She delivers another sharp slap, and at the top of the stairs, I laugh, setting her down when I step inside a nearby room.

"Don't spank me, Hartley. It turns me on."

She lets out a choked noise that sounds like a laugh. When she straightens up, her face is red. "Ugh. Gross."

McKinnon's footsteps thump on the bottom of the stairs and another crack goes off. "Fuck," he curses.

We're in a library, with bookshelves that reach the ceiling, stiff-looking sofas, and a fireplace. McKinnon's footsteps approach, so I do the first thing I can think of—I push Hartley down on the sofa and get on top of her. The back of the sofa is to the door, so unless he's standing right over us, he won't see us.

Hartley's and my faces are inches apart, and her eyes widen. "What are you—"

I press my hand over her mouth and tilt my head to the door. Her heart is racing against my chest as we stare into each other's eyes. At the door, footsteps thump. Red blurs across her cheekbones.

Are you blushing? I mouth with a teasing look, my hand still over her mouth, and her look of outrage nearly makes me laugh out loud.

We stare at each other in silence, barely breathing as we wait. He has to be standing in the doorway, but I'm half-focused, aware of every inch of my body touching hers. Her breasts press into my chest as hers rises and falls with each breath, and I wonder if she can feel my heart pounding. The male, possessive part of my brain likes being on top of her like this—likes pinning her down beneath me and looking into her eyes.

Finally, he leaves, heading down the hall, and despite wanting to spend the rest of the night on top of Hartley like this, I slide off her. She ditches her shoes before we reenter the game.

Ten minutes later, after finding a Nerf gun on a book-shelf, Hartley and I have a stack of Polaroids from players we've hit.

There's a noise at the end of the hall, around the corner. Fast as lightning, I pull her through a nearby door.

It's a dim closet, and tight quarters. I brush against Hazel's chest. The upper half of the door has a stained-glass image, and as the light from the hallway spills through, colors splash over Hazel's face.

My pulse jumps as I think about kissing her earlier. My gaze drops to her lips, so plush and soft. The perfect color of pink.

I wonder if her nipples are the same color. I wonder if they'd taste as soft and sweet under my tongue. If her breath would catch the same way, or if it would be more of a gasp. Or maybe a moan.

My eyes trace over the lines of her dress, the arc of dark fabric over each breast, and the slight swell of cleavage. I rest a hand on the shelf above her head, dragging a deep breath in. This small space smells like her—her hair products, her perfume, everything about her—and it's making liquid heat pool in my groin.

Fuck. I want her.

"What's that look?"

My gaze snaps up to meet her funny, amused smile. My throat works, and I clench my fists so I don't sink them into those soft waves of hers again. Fuck the game. We could just stay in this closet for the rest of the night.

"I'm thinking about how much taller than you I am."

She snorts, and the corner of her mouth slides up.

Fuck being subtle.

"Are you thinking about it?" I ask.

Her breath turns choppy. "About what?"

"When we kissed."

"No." At her side, she rubs her fingertips against each other. "I haven't thought about it once."

"Liar," I whisper.

Her eyes flare. "Rory," she breathes. She says it like she's saying *we can't*, but her eyes search mine.

She wants to kiss me again, too. I know she does.

"Not 'Miller'?"

In the dim, dappled rainbow light through the door, I watch her throat work. "I mean, we're friends now. Right?" Her eyes flick up to mine, questioning. "After Wednesday."

Friends is one step closer to what I want with her, and I'm not going to mess this up.

"Yeah." My voice is barely a whisper. "Friends."

Her mouth eases into a smile of relief, and I want to kiss her again. Once tonight wasn't enough. I don't know if ten times would be enough. No matter how much I touch her, how much time we spend together, it's never enough.

There's a loud rumbling noise, and we snap out of whatever's happening.

"Come out, come out," Owens calls, and Hartley's eyes widen as we listen to the sound of doors opening and closing. He's making his way up the hall, and he's going to find us.

"Rory," she whispers, holding up the Nerf gun. "We're out of ammo."

"Shit." We stare at each other. "We need to run."

She nods, biting her bottom lip, starting to smile.

"Are you having fun?" I ask, grinning, and she nods again, smiling wider. "Good." I take her hand, so soft and delicate in mine. "Ready?"

"Ready."

I THROW THE DOOR OPEN, and we sprint down the hall, away from Owens.

"Oh, ho, *ho*," he calls after us, and Hazel lets out a shriek of laughter that sends happiness and joy streaking through me.

I'm flying. I'm on top of the world with her laughing with me like this. She's holding my hand as tightly as I'm holding hers as we swing around the corner, and this feels like everything I've been missing in life. My pulse pounds in my ears as I take in Hartley's bright eyes and face, flushed from exertion. Her chest rising and falling fast. The slender line of her throat as she swallows, still watching me.

"Hartley," I hiss, picking a fully loaded Nerf gun off a side table.

She gasps in delight, and I feel like king of the universe. I hand it to her. She takes aim, and Owens bounds around the corner. Hartley lets the pellets fly and they hit him in the chest.

He deflates with disappointment. "Come on."

Hartley shrugs, beaming. "Pay up, Owens."

He pulls his Polaroid out of his jacket and hands it to her before hooking his arm around her neck, pretending to choke her as she laughs.

"See you two downstairs," he says, letting her go and handing me his Nerf gun. He lowers his voice and leans in. "McKinnon's on the third floor."

Hartley's eyes light up with competitive focus, and we creep up to the third floor, quiet as thieves, listening with rapt attention as we move through the rooms.

A phone dings in the next room over, and we freeze.

"That's gotta be him," she breathes, looking over at the door that leads to that room. She chews her lip, probably thinking the same thing I am: he could be waiting and ready on the other side.

"There's another door from the hall," I whisper in her ear, smiling when she shudders.

"It's too risky." Her mouth tilts. "This is so stupid."

"Yeah." I nod. "But it's fun."

She nods, smiling up at me.

"I'm going to lure him out."

Her eyes widen in surprise. "What? No."

"Yes." I want her to win this. Fuck that guy. "You want to win, don't you?"

"I want *us* to win." She blinks. "Together."

The thing is, watching Hartley win *would* feel like winning.

"We're a team," she adds, and that's all I need to hear.

"So let me be a team player."

Off her reluctant nod, I walk out and stride down the hallway, hands in my pockets, whistling a cheerful tune. When I pass the room where he's lounging on a couch, texting on his phone, his head snaps up. A moment later, a foam pellet hits my back.

I sigh, and when I turn, his nostrils flare with irritation at my stupid grin. "Gosh darn it. You got me, McKinnon."

Behind him, Hazel steps into the hall, standing tall with eyes full of fire. The hottest thing I've ever seen.

McKinnon gives me a dirty look. "What the fuck is wrong with you? I won, motherfucker."

The crack echoes in the hallway as Hartley sends the Nerf pellet flying, and McKinnon flinches, turning. "What the—"

Hartley's grin stretches ear to ear, and I match it.

"You're out," she says to him.

The look on his face when he realizes we played him? It's fucking glorious.

"Fuck," he snaps. "Stupid fucking game."

Hazel holds a hand out. "Give me your picture."

He rips it off the chain around his neck and tosses it at her. She catches it, watching with a feline grin as he stomps down the hall.

"He was always a sore loser," Hazel says quietly, and her nose wrinkles.

Fuck, I love that she won. "You're ruthless."

She's smiling up at me, and I could stay right here in this moment forever. "I'm a dragon, aren't I?" Her eyes linger on mine, teasing me, lighting my blood on fire.

She glances over her shoulder at McKinnon still walking down the hall, before she loops her arm around my neck and hauls my mouth to hers.

A groan rips out of me from deep in my chest as her lips meet mine. Her mouth is hot, soft, so fucking pliant and sweet and giving as I sink into her. My hands frame her jaw, tilting her open more, and when I suck on the tip of her tongue, she makes a startling, needy moaning noise that goes straight to my cock.

Holy shit. Holyfuckingshit. Hartley's kissing me and there's not a soul around to see.

"Fucking *hell*, Hartley," I rasp between kisses. "You kiss like a fucking champ."

Her laugh is light and breathy against my skin, and I nip her bottom lip, watching the way her eyelashes flutter.

"So do you," she gasps, and I take her mouth again.

While I'm tasting her over and over again like I won't get another chance, my hand drifts over her, touching the sheer fabric, ghosting my fingers over her throat, her collarbone, the swells of her breasts.

Lower. Over those teasing arcs of fabric covering her cleavage. She shivers as I skim over the seam, pausing in the dip between her breasts. She arches toward me, and something pleased and smug twists deep inside me.

"Oh my god."

Her words are a desperate whisper, and I like to think she'd whisper those words exactly that way in the seconds before I make her come. Making her react like this feels like victory. She pretends to hate me, but she's pushing against me for more. It's supposed to be fake, but she's the one who kissed me.

God, she's so sweet. So hot and slick and needy, and I'm fucking dying here, cock straining in my pants as I taste every inch of her mouth.

"It's taking every ounce of my control not to bend you over and fuck you right now." My voice is hoarse as I lean my forehead against hers, taking a deep breath.

She blinks up at me with a swollen mouth and a hot, glazed look to her eyes that makes me even harder, and I run my thumb over her bottom lip. Her eyelashes flutter again, and I feel a sharp pulse of need.

"And if we don't stop, I might just do that."

She tenses before she backs up a step, pulling out of my touch. She blinks, clearing whatever lust I saw in her eyes. "This is fake. I don't know why I did that."

I sink, remembering what she said in the gym when we set the terms. Don't catch feelings.

"Yeah." I nod stupidly.

She looks away. "Sorry."

"No. We were just, um." I clear my throat. "Caught up in the moment. From winning."

"Yeah." She nods, playing with her stack of photos. "Exactly."

I slip my hands in my pockets, searching for my usual swaggering cockiness. If I keep acting like an awkward teenager, she'll know how much she rattles me.

And for the first time, the prospect of something real with Hartley fucking terrifies me. Watching her walk away would crush me.

"It's okay, Hartley." My mouth slides up into a sly grin, and I send her a wink. "I have that effect on women."

She snorts, and my pulse settles.

"Come on," she says, mouth tipping up in a cool smile. "The sooner we finish dinner, the sooner you can go home and jerk off to your own reflection."

And like that, we're back to normal, the teasing back-and-forth we've always had.

CHAPTER 20

HAZEL

AFTER DINNER, a small group of us heads to the Filthy Flamingo. I'm sitting in a booth between Rory and Hayden, across from Jamie, Pippa, and Alexei. Rory's arm drapes over the back of the booth, over my shoulders, and I can feel the heat of him along my side.

I kissed him. I don't even think Connor saw, but I didn't care. I just really, really wanted to kiss Rory again.

The trophy sits on the table in the middle of our group. Every time Connor looked at it during dinner, his jaw ticked in irritation. As soon as dinner was done, he left, muttering about having an early training session tomorrow. I smile to myself.

"What's so funny, Hartley?" Rory murmurs in my ear.

"Just thinking about how we kicked Connor's ass." The way Rory laughed as we ran up the stairs replays in my head. His smile stretched ear to ear, boyish delight radiating from him.

I liked it, and I'm itching to see it again.

I suck in a tight breath. It's pretend. Guys like Rory and Connor, they can have whatever and whoever they want. I'm not going to get attached.

It feels different with Rory, though, and I can't put my

finger on how. Maybe it's that I've got his full attention, whereas with Connor, I was always an afterthought. My thoughts flip to earlier in the closet with the stained-glass window, how I asked if we were friends.

Rory's fingers find my hair, playing with it. Prickles skitter down my spine when he touches the top of my shoulder.

"Have you settled on a date yet?" Hayden asks Pippa and Jamie about their upcoming wedding.

Pippa smiles, fiddling with her engagement ring, and looks at Jamie. The corner of his mouth tips up as his arm slides from her shoulder down to her waist.

"Not yet," she says, still smiling up at Jamie. "Sometime in the spring."

That strange pang hits my chest, the one I feel sometimes when I watch them, and my mind returns to Rory sitting beside me. The gift he got me. How he kissed me when he saw me tonight. How he kissed me upstairs in the hallway so fervently, like I was so necessary to him.

My heart gives another pleasant twang, and I rub it away.

Pippa arches an eyebrow at Hayden. "Are you bringing a date?"

His grin widens. "Nope. I'm thinking about picking up one of your cute musician friends."

She rolls her eyes. "You dog, you."

"I'm not a dog," Hayden protests, laughing. "I never lead girls on. They know I'm not looking for anything serious." He lifts a big shoulder. "It's easier that way, with our schedules and trades and stuff."

My brow wrinkles. I've always lumped him in with the rest of the hockey players who have a new hookup every week because they can.

I'm not looking for anything serious and *it's easier that way* is what I say about relationships, though, and now I'm wondering what his deal is.

With my one-time-only hookup rule, if I were a guy, I'd probably be called a player, too.

"There's something we wanted to ask you two," Pippa tells me and Rory, and I pull my attention back to the conversation. Her hands wring in her lap. "Will you be my maid of honor, Hazel?"

Emotion stings my eyes, sharp and sweet, and I blink it away fast. For the first time, it hits me: my baby sister is getting married. She's fallen in love with a truly great guy who loves her more than anything. A man I actually like and trust, and she's so wildly happy.

All I ever wanted was for her to be happy.

"Of course I will," I tell her, my voice thick. "You didn't even need to ask."

She shrugs, smiling. Her cheeks are pink. "I know. It's just going to be a big day and I need you there."

My heart clenches with love. "Come here," I say, and Hayden and Alexei move so we can slide out of the booth.

She tackles me in a big hug, almost tripping over her dress, and I laugh into her hair, squeezing her as hard as she's squeezing me. Since we were little, that's how we've hugged each other. As tight as we can.

"Love you," she whispers into my hair.

"Love you, too."

We sit back down, and Rory's hand traces the top of my shoulders. He's watching me with a little smile, and my skin goes warm. He saw all of that. I'm not used to him seeing me all hugging and loving. I glance away, embarrassed.

Across the table, Pippa gives Jamie a meaningful look. He clears his throat and turns to Rory. "I need a best man."

Rory's hand stills on my shoulder. "Yeah, you probably do."

Jamie's eyebrows lift. "You up for it?"

A beat passes. "Only if you're sure." There's a hesitant note to his words.

It feels like he doesn't think he deserves this. My heart aches.

"I'm sure." Jamie gives him a nod. "I want you to do it."

Rory relaxes, and his fingers go back to brushing long, distracting strokes over my skin. "You know I'm in."

Jamie sits back. "Good."

"Yeah. Good." I catch the side of Rory's smile.

There's a pause where no one says anything before Pippa gestures between them with exasperation. "Hug each other."

Rory chuckles and Jamie actually smiles as we all move out of the booth. They stand and give each other a masculine, back-slapping hug. When Rory drops back down beside me, it's me who's watching him with a little smile. He shoots me a wink before shifting closer, and his hand lands on the part of my shoulder that meets my neck. A second later, his fingers toy with the neckline of my dress, sending shivers and tingles down my back.

The guys start talking about their upcoming game, but I'm half listening, focused on the tickling sensation of his fingers on me and thinking about the fun we had earlier, bounding up the stairs and laughing like kids. He was so different from the flat, unimpressed version of Rory I see on the ice. He was lit up, glowing from within.

I want to see that version of Rory Miller again.

CHAPTER 21

HAZEL

WHEN WE LEAVE THE BAR, it's chilly and damp outside like it's been raining. I shiver in the night air, and Rory loops an arm around my shoulders, pulling me against him. He's warm, and he smells unfairly delicious.

"We don't need to pretend out here," I remind him, but I'm not moving away.

"You're cold," he says, like that settles it.

We walk in silence, listening to the sounds of the city around us. Music spills out of bars and restaurants. A car horn honks. Two drunk girls stumble, clutching each other and laughing hysterically, and Rory leads me around them with a smile. A group of guys passes, and their eyes go wide at Rory. *That's Rory Miller*, one of them says.

"That was fun tonight," he says, grin turning smug and feral. "Hartley, McKinnon's face when you hit him?" He shakes his head, glancing down at me in admiration. "So pissed."

I snicker. "I knew he'd hate that. He was always like that. Always needed to be the best. Needed to one-up everyone."

An ugly thought bleeds through my mind.

"Did you know?" My voice is quiet as we walk. "Back in high school, what Connor was doing?"

"No." His eyes flare, pinning me. "Hazel. I didn't know."

Earlier, I called him Rory. It slipped out, but it felt so natural. Now he's calling me Hazel, and I love the way he says my name, even when I'm scrambling for ways *not* to like him. The sound of my name in his deep voice makes me want to hear it again.

He shakes his head, eyes still on me, and his tone is firm. "If I ever heard him say that shit, you'd be the first to know." His mouth slants. "If I had sensed any trouble in paradise, I would have taken my shot."

My stomach flutters. Strangely enough, I believe him.

Fuck. That's bad.

Finally, we reach my apartment. Under the maple tree out front, I search in my bag for my keys. "Thanks for walking me home."

Rory slides his hands into his pockets, gaze roaming over the old building. "Invite me up."

Delight and nerves spin together in my stomach. "This again?"

"Hartley," he teases as I roll my eyes, smiling. "Where are your manners? I said I was going to see you home safe and I take this very, *very* seriously." His grin turns roguish. "Besides, I want to see your place."

"You're scheming."

He blanches, looking overly offended. "I would never."

I'm shaking my head to myself even as I unlock the front door. Why am I letting him in? He should go home. "You would."

He smiled tonight, though. A lot. And he laughed and looked happy. We laughed together. So for some reason, I'm holding the door open for him as we head inside.

As we ascend the second-floor stairs, he sniffs and makes a face. "Smells weird."

I shrug. "Someone on the second floor makes a lot of cabbage rolls."

We keep climbing the stairs, and he studies the carpet, stained and threadbare, with fraying edges. "This place is really old."

"It's cheap, and the landlord isn't a creep." I give him a tight smile as I lead him down the hall to my door. "Okay, well, I'm at my door, so. Thanks. Good night."

He tilts his chin at it. "Show me your place."

My stomach pitches with a nervous feeling. Rory comes from money, and he already thinks my building is gross and weird. "Go home, Rory."

"I hate my place. I want to see yours."

"Your place is no doubt a hundred times nicer and a hundred times bigger than mine," I say as I unlock my door. "And I'm sure it smells a hundred times better." The door creaks as I swing it open, and I gesture at the studio. "Ta-da."

Rory steps inside, looking around as I take my heels off. Although I'm fairly tidy, my furniture is shabby, my kitchen is tiny, and the carpet is an ugly brown color.

"You're not staying," I say as he kicks his shoes off.

He slips off his jacket. "Where's the rest of your apartment?" He shoots me a grin, feigning confusion.

"Very funny."

His gaze lingers on my tiny two-seater kitchen table, the couch, and my bed before he stretches his arms out, looking between the walls. "I can almost touch both walls at the same time."

"No, you can't." Yes, he almost can. My face is going red with embarrassment. "You have a big wingspan. Your dick must be huge. Okay, you've seen my place. Time to go."

He gives me a look like I've grown another head, but his eyes flare with amused delight. "What did you just say about my dick?"

Oh god. I'm flustered. Why do I say the weirdest things around him?

He takes pity on me and turns away, studying a picture on my bookshelf of me and Pippa from a few years ago. She has the same one in her place. "Is the team not paying you enough?"

"They pay me enough." Above market rate, which is another reason I'm holding on to this job as long as I can. "I don't like wasting money on rent."

His head tilts as he reads the titles on my bookshelf. "Are you a cheapskate?"

I laugh in frustration. "*No.* I'm saving for when I open my own studio."

Understanding passes over his features, and he glances around my apartment again, wandering over to my dresser.

"That makes sense." He nudges the crystal dragon on my dresser, smirking at me over his shoulder, before he picks up a bottle of perfume, takes the cap off, and sniffs it while his eyes linger on a framed photo. "That's your mom, right?"

It's a photo of her when she was a ballerina, before she was married. In the picture, she's on pointe. Strong, graceful limbs extended with a peaceful and proud smile across her face. Bold stage makeup and a tight, slicked-back bun.

She wanted to throw this picture out because it reminds her of how much her body has changed, but I stole it because she's beautiful here. She isn't beautiful because she's thinner; it's because she's happier and confident.

The photo is a reminder to me, too. Whenever a thought sneaks in about my body or my face, when I worry I'm starting to get wrinkles, or wonder if my boobs are the right size, or if my butt is too big, I think about this photo. She's not beautiful because of her physical appearance; she's beautiful because of who she is. I'd think that no matter what she looked like.

The photo reminds me to love myself as I am. Even if my body and face aren't perfect. I won't allow myself to hate my body like my mom hates hers.

"She looks like you."

I hum, smiling to myself. Everyone says that, and I'm proud that I'm her spitting image. Pippa got our dad's lighter coloring, but I love that I look like my mom.

Rory watches me like he's trying to figure me out, and alarm bells start ringing in my head. Rory's here in my apartment, seeing all my things, seeing who I am.

"Yes, please, snoop away." My tone is dry as I walk over and set the photo face-down. I pull the second drawer open to grab my favorite sleeping shirt.

There's a creak behind me.

"*Rory.*"

He's lying on my bed, hands tucked behind his head. His face screws up in horror. "Jesus, Hartley, *your bed.* It feels like there are rocks in here." He shifts, trying to get comfortable. "But it's also, like, way too soft? Where'd you get this thing, the dumpster?"

My head falls back but I'm laughing. Yes, it's an old mattress, and yes, this is fucking embarrassing.

"The floor would be more comfortable." He moves his hips up and down, and the bed creaks violently. "How do you have sex on this thing?"

"I don't have guys over—"

"Good." He cuts me a hard look.

"—because once they come over," I set a hand on my hip, "they don't *leave.*"

He smiles and exhales all the tension out of his body. His

legs are crossed at the ankles, and his socks are covered in Bigfoots riding bicycles. Weird.

And now his eyes are closed.

"Rory."

"Mmm." Eyes are still closed.

"I want to go to bed." I'm still standing here in my gown.

"So go to bed," he murmurs.

He looks perfectly at ease, like he's over all the time. Like this is his second home.

Something tightens in my stomach. My fake boyfriend is falling asleep on my bed, and I have no fucking clue what to do with that.

"Good night, baby," he murmurs, eyes still closed.

"You're not staying." I stop in the doorway to the bathroom. "And don't call me that."

"Fire-breather."

I laugh despite myself. "When I come out, you better be putting your shoes on." I say this, and yet, I know he won't be.

"You got it."

My sleep shirt barely covers my ass, and there's a warning feeling whispering in the back of my mind, telling me to put shorts on, but I hate wearing anything other than underwear and a t-shirt to bed. I hate feeling all restricted, and I get way too hot.

Fuck that. Rory wants to sleep here, he can deal with what he sees.

Of course he's fast asleep when I come out of the bathroom, or he's doing a damn good impression of it. I lift his arm above his head and drop it. I heard once that this is how doctors check to see whether patients are passed out or faking it.

It hits him in the face, but he doesn't wake up. He's sound asleep.

CHAPTER 22
HAZEL

THE NEXT MORNING, I'm so deliciously warm. Everything is just right, and I'm so fucking comfortable. Rain taps on the roof. I'm on my side with the pillow molded perfectly to support my head and shoulder, and I'm in that hazy zone between asleep and awake.

I sigh, easing back into the warm chest behind me. Clarity cuts through and my eyes snap open.

Rory's spooning me. That's his warm, hard chest pressed up against me, softly rising and falling with his steady breathing. That's his breath tickling the back of my neck.

That's *his* hard, thick length urgently pressing into my ass.

His hand is wrapped around my front, fingers resting just inside the waistband of my panties.

Between my legs, heat and liquid pool, and the familiar twist of arousal stirs low in my belly. I am *very* turned on.

Every muscle in my body tenses and my eyes are the size of dinner plates as I lie there, listening to his breathing. From the steady rhythm, I'm sure he's still asleep.

He shifts, grinding his erection against me, and heat spirals inside me. His fingers brush an inch lower. He's still breathing steadily, still sleeping.

Carefully, I turn my head. His shirt is off. His socks and *pants* are off. He's just wearing tight black boxer briefs.

My t-shirt? It's ridden up to my waist, and my pink panties are on full display, not that that matters when Rory's hand is halfway inside them.

A throb pulses between my legs. God, his hand is so big, fingers dipping inside, resting just above the sensitive areas. My lips press together in a flat line. I'm getting more turned on by the second.

The sex would be hot, I know it would be. Something wakes up inside me, demanding attention.

Once wouldn't hurt, as long as it's only once.

My hips press back into Rory's cock and he sucks in a sharp breath. He's so stiff against my ass. That thing is fucking huge. I'll be sore for days.

Arousal tightens between my legs. I *love* that idea.

A memory from last night flickers in my head—Jamie asking Rory to be his best man—and my thoughts still. They're becoming best friends again. They'll be in each other's lives for years. And Jamie's so head over heels for Pippa, he'll never let her go.

I picture their wedding, and Rory and I are seated next to each other. I picture them hosting dinners, and Rory and I make awkward small talk. Children's birthday parties. Christmas. New Year's. Group vacations.

A cold chill runs through me. Rory's going to be in my life forever, and I'm cuddling with him. We have an end date to this fake relationship, and yet I'm getting far too comfortable.

Connor's ugly words from years ago loom in my head, and I'm out of bed in a shot.

"Good morning." His voice is gravelly with sleep as he squints at me in the morning light.

"Morning." I whirl around, digging through my dresser for clothes.

"Despite your terrible mattress, Hartley, I had the best fucking sleep." He stretches with a low, rasping groan, and my gaze snags on his defined, muscular arms, the carved lines of his pecs and abs, and—

My thighs clench. That thick length that pressed into me earlier strains against the fabric of his boxers.

I meet his eyes, and he winks. He knows exactly what I was looking at, and I don't think he minds one bit.

My clit aches.

I have *got* to get out of here before I do something stupid, like take my underwear off and sit on top of him.

"I'm going to have a shower," I manage, scampering across the room toward the bathroom door.

He shoots me that lazy, panty-melting grin, gaze dropping to my bare legs and probably part of my ass, visible from under the t-shirt, and there's another warm squeeze between my legs. "Want company?"

With his towering height in my tiny shower? "We wouldn't fit."

His grin turns feral and smug. "We'd make it fit."

Heat streaks through me, and my mind whispers *just one time* as my gaze lands on his straining erection again.

It would be so good with him. I know it would.

I don't sleep with guys I know, though. I hook up once and then we part ways. I definitely don't hook up with guys who I'm fake dating or hanging out with on a regular basis or who will be the best man in my sister's wedding.

I slam the door closed and lean against the inside, collecting my common sense.

———

My blood pumps hard as I walk up to my apartment, catching my breath after my run. Moving usually helps clear my head, but today, my thoughts still slingshot around my brain.

This thing with Rory is getting away from me. We can be friends, but we can't be more, no matter how my body responds to him, or how I feel when he lights up like he's actually having fun for once.

I need to remember what this is for him: a chase. He wants what he can't have, and the second he gets it, I'm old news.

"Hazel Hartley?"

Two guys wait outside my building. A delivery van is parked on the street. "That's me."

"Delivery for you." He hands his electronic tablet to me. "Sign here."

My eyes narrow. "I didn't order anything."

The guy glances at the tablet. "Charges went to Rory Miller."

Of course they did. I sign the tablet, and while the delivery guys unload a new mattress and bed frame from the truck, I pull out my phone and call him.

Rory answers the phone a moment later, as I'm holding the front door open for the guys.

"Seriously?" I ask in lieu of greeting.

"You are so welcome."

I don't know whether to scream or laugh as I climb the stairs after them. He doesn't seem weird about this morning, so that's good. I can pretend if he can. "I can hear your stupid smug grin through the phone."

"I'm not sleeping on that lumpy old mattress again."

My mouth falls open in shock. "You're not sleeping on the new one, either."

Especially not after this morning.

"Hartley, I gotta go. The plane's going to take off soon."

"What am I supposed to—"

"The guys will take the old bed." There's an airport announcement in the background. "I'll call you when we land."

I stare at the disconnected call. That dick hung up on me.

"WHAT ARE YOU DOING?"

In our hotel room that night, I swivel in my chair, giving McKinnon an innocent smile.

"Buying gifts for my girlfriend." My mouth tilts. "You don't mind, right?"

His lip curls, eyes on the lingerie website on my laptop. "I never needed to buy her that stuff."

"That's not what I heard."

His smile drops, and I know I've hit a nerve. My curiosity piques but I turn back to the laptop, scrolling and adding things to the cart.

I think about McKinnon touching Hartley, and I feel sick. I think about him waking up wrapped around her, with his hands all over her, and I want to punch something.

She wanted to go further this morning, but something stopped her.

My hand scrubs over my face before I pick up the tiny crystal dragon I've been bringing with me on the road. It's a perfect twin to hers, except hers is blue and mine is green. If she knew I had it, she'd call it a waste of money, but I find myself holding it all the time, thinking about her. I like that we both have them, like they're friendship bracelets or walkie-talkies or something.

Just another fucking thing I can't tell her.

Before I think about it, I'm FaceTiming her, nudging the crystal dragon out of view.

"I'm not keeping it," she answers in my earbuds in lieu of hello.

My mouth tips up and I add more lingerie to the cart. "Yes, you are."

I've never bought a woman lingerie, but picturing Hartley in these scraps of lace is like rocket fuel for my fantasies. She'd never, ever wear it, but that isn't going to stop me from buying it for her.

There's a rustling noise on her end, and my smile creeps higher. "Put your camera on, Hartley."

"Umm. No."

I'm already laughing. She sounds so guilty. "Put your camera on right now."

Her video pops up, and I shake with laughter. "I knew it."

She's lying back against the pillows, grinning, and I just smile at her as a warm, liquid feeling flows through me.

"Okay. I like it. I'm lying on a cloud in heaven. Happy?"

"Extremely."

Her eyes sparkle. "Thank you," she says quietly.

I just shake my head, swiveling in my chair, smiling at her. Her chestnut hair cascades over the pillow, and I remember this morning, when I woke up with her tucked against me.

Jesus, that felt good, her body all warm and soft. "You're welcome."

"I feel like I'm not pulling my weight in this arrangement, based on how often I thank you."

"I like doing this stuff for you."

There's a long pause where we just look at each other, and

my pulse beats harder with the worry that I showed my cards. My gaze roams her face—her lips curved into a small smile, her eyes sparkling in the low lighting of her apartment.

Does she feel the same?

"So, what are we going to do tonight to piss him off?" she asks.

Last night flashes in my head, the way she shrieked with laughter as we ran from Owens. I get an idea.

"Hartley," I say in a scolding tone, glancing over my shoulder at McKinnon on his bed. "We can't. I have a roommate."

"Rory." Fuck, I love it when we use first names. "What are you doing?"

I widen my eyes at her—*play along*—and she sighs, still smiling. "Just watch the sex tape we made. It'll have to do until I get home."

"Oh my god." She shakes her head, but her face is going red. "Unbelievable."

"Alright," I relent. "I can't say no to you." I pick the laptop up and walk to the bathroom, pausing at the door. "You might want to clear out, McKinnon. Hartley and I need some alone time."

He shoots me a dirty look.

"Uh. Miller? What are we doing?" Hazel asks in my ear.

I close the bathroom door behind me and wiggle my eyebrows at her. *FaceTime sex*, I mouth.

Her eyes go wide. "You're kidding."

I gesture that I'm disconnecting my earbuds, and she presses her mouth into a thin line, holding back her laughter.

"Take your shirt off," I say loudly while she glares at me, trying not to smile. My pulse picks up. After a beat, I groan. "God, I miss those tits."

She snorts like she doesn't believe me, but I point at her. She gives me a frantic *what the fuck?* gesture.

Your turn, I mouth.

"Mmm," she moans with an expression like she's eating rotten food. "*Yeah.*" She slaps a hand over her mouth, rolling over with silent laughter as I beam at her.

What was that? I mouth.

She gives me a frantic look, eyes bright. *I don't fucking know.*

"Take it all off." My voice is low and smooth, but loud enough for McKinnon to hear. "Everything. That's it. Let me see you."

"Like this?" she says in a breathy voice that sounds *nothing* like her. Her face goes pink with embarrassment.

My cock stirs, waking up.

"Yeah." My voice is thick. "Like that. Exactly like that."

"And what about this?" Her voice is teasing. Confident. Like she knows exactly what she does to me. "Do you like it when I do this?"

Holy shit.

"Yeah." What's she imagining right now? "I do. A lot. You should do it again." My tongue taps my bottom lip. "And you should touch yourself while you do it."

Her eyes flare with heat. Thank fuck my lower half isn't on camera, because I'm fully hard.

"Are you touching yourself for me, baby?" I ask.

"Uh-huh." Her fingers fiddle with the ends of her hair on camera, but her eyes have this glaze to them that makes me think her mind might be where mine is right now.

"Are you imagining it's me?"

"Yes."

"Good." My mouth tips up in a pleased smile.

That's definitely a flush forming on her face. Interesting. She liked that.

"What do you need right now?" I ask.

"Harder," she breathes, and tingles run down my spine. "I want to go harder. You always make me feel so good."

The hairs on the back of my neck prickle as a shiver rolls through me.

"You know exactly how to make me come so hard," she whispers, and my balls tighten.

There's something about her approving tone that's making me so hard I can't think straight.

"Fuck, that's hot." I swallow, watching Hartley's flushed face as she makes herself breathe hard.

If we were fooling around on FaceTime for real, her hand would be down those pink panties I saw this morning, swirling over her wet clit. She'd be soaked, I know she would be.

"Make yourself come and pretend it's me." My gaze is glued to the screen, and my breathing is ragged. "Touch yourself like I touch you."

She nods, eyes half-lidded as she moans through my laptop speakers.

Jesus Christ. My hand rakes through my hair. I wonder if she'd follow directions like that in real life. If she'd give herself to me, or if she'd fight me every step of the way.

I don't know which way I prefer.

"You, too," she gasps. "Stroke yourself. I want to see."

My cock pulses. Need is coursing through me, rattling in my blood. "I'm not going to last long if you keep making those noises, Hazel." I'm addicted to the lust in her eyes. "You're too hot. You're going to make me lose it."

I don't know what's fake and what's real in this. I'm so hard it hurts, and the second this call is over, I'm going to replay every noise she made while I stroke my cock.

She bites her lip. "Mhm."

"Are you close?"

"Uh-huh."

I'm spilling pre-cum in my boxers. "Good. Keep going. Faster."

I need to hear what it sounds like when Hazel comes.

"FUCK, THAT FEELS SO GOOD," I moan.

Who *am* I? The stupid crystal dragon sits on my dresser, judging me. Nothing's changed since this morning, though, and we're still pretending.

I think.

"What are you thinking about?" he rasps, watching me closely.

God, Rory does a good impression of horny. The low tone goes straight to my aching pussy. His eyes are dark, half-lidded, pinning me, and I wonder if he's thinking about us doing all of this for real.

I am.

I'm thinking about that thick length pressing against my ass this morning and what it would feel like with him on top of me, pushing into me. My mind imagines what the sweet burn of him inside me would feel like.

My underwear is soaked.

"You," I admit. "Inside me. You're so big. The biggest I've ever had."

He wears the laziest, cockiest grin I've ever seen, that bastard.

"How'd you get so good at fucking me, Rory?"

More desire flares in his eyes. He likes when I say things like that, or he pretends to. I'm not sure anymore.

"Tell me how good it feels," he urges, breathing hard and wearing a determined expression.

"When you fuck me, you hit places inside me even I can't reach."

"I bet you're so wet right now."

His pained expression makes me throb between my legs. God, I just whimpered. I'm a mess. I don't care, though. This is the hottest thing I've ever done and it's not even real. I'm not even touching myself. Arousal gathers low in my belly and I press my thighs together, desperate for friction.

A sharp burst of pleasure shoots through me, and my lips part. We need to end this before I actually do come.

"I'm there," I gasp.

"Yes." He leans in, staring hard at the screen. "Yes, baby. Keep going. I need to see you come."

"Come with me."

"I'm close," he groans. "Now, baby."

I let out a cry of pleasure, panting through it and gripping my duvet like it's real, and a ragged, pained groan rips through him.

"Wow," I say, because I can just see it, him making that agonized expression while he comes inside me.

"Holy shit." He blinks, broad chest rising and falling to catch his breath.

We look at each other. What the fuck just happened?

Through the bathroom door, we hear Connor leave.

"He's gone." A sly grin pulls up on his flushed face. "Nice work."

"You, too." I'm still swollen, wet, and aching. I need to deal with this. I can't be talking to Rory while I'm this horny. "I have to go."

He jerks a nod. "Me, too." He clears his throat again. "'Night, Hartley."

"Good night," I say in a weird tone before ending the call.

I toss the phone aside and dip my fingers below the waistband of my leggings. The second I touch my clit, my back arches off the bed.

"Fuck," I breathe, swirling circles through my wetness. "Fuck, fuck, fuck."

My orgasm builds, fills me, expands through every limb before it bursts, radiating heat and intense pleasure from my center while I gasp for air, picturing his intense, focused expression. I'm clenching on nothing, clamping down where Rory's cock should be, where I've imagined it, moaning while my fingers move fast over my soft, sensitive skin.

It's so good, it's so fucking good, and yet it's not enough.

When I'm finally wrung out, pulse beating in my ears and thoughts sluggish, I let out a long breath, roll onto my back, and stare at the ceiling.

That was the strongest orgasm I've ever had.

This is going to be a problem.

"LOOK AT YOU GO, HARTLEY," I drawl as she glides toward me on her skates. "You're kicking those toddlers' asses."

She snorts with laughter and I grin, skating backward in front of her. We're back at the community skate, circling the rink while the disco ball spins and early 2000s pop music plays. After our FaceTime call, I came so hard my vision blurred, and now that she's in front of me, I just want to touch her.

Ward glances over and I take the excuse to slip my hand into Hazel's. She looks down at our joined hands with a small smile before her gaze goes to him.

"Has he said anything?" she asks. "About the captain thing?"

I shake my head. "Ward's a fortress. I have no idea if I'm living up to expectations."

A feeling I can't name twists through me, clawing and nagging. I hate failing. Challenge motivates me, but I don't even know what Ward wants from me. Even with this arrangement with Hartley, I feel like it's not enough to make Ward proud.

She frowns. "I wonder if that's why he paired you with Connor."

"I don't know if that was the best idea." My grin turns wicked. "Hartley, he was in the worst mood after our call."

She laughs but her face goes pink, like she's embarrassed.

"Was that whole thing okay?" I ask.

The long line of her neck moves as she swallows, not looking at me. "Yep."

My eyebrows slide together. "Hartley, if I ever push you too far, just say the word and I'll pull back."

She shakes her head quickly. "You didn't." She's still blushing. "It was fun." A secretive, pleased smile flashes across her face before her gaze meets mine and her expression turns innocent.

The possessive male instinct in me lifts its head, interested, and now I'm wondering what Hartley did right after the call.

"Fun," I repeat, picturing her lying on that big bed I bought her, making the noises I've been hearing for days.

She clears her throat and again glances over at Ward, who's encouraging a kid to skate toward him. "You're a good skating teacher. That has to count for something with Ward."

"Oh, really?" I raise my eyebrow, pulling her closer to me. "You think I'm a good teacher?"

"You're gloating." Her lips curve, and we're back to familiar territory.

"Of course I'm gloating." I puff my chest out and she rolls her eyes. "McKinnon couldn't get you onto the ice."

Ward glances over at us and I slip my arm around her shoulders.

"I like skating with you," I admit before pressing a quick kiss to her temple.

Her scent teases my nose, trickling through me. Her eyes meet mine and the corners of her lips slide up into a small, guarded smile.

"I like skating with you, too."

———

When the skate is over, I take photos with the kids and parents from Ward's group before I head over to Hazel, who's sitting on the side with a quiet smile.

"Hey, Miller." One of the guys from last week's pickup game, Ed, heads to the ice. Guys are already out there, warming up.

I stiffen. "Hey." More players greet me as they head out there, and there's that clawing, nagging feeling again that I can't shake.

Hazel lifts her eyebrows with meaning at the ice, and my instinct to try again fights with my embarrassment at how I played last time.

I can't quit, though. That's not who I am. My blood pounds with the need to figure this out.

"Is it okay if we stick around for a bit?" I ask her, watching the guys warm up.

Her smile lifts higher, eyes full of encouragement. "Play as long as you want."

I step onto the ice and skate over to Ed.

"Room for one more tonight?"

I'm fully prepared for him to let me down easy after how last week went, but he gives me a quick nod and a welcoming smile.

"You bet." He points over to the bench. "Extra sticks on the bench."

Ten minutes later, we've warmed up and split into teams, and the whistle blows. I keep my distance from the puck, playing less aggressively, fighting every instinct my dad has drilled into my head, but the feeling of wrongness persists, like I'm not doing what I should. The guy I'm covering goes for the puck, and I knock it back to one of my teammates.

This feels wrong. I'm not the star, but this isn't even fun. It feels like I'm hiding. There's no point to being here if I'm going to sit on the sidelines.

A memory from the team dinner filters into my head—watching Hazel step into the hall and shoot McKinnon with the foam pellet, winning the game, and the victory in her eyes. The intense, expansive feeling of pride in my chest.

Watching *her* win felt incredible.

The other team has the puck, but I swing past, snagging it before passing to Ed, who's open. I skate to the net.

"Open," I call, and he passes back to me.

The players scramble between me and the net, blocking my shot.

Here's where I would normally score. That's what I'm paid for, that's what I'm trained to do. Ward isn't here, though, and my dad's not watching on TV. There's no media. It's just Hazel, and she doesn't give one shit if I score goals.

I pass back to Ed. Surprise flares in his expression before he sends the puck toward the net. The goalie lunges, but it sails past.

Our team cheers, and Ed gives me a triumphant smile. Something opens in my chest—pride and reward and delight. Happiness. It's the same feeling as sprinting up the stairs with Hazel. It's the tight coil of joy in my chest when she shrieked, and when she slapped a palm over her mouth during our Face-Time call, muffling her laughter.

She watches from the stands with a proud, pleased smile, and I think I just figured it out.

CHAPTER 26

HAZEL

A PACKAGE IS PROPPED against my front door when I get home from skating with Rory.

I step inside, drop my bag, and kick off my shoes, then I cut the box open. Another box sits within the shipping box—pale pink with a white bow around it. I frown. My birthday isn't for months, and Pippa usually warns me if she's sending something to me.

The ribbon is soft under my fingers, and when I slide the lid off the box and move the thick tissue paper aside, my jaw drops.

Three bras and three pairs of lace panties are neatly folded inside the box. The sets—in cream, sky blue, and a pale, delicate lavender—are beautiful, high-quality and constructed with care. Sheer fabric lines the bra cups, and the straps are satin, soft, and so smooth.

My heart lurches with excitement. I never, *ever* buy myself the nice stuff out of guilt, but these pieces are so pretty and feminine that I'm desperate to wear them.

I frown. Who sent me lingerie? In the box, a card sits tucked to the side.

I gasp. *Love, Rory*, the card says.

Without a thought, I'm already phoning him.

"Miss me already? Fine," he sighs, pretending to sound put out. "I'll come over."

"Rory. What the hell? You sent me lingerie?"

Did he think about me wearing it when he bought it? My face flushes.

"I bought it in the hotel room in front of McKinnon. Pissed him right off, Hartley."

The bras are nearly transparent; my nipples would be visible. Heat thrums between my legs. I can totally picture the way Rory's eyes would darken and how his lips would part, seeing me in this.

God, that would be so fun. To get him all worked up like that. I'd tease him until he begs.

What? What am I *talking* about?

I clear the thoughts from my head. "Okay, that's actually genius. But you didn't have to actually buy it."

I brush my fingertips over the fabric. This would feel like a dream to wear, I'm sure.

"Hartley, how many times do we need to go over this? I like buying stuff for you."

My eyes go to the crystal dragon on my dresser, twinkling in the dim lamp lighting. "I'm not wearing it."

That would be weird if I wore it. Even if he never found out, it would be weird.

"What's the matter, you don't like it?"

"It's not that—" I break off. "Whether I like it or not isn't the point."

"So you do like it." I can hear his grin, and another wave of heat pulses through me. "Should I start sending it to your office instead?"

Against my will, a laugh bursts out of me. "*No.*"

"Okay, okay." He chuckles. "I'll just keep sending it to your apartment, then."

"There's going to be more?"

"Oh yeah." He whistles. "Lots."

My lips move, but no sound comes out, because I don't even know what to say.

"I feel like you're going to try to argue, so I'm going to say good night now, Hartley. Good night."

"Good night."

"Try not to think about me when you're trying it on."

He hangs up, and another laugh of disbelief scrapes out of me as I stare at my phone, and then at the soft, lacy contents of the box.

I'm not wearing the lingerie he sent, no matter how much I want to.

THE VANCOUVER FANS brace themselves as the other team takes a shot on Streicher. He blocks it, and Volkov steals the puck, passing to me before I bring it to the other end of the ice.

The fans start hollering, and the energy in the arena intensifies as I approach the net with the puck.

I have a clear shot on the net, and I should take it.

Owens is open, though. Our eyes meet, and I think about the pickup league. I pass to him. It's the same flare of surprise I saw in Ed's eyes, but he doesn't waste a second.

He shoots, he scores.

The arena roars with noise, and ecstasy whistles through my veins as the goal horn blows. Lights flash, sirens blare, and the fans jump up and down.

"Fuck yeah, buddy!" Owens crows as we crowd him, and I laugh at his excitement.

On the bench, Ward gives me a firm nod of approval, then my gaze goes to Hartley, where she's sitting beside Pippa and looking at me with pleased surprise, like she just saw a new side of me.

I think I did, too, and I like who I found.

CHAPTER 28

HAZEL

SOMETHING'S different about Rory when he walks into the Filthy Flamingo after the game.

He's lighter, more relaxed, and there's an easy tilt to his mouth that I mirror as he makes his way to me.

"Hi." My gaze flicks up to his black baseball hat, turned backward. Against his ash-blond hair and bright blue eyes, the effect is intoxicating. "Great game."

"Thanks." He steps into my space. "Now be a good fake girlfriend, Hartley, and let me kiss you."

His lips are gentle, soft, and sweet, and my body relaxes against him. The bar fades away, and there's just the scrape of stubble under my fingers and the tickle of his breath on my cheek. My other hand flattens against his firm chest. His hoodie is so soft, and I wonder what it would feel like to wear it. Every inhale floods my system with his dizzying scent of clean laundry and body wash.

I forget we're in the bar. I forget this is fake.

When Rory Miller kisses me, I forget what it's like to have my heart broken.

He nips my bottom lip, and I pull back before he can deepen the kiss and truly shatter my senses. My face is flushed, and when his finger slides to the pulse point on my neck, his gaze flares with interest as he feels my racing heart rate.

I like him. This is bad.

Also, I'm wearing the lingerie he sent, even though I said I wouldn't.

Bad. So bad. Very, very bad.

"Hartley," he murmurs in a teasing tone. "Nuns kiss with more tongue than that." He arches a knowing brow.

He's goading me, but it's working, and I fist the front of his hoodie and pull him back to me.

This time, I don't hold back. I kiss him as if that FaceTime call was real. He props an arm on the pillar behind me as I taste him, and when I suck on the tip of his tongue, a low, desperate groan rumbles from his chest, vibrating against my fist still holding his hoodie. Urgent, insistent need hums through my blood as his free hand grasps the hair at the back of my head. He tilts my head back to open me up more, and between my legs, arousal gathers.

I didn't expect to like him pulling my hair so much.

"Better?" I whisper, looking up into his eyes.

"Yeah." His breathing is ragged, pupils blown wide. His gaze flicks behind me and his expression turns wicked. "McKinnon."

I stiffen. I forgot he was here.

Rory tilts his chin at Connor. "You should get a better drink. It doesn't look like you like that one."

Connor's expression looks like a storm cloud, but Rory's already pulling me over to the table with the others. Pippa and Jamie are at a bigger table than normal, and sitting with Hayden are his friends, Kit and Darcy. Kit Driedger plays for Calgary, the team Vancouver played tonight, and Darcy is his girlfriend from when all three of them met in university.

"Hey," Rory says to Kit with a playful grin. They played together last season. "Only Vancouver players allowed in here."

Everyone rolls their eyes. "Like that ever stopped you," I tell him, and he chuckles and shakes Kit's hand.

"Good game tonight, Driedger."

"You, too," Kit says with a nod.

"It's hard enough to get this guy out with us without your chirps, Miller," Hayden says. "Darcy had to drag him here tonight."

"Kit likes to go to bed early like a grandpa," Darcy teases, and Rory gives her a big hug hello before she steps over to me, her platinum-blond hair practically sparkling under the dim bar lights.

"I didn't know you were in town," I tell her as we hug. We've hung out a few times after games but I never get to talk to her long enough. "You could have sat with me and Pippa during the game."

"Yeah, Darce." Hayden tips his chin at her, eyes bright. She barely comes up to his shoulder. "Then you could have seen my goal up close like Driedger did." He elbows Kit in the gut and Kit laughs quietly, shoving him off.

"Next time," Darcy says with a shy smile before her curious gaze swings between me and Rory. "I heard about this, but I didn't believe it."

Rory's hand rests between my shoulder blades, and when he looks down at me, his smile is so gentle and handsome. He hasn't shaved in a couple days, and a thin layer of dark blond stubble spans his strong jaw.

"It's true." My eyes lift to Rory's backward baseball hat. His eyes are bright, and the tops of his cheekbones are a little flushed from the game still. With him wearing that hat, I stand no chance against Rory Miller.

People make room, and I move to sit down, but Rory pulls

me into his lap. Jordan swings by with a soda water for Rory and a drink for me, and while he's thanking her, Pippa's eyes widen as she sips her drink, watching us with a smile.

Shut up, I tell her with my eyes.

I won't, she says right back with hers.

I try to slide off his lap, but his hands tighten on my waist, keeping me close.

"No," he murmurs in my ear. "You stay where you are, fire-breather."

Another flush of heat moves through me, and I force myself to focus on the conversation at the table.

"I read an interview with a porn star," Hayden's saying, "and he said if he's having boner problems, he smells the back of his female co-star's neck." He gestures at the back of his neck. "It's a pheromone thing or something."

"No way," Rory scoffs. "That's not real."

"It is," Hayden insists, making me laugh with his earnest expression.

Rory gathers my hair off my neck, moving it aside. My smile falters when his lips press against my skin, and as he takes a deep inhale, his stubble scrapes me.

Shivers run down my spine as he exhales over my skin, and something twinges between my legs.

Rory straightens up, dropping my hair.

"Well?" Hayden asks as everyone watches.

Rory shrugs. "Yeah, I don't know what to tell you, buddy."

Hayden's face falls. "I've been telling this to everyone." Darcy starts laughing, and he tilts his chin at her, giving her a flirty smile. "Come here, Darce. Let's test it."

He makes grabby hands at her and she laughs harder, swatting him away. Kit shakes his head, smiling.

Hayden's eyes linger on her for a moment too long, beaming like she's the best thing he's ever seen.

They're friends. Best friends, he tells everyone. And she's with Kit.

Hayden doesn't look at her like they're friends, though.

She slides against Kit, saying something to Pippa, and Hayden takes one look at Kit's arm around her and glances away, expression tightening.

Huh.

My thoughts are interrupted as Rory stiffens against me. I twist to look at him but he locks me harder to him, jaw tight.

"What's going on?"

"Can you stay still for a second?" His voice is strained.

"What's going on—"

Oh.

A thick, hard length presses into my lower back. My thoughts fizz, and there's another warm twinge between my legs. Rory's hard. Like, really hard. Pressing into me. Hard.

"Oh," I say, staring straight ahead. Every cell in my body is hyperaware of the insistent press of his cock against me.

"Yeah." He makes a hoarse noise.

Liquid warmth pools low in my belly. I picture a thousand dirty things. What it would feel like to fuck Rory. To sit on top of him and ride him. Jesus. My eyes close for a moment and I see it—him holding me down, wrists pinned above my head as he fucks me slowly, staring into my eyes with that lazy, knowing grin as I unravel around him.

My hips shift, searching for friction instinctively, and he sucks in a sharp breath as his hands tighten on my waist.

"Do *not* do that, Hartley," he groans, and his length pulses. "That's not helping."

My skin is too hot, and yet I feel the urge to laugh.

Against my back, his chest rises and falls as he searches for control. "Why do you smell so good?" He says it like it pisses him off, and a warm flush creeps up my neck.

"I just smell normal."

"You definitely fucking don't smell normal, Hartley."

His frustrated tone does weird things to my body. My skin tingles all the way down my back, and arousal tugs low in my stomach.

We pretend to listen to the conversation at the table while I sit very, very still. Jordan swings by and I order some food, still hyper aware of Rory's erection. Eventually, the thick rod against my backside goes away, and I can think again.

"Want one?" I ask him when my fries arrive.

He shakes his head, gaze lingering on them. "No, thanks."

"No drinking, no fries," I list, popping one in my mouth. He's like my mom, always putting herself on a diet.

His eyes linger on my mouth. "My body is my career, and eating junk food isn't going to do me any favors."

Salt bursts in my mouth as I eat. "One fry, though? Is that really going to end your season? Especially when they're *so good*." I quietly moan the last two words, letting my eyes roll back like it's the best fry I've ever eaten.

Rory's eyes darken. "Do that again."

I hold eye contact with him as I eat another.

"Fuck." He looks away when I lick my bottom lip. "That's so hot."

"You know what goes so well with fries? Beer."

He sucks in a long breath. "I haven't had one in forever."

"You played a great game tonight." My brows rise. "I'm proud of you. You should celebrate."

I'm proud of him?

I am, though. For the first time in forever, he actually looked happy out there, and I know it has something to do with the pickup game yesterday.

But I can't say those kinds of things.

"Not that it matters," I quickly add.

"It does." His expression is so serious. "It matters."

My heart gives a happy spin at that.

He looks at the fries, and his eyes spark with teasing. "You trying to be a bad influence on me, Hartley?"

I shrug, still smiling. "Is it working?"

"Yes." He meets my eyes again. "Alright. Hit me."

My grin widens and I hand him my beer before catching Jordan's attention and silently ordering another for myself. When Rory takes a sip, his eyes close and he groans like he just found water in the middle of the desert.

"Fuck," he mutters.

My breath catches, fascinated by the expression on his face. "Good?"

He nods, takes another sip, and sighs, and something warm and pleased weaves through my chest.

AN HOUR LATER, Rory's had *two* beers. His smile is a little brighter, his laugh is a little louder, and his hands roam a little more freely over me, smoothing over my back, resting on my waist, and giving my thigh quick, firm squeezes.

His nose presses to my temple as he takes a deep inhale. "Jesus Christ," he murmurs.

Something about his low voice sends my hormones crashing through my system, demanding horny things.

My mind flicks to him on my bed in just his boxers.

"Are you drunk?" I whisper, giving him a teasing grin.

"No," he laughs against my ear. "Just tipsy."

"Lightweight." I have a stupid grin all over my face. "You have the alcohol tolerance of a Pomeranian."

"Don't bully me, Hartley." He nips my earlobe and my lips part. "It makes me hard."

I'm laughing, but I'm also blushing. His hands tighten on my waist, and one slides down to my hip. Then lower, resting on the crease where my hip meets my thigh. His thumb strokes, and the breath whooshes out of me.

So. Freaking. Hot.

"You're drunk." I can barely get the words out, I'm so turned on.

"I'm not." He presses a kiss to my temple. "I just think you're really, really pretty."

I turn away, smiling and blushing.

"And smart." His stubble scrapes my cheekbone as he presses another soft kiss to my skin. "And you smell good." Another kiss, this one on my jaw. "And I like the shape of your lips." Neck kiss. "And tits." I shudder as he groans against my pulse point. "You've always had perfect tits," he whispers in my ear.

I'm lit up, buzzing as arousal swirls at the base of my spine. "Stop acting drunk or I'm going to take advantage of you."

"Promise?"

I laugh. "I'm going to ask personal questions and find out all your secrets."

He stares down at me with that smirk I want to kiss off his mouth. "When have I ever not answered one of your questions?"

I blink, thinking. He's right; he always answers my questions.

"How many times have you jerked off thinking about me?" I ask with a challenging smile. He'll never—

"Too many to count." His eyes flare with heat, and his eyebrows lift once. *See?* his eyes say. "After the FaceTime call."

Our gazes hold for a beat before I turn away, stomach swooping and dipping. His arm is heavy over my shoulders, a warm, comforting weight.

"I couldn't help myself, Hartley." His lids fall halfway as he grins with whatever memory he's replaying. "The noises you made just—"

"Burger and onion rings." Jordan sets a plate in front of him and I pull back and clear my head with a deep breath.

"Thanks, Jordan," Rory calls after her before he takes a huge bite of his burger, closes his eyes, and lets out a guttural moan of pleasure.

"Holy shit," he groans, and I wonder if that's what he would look like if I were kneeling between his knees, running my tongue up and down his cock.

I look away, shoving the image from my mind, but I'm forced to sit here, watching and listening as Rory basically comes in his pants eating this burger.

"Onion rings," he says with reverence after he eats the first one, shaking his head.

"Yeah." I steal one and dunk it in ketchup. "They're good, huh?"

"Mhm." He looks down at his food, pausing. "I shouldn't be eating all of this. It's inflammatory."

I think about my mom, and how she never lets herself eat dessert. She has a sweet tooth, but she's so terrified of gaining weight that she won't even indulge in half a slice of birthday cake.

My fists clench under the table thinking about that. That she feels like she isn't allowed, that she doesn't deserve it.

"It's okay to enjoy food." I rest my elbow on the table, leaning on my palm, watching him. "And one burger isn't going to end your career, Rory."

He stares at the burger like he doesn't believe me, like he thinks this one burger is going to get him kicked off the team, and I wonder who the fuck put that idea in his head. Sadness pinches me in the ribs, and protectiveness wakes up in my chest.

He eats another onion ring and groans again, and my face heats.

"Can you groan less *sexually*?" I mutter, and he just laughs.

————

"What would you be if you weren't a hockey player?"

We're walking down my street, and Rory has his arm draped over my shoulder, holding me close. Darcy and Hayden were trying to get everyone to go out dancing, but the second the group left the bar, Rory pulled me in the opposite direction, toward my apartment. His tipsiness has worn off, but the evening is cold and he's warm, so I'm letting him tuck me against his body.

We walk half a block before he answers. "I don't know. I've wanted to be a hockey player for as long as I can remember."

We pass under the big maple tree outside my apartment.

I think about his assists tonight and his exuberant grin. "You were incredible tonight."

His Adam's apple bobs as our eyes hold. "Would you still think that if I didn't have the highest scoring average in the league?"

There's something in his eyes that breaks my heart. "I don't like you because of your stats."

"So you do like me." The corner of his mouth tips up, and his eyes lose that vulnerable look. He tucks my hair behind my ear, grazing the shell. "Invite me up."

Energy crackles in the air between us. If Rory comes upstairs, something's going to happen.

I don't care, though. If I reach deep down, beyond all the scarring and scratches I've endured from Connor, I want Rory to come up.

I like him. I don't want to, but I do. Panic rises at that thought, but I shove it away.

"Okay," I say instead.

CHAPTER 30
HAZEL

RORY KICKS off his shoes and heads straight for my new bed, flopping down with a low, satisfied groan that makes me think dirty thoughts.

"That's so much better," he groans again.

The way he's so comfortable in my home makes me feel like laughing.

"Rory, when people come over, they usually sit on the couch."

"People don't usually have their bedroom in their living room."

My mouth falls open, but I'm still smiling. My face hurts, I'm smiling so hard.

"I'm just teasing, Hartley." He winks. "I know you're a good little saver. You'll have your studio in no time."

A pulse of happiness hits me in the chest, and I'm glad I told him about that.

"Thank you again for the bed," I tell him, slipping onto the mattress beside him, folding my legs beneath me.

A soft smile ghosts over his mouth. "You're welcome. Do you sleep okay without all the springs stabbing you in the back?"

I'm shaking with laughter. "Fuck off." I cut a look at him. "But yes."

He's still smiling, watching me. The dim, warm lighting of my apartment is doing incredible things for his eyes and skin.

"I like buying things for you. You should let me do it more often." He props himself on his elbow, frowning at me. "How come you don't wear my jersey to games anymore?"

"I don't know." I shrug. "People already think we're together."

"I bought it for you to wear."

Something thrums low in my belly at his territorial tone. After Connor, I hated the idea of wearing a guy's jersey.

But it's Rory. Everyone wears his jersey at games, but I have this deep-seated, prickling feeling in the back of my brain that it means something to him when I wear it. The memory of his stricken expression during yoga, when I asked the class to think about what makes them feel worthy, flashes in my head.

I care about him, and I think he knows that.

Worst of all, I think he cares about me, too. I should tell him to go home.

Just once, the devil on my shoulder whispers. It's my rule, after all. One time and then we'll never hook up again.

He rests a hand on my thigh, and his fingers drift to the inside seam of my leggings, toying with it. "And I want you to wear it." He holds my gaze. "Please."

It's that *please* that does it for me. And maybe the way his hand feels on my leg, so big and warm. "Okay." I'm hyperaware of where he's touching me and his gaze roaming my face. My heart rate jumps because I can't seem to get it under control around him. "You can be so sweet when you want to be," I say for some reason.

"So can you."

I have to remind myself to breathe as our eyes hold, and my

heart jumps into my throat. I study the elegant lines of his face, his strong nose, his brows, the curve of his lips. He's so handsome with that stubble, and my hands twitch with the urge to drag my fingers over it.

"Besides, it'll piss McKinnon off." He shakes his head. "Fucking McKinnon," he bites out. "He was watching you tonight."

"He just wants to play with your toys. He's always been competitive with you."

He folds his arms over his chest. "He still has a thing for you, and I don't like it. He knows we're together. He shouldn't be staring at you like that."

My stomach does a slow roll at the way he says it, like it's real. Isn't that the whole point of what we're doing, getting under Connor's skin?

"You sound jealous."

His jaw ticks, and our eyes meet again. "I am."

I shouldn't like that he feels possessive over me, but I find myself sliding off the bed and walking to the closet. My stomach is full of butterflies as I tug the jersey off the hanger and pull it over my head.

"Better?" I ask, turning to him, holding my arms out.

The way his gaze flares sends a thrill through me. His throat works as his eyes slowly trace down my form and back up.

"Come here," he says.

The air cracks with tension. Walking over to the bed is going to be a mistake.

I do it anyway.

"I guess that's a yes—" I let out a squeak as he lifts me so I'm straddling him.

He pulls his hat off and sets it on my bedside table, and I

don't know why that's so fucking hot. His hair is messy, and I let myself reach up and run my fingers through it. Soft, too.

Rory has a thousand smiles, I'm realizing. One for every emotion, every possible situation in life, and the one he's wearing right now is a mix of comfort and arousal. His hands settle on my thighs, stroking up and down, pressing firm into my muscles.

"Hi," I whisper, because it feels like we've climbed a level in whatever this is between us, and I'm not sure what else to say.

"Hi, Hazel." He gives me his *Hazel is cute* smile. His hand strokes a little higher, thumbs brushing the seam between my hip and thigh, and my breathing turns ragged. He notices because his gaze flares.

He pulls me down to kiss me, claiming my mouth with urgency and hot desperation. An ache grows behind my clit as his tongue delves between my lips, stroking me.

"I'm thinking about what you taste like," he says between kisses. One hand comes to my breast, kneading and finding my stiff nipple through the fabric of my jersey and shirt.

His eyes flare with heat, and something inside me jumps in anticipation. He's going to see that I'm wearing the pale blue bra and panties he sent.

"And what it sounds like when you come," he goes on, voice low as he nips my bottom lip. "I've been thinking about it for years."

Heat builds between my legs, where I'm spread open across Rory's hips. I'm getting the panties he bought me all wet.

Maybe this will all be easier once Rory gets what he's been chasing.

My heart's beating out of my chest. "Before we do this, um."

I shift to ease the pressure, but his thick ridge rubs against me, sending a streak of need through me, making me lose my train of thought.

He pulls my jersey and shirt over my head, going still. My heart pounds as he stares at the pale blue bra, blinking once, twice before his dark gaze lifts to mine.

"Hartley," he says, with his mouth curving up. "Is that—"

"Yes," I rush out.

The way he's teasing me with his eyes is starting to make me feel embarrassed, like maybe I overstepped. Maybe this looks pathetic, that I'm wearing something he bought me when it was clearly a joke.

"Why?" He holds my gaze, hands sliding up my thighs.

"Because..." I scramble for a coherent thought that isn't related to how wet I am or how fucking horny I'm getting. "Because it was pretty, and I wanted to feel hot."

"And did it work?"

His gaze sears me, and I nod.

It's true—wearing something so beautiful and delicate makes me feel sexy.

Beneath me, his erection pulses, and he lets out a heavy breath. "That is really fucking hot, Hartley." His throat works, and his warm palms return to my breasts, slipping beneath the cups of my bra to toy with my nipples. When he tugs, I feel it all the way to my pussy.

"Oh my god," I whisper, leaning forward to kiss him again.

He devours my mouth, tongue sliding against mine, making my head spin. "What were you saying, Hartley?"

Oh. Right. That. "This will be the first and last time we do this."

He pulls away to look into my eyes. "What?"

"It's just what I do." My shrug is easy and casual, even as I'm tight with need. "I only sleep with guys once. It's easier that way."

He frowns. "And then what?"

"And then we both move on."

When I tell people this, they usually look relieved, but Rory's frown deepens and his hands leave my body. His throat works again as he searches my eyes.

"We should stop," he says.

The arousal in my blood fizzles out like I've been dunked in cold water.

His jaw ticks. "It would complicate things."

Rejection burns through me. He said he's been thinking about this for years. He's slept in my fucking *bed*. I kissed him at the team party, but he kissed me back. He said it was hot that I was wearing the lingerie he sent.

He asked me out at the beginning of the season, before the deal.

He's been chasing me for years, and now he doesn't want me?

Oh. My stomach sinks. He's never seen this much of my body before. He's never touched me like this, felt my tits and stomach and thighs and butt.

Shame whips through me as I climb off him, grab my shirt, and pull it back over my head.

I'm not upset. It's fake. It's a deal. It's not a relationship. Even if the sex would be incredible. Even if I'd come so hard and work to make him come harder than ever.

"You're right." I'm channeling the same woman who told Connor she's dating Rory, the woman with the cool, calm, hardened shell around her. "I don't know what I was thinking. Just horny, I guess."

"Hazel," he starts.

"You should go." I fold my arms over my chest. "It's late."

His eyes flash with something that looks like regret, and when our eyes meet, he looks like he wants to say something, but I take another step back, out of the Rory Miller Danger Zone.

He sits up, wearing a pained expression like I'm killing him. "Hazel."

"It's fine, Rory."

It's not fine. I'm so fucking embarrassed. I've never been flat-out rejected like this, but Rory's used to hooking up with models and actresses. I get an ugly memory of Connor from years ago, asking me if I'd ever consider breast implants, and my stomach recoils.

"Let's pretend it never happened."

HAZEL LOOKS like she wants to sink into the floor as she heads to the front door, and I'm sitting here on her bed, hard as fuck and torn about what to do.

I said *it would complicate things*, but I meant *once would never be enough*.

The second we sleep together, Hartley's done with me.

We have something. I know we do. I think about her telling me she was proud of me after my game and the way she laughed with me at the team party.

And now she's wearing the lingerie I sent her, looking like a goddess sent to tempt me? After she admitted that the gift I got her made her feel hot, hitting the brakes was the hardest thing I've ever done. She looked like mine, wrapped in pale blue lace that I bought.

Possessive instincts charge through me. We're not moving on yet, though. No fucking way.

So I lied, and now she's hurt, and there's an ache in my chest that only grows by the second. My mouth opens to say something, but she lets out a frustrated sigh.

"Rory, please." Her expression is vulnerable like in the gym the day she met with Connor and asked me to give her space. "I don't want to talk about it. Don't make me feel worse. I know you date women who look different—"

"What?" I'm on my feet, moving to her. "What are you talking about?"

Two pink patches appear on her cheeks, and she won't meet my eyes. "I'm just saying that compared to the women who usually date hockey players," she waves a hand over her body, "I look different. I have a normal body. I'm okay with it, and I love my body, but you don't need to drive the stake deeper."

"Hazel." Her eyes go wide as I back her against the door, pressing a hand to the surface over her head, caging her in. Blood beats in my ears.

How could she think that? How could she think she's anything less than perfect? How could I *let* her think that? Since I ran into her last year, I haven't touched another woman. Next to her, no one's as funny or hot or interesting or entertaining.

My fingers circle her wrist and I bring her hand to my erection, watching her eyes flare with heat.

"Does that feel like I'm not interested?" I demand, and her hand twitches on my cock, making my balls ache with need. "Does that feel like I don't think about your body a hundred times a day?"

Her lips part, and I capture her mouth. She kisses me back hard, and relief sweeps through me, followed by intense need.

I'm going to show Hazel how wrong she is. I'm going to worship every inch of her.

Once will never, ever be enough, though.

So maybe we don't go all the way. Maybe I draw it out, take it slow, and never, ever give her enough, so by the time we finally have sex, she doesn't give a shit about her rule anymore.

Maybe I wait until she falls for me.

"I'm mad at you," I tell her, breaking the kiss, and her eyes widen, confused and outraged.

"What? Why?"

"Because I've practically had my tongue down your throat for months, and you still think I'm not interested." I press my hips against hers, pinning her to the door. "Maybe I need to be more clear, Hartley."

Interest rises in her eyes. "What did you have in mind?"

"This rule of yours." I trail my fingers down her chest, brushing over her bra, over her tight nipples beneath it, and she sucks in a sharp breath. "Tell me the specifics."

I draw slow, soft circles on her breasts, and beneath my fingers, her chest rises and falls faster.

"Um." She blinks like she's having a hard time focusing, and I press my erection harder between her legs. Her lips part, and I smile.

"Full sex?" I prompt. "Me inside you? That's the rule?"

She nods, gaze clouding as she sinks her teeth into that full bottom lip.

"So if I were to go down on you, that wouldn't count."

She mumbles something.

"What's that?" I lean in, and my mouth tips up.

"I said no one's gone down on me in a long time." She bristles with irritation, and I smile wider.

Possessive feelings course through my veins. It's wrong, but I like that. I like that I'm going to be the one to make her feel good.

"I don't think that's a good idea," she adds.

Something in her face tells me she thinks it's a *really* good idea, though. She wants this, she just doesn't know how it fits in with her stupid rule.

"And why is that?"

"A guy like you doesn't go down on women." Her eyes dart

around before her gaze lifts to mine, flickering with curiosity and reluctance. "It would be a waste of time."

My smile curls higher. "Really?"

Her throat works. "And you wouldn't know how to make me come."

My mind was already made up, but a switch flips inside me, and the game is on. "You think so? You sure about that?"

She arches a brow, still looking uncertain but clinging to that cool demeanor she wears like armor. "No one's ever made me come like that."

She's so cute, and by the time we're done tonight, she's going to be screaming my name.

"How about a friendly wager, Hartley?"

CHAPTER 32
HAZEL

THIS ISN'T how I expected this conversation to go, and now I've dug so deep I can't get out. Rory's eyes are bright with competition. I just challenged the most determined guy in professional hockey, and he hates to lose.

Why? Why would I challenge him like that?

"What do you propose?" I'm barely whispering. In my ears, my pulse thunders.

His mouth hitches higher. "I bet I can make you come."

In my experience, hot guys aren't that good in bed. They're selfish because they don't have to work as hard to get women. And Rory? He's the best-looking man I've ever met.

There's no way he'll win.

"You think?" And yet, I'm playing this game with him. Weak, Hazel. So weak.

"I *know*."

I can imagine how his tongue would feel, swiping hot, wet circles on my clit, winding me higher. I know how soft his hair is, and I'm itching to tug on it while his head is between my legs.

Holding my gaze, still resting his hand on the door above

my head, he dips his fingers into my leggings and strokes me. I arch, lips parting as heat sears through me.

"Are these the panties I bought?" he bites out, and I nod.

He lets out a low laugh, running the tip of his tongue over his bottom lip while his fingers slide over me, drawing firm circles. The muscles between my legs flex around nothing as pressure builds.

"And you're so wet." His smile is arrogant, like he's already won. The approval in his voice has me tightening up, tilting my hips against him for more friction. My center aches, and I wish he was inside me.

I can't even get a full breath; I'm just taking tiny sips of air. "And what do you get if you win?"

Another slow, wet stroke over my clit. "Anything I want."

My pussy clenches, sharp and fast, and my teeth clamp down on my bottom lip. Why is the idea of Rory taking whatever he wants so hot?

"And if I win?" I'm fighting to keep from moaning as he circles the tight bud of nerves. "If you can't?"

There's that low laugh again, like that isn't even an option, but sure, he'll humor me. "Then you can have whatever you want."

Between my legs, he's drawing the most intoxicating circles. My head spins.

"You said I should eat what I want," he adds with a smirk.

I guess I like playing with fire. I guess I forgot how it feels to be burned. Rory's hands have been on me all night and I'm so worked up, aching between my legs. I'm not thinking straight.

There's a version of me from months ago who hated Rory, the one who's screaming at me to *shut up now*, and I slam the door in her face.

She can wait outside while I make bad choices.

He brings his lips to my ear. "Say yes, Hazel. Let me do something I've been thinking about since the day I met you."

I'm nodding, because consequences be damned. Despite what Rory says, it's just once.

And I'm really, really curious if Rory will win.

His hand slips out of my leggings and he laughs at my noise of frustration, but then he's pulling my t-shirt over my head.

His eyes darken as he stares at my breasts, shaking his head. "If you ever thought I wasn't attracted to you, Hazel," he tugs one bra cup down and pulls a stiff peak into his mouth, and my back arches as a bolt of pleasure hits me between the legs, "you're delusional."

While his mouth is on my nipple, his hands work fast, pushing my leggings down and helping me kick them off before he drops to his knees, looking up at me with a dangerous smile.

"Like this?" I ask as he brushes a kiss on my inner thigh. Self-consciousness streaks through me. I'm standing in front of Rory in two tiny scraps of lace while he's fully clothed and kneeling in front of me, but the look in his eyes is pure heat, pure bliss, as his hands move over my thighs and waist.

"Mhm." A trail of soft kisses up my thigh, over my hip. "Exactly like this. Want to see you in what I bought."

He slips his hand beneath the front of my panties, drags a thumb over my clit, gaze flicking between my face and his hand, and a moan slips out of me. Sharp pleasure courses through me as he winds me higher, and I claw at the door with my nails for something to hold on to.

"Put your hands in my hair," he tells me in a low voice, and when I do, he makes a pleased noise. His thumb is unrelenting and firm, stroking over me, winding the coil around the base of my spine tighter.

Rory touching my clit is beyond incredible—the pressure and speed are perfect, and seeing this big hockey player on the floor in front of me, looking at my body with reverence, feeds my bruised ego and confidence. His eyes meet mine, and the corner of his mouth lifts.

"*Rory.*" It's a desperate plea because, holy hell, Rory Miller is so fucking hot, and I'm soaked.

"Holy fuck, I like that," he says, spreading my wetness over me, swirling, winding me higher. "I like it when you say my name like that, Hazel."

His fingers slide lower, push inside me, and my eyes roll back as the intense feeling rolls through me.

"Fuck," I gasp. I'm so full, and it's only his fingers. What's it going to be like when it's him inside me? I'm going to break in half.

"Tell me it's good, Hazel."

"It's fine at best," I choke out, wanting to tease him even now, but he laughs, and his fingers hook against a spot that makes my vision blur.

Who am I kidding? I'd say anything to make him keep going.

"It's good," I rush out. "It's so good. Your hand is incredible, Rory."

He makes that pleased humming noise of approval again, and my muscles clench around his fingers.

"That's what I like to hear."

With a big arm around my hips, he hooks my panties aside, pulls me toward his mouth, and licks a long line up my seam. Pleasure ripples through me. I should be embarrassed at the needy, desperate noise that stutters out of me, but I'm not. I don't care.

"I knew I'd love that," he growls, and I clench again. His fingers are huge, and my muscles ache around them in the most mind-bending, pleasant way as he slowly strokes in and out of me.

His tongue swirls on my clit, and I'm lost, spinning out. Everything is tightening, tensing, and the pleasure is almost unbearable. Rory's lips close over my clit and his eyes meet mine as he sucks. He lets out the same groan he did earlier tonight when he was eating, that satisfied, ravenous sound that sends electricity through my limbs.

The sensations are overwhelming—the hot, wet pull of his lips on my clit, the stretch of his fingers inside me, and the silken strands of his hair clutched between my fingers. Everything loops together, building in intensity as Rory coaxes me closer to release.

The noises he's making? They only wind me higher. Rory Miller has ascended to a whole new level.

It's never been like this. Never. No one has ever touched me like this, *enjoyed* touching me and making me feel like this.

A tiny flicker of fear moves through me, because this is going to change things with us. It was so much easier to lump Rory in with the rest of the guys I didn't care about.

Like he can sense my worry, he yanks my panties down so he doesn't have to pull them aside. They pool at my feet as he takes one of my hands, interlacing our fingers. My lips part. His hand swallows mine up, but the contact of our palms together while he's on the floor like that in front of me, while he pulls on my clit and looks up at me like my pleasure is his pleasure?

My mind goes blank, and I sink into the needy, intoxicated feelings in my blood.

He sucks on the sensitive bundle of nerves rhythmically, and my fingers tighten against his. My hips tilt against his mouth, desperate for more friction, more pressure.

The first flutters start, but that stubborn part of me digs her heels in. No, no, no. If he actually does make me come, I don't know what that will mean, and I *hate* that he'll get the satisfaction of winning.

"Stop holding back, Hartley."

His tongue sweeps fast, so hot and slick. The heated look of ecstasy in his eyes sends a streak of pleasure through me. His face is flushed, and why is that so hot? He's wearing an expression like my pussy is the best thing he's ever tasted, like he'll *die* if he can't keep doing this. Inside me, his fingers crook, finding my G-spot.

My release closes in on me, building, expanding, boiling over.

"I'm coming," I choke out, working myself over his mouth, and his fingers squeeze mine as searing, blinding heat twists and coils through me. "*Rory.*"

His groan reverberates against me, and I'm still coming. It's arcing through me, making me shudder and shake on his mouth. I think my eyes are closed, or maybe they're open and I'm just so overtaken by this orgasm barreling through me that I don't know the difference. His brow is creased, eyes closed, and I hit another peak, crying out while he squeezes my hand.

The waves subside and my mind clears, and I blink about a hundred times. I usually don't come during hookups.

"Fuck," he says desperately against my clit, breathing hard. "Hazel."

He says my name like a curse, like he's mad, but he stands and backs me against the door, both of us breathing hard. His eyes are glazed, half-lidded and dark, and his cock juts out, tenting the front of his pants. He brings his fingers to his lips, holding my eyes while he sucks my arousal from them.

A shudder rolls through me.

"Tell me it was good," he rasps, inches from my mouth.

"I didn't know it could be like that." I should say something smart and sharp, but I can't think anything. Goosebumps scatter across my skin.

A lazy, smug smile hitches on his gorgeous lips and he

kisses me, stroking deep into my mouth. I never thought tasting myself on a guy would make my pussy flutter like this, but I never thought Rory Miller would kneel at my feet and draw two orgasms out of me, either.

While he kisses me, I reach for his cock, dragging my palm over the hard length. If this is my only hookup with him, I want to hear what it sounds like when he comes for real.

He catches my wrist before he smiles and shakes his head. His cheekbones have a pink wash across them, like right after a game. "Next time."

The words *there won't be a next time* hover on the tip of my tongue. I picture breaking my rule, letting Rory bend me over and fuck me like he said he wanted to after the Assassin game, and my skin prickles.

I've never even had the smallest desire to break my rule, but I can't get that image out of my head.

That's concerning.

"Let's go to bed," Rory murmurs, walking me to the bed with his lips on my neck, pressing soft, intimate kisses there.

This *whole thing* was intimate. I have the urge to make a joke like *I suppose you'll want to stay over now* or *would it be rude to ask you to leave?* but nothing sounds funny, it just sounds mean and callous, and I don't want to be that brittle version of myself right now.

And I want him to stay. I don't know why, and I don't want to think about it too hard.

"I'm just going to brush my teeth." I step out of his touch and reach for a sleeping t-shirt, feeling Rory's eyes on my body as I pull it over my head and walk on wobbly legs to the bathroom. In the doorway, I pause, heart hammering. "I have an extra one. A toothbrush." I clear my throat, and his mouth tips up in amusement. "For you. If you want it. The dentist gives me a new one every time I go for a cleaning, but I like a different type, so I have a bunch of spares."

God, get a grip, Hazel.

Without a word, like he can tell I'm seconds from freaking out, Rory follows me to the bathroom. I can feel his attention as we brush our teeth, and when he leans forward to rinse his mouth, his hand comes to my lower back like it's an instinct.

I lean against his hand.

Don't you dare get used to this, I warn myself.

When we head back to bed, Rory moves to his side, watching me with that smug little smile.

"Told you I could make you come." He pulls me against him, spooning me, and I've never done this part before, either—the *cuddling after* part.

He should leave. I should make him leave. Instead, I reach over and turn out the bedside lamp.

"Don't gloat, Rory."

His low, pleased laugh rings out in the dark as I wonder what the fuck just happened.

CHAPTER 33
RORY

SUNLIGHT STREAMS into Hazel's tiny apartment. When she's awake, Hartley is sharp, confident, and guarded, but asleep, all her rough edges are smoothed over. She's on her side, knee bent forward, hand tucked under her face.

I don't think I've ever seen a girl as pretty as Hazel Hartley.

I didn't know it could be like that, she said last night, and the hairs on the back of my neck rose. There's something about Hazel telling me I'm doing a good job that sticks in my brain.

On the bedside table, my phone starts buzzing, and when I see who's calling, my gut clenches.

"Hi." My voice is quiet so I don't wake Hazel.

"Rory." It's my dad's usual no-nonsense, sharp tone. "Let's talk about the game."

For a split second, I think he's going to tell me he's proud of me. When I do well, he gives me a firm nod. That's it. But it's something, an acknowledgement that I'm not a waste of time and energy for him.

"I don't know what the fuck you were doing out there," he says, and my stomach hardens, "but you need to get your head in the game. They didn't sign you to pass the puck."

Why did I think he'd be pleased?

"Stars score goals," he adds.

And yet, last night, hockey felt like fun. Flipping the puck to the guys and watching them sink it in the net felt like play, and I could enjoy the roar of the crowd instead of resenting it.

Awareness prickles on my skin the moment Hazel wakes up. She's watching me, listening, but I don't look over at her. I don't want to see the look on her face.

He goes through my game, describing each missed opportunity, each assist like he was on the ice with me. He has a hand-written page of notes in front of him and he's checking them off, line by line, because that's what he's always done.

"I don't know what Ward thinks he's doing, but if he keeps this shit up, the Storm aren't headed toward the playoffs, that's for damn sure."

"Ward knows what he's doing."

A beat passes. "Why are you so quiet? You got a girl in bed with you or something?"

My gaze slides to Hazel. Her hair is messy and she looks so beautiful lying there in bed with sleepy eyes. My heart lodges in my throat, and I can feel the worry creasing my forehead. Protective feelings flood me. I don't want my dad anywhere near Hazel. If he said something, even some small comment about how I'm wasting my time with her, I'd do something stupid and rash.

"Right," he mutters, almost to himself. "You're seeing that girl. The physio."

My heart starts beating harder, and the hand not holding the phone is a fist tucked against my side. The photos are all over social media because we planned it that way, and Rick Miller watches my career closer than anyone.

"For all their shit coaching, the Storm have good PR. Get a nice girl on your arm and look like a good captain, and at the end of the season, move on."

"It's not like that." Blood pounds in my ears. What if it *is* like that to Hazel and I'm getting swept up in a fantasy? What if she drops me like it was all nothing? Nausea rolls through me at the thought.

She doesn't trust guys, and she thinks Connor and I are cut from the same cloth.

He laughs, that rough scoff. "Our lives are about hockey first. Don't forget that."

"Not always." My voice is hard. He's describing my nightmare, and yet it's my reality. I'm pleading with the universe.

"Don't let her get in your head. The last thing you want is a girl getting in the way."

I hate how he does this—makes it sound like letting anything but hockey into our lives makes us weak. I *want* Hazel in my head. I like her there, taking up space, watching with that approving little smile. Hazel stepped into my mind, and good things started happening in my life.

"Yeah?" Anger rattles through me, followed by something heavier. Hurt, because he was part of the reason my mom left. Frustration, because I see his pattern and I don't want to be like him. "Is that what you do? Is that why you're still happily married?"

There's a long pause, and I can feel his shock, followed by his own defensiveness. "People get divorced, Rory. Relationships aren't meant to last forever. Grow up and stop living a fucking fairy tale."

I feel like I've been punched in the stomach. "And you're so happy now?"

"What are you on about?"

I don't know why I went there; the words just burst out of me. My teeth grit as I take a deep breath, grappling for control before I unload everything in front of Hazel.

"I have to go," I tell him.

"Alright." His tone is weird, like he doesn't know what just happened, either. "Bye."

"Bye."

I end the call and take another deep breath, inhaling myself back into the present, in Hazel's apartment with her dragon and ballerina photo and closet bursting with bright yoga clothes.

"Was that your dad?" she asks softly.

My gaze swings to hers, searching her face. "You could hear him?"

"No." Her eyes are steady on me. "Just had a feeling."

I make a noise of acknowledgment in my throat, looking straight ahead at her dresser and the perfume bottle on top, but hearing all the things my dad said.

"How do you feel after yesterday's game?"

My dad's disapproval corrodes my stomach like acid. "I feel fine about it." Yesterday, I was on top of the world, but today, I've been yanked back to reality.

She hums, still watching me. The morning sunlight illuminates her eyes, making them sparkle.

My gaze drops to her t-shirt, and I frown. It's too big on her. Is it a guy's shirt? She wore it the last time I stayed over, too. That possessive feeling floods my chest again.

"Whose shirt is that?"

"Mine."

"But whose was it before it was yours?"

She frowns. "What?"

"Did you get it from a guy?"

She breaks into laughter. "What? No."

"Was it McKinnon's?"

Her expression turns baffled. "No. You seriously think I'm wearing his shirt to bed after what he did? Years later? After what I told you last night?" She lifts up on her elbows to stare at me head-on. "Really?"

"Sorry." I wince. "I know you're not hung up on him." The possessive feeling ebbs, fading.

"Jealous," she teases, the corner of her mouth tugging up.

"A little bit," I admit, pushing my hair back. I swallow and look around her place, thinking about another guy being here, in my spot on the bed, and I feel sick. "Sometimes it feels like you're the only good thing I have going for me, and I don't want to share that with some other guy."

I've said too much. I study her face, waiting for her to recoil.

Weak, my dad would say.

"What time is your practice today?" she asks.

"No practice this morning, but I have a training session at eleven. Do you have to get to work?"

A tiny head shake. "Not until ten." She looks like she wants to say something.

"Can I take you for breakfast?" I ask.

Another tiny head shake, but she's starting to smile. "I had something else in mind."

HALF AN HOUR LATER, I'm following her along the Vancouver seawall, dodging strollers and joggers as we run. Gray clouds stretch across the sky, but it isn't raining, and that's a win for November in Vancouver. We're making our way to Stanley Park, the big emerald forest at the edge of downtown. I check my heart rate on my watch.

"Let's speed up," I tell her. "I want to keep my heart rate above one-twenty."

She thrusts her hand out toward me, palm up. "Give me that." She points at my watch. "Your watch. Hand it over." She's breathing hard, face flushed, looking goddamned gorgeous in the morning light. "You keep checking it."

"What else should I be doing?"

She waves her arms at our surroundings. Looking at the ocean, the glass towers, the trees. "This. All of this."

There are a few people sitting on the logs on English Bay Beach, gazing out at the ships in the water.

I point at a seagull eating pizza out of the trash and gasp with overexaggerated awe. "Oh my god. Look at this majestic nature, Hazel!"

She slaps my shoulder, but she's laughing. "Miller, shut the fuck up."

I grin down at her before squinting at a building we're passing. "I just saw a rat. Let's go take a closer look."

"Unbelievable." She shakes her head, flattening her lips, but there's laughter in her eyes. "You know why I like running and yoga and swimming? Because all the other shit in life just disappears. I'm just trying to breathe and not collapse, and nothing else matters. No family shit, no hockey, no McKinnon. Just this." She looks out across the water. "Just trees and water." She tilts her head behind us. "And that seagull eating pizza."

We enter Stanley Park, and the noise of the city dies down as we run down the sidewalk between enormous fir trees. The air feels cleaner, crisper in here, and it's the perfect temperature for running.

"Alright, fire-breather. I'll do it your way."

That nickname makes her glare at me. "Call me that again and I'm going to bully you."

"You know what happens when you bully me."

A huge grin spreads across her face and her chest shakes as she laughs, and the same feeling floods my body as when we were sprinting up the stairs at the team dinner. The feeling I was chasing when I tried playing pickup hockey. And last night, when I flipped the puck to Owens and watched him score.

We run around the park, and I stop caring about my pace or my heart rate. I just run with Hazel. Everything falls away, and it's just us, right here.

"Come on," I goad her later as the entrance of the park comes into sight again. She's lagging a bit, but her pride would never allow her to ask me to slow down. "Is that all you got, Hartley? I thought you were strong."

"I *am* strong," she tosses back, picking up her pace.

I match her speed, and by the time we reach the entrance, we're sprinting. She's not wrong, she *is* strong. She's a lot faster than I would have predicted, but I'm a lot taller.

My mind wanders, and I'm back in that forest with my mom fifteen years ago. My heart squeezes. Worthy, I think Hazel calls moments like these.

I sprint past the entrance sign, two feet ahead of her, and whirl on her with a gloating, victorious smile. "I win." I poke her side. "A little more running and a little less napping on your yoga mat, okay?"

She laughs. "Prick."

"Sore loser." I loop my arm around her shoulders and pull her close as we walk. I'm sweaty, she's sweaty, but neither of us seems to care as we work to catch our breath. "It's okay. I have longer legs."

Her elbow digs into my side. "Don't patronize me."

"It's true." I laugh. "If you were my height, you'd probably win."

"Next time you sleep over at my place," she says, "I'm going to test how long you can hold your breath with a pillow over your face."

My head tips back as I laugh and laugh. "Next time, huh?"

"Whatever." She rolls her eyes, still smiling. "How come we never go to your place? Is it something embarrassing?" Her expression stills. "You don't *actually* have a sex doll, right?"

I snort. "No, Hartley, I don't." I think of my apartment—so cold and empty and soulless compared to Hartley's cluttered, lively shoebox. "My place sucks."

"Worse than mine?"

"Come on." I tighten my arm around her neck, jostling her. "No place is worse than yours, baby."

Her elbow lodges in my ribs again, and I laugh. She didn't tell me not to call her baby, though.

———

"You remind me of my mom sometimes," I tell her later as we walk home, coffees in hand, my arm back around her shoulder. She must be tired from our run because she isn't pushing me off.

Under my arm, she stills, but she turns to me with a curious expression. My focus goes to where her hand touches my side, arm wrapped around my waist, and it's just like that day in the forest when I was a kid, when my mom threw her arm around me and told me she loved me.

When was the last time we talked? Last Christmas, I think. She sent me an email and I didn't respond because I didn't know what to say.

God, I fucking miss her.

"She loves doing stuff like this. Running, hiking, yoga even." I look down at Hazel and wiggle my eyebrows. She's watching me closely. "She'd be all over your woo-woo worthy shit, Hartley."

I wonder what my mom would think of me playing pickup games. I wonder if she ever watches my games on TV.

"Do you see her often?" Hazel asks.

I shake my head. "Not really."

"Why not?"

I bite the inside of my cheek, unsure of what to say. "She left us." Hazel's gaze flares with fury and compassion, so I quickly add, "I mean, she asked me if I wanted to go with her."

My throat's tight as I fight to stay here with Hazel and not go back there to that house, listening as the door closes behind her.

"And I said no. She didn't like how hard my dad pushed me at hockey. Said he was obsessed and making me obsessed." I clear my throat. "And I wanted to make him proud, so I told her

I didn't want to go with her. They tried to do split custody but it was hard with my hockey schedule." My chest tightens. "And I didn't make things easy," I admit. "When I was with her, I'd ignore her or go play hockey until it was time for bed, and eventually I told her I didn't want to live with her anymore."

Nausea rolls through me, working its way up my throat. I was so hurt that she didn't want me and my dad that I made things so much worse.

"Things are kind of different between us now."

That's my fault, and I hate myself for it.

"How old were you?"

"Twelve."

She's quiet for a second. "You were just a kid."

The gentle emotion in her voice pierces a hole in my heart, so I force a laugh and give her a wry, self-deprecating smile so everything doesn't come spilling out. "Hartley, I'm okay."

Am I okay? Sometimes it feels like everything's falling apart.

"I'm one of the best athletes in the world," I continue. "I'm rich as fuck, and I'm very, very good-looking." I wink down at her, but she doesn't smile.

"Do you ever think about what it would be like if you'd gone with her?"

"I try not to."

She frowns.

"I don't want to have regrets." So I try not to think about that moment when maybe I should have gone with her.

She doesn't say anything, just sips her coffee as I walk her back to her place.

"Why'd you do this?" I ask as we turn onto her street. "Take me on a run."

"Because we're friends now." Her eyes meet mine, so bright and blue in the daylight, and she hesitates like she's choosing her words with care. "And because you're good and kind," she says, looking up at me with the most open and sincere expression I've ever seen on her pretty face.

This is who Hazel really is, under all the sharp barbs. I bet she doesn't let anyone except Pippa see this part of her. It's too valuable and precious for someone like me to have.

"And you deserve good things in your life, Rory."

CHAPTER 35

HAZEL

A FEW DAYS LATER, I walk into the gym as Rory's doing bench presses while a trainer spots him. His eyes meet mine from the bench.

"One thousand and one," he manages as I walk past, pushing the bar up. "One thousand and two."

I burst out laughing. He sets the bar on the rack, swings up to sitting, and gives me a broad grin.

God, I'm in so much trouble. When I'm not thinking about him on his knees, licking me, I'm thinking about running with him through Stanley Park. Or about him talking about his mom with that look on his face that breaks my fucking heart, like he misses her. Like he's lost without her. My heart aches.

Or about the way his features hardened when his dad called.

Protective anger slices through me. I'd love to meet his dad and rip him to shreds. So what if he's a Canadian hockey legend? I have a feeling he's the voice in Rory's head when Rory says things like *food is fuel, beer is inflammatory,* and *I'm only worth what my body can do for me.*

Rory deserves so much better than Rick Miller.

"Can we take five?" Rory asks the trainer, who nods.

He walks over to where I'm preparing for my session with Connor and sits on the wooden box I just set down. My stomach flips upside down with excited anticipation. Ever since we messed around, I've been waiting for him to bring it up.

"What are you doing tonight?" he asks. "Let's go for dinner."

I used to find his arrogance annoying. So why do I now find it hot? And why am I wearing more of the lingerie he sent? "I have plans."

He glances at Connor, who just walked into the gym for our session, and stands, stepping into my space. "Give me a kiss," he says to me.

I feel us being watched, which was the point of the whole thing, but my stomach does another barrel roll at the idea of touching him.

When his fingers trace my jaw, I'm done for. I bend toward him like a vine reaching for the sun.

He kisses me with gentle care, soft and sweet, pulling me against his chest. His scent is in my nose, all around me, surrounding me, and every muscle eases as I lean into him. He's too fucking tall and my neck is almost at a ninety-degree angle, but I don't care.

He smiles against my lips, presses one more kiss to my mouth, and looks down at me with affection like I'm the best thing he's ever seen.

"Let me take you for dinner," he says again, and I picture all the things we could do after dinner. Things like the other night, with his head between my legs. Maybe he'd let me touch him, and I'd get to hear what Rory Miller actually sounds like when he comes.

Maybe we'd skip dinner altogether.

No, I scold myself. It was just the one time, regardless of how much I've been thinking about it.

"I can't." I blink, clearing my head, refocusing my thoughts. My skin prickles, and I know Connor's watching and waiting for our session to start. "Really, I can't tonight. My parents are in town."

He looks at me, waiting.

"What?"

"Invite me."

"Rory. It's just my parents." And Pippa, Jamie, and Jamie's mom, Donna.

"I know. I've met them."

Right. New Year's last year, when he and a bunch of other players crashed on my parents' living room floor.

My parents think we're actually dating, though, and Rory getting close with my family feels real. I still don't know what this is between us.

"I can just say you're busy."

"No." He frowns. "I'd like to see them. I like your dad, and I didn't get to talk much with your mom. It would be nice to get to know her." His brow arches. "This is what I want."

"Hmm?"

"I won." His eyes flash with heat like he's reliving me riding his face. "We agreed that if I won, I could have whatever I want."

I let out a laugh of disbelief. "*This* is what you want?" Of all the things he could ask for?

"This is what I want."

He's wearing his soft, sweet, *Hazel is so cute* smile, and I'm struck by how much I like this one. How much I'm going to miss it when we're done with this.

Fuck.

I shake my head because I don't know what to make of this guy sometimes. A laugh slips out of me.

"Fine. Rory, would you like to join us for dinner?"

A broad smile stretches across his handsome face, and I feel like I've won something, because I love that look.

CHAPTER 36

HAZEL

"DREAM HOCKEY TEAM," my dad says to Rory in the restaurant that night. "Go."

Rory leans in with a serious expression, and I smile. "Anyone?"

"Anyone," my dad confirms. "Alive, dead, or fictional."

Rory lists a few hockey players, and my dad's nodding with approval. "Tate Ward," Rory adds.

My dad looks surprised. "Didn't expect that."

"Fastest slapshot in history."

My dad whistles. "I remember. It's a shame he only played for Vancouver for half a season."

"I know." Rory's eyes land on my empty water glass before he refills it from the pitcher, still listening while my dad and Jamie talk about their dream teams. A moment later, his hand lands on my thigh, warm and heavy.

He's wearing a navy blue knit sweater that stretches across his broad shoulders and dress slacks that fit his toned thighs and ass. Except for the team dinners, he's usually in athletic clothes, but tonight, he dressed up. He made an effort, I realize with a warm twist in my stomach. There's product in his hair. He smells nice, fresh and clean. He looks so frustratingly hand-some, and he's trying to make a good impression on my family.

Across the table, Pippa meets my gaze with a little smile, and I look away fast. If she finds out how things have been changing between me and Rory, I'll never hear the end of it, and convincing her that this whole thing is a charade will be even more impossible.

"You've been playing differently," my dad notes, and Rory's fingers tense on my leg.

"Yeah." Rory shifts.

"It's not a bad thing," my dad adds. "You're captain now. It's only natural that your style will change."

"You think?" Rory asks, and my heart breaks.

Rick Miller can burn in hell for the way he's bruised Rory's confidence, but the encouraging smile my dad gives him pushes all my protective rage out of the way, and I just feel grateful.

My hand lands on Rory's and when he glances at me, I give him a little smile.

The guys keep talking, and my mom nudges me. "Rory's very nice."

I smile again. "Yeah. He is."

Jamie's mom Donna leans forward with a cheeky smile. "I always knew you two would get together, Hazel. In high school, Rory would talk nonstop about this tutor of his."

Warmth creeps up my neck and I hide a smile. It feels like he belongs here with all of us tonight, and I like it too much.

"He's a catch," my mom whispers, and the apples of her cheeks pop. "But you're a catch, too."

I chuckle. "Thanks, Mom. Your hair looks nice. Did you get it cut?"

Her hand comes to the ends of her dark hair and she shrugs, bashful. "Just trying something new."

"You look great." I'm blowing on the embers of her self-confidence, urging them to catch.

My name grabs my attention.

"Have you seen her place?" Rory asks my dad.

"The hovel?" my dad scoffs. I give him a flat look, even as I'm trying not to smile. "Yeah, we've seen it."

"I have shoeboxes bigger than her apartment," my mom adds.

"Okay." I narrow my eyes at all of them. "Very funny."

"I can't believe you let her live there," Rory says to my parents.

My dad snorts. "No one tells Hazel what to do."

"Ever since you were a baby, you were hardheaded." My mom chuckles.

"Excuse me." I stare at her, grinning. "I prefer *determined*."

Rory arches an eyebrow. "Stubborn."

"Focused," I volley back.

His arm slips up around my shoulders and he smiles down at me. "All the things I like about you, Hartley."

"Aww." Pippa grins at us. Her phone is out, angled at us.

"Did you just take a photo?" I ask. Rory's arm is still around my shoulder.

"Yep." Her eyes glitter. "Now kiss."

"Pippa." I'm smiling but shooting daggers at her with my eyes. She just smiles wider.

"Come on," Donna calls down the table. "Kiss."

Rory's hand threads into my hair. "Don't be shy, Hartley."

My face is burning as everyone's eyes land on us. People at other tables are glancing over because two of the city's biggest hockey stars and a popular music artist are here. My stomach does a slow roll with nerves and anticipation as my gaze flicks up to Rory's.

"Come on, Hartley." His fingers come to my jaw as he tilts

my face toward his. He's looking at me with such intense affection I think my heart might burst. "Pretend you like me."

I laugh quietly, and then he's kissing me. It's sweet and soft and careful, like I'm precious to him.

When I open my eyes, he smiles at me, and there's a sweet twist in my chest that tells me I'm so, so fucked.

"Perfect," Pippa says quietly, smiling at her phone.

That's what I was afraid of.

CHAPTER 37

HAZEL

WHEN THE SERVER starts clearing the table, I scan my mom's plate. She barely ate anything. A rock forms in my throat, and my mind keeps snagging on that, even as the conversation moves on.

"Rory, what are you doing for Christmas?" Donna asks.

It's early December, and holiday decorations are starting to pop up around the city.

My heart jumps. Rory and I haven't talked about it, but Pippa, Jamie, and I are heading to Silver Falls for a couple days. Jamie needs to be back for the League Classic game on New Year's Eve. So do I, since I promised Rory I'd go with him.

His eyes meet mine. "I'm not sure yet."

He doesn't speak to his mom, and I suspect gruff Rick Miller isn't the kind of guy to dress up like Santa.

My mom gives me a look, lifting her eyebrows, eyes bright. *Invite him*, she's saying.

Here? In front of everyone? My pulse quickens. He wouldn't say no. He'd jump at the chance.

My heart leaps at the idea of Rory hanging out with the family, watching old movies and drinking apple cider while we put up decorations my parents bought before we were born.

I've never brought a guy home, though. It would be another first of mine that we cross off the list together. Rory coming home for Christmas would mean something. We'd make memories together, and it would be another tether to him, another difficult thing to let go of when it's over.

"How are you liking being back in Vancouver?" my mom asks, and I'm grateful we're moving on.

"I love it." His hand slides to mine in my lap and gives me a squeeze. "Hazel and I went for a run in Stanley Park the other day."

My mom sighs. "I need to get back into running." Her hands come to her waist and she widens her eyes at me. "It's hard to keep the weight off in the winter."

My shoulders tense, and that old, familiar pain of hearing my mom insult herself rises. This weight she's apparently gained isn't even visible, but I know from growing up in her home that she weighs herself every morning and keeps a logbook.

"So don't keep it off," I say lightly, playing with my water glass. "Why force yourself to fit someone else's idea of what you should look like?"

Like always, my words ping off her hard shell. She's had a lifetime of our culture's views on how women should look to fortify her beliefs. She waves me off.

"As soon as we get home to Silver Falls, I'm doing a cleanse."

My teeth grit. I can feel Rory's eyes on my face but I stare at the table. I'm a swirling storm of emotions—frustration that my mom bullies herself, that she can't be enough for herself, and embarrassment that Rory is seeing this glimpse into my personal life. All these things I'm trying to keep from him to no avail.

"Lemon, water, honey, and a pinch of cayenne," she continues. "Three days of that and the weight melts right off."

My exhale is shaky. I look to Pippa but she's in conversation with Donna.

"That's not healthy, Mom," I tell her. "You need protein and vegetables and carbs. Real food."

"The cavemen used to go days without eating," she scoffs. "It's good for us. It resets my metabolism."

"There's nothing wrong with your metabolism," I insist, heart pounding. "And then once you start eating real food again, you'll just gain the four pounds back."

My voice is coming out sharp, and I'm aware that Rory is sitting beside me, watching this.

The server appears at our table again. "Are we interested in the dessert menu?"

"No," my mom says.

"Yes," I bite out at the same time, staring at my mom. "They have tiramisu."

"No." Her hands fly up, like she couldn't possibly eat a single bite of dessert.

In my mind, I order the tiramisu. I order *all* the tiramisu in the entire restaurant, and when it arrives, I make her eat it and enjoy it. And then she says *you're right, Hazel. I love my body as it is, and I deserve to eat the things that make me happy!*

"Fine," I say instead. "We should wrap up. I have to be at work early tomorrow."

Shame forms in my throat because Rory saw all of that. He saw me lose my cool. He sees that my passion is helping people feel good in their bodies but I still can't get through to my own mom.

How am I going to have my own studio if I can't help the person I love more than anyone?

Rory excuses himself from the table and when the server

returns, I ask her for the bill.

She smiles at us. "It's been taken care of."

Rory slips past her, taking his seat, and some of the anxiety from this dinner eases in my chest at his kindness.

"Rory." My eyebrows slide up.

He gives me a cheeky grin. "Hazel."

"You didn't need to get dinner."

"I wanted to." To my parents, he smiles. "Next time you're in town, I'd love for you to come to a game."

"Absolutely." Jamie invites my dad all the time, but my dad looks like Rory just made his whole year. He pulls his phone out of his pocket and gestures at our table. "Let's get a photo of all of us."

"I'll take it," my mom says quickly.

I shake my head. "We can get the server to take it."

"No, no." She's already pulling the phone out of my dad's hand. "No one wants to see my wrinkles next to you two."

My breath chokes out of me, and I'm either going to scream at the top of my lungs right here in this restaurant or combust into a million particles of dust out of sheer frustration and anger. Nothing I've said has even made a dent.

We take the photo, and even with Rory's warm, solid hand on the sensitive part of my shoulder, my smile is wooden and forced. There's an uncomfortable lump in my throat as we leave. Outside, everyone hugs each other goodbye and we wish my parents a safe trip home before we all split up.

The entire conversation with my mom replays as I stand on the sidewalk. An angry throb pounds behind my forehead, and my eyes sting.

No, no, no. Shit. I'm about to cry.

"I'm not feeling good, so I'll see you tomorrow." My voice is high and strained.

If I look at Rory, he'll see I'm about to cry, and he can't. I don't cry in front of guys. I don't let guys come to dinner with my parents, I don't let them sleep over, and I sure as shit don't let them see me break.

I don't do any of these things with guys.

"Good night," I say without looking at him and walk away fast.

A hot tear falls and I swipe it away.

"Hazel."

I can't get enough air, and stupid, stupid tears spill over as I think about my mom and how frustrated I am with her. With myself. I've failed her, and she hates herself. She hates her body. She thinks she isn't good enough.

And I look just like her, so what does that mean about me? That I'm beautiful now, but when I'm her age, I won't be?

"Hazel."

He steps in front of me, hands on my arms, peering down at me.

My name rings in the air, strung between us like a taut wire, and I wonder if calling me by my last name was not just his way of being playful, but of keeping a wall between us, because right now, with my eyes all red and puffy and my nose running, I'm totally exposed.

"Look at me."

I clench my eyes closed. "No."

"Yes." The word is so soft, and his fingers tilt my chin up.

I open my eyes, and he's never looked at me the way he's looking at me right now, so openly concerned and careful, like I might shatter. Like he's desperate to make my hurt feel better.

Like he cares.

Maybe that's why I call him by his last name, too. I don't want to care about him.

I swallow. "I'm fine."

"Tell me." His words are gentle, but they're a sledgehammer against my resolve. I'm scrambling to hold the wall up against him, and he's bulldozing it with this sincerity, this *sweetness*.

His deep blue eyes search mine, and then his hand is on my cheek, resting soft as a butterfly.

"What's wrong?" he murmurs, and I'm fucking toast.

"It's my mom." My voice is rough with emotion. "She, um. She says these things about herself that I don't like. She doesn't have very good confidence."

He takes a deep breath. "That must be hard to watch."

My eyes blur but I blink the tears away.

"I hate that our society has made her feel so horrible about herself. I hate that she can't just exist in the body and face she has without feeling like she needs to change everything." I swallow past the gravel in my throat. "And what does it mean about me if I can't help her?"

Rory's expression is so pained, so earnestly concerned, that my heart gives a sharp twist. He drags a thumb across my cheek, wiping the tears away.

"Come here," he says quietly, pulling me into his chest.

My cheek presses below his collarbone, and he brushes his hand down my hair in calming strokes as I listen to his heart.

"It's not fair," he adds.

"It's not."

Another tear falls before absorbing into his shirt. His smell is so comforting, and the vicious pounding in my head is starting to fade.

"I wish I could go back in time and be her friend as a teenager. I'd make her into such a bad bitch."

His chin rests on the top of my head. "I know you would."

I'd tell her she was enough, if I knew her back then. And I'd make her believe it.

"That's why you say all that stuff during yoga?" Rory's

breath tickles my ear. "That's why you want to create a space for everyone?"

I nod against his chest, sniffling. "She likes yoga but says she's not skinny or young enough. She says no one wants to see her in yoga clothes." My voice breaks on another sob as pain racks my chest.

I just want my mom to love herself as much as I love her.

"I look just like her," I whisper, even though I shouldn't. Thoughts like that don't belong in whatever Rory and I are doing.

Outwardly, I'm so confident. Seeing my mom hate her body only fortified my hard shell, but the thought sneaks in through the cracks. One day, I'll look like my mom, and will I still love myself the way I do now? Will someone like Rory still find me beautiful?

Connor didn't, and I was nineteen. What about when I'm sixty?

Rory peers down at me, and I've never seen care in anyone's eyes like this. "You're so beautiful that it makes my chest hurt."

My heart pounds.

"And even when we're a hundred years old," he whispers, "I'll be flirting with you to get your attention."

It's funny, how he knows exactly what to say. How they're just words, but they heal one of the cracks in my heart.

We stand on the sidewalk for a long time, wrapped tightly together while people maneuver around us.

"You're incredible at what you do," he murmurs into my hair, and the words sink right into my heart, dissolving into my blood. "Keep trying with her. One day, she might surprise you."

I swallow, resting against his chest, listening to his steady heartbeat.

I want to believe him so, so badly.

CHAPTER 38

HAZEL

"THANKS FOR WALKING ME HOME," I say to Rory as we approach my apartment. It's a clear night, so the stars are out, sparkling in the dark sky.

I wait for him to tell me to invite him up. I'm not sure what I'll say this time.

"Let's go for a run," he says instead. "Just a short one." His hands are on my shoulders, and he's leaning down to meet my eyes. "Two blocks."

I snort.

"Ten feet." His eyes plead. "We can run to the corner and back if you like. Come on, Hartley." He glances to my apartment's window. "You still have that gym bag I left the other day? You didn't burn it?"

"Haven't gotten around to it yet," I say lightly, but he doesn't laugh like I want him to.

He's giving me that look again, the same one from the day we argued at the skating rink and he came after me, and the same one from earlier tonight. Like he needs me to be okay, like he'll do anything to fix this hurt in my heart.

"Why are you doing this?" I breathe.

"Because you did it for me." He searches my eyes. "So let's

shake it off together." He brushes a soft, sweet kiss on my mouth, and my heart lodges in my throat. There's such careful attention, such protectiveness in that little touch.

My eyes sting, but not for the same reasons as before.

"Okay?" he whispers.

I nod. "Okay."

He smiles. "That's my girl."

Ten minutes later, we hit the pavement. It's cool out and quiet as the city winds down. We stick to side streets until we reach the seawall. While we run, I replay what my mom said, and what I said.

"Alright, Hartley," he says after ten minutes of silence. "I'll make you a bet."

We're running along the sidewalk that overlooks English Bay, and the golden streetlights cast shadows on his features.

"A friendly *competition*," he adds, and the corners of my mouth kick up.

"I've heard that before."

"I know, and you lost. Badly."

"Shut up." I'm smiling, forgetting all the stuff at dinner. Forgetting how I cried in front of him.

"This is your opportunity to even the score."

The stubborn part of me says *don't take the bait,* but my competitive side wants more. "What's your offer?"

He points at a sign at the end of this stretch of seawall, bordering the beach. "Let's race to that sign."

Normally, he's faster than me. He's tired from training today, though. I might be able to beat him. "And if I win?"

His smile is smug but his eyes are hot. "I'll text you something sexy."

Awareness shoots through me, but I keep the cool mask on my face. "Oh?"

"Yep. Something to keep you warm when I'm away."

The team is traveling for away games for the next two weeks. A thousand images play through my head, and my pulse beats between my thighs. "And if *you* win?"

There's a beat of silence, and I feel like I can't get enough air as I look up at him.

"I'll leave that up to you," he says with a lazy smile. "Whatever you think is fair."

My heart pounds harder. He basically offered me nudes, so it would only be fair if I sent one back. My stomach flutters at the idea.

"You ever send McKinnon anything?" he asks quietly.

I shake my head, letting out a heavy exhale. "He asked but, um. I never wanted to."

I never trusted him, I realize. Deep down, I knew something was wrong. Maybe not that he was seeing girls behind my back, but I knew I was an afterthought.

His eyes sharpen, pinning me. "Interesting."

"Yeah." I swallow, nerves dancing up and down my spine, sending shivers through me.

What would I even send? I think about the lingerie that keeps showing up at my apartment—the lingerie I keep wearing. He likes softer colors, it seems, because everything is pastels. Pale pinks, blues, lavender, mint green, cream. A light pink lace bodysuit arrived yesterday, and I stood in front of the mirror in it, brushing my fingers over the soft, sheer fabric.

I looked incredibly hot in it, and that's what I'd wear.

A streak of nervous energy hits me in the stomach at the idea, and when I look up at him, he's still watching me with a challenging, curious expression. My stomach flops again.

If we do this, one of us is getting a photo. We're stepping past the territory of pretending. A lot of tonight has felt like that.

His eyebrow arches. "Only if you want, Hartley."

Something stubborn, competitive, and playful courses through me, and my nerves fade. I want the victory to lord over him, but more, I want to see what he sends me.

Losing is not an option.

"Fine." I bite my bottom lip, and his eyes follow the motion. "Get ready to have your ass kicked."

A broad grin stretches across his face, and I mirror it even as a voice in my head asks if I'm a fool for thinking I'll win.

"Ready?" His legs bend, preparing to sprint, and I match his stance.

"Yep."

"Go."

We're off, sprinting, and even as competition rushes through me, I'm filled with laughter, light, and joy. Our feet hit the pavement fast. Someone moves off the path to give us space.

"Sorry," I call over my shoulder.

"Yeah, sorry," Rory adds, laughing.

We're a hundred feet from the sign. Rory's a few feet ahead of me, so I dig deep. My legs burn and my lungs sear with the need for more oxygen. I don't think my blood has ever pumped this hard. I've never run this fast. I'm flying. I'm filled with color and light, and when Rory looks back at me over his shoulder with that perfect, handsome smile, I know he's flying, too.

We're almost at the sign. Fuck. He's going to win, and I *can't* lose. Not with these stakes. I panic, and with one glance at the sand beside us, I summon all my energy and shove him.

Not my proudest moment. It's a soft landing, though, so he won't get hurt.

With a grunt of surprise, he stumbles but doesn't fall—his stabilizer muscles are too strong—but I take the lead. I run harder and slap a hand on the sign.

When I turn, I see him flop down to sit in the sand, chest

rising and falling fast, laughing.

"You dirty little cheater," he calls, brushing sand off as I loop back to him, heaving for air.

Fuck, that was close. Why did I even agree to that?

Because Rory flicks at something inside me that makes me want to play with him. He knows exactly how to get me going.

I grin at him, still sitting in the sand, and extend a hand, but he pulls me down beside him. I'm filled to the brim with gratitude because this actually made me feel better. Or maybe it's being with Rory.

We're both breathing hard still, damp and sweaty, but I smile at him. "Thanks."

"Don't thank me yet. You haven't even seen the picture."

I choke out a laugh as my stomach swoops in anticipation. As we get up and walk home, I think about earlier at dinner, when my mom asked Rory what he was doing for the holidays.

"So," I start, "about earlier."

"Which part?"

"The Christmas part."

He sends a curious glance at me, the corner of his mouth tipping up.

"I know you probably have plans," I say, fiddling with my fingers.

"I don't." His eyes linger on me, bright, interested, and patient, like I'm a flighty bird and he's gently waiting with his hand out for me to gather the courage to land.

"Right."

God, why is this so hard? Maybe because Connor always gave me the impression that I was being clingy when I tried to make plans with him. Just blurt it out, Hazel.

"It's short notice and maybe there aren't even any flights left"—I don't know why that thought is so disappointing—"and the guest bed at my parents' place is worse than my old one"—

he could sleep in my twin bed in my room, but it would be cramped, although maybe that would be hot and we'd mess around more—"and you'd probably be bored in a small town—"

"Come on, Hartley. Spit it out."

"Do you want to spend Christmas in Silver Falls?" My heart beats up into my throat.

He arches a teasing eyebrow. "With you?"

I huff a laugh. "Yes, Rory. With me."

"Taking this fake dating thing a little far, aren't you?"

My stomach drops. Of course I am. Of course I got carried away. Earlier, when he comforted me, I thought... I don't know what I thought. "It would look weird if you didn't come with me," I lie.

Coward, my brain whispers.

Under his scrutiny, my pulse speeds up.

"You're right." He puts his arm around my shoulders and pulls me to him, and I relax. "We should keep up appearances."

"You can say no."

"I don't want to." He tugs on a lock of my hair. "And now I'll get to see you open the presents I got you in person."

"Presents?" I light up. "Multiple?"

I've already bought him a couple things, but I wasn't sure how to bring it up.

"Yep." His eyes narrow with mischief. "It wouldn't be weird if I gave you lingerie in front of your parents, right?"

I burst out laughing, all tension from earlier disappearing. "No, I'm sure that would be totally fine and not awkward at all."

"Great. I'm looking forward to it."

My heart lifts. I know he's joking about the lingerie, but the idea of Rory in my parents' home, spending time with my family?

I'm looking forward to it, too.

CHAPTER 39

RORY

LATER IN THE WEEK, I'm lying in my hotel bed, scrolling through my text chat with Hartley. We played New Jersey tonight, and when our right winger scored after my assist, I felt another rush of that light, victorious feeling I've been chasing.

I should be sleeping or reviewing game tape for tomorrow's game, but instead, I'm thinking about Hazel.

When she asked me to come with her for Christmas, she was doing that finger-twirling thing. She was nervous.

Keeping up appearances, my ass. She likes me. She isn't ready to admit it, but I can be patient.

I scroll through our chat. She didn't respond to the link I sent with a studio for rent.

Did you see the studio I sent?

The typing dots pop up, disappear, and pop up again. *Yes. Thanks.*

And?? She sends a shrugging emoji, and I frown. *Too expensive?*

It's expensive but not outrageous.

Too big? Too small? The listing said the space has two studio rooms.

No. It's a good size.

I shake my head at my phone, confused. *Let's check it out when I get home.*

I don't think I'm ready yet.

I remember what she said after the dinner with her family while tears rolled down her face, about how if she couldn't help her mom, how is she supposed to help other people, and my chest hurts. The need to make this situation better for Hazel claws through me.

You're ready, Hartley. What does Pippa think?

I don't really talk to her about this stuff. She's busy with her own career.

I let out a heavy exhale. *I think you should talk about it with her, and I think you're ready.*

Hazel admitting these things to me has to mean something, though. This thing between us might be more than she lets on.

The typing dots appear, disappear, and appear again before her next message pops up. *I seem to remember winning a bet.*

I shake my head, laughing. I've been thinking about it all week, and the photos are ready to go, but...

I wanted her to ask. I wanted to see a little sliver of desire from her. I still get hard thinking about her saying *I didn't know it could be like that* after I ate her pussy like my life depended on it.

She's asking, though. I grin at my phone. *You cheated.*

Now who's being the sore loser?

Put my jersey on, I text back. Christ, I love sparring with her like this. *It'll turn me on.*

Wow. Your ego, Miller.

A laugh chokes out of me. I wish I was in her bed, watching her try not to smile. We had a game Wednesday, so I couldn't attend her online yoga class. I feel like I haven't seen her in forever.

The picture pops up in our chat. She has her back to her

bathroom mirror in the photo, peering over her shoulder with a little smile, *MILLER* across her back in bold letters.

Possessive satisfaction curls through me.

You're beautiful, I text.

Are you talking to me or the jersey?

My smile turns high-watt. I'm buzzing, warmth spreading through my chest and over my skin. *Why can't it be both?*

Excitement and nerves thrash through me as I go to the last photo in my camera roll, a shirtless picture I took in front of the mirror yesterday. My phone makes a whooshing noise as the photo sends, and a moment later, she responds.

Wow.

I suck a breath in. *Hartley, I seem to remember you saying I don't have an eight-pack.*

I can feel her cute little huff through the universe. *I don't remember saying that.*

My eyebrows lift as I wait, smiling. She totally fucking does remember.

You're shameless, she says.

My smile lifts higher. *Say it.*

The longest pause in the world stretches out, and I scrub a hand over my face with impatience.

You have an incredible body. Happy?

My lungs expand, filling every corner of my chest, and I grin like a fool at my phone.

———

The next afternoon, I'm on the plane with the rest of the team, waiting for takeoff and debating whether to send Hazel the shirtless photo I took this morning.

I read over our text conversation and her response to the picture I sent last night, and hot possessiveness courses through me at the idea of her staring at my picture, getting turned on.

Ward claps me on the shoulder as he walks past my seat, and I slip my phone away.

"Nice work out there tonight, Miller," he says with a nod and a quiet smile, and I straighten up. On his phone beside me, Streicher pauses, listening.

"Thanks, Coach."

"Whatever you're doing, keep it up." His eyebrows bob before he keeps walking, and I watch his tall form disappear down the aisle.

Every game, my dad's voice gets quieter. Instead, I picture Hazel giving me that proud smile. During games, I look to Ward on the bench, and when I pass the puck and help the other guys score, he always wears the same stoic expression, eyes glinting like he's pleased.

"You weren't in the gym this morning," Streicher says from the seat beside me.

"Uh, yeah. I went for a run around the waterfront instead."

He frowns. It's unusual for me to skip a workout. "Why?"

I run a hand through my hair. I woke up to an incoming call from my dad but let it go to voicemail. I still haven't checked it. "Hazel makes me go for runs sometimes with her and it's, uh." I shrug. "Nice. To not think about hockey all the time." I swallow. "And just talk and stuff."

He stares at me. "You miss her."

I think back to the past few days, how often I wonder about her or have the urge to text her. How I can't wait to see her again. "Yeah. I do."

Streicher turns back to his phone, and I read over my conversation with Hazel. Before I think too hard about it, I send her the photo I snapped this morning, lying in bed with the light streaming in.

Stop teasing me, she texts a moment later, and I burst out laughing. Players look over and I clear my throat, stifling my laughter.

Your turn, I respond, grinning like a dumbass.

A photo pops up—she's in her apartment, sitting on her yoga mat with her feet together, stretching, full lips curving up. She's wearing a loose sweater and leggings, silky hair up in a ponytail, and no makeup.

My heart skips a beat. She's gorgeous.

Not what I had in mind but still cute as hell.

I study the photo, desperate for any scrap of Hazel I can get. The dragon I gave her sits on her nightstand now. Does that mean she misses me, too? Her bed looks huge and comfy and I cannot fucking *wait* to get back to her and flop down on it.

My eyes land on Hazel again. The shoulder of her loose sweater has slipped aside while she stretched, revealing a pale purple strap.

The pale purple strap of one of the pieces of lingerie I bought her. Proud male satisfaction charges through my veins.

Hartley, are you wearing one of the lacy things I bought you?

Her response is immediate. *Yes.*

CHAPTER 40
HAZEL

I'M PLAYING WITH FIRE.

I needed to make sure it fit, I text like a dirty little liar, closing my eyes and leaning my forehead against the bed.

First, it was the photo the other night of him in front of the mirror, looking smug and ripped and fuckable. I thought about that picture all goddamned day. I thought about it when I woke up this morning, aching between my legs, at work when I was trying to focus, and this evening during his game.

This fake dating thing? I suck at it, and my one-time-only rule? This is pushing it.

I'm not breaking the rule, though. I'm bending it. A shirtless picture of him isn't sex. Wearing pretty lingerie isn't sex. It's fine.

I pull up the photo he just sent. He must have taken it this morning, because in the picture, he's lying in a hotel bed, hair messy and eyes sleepy. The morning light makes his eyes glow, and he smirks like he knows I've been thinking about him. The sheets are rumpled, and I can practically hear the groan he'd make stretching out against them.

Pictures like this, where he looks intensely hot? They're dangerous. I can't look at them, but I can't look away, either.

Deep inside me, it feels like a new version of myself is waking up.

And does it fit? he asks.

Yes.

Prove it.

My eyes go wide and a thrill shoots through me. He wants another? *No way.*

Why are you wearing it?

I already told you. Plus it's pretty. And I feel hot in it.

It's not just that, though. I miss him. When I wear the stuff he selected, I feel closer to Rory.

I don't know what to do about that, and I don't know how it fits into this fake dating thing we're doing or the one-time-only rule I have for myself.

Please, Hartley. Please send a picture. I'm begging here. Show me.

My breath catches, turning ragged, and heat spreads up my chest and neck. I'm quickly losing control of this situation, but the desperation in his texts melts my resolve.

A photo isn't fucking. I'm still in control. We're just playing around.

I let out a delirious laugh. I can't believe I'm about to do this. I pull my sweater off and lie down on the bed, heart pounding as I open my camera app and lift the phone.

The photo doesn't even show my face, just my shoulder, the top of my cleavage, and my hair spread across the pillow, but still, it's the sexiest picture I've ever taken. Hesitation rises in me, but I picture Rory's expression when he sees the photo—a slack jaw, pupils blown wide—and I send it.

His text appears immediately. *Jesus Christ, Hartley.*

I bury my burning face in the pillow, smiling.

———

The next evening, I receive another photo.

He's shirtless in the mirror, clad in just those tight black boxer briefs. My eyes linger on the sharp V cuts above his hips, the trickle of hair into the waistband, and the toned flex of his arms. He's smirking like he knows how hot he is.

Heat twists low in my belly, and I head to my closet to pull out another piece of lingerie—a baby blue balconette bra with a matching lace thong and garters.

It's just a picture, I tell myself as I set my phone up and snap the picture of my back, hair draped across my shoulder, lacy strap visible. It's just for fun. I'm always telling my students that they deserve to feel good, so why can't I? Sending sexy pictures to Rory and seeing his admiration of my body makes me feel hot. That's all.

I won't let it get away from me. I know what I'm doing.

My pulse jumps when his response arrives, and I flush with pleasure.

Holy fuck, Hartley.

CHAPTER 41

RORY

GOOD GAME TONIGHT, Hazel texts a week later while I sit in a bar with the guys, celebrating the game. She and Pippa are on their weekend away at Harrison Hot Springs.

We won the game tonight four-nothing, and not a single one of those goals was mine. I smile down at my phone. A half-full beer sits on the table in front of me after Owens shoved it in my face.

One beer isn't going to ruin my career, and it's so good. So fucking good.

You watched my game? I reply.

Her typing dots appear, disappear, and appear again. I hope she's getting flustered on the other side.

It was on in the background.

My grin widens. *You watched my game.*

Christ, I miss her, but the photos we've been sending back and forth? My cock stiffens just thinking about them. Prickly, guarded Hazel, sending me glimpses of the lingerie I bought her. Every time my phone chirps with her text tone, my balls tighten in anticipation.

I haven't jerked off this much since I was a teenager. I scroll up to the photo she sent this morning of her cream-colored lace panties stretched over the long line of her hip, and I scrub a hand over my face.

Hazel Hartley has me under her thumb, and I love it.

Something on the TV screen behind the bar catches my eye —my dad. He's in the studio as a guest commentator. Replays roll of the Storm game, and a familiar weight settles in my gut. They replay me passing to another forward before he snaps it into the net.

That play was everything I love about hockey—speed, skill, and luck. Teamwork, too, I guess. Fuck, that was a nice goal.

"What a waste," the captions read as my dad talks.

Pain rips through me. I hope Hazel isn't watching this.

"I know he's my son, but Rory Miller is a weapon on this team, and Ward's using him to prop up other players," my dad continues, and my molars grind. "Ward makes Miller captain but has him passing to other players like they're at summer camp."

"Don't," Streicher mutters beside me, staring at his own phone, probably texting Pippa.

"What?"

He tips his chin at the TV before meeting my eyes with his usual serious expression. "Don't watch that shit. It doesn't matter what they say. They're not on the ice with us."

"He's right, though." I rub the back of my neck. "I was traded to the team to score goals and win games."

Streicher watches me for a long moment, frowning. "Why don't you leave that up to Ward?"

"I just want to be a good captain," I admit to my oldest friend. I blow a long breath out. "What would you do in my position?"

He shrugs his big shoulders. "I'd do whatever Ward thought was best. I trust him."

"Me, too." The urge to make Ward proud fights with my need for my dad's approval. "I don't understand him, though."

Streicher makes a noise that sounds like a snort. "Me neither. I think he's got a plan, though."

My mind wanders back to tonight during the game, after my assist. Ward met my eyes and dipped his chin in approval at me.

"How's stuff going with Hazel?" Streicher asks.

"Good." Really good. I think about us racing to the sign on the beach, her shoving me, and me laughing. Falling asleep beside her. Her sending me the hottest pictures I've ever seen in my life.

Too good, actually. Better than I ever imagined it could be. It's not just the photos we send back and forth, and it's not just that I jerk off daily thinking about her and only her. It's that I think about her constantly, and I can't wait to get home to her.

A realization looms at the edge of my consciousness. My feelings for Hazel grow every day, and I've never felt like this. This could all be over in a heartbeat, though. Just because I'm trying not to be like Rick Miller doesn't mean it's working.

"Still pretending?" Streicher asks, glancing at my phone.

I've got a photo of Hazel from this morning pulled up. She's wearing a toque, and her cheeks and nose are pink from the cold. My chest feels tight and warm.

The realization I'm avoiding starts pounding on the door, demanding attention. I don't know what this is to Hazel. We still have a deadline on this thing between us.

"I don't know." I clear my throat as my chest pulls tight.

Streicher makes a noise of acknowledgment like he isn't fucking surprised, and I have the urge to grab him by the shirt and shake him.

"Why didn't you warn me?" I ask, keeping my voice low so the guys don't overhear.

Streicher gives me a disinterested look. "Warn you about what?"

My mind goes to Hazel crying on the street after her family dinner and the unbearable pain of seeing her hurt and disappointed like that. The urge to fix things, the need to make everything better. I shake my head, at a loss for words. "That it was going to be like this." I exhale a heavy, frustrated breath, meeting his eyes. "It's different with her, you know?"

He watches me for a long moment. "Good." He sets his phone down. "You mention this to Hazel yet?"

"Nope."

"Are you going to?"

"I don't know." If she doesn't feel the same way, it'll ruin everything we have. "It's fake to her."

We stare at the TV for a beat. "At least give her the option of rejecting you instead of doing it yourself."

There's a long, low whistle, and I look up to see McKinnon standing over us, watching the TV.

"Too bad," he says as they show my goal stats this season compared to previous years. "Maybe if you spent more time training and less time crying and jerking off to pictures of Hazel, your stock wouldn't be crashing."

If Hazel said the thing about me crying and jerking off, I'd laugh, but because it's her fuckface ex, I just stare at him, territorial anger simmering inside me.

"Need something, McKinnon?"

Streicher gives McKinnon a cold, intimidating stare, but McKinnon ignores it, dropping into the seat across from us.

"Nope." He smirks, eyes red and bleary. "I can see the appeal of it, though." He slurs like he's drunk. Thank fuck Ward took pity on me and gave me my own room for this leg of the trip.

"What are you talking about?" Streicher's tone is flat and unimpressed.

Connor just smirks right at me. "Miller will find out soon enough." He catches the attention of a passing server. "Get me another beer, would you?"

My fist clenches with irritation before I give the server an apologetic look. "Thank you," I tell her before shaking my head at him. "Use your fucking manners, McKinnon. Don't make the team look bad."

He scoffs, leaning back in his chair and staring at the server's ass as she walks away. "She's fine. She likes me. If you give them too much attention, they get clingy." He burps into his fist. "But if you leave them wanting more, they work harder for your attention." His gaze swings to me, eyes full of hate. "It worked for Hazel."

Even as protective rage roars through me, I keep my expression relaxed and amused. "She's moved on, and you should, too. It's getting sad."

Fucking asshole.

McKinnon winces and makes an exaggerated pained noise. "My groin sure is sore after the game," he says, grinning at me. "I'll need Hazel to work on it all week."

The simmering rage in my veins boils over, and I clench my teeth so hard my molars hurt. "Watch it, McKinnon."

His drunk smile pulls higher, and my blood pounds. Thank fuck Hazel isn't around to hear this.

I lean in so only he and Streicher can hear me. "If you make her uncomfortable, I will fucking end you."

My teeth grit. I've never hated someone the way I hate this guy.

McKinnon widens his eyes, pretending to be scared. "Wow. Someone's got it bad." He laughs to himself, and the sound makes me sick. "You always did have a thing for my girl, didn't you?"

His arrow hits me right in the chest, and anger rolls through me like a storm.

"She's not your girl," I say in a low, deadly voice, on my feet with my fists clenching and my shoulders tight. "Hazel is mine."

"Like I said." His eyes glitter with ugly condescension. "You'll see."

On the edge of control, I drag in a deep breath and look around, making eye contact with Ward across the bar with the other coaches. The goalie coach is talking, but Ward watches us with interest.

I'm the captain, and if Hazel were here, she'd encourage me to be the guy Ward thinks I can be.

"Drink some water, McKinnon." I nod good night to Streicher and he lifts a hand as a goodbye.

In the elevator, I pull in deep breaths, letting them out slow. Fuck, I hate that guy, but what I said about Hazel being mine? It was the truth.

I scroll through our texts, all the fucking incredible photos she's sent me over the past week. Hartley's body is a dream, with smooth curves, swells of cleavage, the gentle dip of her hips—even her collarbones are gorgeous. She has a freckle right over her left breast that I think about licking every time I get a photo where it's visible.

That *she* feels hot and desired while taking these photos is what makes me hard, though. Thoughts of McKinnon and my dad fade away as I send her another one.

Her response comes immediately.

It's a picture of her on her front, hair falling forward and breasts against the duvet. The soft curve of her ass is visible, and need flows through me, making my balls tighten.

*Is that all you've got, Miller? *yawn* Even with all your pretty muscles, I'm getting bored.*

My smile curls higher. I don't know whether it's the two beers I had or the possessive feelings from tonight, but the urge to ramp things up with Hartley courses through me.

She may not know it yet, but Hazel Hartley is mine, and tonight? I'm going to show her.

CHAPTER 42

HAZEL

THE PHOTOS HAVE ESCALATED and I've completely lost control of the situation. I've become addicted to the pictures Rory sends, and his responses to the photos *I* send in return.

I thought about that photo all day, Hartley.

God, you're so fucking hot.

I came in the shower thinking about this one, he said about a photo of me wearing a plum-colored bra, my cleavage on full display, before he sent back a photo of himself shirtless, grinning as his erection strained the fabric of his boxers.

Lying on the hotel bed beside Pippa, I scroll past the photo of him just out of the shower, water droplets on his skin, towel low on his waist and the outline of his thick arousal clearly visible, and the photo I sent back of me lying in bed, stretched out on the sheets wearing a delicate cream lace set.

My phone buzzes as another picture arrives. He's naked, holding a towel in front of him, all the muscles down his hips and thighs on full display. Water droplets cling to his chiseled chest, and I twinge between my legs. My response is a picture of me lying on my front. No face, just cleavage and my ass in a midnight-blue thong the color of his eyes.

Excitement jitters through me as I pause on that picture

and press my lips together to hold back the grin. I'm floating with warm, liquid feelings.

This is fun, I realize. It's exciting and playful, and I've never experienced this in regard to sex.

Pippa flips to postgame press from the Storm game.

Be a good boy and drop the towel, I text before scrolling back to the picture of him fresh out of the shower.

And now I'm baiting him for more. Unbelievable.

"You've been seeing Hazel Hartley, a physiotherapist with the Storm," a reporter says to Rory.

His hair is damp from his shower, the tops of his cheeks are still flushed from the game, and his mouth tips up in an effortless smile.

"Jamie Streicher will be her brother-in-law soon. Could there be another wedding in the family's future?"

Pippa clasps my hand, and I'm frozen as the corner of his lip slides a half inch higher. *"Yeah. There could."*

My heart is in my throat. He's telling the press what he needs to so he can look like a solid captain. It's not real. And if it were real, well, no one would actually say that about a girl he's been seeing for a couple months.

Rory would, an annoying voice says in my head. He's intense and impulsive and goes after what he wants. He thinks with his heart on his sleeve.

It's not real, but I'm smiling as I send him another picture.

"Did you bring a charger?" Pippa holds her phone up. "I forgot mine and my battery's almost dead."

"In my bag."

She slides off the bed, and I scroll up through our text chat. We talk every day, sometimes sending each other photos—his from the road and mine from work or hanging out with Pippa or in my apartment.

The guys' flight gets in late Monday night, so I won't see

him until Tuesday, and liquid heat pools inside me at the idea of finally seeing him in person after two weeks of torturing each other.

"Hazel."

Pippa stands over my bag with an accusing look, smiling ear to ear. She reaches in and pulls out a fistful of lingerie.

My mouth flattens, and I give her a guilty wince.

"*Hazel.*"

I start laughing. "Get out of there."

Her mouth falls open but her eyes are still lit up, bright and sparkly with amusement. "Why do you have an entire bag of lingerie for a weekend with *me?*"

"No reason." I scratch my neck, looking away.

She starts looking through the garments. "This is nice stuff, too." Her brow goes up.

I jump up and snatch everything from her, tucking it back in my bag as she flops back down on the bed, still smiling. "Rory bought it, didn't he?"

My face is burning hot. I shrug at her. "Yes. Okay?"

"Hmm." She narrows her eyes, smiling.

"What."

"*Hmmmm.*"

A laugh bubbles out of me. I'm still blushing. "Pippa."

"Interesting. Very, very interesting."

I fold my arms over my chest. I think I'm smiling, too. "Say what you want to say."

"You said it was fake."

My heart squeezes up into my throat as I blink about thirty times. "It is."

"So why is he buying you expensive lingerie that no one can see?"

The silence stretches for too long for there to be a reasonable explanation.

"Hazel!" she bursts out. "Are you two messing around?"

"I don't know," I burst back. "Sort of. Not really. He sleeps over. We fooled around once but he wouldn't let me touch him and we"—I wince—"send pictures back and forth?"

It doesn't sound great out loud.

She looks like I told her unicorns were real. "What kind of pictures?"

"Sexy ones," I admit, sounding strangled.

Her head tips back, laughing. "I knew it. You like him."

"I don't know." My heartbeat feels erratic and I force myself to shrug.

"You do. Admit it."

"Fine." I shrug again, eyes darting around the room. "I like him."

Fuck. I said it. My throat knots. I really need to get a hold of this thing. It has an expiration date.

"I like him," I repeat, worrying my bottom lip.

Her expression softens. "Why do you say it like it's a bad thing?"

There are a million things I can't say out loud. Because he can have anyone, so why would he choose me? Because I'm just waiting for the thrill of this to be over for him.

Because I'm ordinary, and guys like Rory Miller are extraordinary.

"I invited him home for Christmas." I'm still putting the finishing touches on his presents, but I can't even use him coming home as an excuse since I bought them before I asked him. "I don't do this kind of thing."

Pippa's eyes are soft and watchful, and I love her so much because there isn't a lick of judgment in her expression, but at the same time, I feel like she can see deep inside my head. "What if you did, though?"

My stomach tightens.

"Don't you want more?"

I think about what Rory said in postgame press tonight and how it didn't sound fake. When I put the past behind me, being with Rory is effortless.

No. It's more than that. It's incredible.

I don't answer Pippa's question, but she can see it all over my face.

"He fit right in with us at dinner," I say instead. My mouth twists as I think about him and Dad talking, and how at ease Rory looked. "His family isn't like ours."

She gives me a small smile like she can see something I can't.

"I got upset afterward," I admit. "I started crying on the street right in front of him."

Her eyes widen. "Why?"

Shame and worry clog my throat as I swallow. "Because of Mom. The stuff she was saying."

Pippa hums, nodding.

I think about what Rory said, how I should talk to Pippa about it, and I pull my knees closer to me, tracing the edges of my phone case. "It's supposed to be my calling." My brow knits. "Helping people feel good about themselves and their bodies."

She sighs. "These things have been the truth to her for her entire life." Pippa plays with the duvet, running her fingertips over the seams. "Change takes time, and we don't know what's going on in her head." She squeezes my knee. "Keep being a safe place for her to land. When she's ready, she'll let you know."

I nod, looking away and blinking fast as my eyes sting. "When did you get so wise?" She laughs, and I grin at her. "Love you."

"Love you, too," she whispers.

We settle back against the headboard and put *Bridesmaids* on. Halfway through the movie, my phone lights up.

It's from Rory. My eyes go wide. A video. This *thing* we're doing has escalated to videos. The video thumbnail shows him seated in his hotel room, shirtless. Anticipation thrills through me, and my curiosity is at an all-time high.

"What's that?" Pippa asks in my ear, and I jump, jerking my phone away to hide it. The smile she gives me says she knows exactly what it is.

"Nothing." My voice is strangled and my eyes dart around. I look *so* guilty.

She wiggles her eyebrows. "He's sending you videos now, huh?"

"No." I shake my head, staring at the video thumbnail. "I don't know. Yes."

"Are you going to watch it?"

God, I want to.

I gesture at her. "It's weird."

"I'll go for a walk."

"Pippa, *no*." I'm laughing now, too. "I can't." My gaze lingers on the thumbnail again. Every instinct in my body is pleading with me to watch this video. "If I watch it," I admit, "I might like it too much."

Her eyes are still lit up with entertainment as she nods in an understanding way, mocking me. "And you might send one back?"

I choke. "No."

Yes. That's exactly what I might do.

Shit. This thing has boiled over. This isn't even close to being fake. Panic skyrockets inside me and I toss Pippa my phone.

"Take it."

She gives me a strange look. "*I'm* not going to watch it."

"No." My expression turns pleading. "Take my phone. At least until we get home tomorrow. I'm thinking about him too much. I'm—" A frustrated noise comes out of me. This is embarrassing. "I'm like, reading over our text chats every day. I look at all the photos he sent and think about them the rest of the day. I need to clear my head and get this thing under control again. Please. Take my phone."

My pulse still races, and I think about Rory and myself running through Stanley Park, laughing. It would be the best thing that's ever happened to me, and then he would get sick of me, and all I'd be left with is a closet full of lingerie and stale memories of the good times.

"Please, Pippa."

She puts my phone on airplane mode before tucking it away, and we spend the rest of the evening watching the movie and eating hotel room snacks from the minibar.

I lie in bed until the early hours of the morning, thinking about what's on that video.

CHAPTER 43

RORY

THE NEXT EVENING, I'm in the airport, staring at my phone with a frown, knee bouncing.

"Miller." Ward glances between my face and my phone.

"Hey, Coach." I straighten up.

"Everything okay last night?"

My gut tightens but I give him a quick nod. "You bet."

He means the stuff with McKinnon at the bar, and not that I sent Hazel a video of me jerking off and moaning her name, but twelve hours later, she still hasn't responded.

Fuck.

Ward keeps staring at me, and it feels like he's digging through my head. "My door's always open," he finally says before moving to his seat.

I turn back to my phone, staring at our chat. Stupid. So fucking stupid. I went way too far. Hazel's horrified, disgusted expression floods my mind, and I groan, turning out the window to stare at nothing.

We were going to spend Christmas together. Things were going so well, but I fucked it all up because I was feeling possessive and horny.

"There's my little ray of sunshine." Owens drops into the

seat beside me, holding one of those big fantasy novels he's always reading. He flinches at my expression. "Someone's grouchy. You going straight to Hazel's tonight after we land so she can make you feel better?"

I had planned to, but the message in her silence is loud and clear: *fuck off, Miller.*

Tomorrow, I'll apologize and we'll go back to playing pretend, but for now, I'll give her space.

"No." I put my phone on airplane mode and toss it into my bag, chest straining. "I'm not."

CHAPTER 44
HAZEL

WHEN I GET HOME from my weekend away with Pippa, my sole focus is getting inside my apartment and watching the video Rory sent with my fingers on my clit. My footsteps thump on the stairs as I hurry to the third floor, keys in hand, but when I reach the landing, a package sits on the floor, leaning against my door.

My stomach flutters and I bite down on my smile. Another? He must be as addicted to those photos as I am.

Inside my apartment, I tear the package open, excitement drumming in my veins, but when I push the plastic wrapping aside, my expression turns disgusted.

I hold it up and a laugh bursts out of me. Until now, Rory's taste has skewed delicate, sweet, sheer, and lacy. Everything has been high quality and carefully constructed from soft material that feels incredible to wear.

This piece of shit looks like it's going to fall apart any second.

It's all black straps, stringy and confusing. My nose wrinkles. I'm not sure which hole is for the neck and which are for the legs.

"What the fuck?" I murmur, laying it out flat.

This thing is so ugly. It looks like a spiderweb. How am I supposed to wear it? I burst out laughing again before I take a photo.

Not sure about this one, Miller. It needs an instruction manual.

"WHERE TO?" the driver asks when I get into the taxi at the Vancouver airport.

I rattle off my address, and we drive in silence while I stare out the window.

The charity skating event is tomorrow. Will she still show up, after the video I sent? Even though she'd never admit it, I know she's proud of learning to skate. My stomach sinks lower with disappointment.

My phone chirps with the ring tone reserved for Hazel. My pulse jumps as I pull it from my pocket, expecting the worst. Expecting her to tell me we're done, or that she never wants to talk to me again.

Instead, it's a picture of some weird mess of black yarn on her duvet. Or maybe they're shoestrings. My face screws up in confusion.

Not sure about this one, Miller. It needs an instruction manual.

"What?" I murmur, zooming in.

Within the mess of shoestrings is a clothing tag. My gut drops through the floor.

It's not shoestrings. It's lingerie, but I didn't buy that for Hazel.

You'll see, McKinnon said yesterday.

Jealous rage thunders through me. He sent her a fucking piece of lingerie. I regret not punching McKinnon in the face last night as I stare daggers at the picture.

I'm going to kill that guy.

First, though, I'm going to make sure Hazel knows exactly who sent it.

"Change of plans," I tell the driver. "I'm going to my girl-friend's place instead."

I rattle off Hazel's address and fold my arms over my chest, seething with jealousy and possessive feelings as we drive.

Hazel is *mine.*

"*THIS VIDEO IS for my girlfriend, Hazel Hartley,*" Rory says in the video in a low voice that makes my pussy clench, "*who I've been thinking about a lot these past few weeks.*"

I lie back against my headboard, and the breath whooshes out of me as my eyes land on his dick, fully erect and resting against his flat stomach. I suddenly understand exactly why Rory's so arrogant.

His cock is perfect—a long, thick length with a swollen head that I imagine wrapping my lips around and sucking on. My thighs press together. With his ridged stomach, roped biceps, toned arms, and big hand resting around the base of him, he's the definition of virility.

Rory Miller, the god of making me super horny.

It's only a matter of time before we have sex, and sparks move down my spine at the idea of Rory inside me. Him on top of me, notching himself at my entrance before he slides inside, stretching me in the most mind-bending way with his thickness. I'm still fully clothed, but they feel too tight, too restrictive as I watch him in his dim hotel room.

"*And who I miss,*" he continues with a small smile, stroking himself slowly, "*very, very much.*"

My mouth waters, and I picture running my tongue up his cock while he watches in fascination. Heat gathers low inside me and my nipples prick.

"And who I can't wait to fuck."

His hand works so torturously slowly. Is he doing this to drive me insane? Or maybe it's because this is how I'd stroke him, keeping him on the edge of pleasure until he can't take it anymore.

Wetness blooms between my legs and I squirm, running my hand over my thighs. The second Rory gets home, I'm fucking pouncing on him.

"Hold on," he murmurs, squinting at something behind the phone. *"Just propping up a photo of myself to look at."*

A laugh bursts out of me and I'm flushing with silly, light feelings as he winks at the camera. I'm alone in my apartment, grinning at my phone like a dork.

I wish he were here on my bed so he could see how much I'm enjoying this. My hand slides over my panties and rests on the soft lace. I'm warm, swollen, and soaking wet, and there's a streak of electricity through me when I press harder against my clit. I clamp my lips together to hold in a moan as Rory strokes himself at an excruciating pace.

His head tips back, eyes closed while he works his length. *"I think about my tongue on your pussy every hour of the day."*

So do I.

A shiver runs through me, and I rub a soft circle over the damp fabric, shuddering. I'm going to come so hard from this.

He strokes faster, nostrils flaring as he sucks in a sharp breath. Heat stirs through my limbs, and I move my fingers faster, matching his pace.

"We're doing this again," he tells me. *"This is going to make me come so fucking hard, Hazel."*

A moan slips out of me and my hips tilt forward as I rub

tight swirls over the lace, drawing this out, wishing my hand was his and that I was the one stroking his cock.

If he sent me this video to push me over the edge, to force me to admit I want to fuck him, it worked.

A groan rumbles from deep in his chest, and he wears the most delicious frown as every muscle in his torso tightens. His hand moves fast over his cock.

"*I'm going to come,*" he murmurs, head tilted back, the long line of his throat working. Every sensation in my body heightens and my lips part with pleasure at his strained expression.

Watching Rory jerk off is the best thing I've ever seen. Urgent, insistent pleasure builds between my legs. I'm so close.

His eyes open and he looks at the camera, looks right into my head, before he sends me the cockiest, smuggest grin and nudges the phone with his free hand.

There's a clacking noise, and now the only thing visible on screen is his hotel room ceiling.

"*Fuck, baby,*" he grits out, and my eyes are wide as I listen to the sound of him stroking himself.

Listen, not see. I blink at the screen in disbelief. Did he actually—

That fucking *dick.* He did that on purpose. He did that to tease me, to wind me up and then leave me aching for him. I nearly scream in frustration. I'm too horny, too worked up and desperate and wet and needy.

I just need to come. And I still haven't seen *Rory* come, which pisses me off.

I close my eyes, picturing what I wanted to see from the video. Picturing his cock pulsing, his abs tightening, and him spilling hot cum all over his stomach. I imagine his chest rising and falling fast as he catches his breath, shooting me a sated, glazed look, the same one he gave me after I rode his face.

Pressure builds and I'm about to come—
There's a knock at the door, and I freeze.
"Hazel," Rory thunders from outside. "Let me in."

THROUGH THE PEEPHOLE, I see Rory on the other side of the door, wearing a murderous expression, arms folded. My heart starts pounding but I open the door.

"Hi." My skin prickles as his gaze moves down my body, flaring with heat. There's a hard set to his jaw, and his nostrils flare. "I didn't like the last thing you sent and I'm not wearing it."

"Good." He steps inside with an expression like a storm cloud, eyes flashing with possessive fury as I shut the door. "Because I didn't send it."

My whole body goes cold and tense. "What?"

When he meets my eyes, my stomach wobbles from the way his flash.

"Who bought it?" I whisper.

"McKinnon."

My stomach turns inside out, and I gag. "*What?*"

"Are you okay?" His hands land on my upper arms, and worry flickers through his eyes as he scans my face. "What can I do to make this better?"

I'm grossed out by what Connor did, but my body is still

humming, twitchy and agitated from watching the video before Rory got here. "I'm okay."

Rory being here, his fresh scent teasing my nose and his hands on me, it's making it better.

"You being here is helping," I admit.

He closes his eyes, letting out a pained exhale. "I'm feeling really jealous right now, Hartley, and I feel like I'm going to do something stupid."

Wicked delight curls inside me, and I bite my bottom lip. "Like what?"

"Like send you a video of me jerking off." A muscle tightens in his jaw. "I'm sorry." He looks away, and it's the same remorse from when he gifted me the weekend away with Pippa. "I went too far."

I make a face, confused, before it hits me: I didn't respond. He sent the video and I disappeared.

"I didn't respond," I say on a sigh. "Shit."

Oh god. Hazel, you asshole. Of course he thinks he went too far.

His tongue pokes in his cheek. "If you want to go back to the way things were before, we can." He looks down at me with such earnestness my heart cracks open.

I can't believe I ever thought Rory Miller was an asshole. He's not. He's just not.

"I just watched it," I blurt out, pressing my thighs together. I can still feel how wet I am.

His gaze sharpens, fingers flexing on my shoulders. "Really."

"You didn't go too far." I sound breathless, and I can't get enough air as our eyes hold.

"Two years, I watched you with that prick." His eyes flash. "I hate that he still thinks he has you."

"He doesn't." I'm not sure what we're doing here anymore

but I have an overwhelming need to prove to him that Connor doesn't mean anything.

Between the strange friendship we've developed and the flirting that feels like fun, things with Rory are so different than they ever were with Connor.

My skin's prickling. The last two weeks of photos and flirty texting have driven me to the brink of horniness, and now I want to do something about it.

I *need* to do something about it.

Lifting up on my tiptoes, I kiss him. My hand flattens on his chest, rubbing slow circles over his heartbeat as I walk him backward to my bed, giving him light, sweet kisses.

"Sit down and close your eyes," I tell him when the backs of his knees hit the bed.

His features are strained like he's holding himself back, but he gives me a funny smile, and that playful spark is back in his eyes. "Why?"

"Do it." I push against his flat stomach. "You'll be happy you did."

He drags a breath in and smiles like I'm killing him before sitting on the edge of the bed and closing his eyes, propping his elbows on his knees. In my closet, I find my favorite piece he sent—a pale pink lace bodysuit, sheer and delicate and soft with tiny straps.

My clothes swish against my skin as I take them off, and I pull the bodysuit on with care. Like the last time I put it on, it feels like a dream to wear. It's the perfect size, like it was made to my measurements, and against my skin, the lace is luxurious.

"Don't peek."

I turn, and he's resting his chin on his palm, gaze hot and intense.

"I'm not," he says, eyes raking down my body.

Goosebumps rise across my skin. As I approach, he pulls

me between his legs. His hands come to my hips before sliding down and into the bodysuit, palming my ass, and I sink my fingers into his hair.

I try not to think about why I want to comfort him so badly, why I want him to realize Connor's nothing to me. I'm not thinking about my rule and what this means. I'm not breaking it. I'm not getting attached. I'm just letting myself enjoy this one tiny moment with a guy I know I'll have fun with.

"I missed you," he murmurs, resting his forehead against my stomach, hands flexing on my ass. "Did you miss me, Hazel?"

I shouldn't have, but I did.

"Yes," I admit.

He presses a kiss to my stomach, flicking his hot gaze up to me. "Good."

He pulls me into his lap, one hand spanning the width of my thigh to keep me there and the other roaming my body, smoothing over the low back of my bodysuit, the high-cut thighs, the thin satin straps. I cling to him, watching his look of hot admiration as his hand rakes over me.

Having a hockey superstar look at me like this is doing *incredible* things for my confidence.

"This one was a good choice," he says in a low voice, playing with the strap, dragging his fingers over my neckline.

Through the thin fabric, my nipples pinch. I press a kiss to Rory's neck, the stubble prickling under my lips. "You have great taste."

He stares at me, eyebrows lifting with that constant, steady, teasing smile, like he has a secret. "I know."

I pull him down to kiss me, and a soft moan slips out of me as he coaxes me open, tasting me, exploring and claiming my mouth.

"Better?" I whisper between kisses.

"Uh." Another pained noise in his throat, a frown between his brows. "Not really." He pulls me harder against him, and I feel the thick, hard length pressing into my stomach.

My breath catches, and warm pressure squeezes at the apex of my thighs. My hand comes to his and I place his palm against my breast, urging him on. Everything inside me tightens when his fingers find the stiff peak, toying and tugging and rolling and driving me absolutely fucking nuts.

He shakes his head, staring at my breasts with a look of awe. "Your tits are beautiful."

I laugh, even as I'm coiling up with need. "What about now?" I ask again, biting back a moan as he toys with my nipples. "Is this better?"

"No."

"What would make it better, Rory?" I don't know why I'm acting like this, trying to find out what would satisfy him.

His hand slides between my legs, and I suck in a breath and let it out on a moan as his fingers press and circle my clit over the damp lace.

"Hartley, you're drenched."

I PRESS my lips together to hold in the moan as his hand works exactly the way I need. My face is buried in his neck, huffing in his scent as his hand massages my pussy into another state of consciousness.

"Still feeling jealous?" My voice is thin as he slips his fingers beneath the fabric, and our moans mingle as he drags friction over my clit. "Oh my god," I breathe against his warm skin. Heat builds under his fingers, swirling and gathering at his touch, and I see my release on the horizon.

He makes a low, pleased noise, hand working steadily with flat fingers, wide and firm circles, exactly the way I touch myself. I don't know how the hell he knows.

"This is helping," he says.

"Good." My lips run up his jaw to his ear. "Keep going, then."

He reaches over his shoulder and pulls his shirt off before shooting me another knowing grin and getting back to work with his hand between my legs. "Give you something pretty to look at while I get you off."

So sure of himself. It only drives me higher. His fingers

swirl and the spring of tension around the base of my spine winds tighter and tighter.

"Only one thing will really help, though," he murmurs.

His fingers sink into me, and every nerve in my body lights up. I can't think, I can't speak other than the breathy, needy noises slipping out of me, and I stare wide-eyed into Rory's eyes as he pushes his long fingers into me, not even giving my body time to accommodate him.

"Oh," I gasp as heat shivers through me.

He isn't gentle, and I like it. He watches my reaction closely and I know any sign of pain or discomfort would stop this whole situation, but that's the last thing I want.

I want him to keep doing this. I love his expression, like he's had a taste of control for the first time and needs more.

"Is this okay?"

"Yes." Rory holding me on his knee and taking what he needs lights up my whole body. "Take what you want, Rory."

He groans, jaw tight, pinning me with his focus. "This is exactly what I want. I want to keep you here like this." His gaze drops to where his fingers are deep inside me, touching a part of me I've never been able to reach. "I love it when you're a good girl for me like this."

Pleasure unfurls through me and I clench my teeth, breathing hard. This might be my kink, watching Rory get what he wants.

"You're close."

"No, I'm not." Yes, I am, but how much further can I push him? "The last time was a fluke."

His hand moves to the back of my head, and when his fingers thread into my hair, pulling a fistful tight, light blooms through me like a sunrise. It doesn't hurt, not at all, but with his strength, his size, and the knowing, focused look in his eyes, the message is clear.

"You're not going anywhere," he says, gaze raking over me like his control is fraying. "You're going to sit on my lap and come on my fingers like I've been thinking about for weeks."

Rory's expression is awestruck and curious, like he's surprised himself, pupils huge and mouth slanted up in a reluctant smirk that tells me he's enjoying this very, very much.

When I clench up around him, he smiles more.

"Yeah. That's what I thought."

I'm always in control. Always. But him holding me down in his lap, stuffing me full of his fingers while I spiral higher and higher—it's working for me. He tilts my head back another inch, baring my throat, and his smug grin slides higher.

"Oh, no," he says in a low, teasing voice. "You're not going to come, are you?"

On a broken exhale, I shake my head, still clinging to his gaze.

"Because you don't do that with guys, right?"

"Right." My eyes start to close but his grip on my hair tightens.

"Open your eyes and look at me." Against my hip, his steel cock presses with urgency. "You're making a mess on me, Hartley."

He crooks his fingers, finding that spot inside me that makes me lose my mind, and my nails dig into his pecs as pleasure arcs through me.

"I love how you try to fight me," he says in my ear, nipping the sensitive skin between my neck and shoulder. "You don't know how many times I thought about this when you were tutoring me."

I bite back a moan, imagining us doing this in the library, me trying to be silent while his fingers stretch me out and make stars dance behind my eyes. The pressure inside me coils tighter and I'm starting to shake against him.

"Don't stop," I moan against his shoulder as he works my G-spot. My pleasure bears down on me, circling closer and closer.

"God, Hartley," he growls as my toes start to curl, "I needed this so bad."

Around his fingers, my muscles tighten. He grips my hair harder, tipping me back farther to look up into his eyes while he wears that wicked, knowing smile and brings his thumb to my aching clit, rubbing tight, fast circles.

I can't hold off any longer.

My orgasm hits me hard, bursting behind my vision and sweeping through me. I'm gasping words like *please* and *yes* and *Rory* and *oh god* while he watches me unravel on his knee, shaking and shattering and sobbing at how fucking incredible the waves of pleasure feel. He doesn't let up from my G-spot, doesn't stop his fingers from delving in and out as I clamp around them, and even while blood is whooshing in my ears and my face is in his shoulder, I can hear how wet I am as he fills me again and again.

When I slump against him, catching my breath, his mouth is on my temple, on the shell of my ear, my neck, my cheek. I tip my face up to him, feeling drunk and drained in the best way, and he smiles against my lips.

"Good job me," he says, and I laugh silently.

"So cocky."

"Mhm."

He lifts his hand and sucks his fingers off, and another wave of heat ripples through me as he lets out a low groan. Against my hip, his cock pulses.

God, that shouldn't be so hot, but it is, seeing him love my taste like that.

"What's your favorite position, Rory?" I whisper, running my lips down his neck. More than anything, I want to see him lose it. My hand comes to his cock and a hoarse groan rumbles out of him when I stroke his length over his pants.

"Whichever one makes you come the hardest."

"Good answer."

Here we fucking go. I adjust on his lap, straddling him, giving him a coy, teasing smile as I push his shoulders back so he's lying down. His cock presses between my legs, straining against his pants, and I smile at the tortured expression on Rory's handsome face.

"But we're not doing that tonight," he adds, dragging in a deep breath, gaze dropping to my chest and then the damp fabric between my legs.

I lean down, running my mouth over his chest in soft kisses, holding his gaze. "I want to." Against his erection, I grind down, already feeling the stirring ache again.

There's something behind his eyes, something he's holding back from me. Something vulnerable he doesn't want to say as his throat works.

"What's the rush?"

I pause. It's the second time I've offered him sex and he's turned it down. I'd feel rejected if it weren't for the way he looks like he's seconds from losing control. The stiff length pressing against my pussy helps, too.

He wants this, so why's he holding back? I'm not sure how this fits with the *Rory's just interested in a chase* narrative I've been chanting to myself.

Guys don't do this. This doesn't make sense.

His hands come to my hips, his mouth lifts into a sweet smile, and dread settles in my stomach.

Oh god. He's dragging this out because I told him that I fuck a guy once and never again.

I can't think about what this means on his end. I can't think about what he wants. It's going to give me ideas.

Maybe this is a good thing, not sleeping together. Rory's so much more than I expected and if I have sex with him, I might fall in love with him, and that can't happen. I can already feel it starting—this urge to be the loving, encouraging person he needs in his life.

It would be so bad if I fell in love with Rory Miller. It would break me into a million pieces.

He deserves good things, though, and an insistent desire to please him and make him feel good loops through me, so I trail my fingers down his chest and flat stomach, brushing along the V cut into his hips, closer and closer to his waistband as his eyelids droop.

"What, then?" I ask softly, dipping down to kiss his throat. "What do you need?"

His exhale is ragged, and his throat works again.

"What did you think about while you were away?"

His eyes close, and when they open, his gaze sears me. "You lying on the edge of the bed and me fucking your throat."

The noise that slips out of me is pure want. "So take what you want, Rory."

CHAPTER 49

RORY

"FUCKING FINALLY," Hazel says when I pull my pants and boxers down and my cock springs free, hard as fuck and beading with pre-cum.

Every muscle in my body is tight with anticipation. She told me to take what I want, and the urge to fuck her has my cock so hard it hurts. My balls ache with need as I grapple for a reason why we shouldn't do what we both want.

Her hand wraps around my length, and I stop thinking.

"Your cock is gorgeous," she whispers, kneeling on the bed and stroking me, and a groan rumbles out of my chest.

"Yeah?" My hands are in my hair, tugging. Hearing my sharp-tongued Hazel lavish my dick with praise makes my scalp tingle.

"Mhm." She smiles at it as she strokes before she leans down to lick the moisture off the tip, and a bolt of lust streaks through me.

"Fuck," I choke out, and she sends me a wicked grin. "Hazel."

I don't even have the words to tell her I can barely hold off, that I'm straining for control, but somehow, she knows. Her smile is catlike as she moves to her back, head hanging off the edge of the bed.

I won't survive this.

"Well?" she says, still smiling. "What are you waiting for—"

She moans as I push my cock between those pretty pink lips.

"God, *yes*." Shiiit. It's been a long time for me, but I still know it's not supposed to be *this* good. Her lips stretch as I stroke all the way to the back of her throat, slow and careful, before I pull back. Her tongue flattens, dragging against the sensitive nerves, and a shudder rolls through me.

So fucking good like this. Her mouth, it's heaven. I can't string two thoughts together.

My hand lands on the bed beside her for balance. Each thrust into her mouth shoves me closer to coming.

Hazel wouldn't give me the time of day, didn't even like me, and now she's moaning around my cock.

"Such a good girl for me, letting me fuck your mouth," I groan.

My free hand drifts between her legs and my balls tighten when I feel how wet she is still. Her hips lift, chasing friction, and I can't fight the lazy grin. My fingers sink deep inside her and she moans around my dick, making my abs tense.

"Yes," I rasp, drawing my fingers in and out of her tight pussy in time with my cock in her mouth. "This, Hazel. This is what I need."

She hums around me and I let out a noise of anguish and pleasure, deep and guttural. I feel like an animal, fucking Hazel's mouth like this. Every primal, possessive urge rises to the surface. Her hand comes to my base, stroking, and my attention snags on how her lips stretch around me. I'm too big for her mouth, and the realization sets off another wave of heat through me.

Jesus fuck, I'm so close already.

I try to slow my strokes, but the urgent need to come lingers, pushing me harder. Like she can sense me holding back, Hazel sucks hard, cheeks hollowing out, and a desperate moan slips from me as I curl over her. I find that sensitive spot inside her, working it hard, and she clenches.

The pressure at the base of my spine expands, and I'm shaking with the need to come. My thrusts in and out of her mouth turn jerky.

"Can I come on your tits?" I beg. "Please?"

"Mhm," she moans, and my mind starts to splinter.

With my eyes on her lying beneath me like a fucking goddess, I pull out and stroke myself hard. Pleasure fires through me, racing through my blood, searing up my spine as I come, shooting all over the perfect swells of Hazel's breasts, covered in soft pink lace. My whole body is tight as I pulse, waves of desire radiating through me.

Stars burst in front of my eyes; I've never come so hard in my life.

My caveman brain likes the way she's covered in my come. A shudder of satisfaction rolls through me. Mine. Hazel's mine. Wearing the lingerie I bought her.

I climb over her and kiss her hard, claiming her mouth, and her tongue tangles with mine, meeting me with every stroke. A dirty, depraved idea sneaks into my head, and I don't have the self-control to keep it to myself.

"Are you on birth control?" I ask, still breathing hard.

She nods. "I have an IUD."

My hand comes to her chest, swiping my fingers through my own release, and I hold her eyes as I bring my hand between her legs and sink my fingers back inside her.

Her eyelids drop halfway, and a desperate noise falls from her lips.

"There." My voice is low. "That's better."

Something hot and urgent shoots through me, and I crook my fingers against her G-spot, watching her pretty, flushed face as her eyelashes flutter.

"Oh, *fuck*," she gasps, tightening up.

The need to possess her has me by the throat. Another high, breathy moan slips from her lips as I fuck my cum inside her. Her nails dig into my biceps, and I wear a satisfied, smug smile.

Her eyes flare, going wide, and she ripples around my fingers. "This doesn't happen," she gasps, holding my arm tighter.

Oh, fuck. She's going to come again. My skin prickles with anticipation.

"One more?"

She nods, blinking, tightening, and my instincts sharpen. I adjust my hand so my palm bumps her clit, and there—her head tilts back and her lips part. My fingers delve fast as she clenches. She's saying "Yes, Rory" and "Oh my god, that's so good" and "Just like that, baby," and my blood courses with electricity.

I'm addicted to pleasing Hazel, it seems.

She rides it out on my hand, and her gaze turns desperate. "Kiss me," she begs, and our mouths crash together. She moans against my tongue, soaking my hand, and I slow my movements as I feel her start to come down.

"What the hell, Rory?" she breathes with soft surprise. "That was so..."

She doesn't finish the thought.

"Yeah." I swallow, pulse beating in my ears. I can already feel the sleepy, sluggish post-orgasm haze settling in my body.

After we clean up, Hazel curls up against me in bed, her

head on my chest, her hair brushing my skin, and her scent in my nose.

"Good night," she whispers, and I press a kiss to the top of her head.

"Good night."

I want to say more. I didn't know fooling around could be like this. It doesn't feel like fooling around; it feels like—

I'm not ready to even think that. Not when there's a chance she doesn't feel the same way.

So I just lie there, hoping that inside her head, she feels the same way.

THE NEXT DAY, I arrive early at the arena for the charity skating event and take a seat near the entrance to the rink, where I'm meeting Rory after he's done training.

My stomach pitches with butterflies. Rory, whom I wasn't supposed to mess around with because this whole thing is fake, but whom I can't stop thinking about.

My phone buzzes in my jacket pocket, yanking my thoughts back to the present.

It's a text from one of my students, Laura, with a link to a studio space for rent. I've confided about my future dream with her.

The owner is a family friend who lives in Iran, she texts. *He'll be back in town for the holidays and he wants to rent the place out fast.*

I open the link she sent. Two decent-sized studio rooms, a spacious front entrance, and three smaller side rooms, two of which could be used as physiotherapy or massage rooms. The rent is expensive but the location is stellar, only two blocks from the Skytrain. It's in a new building, so it probably has excellent accessibility.

Interesting. A place like this would go fast.

Am I ready, though? Reluctance rises in me.

In my hand, my phone buzzes, and my heart jumps at the name flashing across the screen.

"Hi, Mom," I answer.

"Hi, honey." Her tone is warm. "Is this a bad time?"

"Never. I'm about to go to a charity skating event with the team, but it doesn't start for a bit."

"Skating?"

I smile at the ice, where event staff are setting up. "Yep. Skating. Rory taught me."

And tomorrow afternoon, Christmas Eve, we're flying out to spend Christmas with my family. I'm in so fucking deep.

She makes a pleased noise. "The photos of you two from when we had dinner together are so sweet."

The family dinner. My stomach wobbles as I remember what Rory and Pippa both said. I know I need to bring it up, and that I can't avoid it forever.

Keep being a safe place for her to land, Pippa said.

"I wish I'd gotten a photo with you," I admit.

She makes that joking, dismissive noise she always does. "Next time, after I've gotten rid of the vacation weight."

I shouldn't be surprised, but it's a tiny cut to my heart every time she says those things. The words lodge in my throat, but I force them out.

"I don't like when you make comments about dieting and needing to lose weight."

"Honey, that's because you're thin."

"No—" I catch myself, trying to keep my cool. "You're beautiful, and it's hard to hear you insult yourself."

"So I want to go running more, so what?" She laughs but it's brittle. "I feel better when I'm thin."

"That's what I'm saying." I sigh. "I want you to feel amazing regardless of what size you are. You're so many things,

Mom. You're funny and smart and an incredible mom, and none of those things have anything to do with your weight. It's fine if you want to be skinny, but you're still beautiful and amazing if you aren't."

She's quiet, and I reach past all the reluctance, down to the most vulnerable parts of myself.

"I love you," I tell her. "And I want you to love yourself as much as we all love you. I want you to take a dance class and feel the same joy you used to feel—"

"Dance class?" Her tone is weird and tight, and my stomach knots.

"There's a dance studio in Evergreen." The town next to Silver Falls. "They do adult classes on Thursday evenings."

She scoffs, crushing me. "So I can wear a leotard and have everyone stare at me?"

My face falls. "People just wear normal workout clothes. They do barre exercises to pop music." My voice gets quieter because I know this isn't working.

"You're always going on about how we're the boss of our own bodies." Her tone is sharp. "So let me say what I want about myself."

My mouth clamps closed, and silence stretches between us.

"I should get going," she says.

"Okay." Cold misery settles in my stomach. "Bye. Love you."

"Love you, too. Bye."

The call ends and I sit there, staring at nothing. I failed her. Again.

"Hey."

I jolt to find Rory towering over me in his Storm jersey and skates. The tension around my heart loosens. "Hi."

He tilts his chin to the phone in my hand. "Everything okay?"

When I don't answer right away, he sits beside me, arm coming up around my shoulders to pull me into him. I melt against him.

"That was my mom."

"Yeah?" He watches my eyes with concern.

"We had another argument."

"I'm sorry, Hartley." He lets out a heavy breath with a heartbroken expression, like my pain is his pain, and even though I'm upset from the call with my mom and I don't know what the fuck I'm doing with Rory these days, the look in his eyes makes my heart expand.

He gives me the softest, most affectionate kiss, and all the stuff with my mom fades to the background. His fresh scent surrounds me and I smile against his mouth.

"You always make me feel better," I whisper.

"Good." He smiles, and I fall a little harder for him.

The text from earlier snags in my thoughts. "A student sent me this." I open the link and hand the phone to him, watching as he scrolls through.

"This is nicer than the studio I sent you."

"More expensive, too."

"And a better location. Close to your apartment *and* mine."

My stomach does a slow roll. It shouldn't matter that Rory's apartment is close to this space—I haven't even seen his place—but deep down, it does. I love that he thinks about these things, even if I'm not ready to.

"I don't know." My brow wrinkles.

"Okay." He hands my phone back, and his gaze is steady and encouraging. "For what it's worth, I think you should take a look. There's no commitment in just seeing the space." He nudges me, mouth tipping up. "I'll go with you."

I can picture it—us viewing the space together—and the image makes it so much less terrifying. "I'll think about it."

He winks. "Good." He glances to where kids, parents, and players filter onto the ice. "Ready to go show them what you've learned, Hartley?"

I nod and smile. "You bet."

He pokes his tongue in his cheek, hiding a smile. It's his *I've done something bad* grin.

"What's that look?" I ask, raising my eyebrows.

"I hung the spiderweb thing in McKinnon's locker stall."

I burst out laughing so loud people glance over before clapping a hand over my mouth.

"I'm surprised you were able to hang it up." He shredded the thing.

His eyes spark with mischief as I shake with laughter while he laces up my skates, and when he stands and holds a hand out to me, I take it without hesitation.

CHAPTER 51

HAZEL

HALF AN HOUR LATER, I'm skating around the rink, a kid clutching either hand, while Rory skates backwards in front of us. On the other end of the ice, Jamie teaches kids to goaltend using a wiffleball as Pippa takes photos. Music's playing, and the kids, parents, and players all seem to be having a blast.

"Are you trying to steal my girlfriend?" Rory asks the kids holding my hands, and they giggle.

He wears his *Hazel is cute* smile. My skin tingles with delight.

The kids want to skate with Rory, so I head to the boards and watch with a smile as he has them hold his hockey stick while he pulls them around the ice. He's unbearably cute, laughing and teasing them, light shining out of him.

Rory would be a good dad. He'd be nothing like his own father. There's a warm tug in my chest at the idea of kids who look like Rory, bright-eyed troublemakers with hearts of gold. The image of him chasing them around our house, playing with them, makes me ache with affection.

Our house? Oh my god. Are these kids now *our* kids?

I've never really thought about having kids. They felt so far away, and with the way I normally date, it didn't seem within reach.

Again, something tugs in my chest, and I rub my sternum. I shouldn't be thinking about Rory as a dad. That seems dangerous.

Someone catches my eye, and I try not to make a face. Connor's across the ice taking photos with parents while the woman he brought watches. She has curly blond hair, a bright smile, and his name on the back of her jersey. A kid asks her a question, and she leans down with a gentle smile.

She seems nice. I wonder if she knows how horrible Connor is.

Bells start jingling, and the kids swarm the entrance, where Alexei appears wearing a Santa costume. Hayden, dressed as an elf, is right behind him. The kids lose their minds as Hayden pulls presents out of Alexei's big red bag.

Darcy skates up with a shy smile and I light up in surprise as she takes a spot beside me against the boards, giving me a quick hug.

"Good to see you," I tell her. "I didn't know you were in town. Is Kit here too?" Sometimes players from other teams drop into these events.

"Over there." She points him out, dressed as a reindeer, helping Hayden and Alexei.

"Is that lipstick on the end of his nose?"

She laughs. "We had to improvise at the last minute. Hayden never gives us a warning about these ideas."

"Are you here for Christmas?" I remember Hayden saying Darcy's from Vancouver, like he is.

"Yep. We played Seattle last night, so Kit's spending tonight here to see my family before he flies out to Ontario for Christmas." Seattle is a two-hour drive from Vancouver. "Hayden and I will probably spend most of the break playing

Legend of Zelda like back in university." She grins. "We used to
play for hours. Kit would hide the controllers so we could get
some studying done. I'm looking forward to hanging out with
him. We don't get to see him enough during the season."

Again, I think about Rory coming home for Christmas, and
I'm so glad I asked. There's no way I could let him stay here
alone.

"You and Kit have been together since university, right?"

"The first week of school. Feels like forever ago." She
watches the guys out on the ice. "But also, sometimes, it feels
like we all just met yesterday."

Her eyes track them as they skate. Hayden grins over at her,
waving, and she waves back with a beaming smile.

I study her for a moment. I've never seen her without
Hayden and Kit nearby, but I think she might be shy. There's
something about Hayden's boisterous friendliness that puts
people at ease, though, and I think being around him brings her
out of her shell.

"Did you and Hayden ever go out?" I ask, because I'm a
nosy bitch.

Her eyes widen. "Oh my god. No. *No.*" She laughs. "His
type is like, tall supermodels with dark hair, and I'm the girl
who did a whole degree in math." She laughs again, rolling her
eyes at herself, before she pauses, a tiny frown forming
between her eyebrows. "I thought he was going to ask me out in
the first week of school but..." She shakes her head at herself.
"Anyway, like I said." She gestures at her petite frame with a
self-deprecating laugh. "Not his type. Guys like Kit are more
my speed."

My eyebrow goes up because that's *not* what I asked, and
now I'm curious as hell, but she catches herself.

"And I love Kit." Her eyes go to him. "Is it hard, having my
life revolve around his? Of course. Do we feel like roommates

sometimes? Yes. But we know each other so well and—" She blinks. "I can't imagine not being with him."

Her words feel strange, like she's tiptoeing around what she really wants to say.

"I think this is just what happens when you've been with someone for seven years. It's fine." Her expression tightens like she's embarrassed. "I'm rambling. Can you talk now, please, so it doesn't get weird?"

I start laughing, because even if I'm slightly concerned with what she said, Darcy is adorable. "What do you want to talk about?"

"You and Rory," she says pointedly. "I want to know all the dirty details." I laugh harder as her eyes go wide with excitement. "Seriously. I want to know all the TMI stuff. My life is boring, Hazel. I'm living vicariously through you."

"Well," I chuckle, thinking about riding his hand last night. Definitely can't tell her about that, although I'm sure she'd love it. "It's really fun. He's different from what I expected."

"He looks at you like you're a dessert he's about to devour."

My face warms.

"Enjoy it," she says, smiling. "This is the fun part, when you can't get enough of each other."

I think about this phase ending, and my heart aches at the idea of Rory's eyes flicking over me with disinterest. His teasing used to irritate me, but now I'd miss it.

A massive blur of red and green comes to a sudden stop in front of us, spraying ice against the boards.

"Oh my god. Come here." Darcy reaches up and rubs her thumb down Hayden's jaw. Her head barely comes to his shoulder. "You have glitter all over. Where did you even get this stuff?"

He obediently leans down for her while she brushes it out

of his stubble. "Pippa put it on me." He gives her a flirty smile. "Aren't I the prettiest elf you've ever seen?"

She's blushing. "You're definitely the biggest elf. You'd weigh the sleigh down."

Hayden puffs his chest out. "I'm taking that as a compliment."

They grin at each other, but there's something in Hayden's eyes as he looks down at Darcy. His gaze lingers on her, flooded with the same warm, affectionate longing I see in Rory's eyes when he looks at me.

Kit skates up beside Darcy. "You two look like you're getting into trouble."

He wraps an arm around her waist, and Hayden's eyes drop to it before he glances away.

"Just the usual." Darcy smiles at Kit, nudging him with her elbow. "You were having fun out there, huh?"

"I was." He rubs the back of his neck, sending her a quiet smile. "I'm looking forward to it."

"Teaching kids to skate?" Darcy asks, chuckling.

"No." He gives her a shy, meaningful expression. "Having kids. A bunch of them. Going skating with them and stuff."

Her smile drops like it's the last thing she expected him to say.

Hayden laughs, but it seems forced. "Jumping the gun a bit there, aren't you, buddy?"

"Yeah." Darcy does her own uncomfortable laugh. "That's pretty far away, Kit."

He shrugs. "I don't know. Not that far away."

Her features tighten, eyes flaring with worry and apprehension, and Hayden looks between them like he's seen a ghost. No trace of his former smile on his boyish face.

"We'd get married first," Kit adds.

Darcy blinks like she doesn't know what to say, and when Connor and his lady friend skate up, she looks relieved.

Connor says hello to everyone before lifting his eyebrows at me. "Hazel." His eyes rake over my jersey, flickering with distaste. "Have you met my girlfriend, Sam?"

Darcy, Hayden, and Kit must sense the weird energy because they mumble an excuse about helping Ward with something and leave.

A laugh slams against my vocal cords but I hold it back. Sam is smiling at me in a way that tells me she's lovely and kind, and I don't want to be rude.

Saw this and thought you'd look hot in it. That's what the card said. He sent that gross lingerie when he likely had a girlfriend.

Gross. Just gross. But that's not her fault.

"Hi, Sam," I say with a warm smile, shaking her hand. "I'm Hazel. So good to meet you."

"You, too." She beams at me, and there's a sour feeling in my stomach. Why is she with him? Doesn't she see what he's really like?

I didn't, though, so how can I fault her for not seeing it either?

"Do you live in Vancouver?" I ask, and Connor's expression darkens a fraction.

He doesn't like me being friendly with his new girl, but I ignore him. As we chat, Connor clears his throat and puts his arm around her shoulders, watching me, but I just smile at them.

This asshole's trying to make me jealous, but instead, I just feel like laughing.

After a few minutes of friendly conversation while he glowers at us, he gives her a tight smile. "You want to keep skating, babe?"

She nods and smiles up at him, and without another glance at me, he pulls her away. She waves goodbye over her shoulder.

I wave after them, feeling tired of this game we're playing. When I think about what Connor did, I don't feel angry anymore. I want to move on.

Rory comes to a stop beside me, watching after Connor and Sam. "What the fuck was that?"

"He brought a girl. She's nice, actually." I slip my hand into his, and he looks down at me, expression clearing. "I don't care about them," I tell him, giving him a soft smile.

Memories of last night flash into my head, me sitting on his lap while his fingers curled inside me with that clouded, intense expression. My eyebrow arches as I give him a cool, flirty smile.

His gaze sharpens and he lifts his brows in interest.

"What are you doing tonight?" I ask lightly, still smiling.

"You." He winks, and I burst out laughing.

"Good." Finally.

A gaggle of kids shuffle up to us, interrupting. "Can you teach me how to skate backward?" one kid asks Rory.

Rory leans down, setting his hands on his knees. "I sure can." He looks to a little girl standing beside the boy. "You want to learn, too?"

She points a chubby finger at me. "I want her to teach me."

Rory winces. "She isn't very good."

My mouth falls open and I laugh. "Not very good? That's only because I had a bad teacher."

He grins.

"He's always trying to hold my hand," I tell the kids, wrinkling my nose.

"Ew," the boy says, and the girl giggles.

Rory and I smile at each other, his eyes spilling over with light and affection.

"How about a friendly competition, Miller?"

Five minutes later, the orange cones are set up on the ice and players and parents line up behind us to take their turn racing through an obstacle course. Rory and his teammate, a boy with glasses and an adorable gap between his two front teeth, finish to a round of cheers.

I smile down at the little girl clutching my hand. "Ready?"

With her eager nod, we're off, only skating as fast as she can while everyone cheers for us. I look over to Rory and stick my tongue out at him, and the kids laugh. We're weaving through the cones, and she's a little wobbly on her feet, so I skate backward, holding her hands the way Rory did for me the first time.

"Look at those moves, Hartley," Rory calls. "You must've had an incredible teacher."

I laugh, but as I grin back at him, something catches under my skate. One of the cones. I suck in a sharp gasp, stumbling and dropping the girl's hands as my skate slips again.

I hit the ice, knocking the wind out of my lungs, and white-hot pain shoots through my ankle.

CHAPTER 52

RORY

PEOPLE DESCEND ON HAZEL, crowding her.

"Everyone back off!" My voice booms around the arena as I hurry over at full speed. People give her space, but not fast enough. "Move the fuck back!"

"Dude, there're kids around," Owens mutters to me.

I don't care. My pulse pounds in my ears as I crouch down to Hazel, looking her over, moving my hands over her limbs.

No blood. Her ankle is still on straight. It doesn't seem like anything is broken.

"Rory, I'm fine," she says, but she's wincing. Hazel is in pain and she's wincing, and it's my fault.

I said I wouldn't let her fall. Fear leaks into my blood, making my chest hurt.

"She needs a stretcher." My voice sounds different. Tense and sharp and loud.

Hazel puts her hand on my shoulder, and I can feel how wild my eyes are. She puts on a reassuring smile.

"Rory, I don't need a stretcher," she says softly. "I'm okay. I just slipped."

I take her hand, the one she used to break her fall, and inspect it. The heel of her palm is red. My fingers skim over the delicate bones of her wrist but nothing seems amiss. Swelling, but not broken.

"Alright." The medic crouches beside us. "What hurts?"

"I'm okay—" she starts.

"Her ankle and her wrist," I answer. "And probably her tailbone. We need to go to the hospital."

She hit the ice so hard I heard her teeth clack. My mind keeps replaying her eyes going wide as she fell, the way her lips parted with worry, and my chest tightens again.

"She might have a concussion," I add.

I don't miss the look she exchanges with the medic. "I don't have a concussion," she says, "and I definitely don't need to go to the hospital."

"Yes, you do. You could have a fracture." My throat knots.

Hazel is hurt and it's because of me.

I can hear myself, I can hear how insane and upset I sound, but right now all I care about is making Hazel feel better. Making sure she's okay. Protective instincts fire through me.

Fuck.

Behind us, the kids, parents, and players watch me lose my mind. Ward meets my eyes and arches a brow.

I look to Volkov, waiting nearby. "Call Dr. Greene."

He makes a face. Georgia Greene is one of the team doctors, and Volkov can't stand her, but I don't give a shit about that right now.

"Call her," I snap, and he frowns but pulls his phone out.

"Can you stand?" the medic asks Hazel.

"No, she can't stand." I'm already scooping Hazel up with care, clutching her tight to me as I slowly skate to the bench. My brain is stuck in caveman gear—make her feel better, get her safe, get her warm, and make her comfortable. Take her pain away.

"Rory." Her uninjured hand flattens on my chest, smoothing over me in soothing circles.

She's my whole world, and I let her fall. My teeth grit.

"We're going to see Dr. Greene." Off Hazel's exasperated expression, I glare down at her. "No arguing."

Hazel sighs as I step off the ice and head to the medic's room.

CHAPTER 53
HAZEL

THAT EVENING, Rory carries me through the door of the Filthy Flamingo, and everyone cheers.

"You made it." Pippa grins between us and Streicher raises an eyebrow as Rory gently sets me on the chair beside my sister. Kit, Darcy, Hayden, and Alexei all call out their hellos, crammed into the booth.

It's the last time everyone will see each other before the holiday break, and most of the players and their partners are here, talking and laughing, crowding the bar. Jordan's strung Christmas lights up on a small tree in the back corner, and cheap, sparkly, old-school tinsel drapes over the frames and photos.

"We're only staying for an hour," Rory mutters before crouching down to inspect my wrapped ankle. "And then I'm taking her home to rest."

I watch him check the tensor bandage. He did this when Georgia, the doctor, saw me, too, and demanded she get a second opinion to make sure it wasn't a high sprain. For the past two hours, Rory's worn a worried frown, and while it's adorable as hell, my heart hurts because I know he thinks it's his fault.

My hand lands on his shoulder and I give him a squeeze. "Why don't you come sit up here with me?"

He glances up at me with hesitation, and I suppress a smile because for a moment, it actually looks like Rory would prefer to sit on the floor beside my ankle, guarding it, but he stands, and after he retrieves a bag of ice from Jordan and places it over my propped-up ankle, he finally takes the seat beside me.

My stomach dips as he loops an arm around my waist, tugging me close.

"Why are you acting like this?" I ask softly, gaze lingering on the lock of hair that's fallen into his eyes.

They pitch with worry. "I said I wouldn't let you fall."

Oh, god. My heart. "It's not your fault. I don't blame you. It was just an accident."

"I hate seeing you hurt." His throat works and he frowns at my wrist, bandaged up. It aches, but it's barely noticeable compared to what his pained expression does to me.

"I'm fine, I promise." I wiggle my fingers to show him. "Did you have fun today?"

"Besides when you took a decade off my life?"

I laugh, and he finally cracks a teasing smile. My stomach flutters at the sight of it.

"Yes, I did." He winks, mouth still curved up with reluctance. "Thank you for coming."

I give him a warm look. Behind Jamie and Pippa, I spot Connor at another table, sitting with a few players, but the girl he was with today, Sam, is nowhere in sight. Our gazes meet and his eyes are red and unfocused as he downs the rest of his beer.

Something recoils inside me. He's drunk. Some people are cute and sweet and silly when they're drunk, but not Connor. From what I remember, he gets childish and pushy.

I shove the thoughts of him away. He doesn't matter.

"Seeing you with the kids was so cute," I tell Rory, refocusing on him. "You're so good with them."

He makes a thoughtful noise. "If I wasn't a hockey player," he says, shrugging with a smile I might call shy, "I think I'd be a gym teacher. It's fun, teaching kids how to skate and playing around with them." His eyes slide to me, teasing, but there's something vulnerable and honest behind his gaze. "Would you still like me if I were a gym teacher?"

My heart twists in half.

"Of course." I give him a cool smile. "You'd look so good in the shorts."

"I do have great legs, don't I?"

We grin at each other, and his eyes are bright under the Christmas lights in the bar. Finally, he's starting to relax and seem like himself again.

"I would, though," I add quietly. "Like you if you were a gym teacher, that is."

His expression softens as he searches my eyes.

"You're a catch. And you'd be a catch even if you didn't play hockey."

Rory Miller is so much more than a hockey player, but I don't know how to say that without spilling everything to him.

He takes a deep breath like he wants to say something, but instead, his throat works and he just smiles. I don't know how to categorize this one; it's sweet, affectionate, and wistful. He's gorgeous when he shows me this smile.

Rory brings his mouth to my ear before he gives me the lightest nip on my earlobe, and my breath catches. "Love it when you pump up my ego like this, Hartley."

My stomach flutters. "Like you need it."

He presses a kiss to my temple, warming me with another quiet laugh. "From you? I need it." His voice goes low and liquid, and there's another flutter low in my belly.

"Maybe later tonight, you can show me what else you're good at, besides hockey."

His eyes flare with heat but he shakes his head. "That's not happening tonight."

I balk. "Why not?"

"You need to rest."

I hold his gaze, challenge rising in my eyes as my mouth slides into a knowing smile. "We'll see." I bring my lips to his ear, lowering my voice. "There are a couple pieces you sent that you still haven't seen."

His eyes dip to my mouth, darkening, but he pulls his gaze away, taking a deep breath like he's trying to block out the dirty thoughts of what we did last night.

"Hartley," he groans. "Please don't make me hard in public."

I just chuckle, turning back to the conversation at our table.

"We fly out tomorrow night," Pippa says to Hayden, gesturing at Jamie, Rory, and me. "Although," her eyes linger on me as she chews her bottom lip, "I don't think you should go anymore."

"What?" My jaw drops in outrage. "I'm not missing Christmas."

"Pippa's right," Rory says in a firm, no-nonsense tone, that heartbreaking worry back in his gaze. "They'll have snow in Silver Falls and I don't want you to slip on your crutches."

Disappointment flows through me in waves. I've never missed Christmas with my family, and all those images I daydreamed about that included Rory? Gone.

His fingers tense on my waist. "I'll stay at your place and take care of you."

My heart lifts, not knowing what to say as I look up into his pretty blue eyes.

"Don't be stubborn, Hartley," he adds, watching me like he hopes I'll say yes.

"Okay." I nod, blowing out a nervous breath. He's going to be *staying with me*. Not just crashing in my bed. This is getting more real by the day. "I'd like that."

He smiles again, softer this time, and gives me a gentle kiss. "Good," he whispers against my mouth. "I'm going to make you rest, Hartley, even if I have to tie you to the bed."

My eyebrows wiggle and I grin against his mouth, and from his huff of laughter, he likes that idea just as much as I do.

After convincing Rory I don't need him to carry me to and from the ladies' room, I make my way back through the crowded bar to our table.

I bump into someone, and a wave of hot beer breath hits me in the face.

"Hey."

I recoil at Connor's bleary gaze. He sways on his feet, wearing an unfocused frown.

"Hi." My tone, expression, and body language say *go away*.

"Did you get the thing I sent? You never thanked me."

A gross feeling skitters over my skin. "Don't send stuff like that to me."

At the table, Rory watches, tense and on high alert.

"That's not okay," I add. "Even if I wasn't dating Rory, that wouldn't be okay. We work together." I give him a *duh* look. "Being professional, remember?"

I start to crutch past him, but he sighs and puts a hand on the bar counter beside me, blocking my path to the table.

"I saw the way you were looking at me today," he slurs.

Nausea and discomfort roll through me. His hot, wet beer

breath slithers over my skin again, and I look to Rory, who stands. Connor takes an unsteady step, smirking down at me, and I step back with my crutches but hit the counter. There's a chair behind me, and I'm blocked in.

Alarm races through me and my lungs tighten. Rory makes his way over, trying to get around people, but the bar is crowded and loud.

"I wasn't—"

"You were jealous." Connor goes on like he didn't hear me, still giving me that weird smirk. "It's okay. That's the little game we're playing here." He hiccups.

"I wasn't jealous." My voice comes out sharp. I'm gripping the crutches harder than I need to, nails digging into the foam. "I don't care if you have a girlfriend." I gesture with my crutch for him to get out of the way. "Move."

He steps closer and I shrink back, but there's nowhere to go. I'm backed against the counter. My pulse skyrockets, pounding in my ears. I search for Rory but Connor's in my way, moving in front of me, mouth on mine—

A horrified, revolted sound falls out of me and I flinch back, every cell in my body recoiling. Commotion explodes in the bar —noise and movement and energy. On instinct, I lift a crutch and swing it at his ankle. It connects with the bone and I feel the impact up the length of the crutch.

"Don't fucking *touch me*," I bite out just as Rory hauls Connor off me with a murderous expression.

"Mother*fuck*." Connor hisses in pain as Jamie and Hayden pull him back. "She hit me."

"Get him the fuck away from her," Rory thunders, searching my eyes with a frantic look. His chest is rising and falling fast and a muscle ticks in his jaw. "Are you okay, baby?" His hands come to my jaw, tilting it up as I nod.

"He kissed me," I say, almost to myself, and I can feel my

lip curling with disgust as I replay the gross beer smell, the feel of his lips mashing against mine. I swallow, pulse still racing. Behind Rory, Connor tries to shove Hayden off, but Hayden holds tight. For once, Hayden isn't smiling. He wears the same furious, stony expression as Jamie.

"I know." Rory's voice is sharp like a knife but his gaze stays locked on mine. "I'll fucking kill him."

PROTECTIVE RAGE BURNS THROUGH ME.

We never should have come here. We should have gone straight to Hazel's place so I could tuck her into bed and keep her safe.

I take in the angry flush coloring her cheeks and the way her nostrils flare, and the urge to make it better fires through me like a bullet.

I was supposed to prevent stuff like this. That was the whole point of our agreement.

"I'm okay," she says. Her throat works again. "Pissed off, but fine."

Everyone in the bar is either staring at us as I help her to her seat or at McKinnon, still trying to shove Owens and Streicher off as they hold him like sentinels. They're almost as furious as I am, and beneath the jealous rage, a pulse of gratitude hits me. Even if I wasn't here, they'd stick up for Hazel. They know what she means to me, even if I've never told them explicitly, and they care about her.

When she's seated, I give her a kiss on the top of the head. "You okay here for a moment?"

She nods, and I give her another kiss before straightening up and stalking over to McKinnon.

"Wrong move, McKinnon," I call as I approach, shaking my head, feeling wild and out of control.

He hurt my Hazel. *My* Hazel. He thought he could help himself to her. He sent her *lingerie.*

This ends now.

He shakes his head, wearing a stupid grin that makes me want to break every bone in his body. "She's got you fucking *whipped.*"

"Shut the fuck up," Streicher growls. "She's your physio, and he's your captain."

McKinnon burps. He's fucking wasted. "Whatever."

I grab the front of McKinnon's shirt, hauling him up straight so I can look him in the eye. Everyone in the bar is silent, listening and watching as tinny Christmas music plays.

"You don't fucking touch her," I tell him in a deadly calm, lethal voice as my pulse races. "You don't go near her. You don't *look* at her. You're nothing to us. This stuff?" I gesture at the bar. "You don't show up for these things anymore. You're going to pull that shit? You're not part of the team."

He's breathing hard with the ugliest, most resentful expression.

"I can't kick your sorry ass off the team but I can make sure you never bother Hartley again," I continue. "Ask for a new physio or I'll do it for you."

Silence stretches between us, and in McKinnon's eyes, I see something settle. Defeat, I think.

"Understand?" I give him a shake, and he stumbles.

"Fuck you," he spits.

My blood simmers, crackling with energy. Every primal, male instinct in me wants to hit him.

He's wasted, though, and it's not a fair fight. *Captain*, Streicher called me. I'm trying to be the guy Ward wants, and I can't hit a guy who can barely stand up straight. Hazel watches with a worried look, and that settles it.

"Go home," I tell him in that same deadly calm voice before letting him go. Streicher and Owens escort him out of the bar but I'm already at Hazel's side, leaning down.

"Rory, what are you—" She lets out a yelp of surprise as I haul her over my shoulder, careful not to bump her ankle.

I've got one arm wrapped around Hartley, holding her steady, and Volkov places the crutches in my free hand. "I'm taking you home and you're not going to argue," I tell Hazel.

I need to get her out of this place. My blood is pounding with the need to get Hazel home, get her safe, and get her all to myself.

She doesn't say a word, and Pippa's eyes are wide as she watches us leave. Even Jordan's eyebrows are at her hairline.

"Have a great break, everyone, and nice work today," I announce to the silent bar, carrying Hazel out the door. "And Merry Christmas."

CHAPTER 55

HAZEL

I WAKE up on Christmas Eve morning to Rory gently moving a pillow under my ankle, elevating it while I sleep. I open one eye, squinting in the bright morning light as he walks to my kitchen, studying his muscular back and broad shoulders while he rummages through the cupboards, pulling out the coffee. His ass looks so good in those tight black boxers.

It's nice watching him move around my kitchen like he's at home here. In the middle of the night, I woke up and reached for him and he was right there, curled around me, warm and solid and steady.

He glances over and does a double take.

"Hey, Hartley." He walks over, and I let my gaze wander down his body, counting every well-earned ridge and groove.

There's a twinge between my legs when I think about what we did the other night and how hard he made me come. My gaze flicks up to his but he's frowning, concern furrowed in his brow as he looks me over.

The bed dips as he sits beside me, picking up my wrist to check the swelling. "How's it feeling today?"

"Better." I test my ankle out, flexing and pointing as much as I can. There's a sharp streak of pain as I hit the limit of motion, and Rory's eyes widen when I suck a breath in. "It's okay," I reassure him. "I'll stay off it today. You can wait on me hand and foot if you like."

He makes a noise like a growl, and I shake with laughter.

"Not funny, Hartley." His throat works and he studies me warily. "You think you'll ever want to go skating again?"

I blanche. "Of course. After all the time you put into teaching me?" I slip my hand into his. "Besides, it's our thing."

He raises an eyebrow, starting to smile. "Our thing?"

My heart does a little jump, and I nod, smiling back at him. "And seeing you go psycho over me is kind of adorable. You told like, six kids to fuck off."

He laughs, cringing. "I really did that, didn't I?"

"Mhm." God, he's so pretty like this, shirtless and hair all rumpled. "Careful, Miller. People might think you really like me."

His gaze swings to mine and his mouth tips up like he has a secret. "I do like you."

There's an urgent, insistent hum in my chest, but I just hold his gaze.

"And I think you like me, too," he says, smiling more, eyes on me like nothing else exists.

I like it when he looks at me like that.

"Hmm." I smile at him. "Maybe I do."

He nods, still smiling, before something cold cuts through his gaze and he frowns. "About McKinnon."

"Ugh." The noise of disgust slips out as I make a face.

Rory drags a deep breath in and I catch a glimpse of that furious, protective version of him from yesterday. His hand squeezes my thigh, warm and steadying.

"You okay?" he asks in a low voice, watching me.

I have a feeling that if I said no, he'd do whatever it took to make it better. Seeing him lose his mind yesterday was just—

I don't know what it was. I shouldn't like it so much, but I do. I love seeing Rory Miller lose his fucking mind over me.

"I'm fine. Connor doesn't matter. He's gross and I'm glad you told him to find a new physio." The breath whooshes out of me. "And for the millionth time, I wonder what the fuck I ever saw in him."

Rory's jaw ticks, and it's laughable how much better a boyfriend he is, even when we're faking. Even when we've moved into something that doesn't feel like faking.

"But I'm fine. Truly."

"Good." He leans forward, careful not to put his weight on my ankle or wrist, and gives me a quick kiss.

When he sits up again, he frowns.

"Why's it so cold in here?" he demands, stalking over to the thermostat. "I keep turning it up but it's freezing." He moves to the radiator, hovering his hand over the elements before giving me an outraged look. "The heat isn't working."

I gesture at the front hall closet. "There's a space heater in there."

His outraged look intensifies. "Hazel."

"What?"

He stands, putting his hands on his trim hips, and my gaze lingers on those V muscles pointing into his waistband. Heat builds between my legs and I squeeze my thighs together.

Being around Rory is making me hornier by the second. It's the way he smells, the way his morning voice sounds, the way he kept a protective arm around me all night.

Even his messed-up bedhead is fucking hot.

"Wow." He folds his roped arms across his chest, amused. "Really?"

I raise an eyebrow. "What?"

"You're ogling me."

I bite back a laugh as electricity thrills through me. "You don't look like you mind."

"Of course I don't." He gives me that lazy, flirty smile that makes my pulse stutter before his grin drops. "Okay, but it's really cold in here." He glances through the window up at the sky. "It's supposed to go below freezing today."

I point at the closet again but he cuts me off.

"We are *not* using a space heater." His expression says he means business, and I bite back another smile.

"I like it when you're bossy."

At my bedside table, he picks up my phone and hands it to me. "Call your landlord."

"He's in Greece for the month."

"So call whoever does these things when he's away."

My smile pulls into a reluctant wince, and Rory knows immediately that there is no guy who does the maintenance when the landlord is away.

"*Hazel.*"

"This is why my place is so cheap."

His head falls back and he groans loudly, like I'm the most frustrating person alive.

I just smile at him. "Your eyes are so pretty in the morning light."

He gives me a side-long look, sighing, but he's starting to smile. "Don't distract me."

"Is it working?" He rolls his eyes, and I think I like this flipped dynamic between us. "That means yes."

He runs his fingers through his hair, glancing around my place. "Where's your overnight bag?"

"Why?"

He finds it in the closet, pulling it out and setting it on the bed. "We're going to my place."

"WOW."

In the foyer of Rory's apartment, my jaw drops. I take a few steps forward on the crutches, looking around.

"You've been holding out on me, Miller."

Behind me, holding my bag, he watches me, his gaze unsure and assessing. "Yeah?"

I nod, eyes bouncing from the warm wood flooring to the giant green L-shaped couch to the midday sun streaming through the impossibly tall windows. Snow is starting to fall outside. A massive TV hangs between two built-in bookshelves that reach to the ceiling. There's nothing on the shelves, though.

I frown, scanning the sparse living room with two lamps, the big sofa, and a coffee table, and then the large, open-concept kitchen with a massive island and gleaming appliances.

I tilt my chin at the bookshelves. "You're supposed to put things on those shelves."

"Like what?" The corner of his mouth kicks up.

"Photos and trinkets and books." There's nothing on the walls—no art or framed pictures. No blankets thrown over the couch. I crutch farther into the apartment, down the long hallway. A door at the end leads to what looks like the master bedroom, and Rory's soft footsteps follow behind.

At the doorway, I take in the king-size bed with a forest-green duvet. Warmth twinges in my stomach because I'm going to sleep in that bed tonight and it's going to be the best sleep of my life. The windows overlook the city, same as the rest of the apartment, and on the balcony sits a hot tub.

Still no framed photos. No plants. No patio furniture. A lamp and a nightstand and his hockey bag from a few days ago, but that's it.

He has a fireplace across from the bed, which I'm totally going to turn on later, but his place feels so blank. Silent. Empty. Rory Miller is brimming with personality, overflowing with it, and yet his apartment is nothing like him.

Something sparkly on his bedside table catches my eye, and my lips part in surprise.

"What are you—" he starts before he sees what I'm crutching over to, and a guilty expression passes over his features.

I pick up the tiny crystal dragon, almost an identical twin to mine except this one is green, not blue. My heart does a funny flop, and a smile spreads over my face before I lift my eyebrows at him.

"What's this?"

He shifts, mouth curving into a reluctant, playful grin. "That's a dragon," he says simply.

"I can see that it's a dragon, Rory." I'm still smiling like a fool, but I narrow my eyes at him. "Do you have a shopping addiction?"

He chuckles, taking a seat on the bed. "No."

I turn the trinket, watching it scatter light on the wall. "So why do you have it?"

I think I know the answer, but I want to hear it in Rory's deep voice.

Sitting on the bed, he keeps his eyes steady on me. He lifts one big shoulder, giving me the sweetest, most innocent expression. "I bring it on the road because I miss you."

My heart sighs and flops over. I can't. He's too much, and I don't know what to do with this fluttery delight in my chest.

I tamp down the smile pulling on my mouth. "So you're saying that this dragon has seen some horrible, depraved things?"

He chokes out a laugh, light spilling out of his eyes as he shoots me a flirty grin. "Oh, yeah. That dragon knows all my kinks."

A sizzle of heat sears down my spine. I'd like to know all Rory's kinks, too. I remember how he licked me between the legs like I was the best thing he ever tasted, and another shiver rolls through me.

I set the dragon back down and dig into my own bag on the floor before I pull out what I carefully tucked into my balled-up socks when Rory wasn't looking and set it beside his.

His eyebrows go up in delight. "You brought yours?"

I shrug like it's nothing. The truth is, I love that stupid little overpriced dragon. The red eyes make me laugh, and seeing it before I go to sleep makes me think of Rory.

"Whatever," I say.

His gaze sharpens, and a predatory smile spreads across his mouth. "Does it know *your* kinks?"

Even as my face goes warm thinking of all the times I used my toys or touched myself to the thought of Rory, I'm laughing. "Oh, yeah."

He runs his tongue along his bottom lip, watching me with interest. "Maybe our dragons can talk."

"Maybe." I give him a cool smile, and the interest in his eyes intensifies.

Oh. Something thunks hard in my head like a book dropping onto the ground. We're flirting. When I give him that cool little smile, I'm flirting with him.

I've been doing this for years, all the way back to when we were teenagers studying in the library.

"You okay there, Hartley?" His voice is almost a purr as he wears a knowing smile.

God, I want him. My heart beats like a hummingbird.

"You want to take a nap?" I ask softly, running my hands up into his hair. It's so soft and thick and the strands feel like heaven between my fingers. Under my touch, he shudders, and he can tell from the tone of my voice that if we got into this bed, the last thing we'd be doing would be napping.

His eyelids droop and he leans into my touch, and I think it's going to happen, but then he groans.

"I want to." His gaze drops to my ankle and he sighs through his nose, a frustrated noise that makes me want to play with him more. Push him closer to his breaking point. "But you need to—"

"Yes, I know." I sigh, feeling flushed. "I need to rest."

Rest is the last thing I want to do. God, it would be so hot, seeing Rory Miller break.

He walks into his closet, and I pick our dragons up, holding one in each hand.

"*Please have sex with me,*" I make my dragon say to his, using a high, girly voice, before holding his dragon up and affecting a low, masculine voice.

He returns to the bedroom holding a hoodie.

"No," I continue. "*You're a fragile little lady, and I'm afraid I'll hurt you with my huge—*"

"That's enough out of you," Rory laughs, taking the dragons

from me as I dissolve into laughter. He's shaking his head, grinning at me. "Come here."

He gestures for me to lift my arms, and when he pulls the hoodie over my head, I get a lungful of his comforting scent.

"Now you're trying to dress me, too?" I ask, smiling down at the hoodie. It's huge on me, worn soft from washing.

His eyes spark. "Didn't want you to get cold."

Desire swoops through me. Why, *why* is a man taking care of me so hot? There's something about his sweet, caring nature that makes me want to write my name on him and fuck his brains out.

I lie down on the bed and he takes the spot beside me, propped on his elbow, eyes flickering with heat.

"Is seeing me in your bed turning you on?"

He lets out a heavy breath. "Yes."

Heat rushes between my legs, thrumming. "Good. What are you going to do about it?"

His eyes drop to my mouth and a tortured noise rumbles in his chest.

"You said you'd take care of me," I whisper.

His eyelids close and he sighs. "I did say that, didn't I?"

"Mhm." My hand comes to his cock, already hard and straining against his pants, and I give it a slow stroke.

He groans, hips jerking into my hand, and his eyes burn, molten hot. "Fuck. I can't say no to you."

"So don't." A string plucks low in my belly, making me ache.

"Come here."

He nudges me so I'm on my side before he moves behind me, spooning me, surrounding me with his hard chest and broad shoulders. I sink back into his warmth, and he pulls the duvet over us.

I moan at how comfortable this is, but my breath catches

when he loops a big arm beneath me and slides his hand into my shirt. His lips are on my neck, his breath tickling my skin as he tugs my bra down and finds a nipple.

"Better?" he asks in a low voice.

"Almost." Heat swirls inside me, and I grind back against the thick erection pressing into me, pulling a deep groan from him. I can feel myself getting wet already from the way his fingers are toying with my breast.

His other hand sneaks into my leggings, stroking over me. Sparks jolt through me at the contact, and I arch against him.

"How about that?" His tone is so cocky and smug.

I clutch his arm across my chest and my breath catches when he pinches my nipple. This is fooling around on another level. I'm somehow insanely comfortable and aching with need, inhaling his masculine, clean smell with every breath.

"You know it's good," I bite out, sounding breathless. "I need more."

His hand stills between my legs, and his finger rests on my clit. Not moving. Just touching lightly. I buck against him, seeking friction, but he pulls away, still barely touching me.

"Rory," I whine, writhing.

"You going to be good for me over the next few days?'

I growl, and his laugh grazes my cheek.

"You going to stay off your ankle and let me take care of you?"

"I swear to god, Rory—"

He pinches my clit, and my teeth clench at the lust roaring through me. "Fine. Yes. Okay. I'll be good."

It's not fair that messing around with him is both the best sex I've ever had and the most fun.

His lips skate over my neck, and he nips me. "You sure?"

"*Rory.*"

He laughs, and his fingers start to swirl. I sink against him as warmth courses through me and my muscles tighten.

"How's this?"

"So good," I moan. My heart races, and Rory's hand works faster, circling exactly the way I like it, flat fingers, not too fast, not too hard.

"You going to come for me?"

"Of course." I can already feel myself fraying, nerves firing with sensation.

He makes a low noise of pleasure. "Good."

The pressure builds between my legs and I turn my face into the pillow. When I suck a sharp breath in, Rory's scent goes straight to my brain, and I clench up. In my ear, he groans with pleasure as he touches me, and the heat between my legs spills over, coursing through me, radiating through my limbs. The entire time, Rory holds me tight against him, whispering in my ear about how much he likes me being here, how pretty I am, and how much he loves watching me come.

"Oh my god," I whisper as my release subsides. "You're so good at that."

Rory smiles against my neck, but when I turn and reach for his erection, he's off the bed in a flash.

I arch a brow, feeling cold without him against me. "Get back here."

"No." He leans down to give me a kiss but steps away when I reach for him again. "I have errands to run, and you're going to rest like you said you would."

I blink in outrage, gesturing at the thick ridge between his legs. "You're hard."

"I'll survive, Hartley. You've been making me hard for years, and it hasn't killed me yet."

A laugh falls from my lips. My mouth is watering, thinking about him fucking it again.

"We had a deal." He gives me a hard look, but he's smiling as he drops another kiss to my lips. "So be a good girlfriend and stay off your ankle so I'm not worried about you."

Girlfriend, he said. Not *fake girlfriend*.

"I was coerced," I call after him as he winks and strides out of the room.

I should be warning myself that this has an end date, and that we haven't addressed what's going on with us. I should be freaking out because Rory fits into my life seamlessly, and if it goes south, he's going to tear a hole so big it'll be impossible to repair. I could do my typical mental gymnastics, telling myself that he didn't mean to say that, that it was just a mistake.

Instead, I smile out the window and listen to the front door close, already excited for him to get back.

CHRISTMAS CAROLS PLAY in the grocery store while I load things into my overflowing cart.

Keep Hazel warm, keep Hazel fed, keep Hazel happy. I'm in protector mode, and I love it. Taking care of her feels right and natural.

I normally spend the Christmas break in the gym or taking advantage of the empty rink schedule, but the idea of curling up on the couch with Hazel tonight blows all of that up. I used to hate my apartment, actively avoiding the empty, lonely penthouse overlooking the city, but with her there?

I can't wait to get home.

I'm loading the groceries into my car, snow falling around me, when my phone buzzes with a call. I'm expecting something regarding the dinner I've ordered for us from a local restaurant, but my stomach tightens when I see the name flashing across the screen.

Dad.

Already, the weight settles in my gut. We haven't talked in a couple weeks, and I forgot this feeling that floods my system when we do.

"Rory," he says when I answer. "I've been reviewing your recent games."

My eyes close. All we fucking talk about is hockey.

"I'm coming to a practice," he says. "I need to see what Ward is putting in your head."

"No." Anxiety shoots up my throat. "He runs closed practices. He doesn't like spectators. He says it's distracting."

I don't know if that's true, but I've never seen someone outside of the organization watching our practices, and I sure as fuck don't want my dad there taking notes.

He sighs. "Well, I'm coming to the League Classic next week, then."

I'm looking forward to the game on New Year's Eve. I booked a super nice suite, because yes, even now, I'm shamelessly trying to impress Hazel. The game is our deadline for this agreement to get back at McKinnon, but it's gone so much further than that.

She has feelings for me. I know she does. The League Classic weekend will be special, so I don't want my dad there, telling me all the reasons I'm not good enough.

"I don't think that's a good idea," I tell him, rubbing the back of my neck.

There's a long pause on the other end of the line. "What's going on with you lately?"

Hazel. Hazel's what's going on with me. She's become my entire life, but my dad would never understand that.

"You're different this season," he adds, a note of frustration in his voice. "You're playing differently, you're acting differently... I don't know who you are anymore. Where's the star, Rory?"

He's long gone, and I'm happy to see him go. "I don't know what to tell you."

"It's that girl."

"Hazel." That protective feeling rises through me. "Her name is Hazel."

"You're distracted."

"I'm not distracted, Dad." Am I distracted if I feel like everything I've ever wanted is shifting into place? This conversation isn't going anywhere. "I need to go."

"Big plans tonight, huh."

There's something in his voice that makes me frown. Resentment, or loneliness or something. "Yeah. I'll talk to you later."

We say our terse goodbyes and I finish loading the groceries into the car. My mind wanders to the girl waiting at home for me, and the anxiety fades.

My dad's right—I am different, and it's because of her. With Hazel by my side, I'm nothing like him. Maybe I never was, and she showed me that.

Footsteps crunch in the snow, and two women walk past, carrying a Christmas tree.

"Merry Christmas," one of them says with a big smile.

I nod back, staring at the tree. "Merry Christmas."

On the other end of the parking lot, snow falls on the remaining Christmas trees, and I smile.

Hazel's missing Christmas with her family, so I'm going to make this one memorable.

CHAPTER 58

HAZEL

WHILE RORY IS OUT, I wander around his apartment, snooping through his closet and bathroom and buying home items for him with the credit card he left for me in the kitchen. With the fireplaces on, his apartment is warm and cozy, but without him here, I feel a weird panging ache in my chest.

I return to his bed, gazing out the window with the neckline of his hoodie pulled over my nose, inhaling him. Outside, snow blankets the city in white.

I wake sometime later to a dim bedroom splashed with warmth from the flickering fire and a muffled thump from the other room. I'm cozy, warm, and sleepy, and Rory's scent from his hoodie is in my nose, making me sink farther into his bed. I glance at my phone—it's just after five in the afternoon. The duvet is now on top of me, and a glass of water sits on the nightstand.

"Rory?" I ask, squinting into the light as I crutch down the hall to the living room.

I stop short, jaw dropping.

"How the fuck does that work?" Rory mutters to himself, fiddling with something with his back to me.

I don't know where to look first. Maybe the plaid wool

blanket lying across the back of the couch, or the garland and twinkle lights strewn across the fireplace mantel above the fire. On Rory's oversized TV, the fireplace channel is also on, which is so weird and so Rory.

A dozen candles sit in stained glass votives on the coffee table and around the kitchen, and Rory's wearing a hideous green and red knit sweater that he somehow manages to make look hot. There are poinsettias everywhere. The entire place smells like the hot apple cider drink my family makes every year at home, and there are pine needles all over the floor.

Between the bookshelf and the window, an enormous fir tree stretches to the ceiling.

When he turns, there's that assessing, cautious expression on Rory's face again, the look that makes my heart beat faster.

"You bought ten poinsettias and you're wearing an ugly Christmas sweater."

He grins, tilting his chin to a bag near my feet. "Got you a matching one." He walks over, and yeah, he does look really, really hot in that stupid sweater. "You didn't think I was going to wear it alone, did you, Hartley?" His eyes glitter as his grin hitches higher. "We have to match."

"You bought a tree." My voice sounds funny, thin and breathless. "It looks like Christmas threw up in here."

"Is that a good thing?"

I sigh, taking it all in, glancing over at the kitchen, breathing in the familiar, sweet cinnamon smell filling the apartment. "That's the same recipe we make at home, isn't it?"

"Mhm." His eyes are warm. "I called your parents earlier."

That girl from a few months ago, who hated Rory Miller? She shakes her head and walks away because I'm way too far gone to help.

Christmas decorations. He bought decorations. All of them,

from the pile of boxes in the corner. My heart explodes into a million pieces all over the floor.

"Why?" I ask, blinking away the sting in my eyes.

He steps behind me, looping his arm around my waist and pressing a warm kiss to the side of my neck. "Because you wanted it, Hartley."

If my heart is a house, Rory now lives there.

I'M in love with her.

Hazel's eyes are bright as she takes in the living room again, smiling, and a warm pulse of happiness radiates through my chest.

I'm in love with her, and I'd do anything to make her happy. And this look of elation on her face as she smiles up at me—it's everything I've ever wanted.

"Thank you," she says, resting her palms on my chest. "This is amazing, Rory." She presses her lips together, gaze lingering on the tree. "You just—"

Our eyes meet, and her full mouth tips up into a pretty smile. I think maybe I've always loved her, because this feeling in my chest isn't new. I just have a name for it now.

"You make everything better," she whispers.

My throat knots with emotion, and I wonder if anyone ever told Rick Miller he makes everything better. If my mom ever felt that way about him.

My fingers thread into her hair, and I brush a soft kiss to her mouth. "So do you, Hartley."

When she pulls back, I search her eyes for any sign she

feels the same way. Behind the warm affection there, worry flickers.

Good. She's worried because it feels real to her, and she's never been here before with a guy. Another pulse of something sharp and sweet pangs through me, and I tuck a lock of hair behind her ear.

She knows how I feel. She has to by now, and when she's ready to hear it, I'll tell her.

"You want to decorate the tree with me?" I ask, and she nods, smile stretching ear to ear.

———

"I'm not too heavy?" Hazel asks that evening as I give her a piggyback ride along the seawall.

Snow falls around us, coating the sidewalks, and traffic is almost nonexistent. It's just us and a few other people out walking, enjoying the sight of the water and forest in the snow.

All afternoon, Hazel flipped between begging to go outside and threatening to wear only lingerie for the next two days to test the limits of my control, so now I'm carrying her, because there was no fucking way I'd let her use crutches on snow. Most of the sidewalks aren't shoveled, and it's slippery.

I snort, giving her a flat look over my shoulder. "Don't insult me, Hartley. You weigh nothing."

She chuckles. My boots crunch in the snow, and I inhale a deep breath of cold, crisp air coming off the water.

"My dad called today," I tell her for some reason.

Her arms tighten around my neck. "How'd that go?"

"Uh. Not great." I make a face over my shoulder at her. "He says I'm different this season."

"You are."

"Yeah." I sneak a glance at her. "I'm okay with it, though. I feel better, playing the way I do." My thoughts flip to the moments after I assist a goal, the sheer elation on my teammates' faces. "Those guys on the team are like my brothers, you know? They matter."

We're quiet as I walk, and I keep thinking about my team and this deep urge in my chest to be the best captain I can for them.

Hazel gives me a squeeze. "Put me down for a second."

I lower, easing her down to her feet, keeping a hand on her at all times to support her, and she turns me to face her. Her nose is pink from the cold as she smiles up at me, snowflakes catching on her toque, hair, and eyelashes.

"I'm so proud of you," she says, and I memorize this moment to keep with me forever, this quiet stillness with someone I never thought I'd have.

"It's like we're in a snow globe," I whisper, and she smiles as I lean down to kiss her.

———

"Hayden's going to come by to get my keys in an hour," Hazel says about a block from home.

Home. She doesn't live there, but maybe one day. My heart lifts as I picture it—our crystal dragons sitting beside each other, her hair products in the bathroom, her clothes hanging in the closet. Her scent in the bed.

My thoughts snag on what she said and I wrench around to look at her over my shoulder. "Why?" My brows knit together and there's that possessive urge again. "If you need something from your apartment, I'll get it. Anything you need, Hartley, I'm your guy." I try to keep my tone light so she doesn't think I'm being a territorial asshole.

Her arms squeeze my neck. "You can't do it because I need him to pick up your Christmas presents."

"Christmas presents?" I straighten, starting to smile. "For me?"

She laughs. "Yeah, baby. For you."

Baby. She called me *baby*. My grin broadens, and a light, buzzy feeling pings around my chest.

"What did you get me?"

She laughs again. "I'm not telling. You have to wait until tomorrow."

"Hmm." My eyes narrow as I walk, brimming with curiosity.

My lips part, and I'm about to start guessing out loud when an older woman with long blond hair steps out of a store and nearly bumps into us.

"Oh, excuse me—" she starts, but then our eyes meet.

My stomach drops through my feet, and my whole body tenses.

"Mom."

CHAPTER 60
RORY

MY HEART BEATS in my ears as my mom and I stare at each other.

"Rory," she breathes, eyes roaming my face like she can't believe it.

She looks older. There are a few more lines around her eyes, and her face is thinner, but her hair is the same. Long and a little curly. And her irises are the same dark blue as mine.

My heart aches.

"I'm Hazel," Hazel says behind me, peering over my shoulder.

My mom's gaze lifts and she blinks, like she just noticed the woman clinging to my back. She smiles a little as I set Hazel on her feet again. "Nicole."

They shake hands, and something in my brain trips. Hazel wraps an arm around my waist, holding me tight. My mom notices, and something softens in her gaze.

"Lovely to meet you, Hazel," she says. Her eyes drop to Hazel's foot, hovering off the ground as she balances on one leg. "What happened there?"

"Rory bodychecked me."

I choke, and Hazel grins up at me with teasing in her eyes.

"I didn't bodycheck her," I add, glancing at my mom. "We were at a skating thing for the team and she fell. She sprained her ankle." I send Hazel a hard look, but she just smiles more. "I'm trying to take care of her, but she won't sit still and rest like she's supposed to."

Hazel rolls her eyes. "Rory, it's snowing. You can't expect me to stay inside when it snows, like, twice a year here."

She's joking, but there's a protective edge to her gaze. She's trying to make us comfortable by joking around, I realize.

If it's possible, I love her a little more.

My mom watches on, wearing a funny expression like she's amused and surprised, but heartbroken. "I agree. Snow means you have to go outside." The side of her mouth lifts. "You used to love going outside in the snow," she says quietly. "You would make a snowman every year."

Pain racks through me, and I swallow past the rock in my throat. She gave that all up when she left, and I've squashed any hope of a relationship.

I want to ask her a million questions about her life. I want to tell her all about Hazel and hockey and how I think everything may have gotten fucked up with us because of me, but the words lodge in my vocal cords, and I turn to Hazel.

"We should get home."

My mom blinks, standing taller. "I'm having a Christmas party." There's a rushed, frantic edge to her words, like she doesn't want it to end like this, either. "Tomorrow afternoon. Just a casual gathering, a few friends. You don't have to bring anything, just yourselves." Her demeanor dims, like she's bracing herself for me to say no, before she takes a deep breath. "I'd love for you to be there," she tells me before her gaze swings to Hazel, brightening. "You too, Hazel, I'd love for you both to be there." Our eyes meet. "If you want."

Hazel watches me with concern and fire in her eyes, like she's ready to strike if I need her.

Want to? she asks with her eyes.

I shouldn't, because I've done enough damage with the relationship between me and my mom, but there's that ache again in my chest.

Maybe it doesn't have to be this way. Maybe I can show her I'm not my dad.

When I give Hazel a barely perceptible nod, she lights up.

"We'd love to come," she tells my mom.

Her face relaxes with visible relief, and she lists off the time and address.

I nod. "I remember."

"Of course." She shakes her head to herself. "Of course you do." She takes another deep breath, looking me over again. She looks like she wants to say more. "Well—"

Without thinking, I rush forward and give her a hug. She's stiff for a moment before she relaxes, clutching me hard, and her painfully familiar scent makes my chest hurt. I pull back before I do something stupid, like tell her I miss her.

"See you then."

"See you then," she whispers as I lean down for Hazel to climb onto my back.

I carry Hazel away, heart pounding, and just before we turn the corner, I look over my shoulder to see her standing there, watching us.

CHAPTER 61
HAZEL

ON CHRISTMAS MORNING, I wake to Rory carrying a tray into the bedroom.

"Good morning," he says, crooking a grin at me.

He's shirtless, wearing black dress slacks and a black bowtie. I burst out laughing.

"What are you wearing?" I ask as he sets the tray on the bedside table.

He hands me a mug. "What, you don't like it?" He flexes his pecs and I smile harder. His hair is rumpled and his eyes are sleepy but affectionate.

How did I never see this in him, this kind, hilarious, gentle man? My life with Rory is so full, bursting with bright color.

"You look like a stripper."

"I need a backup in case hockey doesn't work out."

He flexes his biceps, shooting me a flirty smile, and I sip my coffee, humming with happiness. Almond milk latte, my favorite. Is this what being in a relationship is like? It seems too good to be true.

"Thank you for the coffee. Wait." I frown. "You don't have an espresso maker." My gaze slides to the chocolate croissant on the tray.

Rory shrugs, settling on the bed on his side. "I found a place nearby that was open today."

"You didn't need to do that." My heart pulses again, warm and delighted. "How long have you been awake?"

"A couple hours." He looks out the window and worry flickers through his eyes.

My mind goes back to yesterday, when he and his mom looked at each other like they each had so much to say. How he looked so lost.

My protective instincts were on overdrive, seeing the woman who was supposed to love him with everything she had, but who left him. Her expression was full of yearning and regret, though.

They miss each other, and they want a better relationship, but they have no idea how. I'm sure he's freaking out about going to her place later today.

I set the coffee aside. The need to comfort and distract him has me moving closer on the bed, trailing my fingers through his bedhead. "Your hair is wild."

"So is yours."

"I like it."

His eyes move over me, warm and soft. "I like it, too."

Heat pulses through me, and I'm flooded with the urge to take care of Rory like he takes care of me. To distract him from his worries and to fill this holiday with good memories.

My hand grazes his neck, flicking the bowtie and making him smile. I drag a slow line down his chest, his abs, until I reach his waistband. I trail lower, brushing over the hardening length between his legs.

His abs tighten, and he sucks in a reluctant breath, eyes going to my wrist.

"My wrist is fine." I flick the top button of his pants open and slide my hand inside his boxers, palming his erection.

"Oh, fuck," he breathes, bucking into my hand.

I love the way his lips part and how his half-lidded gaze stays on me, watching me with fascination.

"What are you thinking about?" I ask lightly as I stroke him.

"Fucking you," he says on a groan.

"We both know you wouldn't last one minute inside me."

"Fuck," he laughs, and his cock pulses in my hand. "Of course I wouldn't. Can I touch you?"

"No."

He makes a frustrated noise, and I smile. Heat flows through me, landing between my legs, making me wet, but toying with Rory is too fun.

"Take your pants off."

He hurries his pants and boxers off, and his cock springs free, already beading with moisture at the tip. His eyes spark with hot amusement as he pulls the bowtie off and tosses it aside.

When I climb on top of him, his smile drops. "Your ankle—"

"Rory." My hand sinks into his hair and I grip the strands, straddling his lap and forcing him to look at me instead of my foot. "Shut up," I say gently.

He nods, eyes going glassy. "Okay."

I smile again. This is fun.

"I love when you do what I say," I tell him, reaching down to pull my t-shirt off.

And I *love* the way his eyes darken when he stares at my chest. My nipples prick under his gaze. When I take his hands and set them on my breasts, his jaw flexes.

"You have the best tits," he murmurs, running his warm palms over them, playing with the tips.

"I know."

His breath catches when my hand returns to his cock, stroking him slow and firm. Under my lips on his neck, his skin is hot, his pulse quick, and his breathing shallow. His lips find mine, kissing me with hunger. Between his hands all over me, in my hair and on my breasts, the way he kisses me like he'll drown without me, and the low, desperate noises coming from him, I'm aching with arousal.

But I like playing with him too much. My hand speeds up.

"Slow down."

"No."

"Please," he gasps, and his thighs tense, fingers pinching my nipples and sending a hot streak of electricity to my pussy.

I arch an eyebrow. "No."

"Hazel." His voice is rough, pleading. "I don't want to come yet."

My blood sings with power, and I wear a wicked smile. "So don't come yet."

His head falls back on a groan. I grin wider, working my hand around him faster.

"You're so hot like this," I whisper, taking in his flushed cheeks, hazy eyes, clenched teeth. "You're so fucking beautiful, Rory."

"You don't even *know* how beautiful you are," he grits out. "The second I saw you last year, I lost interest in every other woman on the planet."

My skin tingles with delight. I can't help it, I love to hear that. "Good."

A thought occurs to me. I'm not sure if I want to know the answer, but I ask it anyway.

"When was the last time you had sex?"

He's breathing hard as our eyes meet, and something flashes in his expression. He hesitates, and I squeeze his cock, making his nostrils flare.

"When?"

"Last summer." His throat works. He leans forward to press his lips to my neck, inhaling me.

"A year and a half ago?"

He nods, nipping the sensitive skin between my neck and shoulder, and a heavy emotion surges in me. Hope, I think, or maybe affection. Possession. The idea that Rory is mine and all mine is so sweet and necessary, I'm scared to even think about it.

Instead, I move back, settling on my knees between his legs, and lick a long line up his cock. His groan is tortured, shaky, and desperate, and I swirl my tongue over the swollen tip, humming at the way he tastes.

At his sides, his hands make tight fists.

"You're doing so good," I murmur before sinking my mouth around him, and his cock pulses against my tongue.

My free hand wraps around his balls, pulling another deep, hoarse noise from him. His fingers are in my hair, tensing with gentle weight, and I suck hard.

"Oh, fuck, fuck, fuck, Hazel. I can't—" He breaks off on a broken moan when I take him to the back of my throat, hollowing out my cheeks.

The desperate edge to his voice? He's close.

I'm cruel, so I pull off him for a moment. His eyes are feverish, hair a fucking mess, sweat beading on his forehead.

"Don't come," I remind him before taking him back into my mouth, smiling around his thick length as he makes tortured noises.

I suck as hard as I can, and he stiffens. His balls tighten, and a second later, hot, salty light floods my mouth. His hips jerk, pushing between my lips, and I swallow his release with greed. My blood thrums between my legs, pounding through me with satisfaction and pride.

"Sorry," he gasps, pulling me to his chest. "I couldn't help it."

"I know." I laugh. "I wanted you to come."

"You're the devil." He's still catching his breath, but he's smiling.

"You love it."

"I do."

His sated expression flickers with heat, and his hand drifts between my legs. My toes curl at the burst of sensation.

"My turn?"

I nod, arching into his touch. His hand comes to my waist, and he slides down the bed beneath me before his lips are on my clit.

"Oh, fuck."

"Mhm." His eyes close as he drags his tongue over me.

Fire races through me as I ride his face—I'm so worked up from going down on Rory that this won't take long. My hips tilt in rhythm with his mouth, and pressure gathers between my legs. His mouth is slick, hot, and the perfect amount of pressure, and when he looks up at me, something unfurls in my chest.

"Rory," I moan.

His hands slide to mine, fingers interlacing, and the stupid little affectionate moment winds me higher. This is so much more intense than any hookup I've ever had, and we still haven't had full sex.

The thought fades away as his lips wrap around my clit and he sucks hard. My muscles flutter, he moans, and the ache behind my clit bursts, soaring through me, making me gasp and work myself shamelessly over his mouth. Pleasure rolls through my limbs, and every thought explodes into dust. Throughout, he grips my hands, steady and strong.

When my release fades, I lift off him, climb down his body, and collapse on his chest. Both of us breathe hard, hearts pounding against each other.

"Best Christmas ever," he whispers, grinning, and I dissolve into laughter.

CHAPTER 62

HAZEL

AFTER RORY CARRIES me into the shower and insists on washing my hair for me to "give my wrist a rest," we move to the living room.

Excitement flutters through me as I set the stocking I made him in his lap.

"You did this?" His fingers trace the gold stitching of his name.

"Of course."

On the couch beside him, I pull the blanket over my bare legs and watch with a smile as Rory opens his stocking, setting the items one by one on the coffee table with care. Deodorant, gum, Lindt chocolates, wool socks, an orange, and lip balm.

He chuckles at the plastic key chain I bought the other week—a tiny dragon with a pissed off expression and flames coming out of its mouth.

Amusement sparks in his eyes. "Is this you?"

The apples of my cheeks ache, I'm smiling so much this morning. "I bought it so you could bring it on the road, but that was before I saw you already have a dragon of your own."

He studies the cheap piece of plastic, turning it over with a smile. "I love it."

He reaches back into the stocking and pulls out a can of room-temperature beer, grinning at it in surprise.

"I like this kind," he says.

"I know." I kiss him on the cheek. My mom always puts beer in my dad's stocking. I understand the appeal.

"Thank you, Hartley." He sighs, looking at all the stuff lined up on the table before he shakes his head. "I didn't expect this."

My throat closes up with emotion. Even if this all falls through, even if Rory loses interest in me and moves on to someone else, I'll remember moments like these.

I don't regret any of this. Rory deserves to be shown that he's loved.

He kisses me again and I smile. "Thank you," he says.

"You're welcome." I wrench around, pointing at the larger present, a wide, flat rectangle wrapped in blue paper with dancing reindeer. "That one next."

Rory heads to the tree, still wearing a funny, curious smile as he carries it over. He tears the wrapping off, revealing a framed navy and gray jersey—an older Storm jersey. His brows knit as he pushes the paper away, and he stares, taking in the autograph on the number.

My heart beats hard, praying he likes it.

"You framed Ward's jersey for me?"

I can't tell how he feels about it. "You don't have to hang it up or anything. No one has to know that you have it. I just—" I break off, scrambling to remember why I chose this as one of his gifts. "You said he was your idol. You said making him proud this year matters. I wanted to get you something that reminded you of what matters."

His earnest, searching expression cracks into a brilliant smile, and he beams at me before looking back at the framed jersey. "I fucking love it, Hartley."

My whole heart lifts. Admiration fills his eyes as he studies the autograph.

"Did he sign this for you?"

I nod, smiling. "He was happy to."

Rory makes a pleased noise in his throat before he sets it down and gives me a kiss.

"Thank you," he says against my lips.

"You're welcome." I can feel the goofy, happy look all over my face as the warm, buzzy feelings flow through me.

He sits up. "My turn."

"No." My eyebrows shoot up, and my stomach flutters as nerves flood my system.

He gives me a curious look.

"Um." My fingers twiddle together, fingertips rubbing fast circles. My eyes dart over to the tree and I point at another gift. "I have one more for you."

"You're spoiling me," he says, shaking his head as he retrieves the gift I pointed to. Back on the couch, he tears the wrapping off.

It's the photo of us in the high school library, except instead of being cropped like it is on his phone background, it's the full picture. Us sitting side by side at one of the library tables, books and papers scattered in front of us, me wearing a guarded, reluctant smile and Rory grinning ear to ear with his arm thrown around me.

Rory hums, studying the photo with a look I can't read.

"You can put it on your shelf." I shift under the blanket. Maybe it's a weird gift. I should have run it past Pippa to see if he'd like this kind of thing.

He tilts the photo to me. "I liked you then."

Flutters scatter throughout my chest. "I liked you then, too, I think."

We smile at each other.

"I love it, Hartley. Thank you."

He stands, walks over to the bookshelf, and positions the picture at eye-level. When he glances over at me, his mouth tilts and he winks.

"Perfect," he says.

I could melt right into the couch, I'm so relieved and happy.

A moment later, he drops a small gift into my lap and flops down on the couch beside me, watching me with bright eyes. "Your turn."

The box is small, barely bigger than my palm, and I tear the wrapping away to reveal a velvet jewelry box.

My pulse takes off at a sprint.

"That better not be a fake engagement ring," I blurt out, even though I know it isn't.

I think.

His eyes sharpen and his grin turns feline. "What if it is?"

"Rory." My face heats and his grin widens.

"You're so easy to fluster, Hartley." He tilts his chin at it. "Just open it."

The velvet is soft under my fingers as I crack it open, and inside are two sparkling stud earrings, stones the color of my eyes. My breath catches, and for a long moment, I just stare at them.

"You hate them."

"No," I rush out on a light laugh. "How could I hate them? They're beautiful."

There's a feeling in my chest as I meet his cautious smile—a flipping, turning, rolling as Rory and I look at each other.

"Don't say it's too much or too expensive." His eyes are so soft, like the velvet box in my hand. "I was thinking about you when I saw them, and I like buying things for you and making you happy." He exhales slowly, eyes still roaming my face. "And you deserve something beautiful."

It's so cliche, me falling for a rich guy who loves to buy me things. I'm more evolved than this. I can buy my own damn earrings.

It's not the cost, though. It's that he was thinking about me. It's the gesture, because Rory Miller is turning out to be so fucking *caring* and *kind* and *sweet.*

"You were thinking about me?" The corner of my mouth turns up, and I glance down at the earrings again. They really are gorgeous. I've never owned jewelry like this, and I'm already terrified I'll lose them.

"Constantly," he says, almost reluctantly, like he wishes he didn't have to tell the truth.

My heart falls out of rhythm, excited and pleased. "These are too pretty to wear."

"Hartley. Wear those earrings. If you lose one, I'll buy you another. I'll buy you ten."

I snort. I don't know what that means that he can basically read my mind.

"Try them on." He settles back against the couch, finally looking at ease in his own home. "Let's make sure they fit."

I huff a quiet laugh as I slip the earrings out of the box and put them on. When I turn back to Rory, his eyes warm with affection.

"Gorgeous," he says in a low voice.

"Pippa has ones like these, I think." My heart warms at the idea of having earrings that match hers.

"Same stone, different design," Rory says. "Same jeweler."

He got the jeweler recommendation from Jamie. He put effort and planning into this.

My stomach flutters and I bite back a smile, leaning over to kiss his cheek. "Thank you."

"You're welcome." He leans forward to pick a green envelope off the coffee table before handing it to me.

My eyes narrow as I rip it open. "Another weekend away with Pippa?" I ask, wiggling my eyebrows, and he smiles to himself. I pull the paper out and read his scratchy, masculine writing.

It's for five coaching sessions with the woman who started the body-positive dance studio in New York, the one who inspired my dreams.

My gaze whips to his. Months ago, when he was first teaching me to skate, I mentioned her once. I didn't even say her name.

Just when I think I've seen all there is to see with Rory, he pulls something else out of his back pocket.

"I didn't know she did coaching," I breathe, rereading his card.

"She doesn't." He rubs the back of his neck. "But it wasn't that hard to convince her, once I explained what you want to do and she looked at your website."

"She looked at my website?" I chew my lip, heart beating wildly.

He nods, mouth tipping up into a cautious smile. "Did I go too far?"

My emotions pitch and swoop inside me. Even if I'm uncertain about my abilities, Rory believes in me and my dreams. No one's ever done this kind of thing for me.

"No," I whisper, running my finger along the edge of the card. "You didn't go too far."

Rory sits back, watching me, looking so handsome in the morning light, and I want to say a million things.

"Come here," he says, and I carefully climb over so I'm straddling his lap. He's warm under me, and I let my hands skim up his chest, up his neck, until my fingers sink into his messy hair.

"Thank you," I whisper before I press a light kiss to his mouth. "I love it."

He hums against my lips, a low, satisfied noise that rumbles through his chest, and I fall deeper into whatever this is with Rory Miller.

"I SHOULD HAVE KNOWN you'd drive something like this," Hazel says that afternoon as I pull out of the parking garage.

I toss a grin over at her, turning on her seat warmer. "Fast, powerful, and incredibly good-looking?"

"Showy and expensive." She snorts. "And only *you* would drive a car like *this* in the snow."

"Hey, I have snow tires." I change gears in the sports car, winking at her with a lazy grin as the engine purrs louder, and she rolls her eyes, hiding a smile. "Can you drive stick?"

"Nope. My dad wanted to teach us but Pippa and I both refused."

The streets are quiet as we drive. "Do you want me to teach you?"

"Rory." Her eyes flick over to me. "I'm not driving this car."

"Why not?"

She balks, probably about to protest that it's too expensive or something.

"You might need a car for something."

It's fucking cute how she does that rapid-blinking thing when she's flustered. Like this morning when she saw the box and thought it was an engagement ring. It almost makes me want to buy one to see what she'd say.

Who am I kidding? That's not the reason I want to buy one.

"I'll rent a car if I need one," she insists.

"Okay." I sigh like she's worn me down. "I'll get another car." I pull onto the bridge to North Vancouver, and my gut tightens with nerves. "What kind of car do you want?"

She shakes with laughter. "You're relentless."

My thoughts wander to my mom, and another round of nerves pitch through me. My fingers drum on the steering wheel in anticipation. Do her friends even know about me? Does she have a partner? Does she still go hiking in the trails? It's like she's a stranger. But the way she looked at me yesterday, it felt like—

My exhale is heavy. It felt like she didn't want it to be that way.

She left, though, so now I don't fucking know what to think. I don't know what I'm doing, going to visit her today.

Hazel's hand lands on my thigh. She can see right through me, and she knows I'm nervous about today.

I wonder what else Hartley knows. I wonder if she realizes I'm in love with her.

"I'm glad you're coming with me today," I admit, glancing between her and the road.

Without Hazel, I'd make some excuse and then lift weights until I was too tired to think. With Hazel, though, I haven't felt the urgent, clawing feeling that I'm not doing enough for hockey. If I asked her about it, she'd say I can take three days off without ruining my career, and I'd agree.

"I need you," I add, inching closer to the secret I'm keeping from her.

Hazel's changed my life in ways I couldn't predict, and being with her is so much more than I expected.

She watches me, and I worry I've pushed it too far, but she just gives me that soft, sweet Hazel smile I've unearthed in the past few months.

"I'm happy I'm here, too," she says, giving my leg another squeeze.

CHAPTER 64

RORY

WHILE MY MOM bustles around the party, topping up drinks and chatting with people, I sit beside Hazel in the living room. My mom bought this house a few months after she left, and I've been here twice. No, three times. I spent most of my visits practicing slapshots in the driveway, ignoring her.

"Hazel," my mom says, taking the seat beside her. "What do you do?"

Her hand slips into mine, anchoring me. "I'm a physio for the team."

They talk about Hazel's work and her yoga practice, and my mom gives me a warm look when Hazel shows her the earrings I bought.

"How are you liking the Vancouver team, Rory?" my mom asks, and the room seems to quiet down.

"Good." I send her a quick glance. "Streicher's on the team, so it's nice to play with someone I know." I shift, aware that everyone in the room is listening to our conversation. "And I like playing for Ward."

My mom nods, humming. "Didn't you have his poster on your wall?"

Hazel smiles up at me, and I try to smile back, but my face feels rigid. "Yeah."

She hums again, and we fall quiet. She looks at her hands in her lap before glancing over at me. "Jamie and his mom are doing well?"

I nod. "Yep."

"He and my sister are engaged," Hazel adds, and my mom lights up.

"I saw he was engaged but I didn't know she's your sister." My mom's gaze flicks between us, hesitating like she wants to say more. "Congratulations to them."

Hazel runs her thumb over the back of my hand, and a few knots inside me untie. I don't know how I'd do this without her.

"Jamie's a surly grump," Hazel tells my mom, "but I couldn't ask for a better brother-in-law."

My mom chuckles. "He was always quiet and serious. Nothing like Rory. I guess that's why they were good for each other."

I don't know what to say. Everything we talk about is from the past, but I don't want to talk about hockey. She hates hockey.

This is awkward. I open my mouth to ask if she still makes jewelry, but the doorbell rings, and she jumps up like she was waiting for an out. She opens the door and more of her friends pile in.

"I'm so glad we could make it," her friend says, hugging my mom. "When you called yesterday—"

"Oh, yes, yes." My mom cuts her off, eyes darting over to me and Hazel. "So good to see you."

Her friend sees me and gasps, hands on her mouth and eyes wide. "Is this Rory?"

I give her a tight smile. "Hi."

"My god," she breathes. "He's Rick's twin!"

So fast I barely catch it, my mom winces, and my heart sinks.

"I need to, uh," I start, getting to my feet, not meeting Hazel's searching gaze. "I'm going to grab some water. Be right back."

I sense Hazel's eyes on me the entire way to the kitchen. At the kitchen sink, I pour a glass from the tap, down it, and pour another, staring out the window into the back yard.

What am I doing here? I'm just ripping open old wounds. The way she reacted when her friend said I looked like my dad was everything I needed to know.

This was a huge fucking mistake. I don't know what I thought was going to happen, showing up. Did I think suddenly we were going to be different people? That we could start fresh or something?

Pathetic, Rick would say.

I think back to the day she left, when she asked if I wanted to go with her. Everything would be different if I had said yes. I'd know my own mom. I wouldn't play hockey, though.

"Rory." My mom steps into the kitchen wearing a strange expression.

The kitchen feels too small with just the two of us, but at the same time, my gaze clings to her, taking her in. My mom. My heart hurts, looking at her. Even though she's right in front of me, I miss her.

I wish we *could* start fresh. I just don't know how.

She gestures over her shoulder, shaking her head. "I'm sorry about what Erica said. About you looking like your dad."

I take a drink of water, just for something to do with my hands. "Everyone says it."

"I always thought you looked more like me."

Silence stretches between us. I can smell her perfume—the same one she used to wear when I was a kid.

"How's your dad?"

"Uh." I rub the back of my neck, thinking about our call yesterday. "He's good."

"Is he in town for the holiday?"

I shake my head. "Back in Toronto. He's not much of a Christmas guy."

She nods like she remembers before her expression changes. "He used to be, when you were really little. He loved doing all the Christmas stuff with you."

I make a face. That doesn't sound like him.

"Honestly, Rory, he was." She sighs. "Your dad loves you. I hope you know that. He shows it the only way he knows how."

My dad loves *hockey*. He loves being the best and anyone connected to him being the best, but I shove that all away.

"I should get back—" I start.

"Are you happy?"

The question stabs me in the heart, and I don't know why. She waits, watching my face. "Yeah. I am. Hazel's..." I trail off, looking to the living room, where we can hear everyone talking and laughing. "Hazel's amazing."

My mom's worried expression melts into a smile full of affection. "She's lovely. You seem perfect for each other."

I just nod. I want to tell her how I've liked Hazel since high school and how we did this whole faking it thing to piss off her ex, and how I'm in love with her and have no idea what to do or when to tell her.

Instead, I stare at the water glass on the counter and nod again. "I hope so."

It's quiet again in the kitchen, and I take a step to go back to the living room.

"I have a gift for you," she says quickly behind me.

My eyebrows go up as she hustles into the living room and

returns holding a small gift box. "It's not much, but—" She hands it to me, flustered. "Well, just open it."

I pull the lid off and push the tissue paper aside. It's a knit sweater, a navy blue with flecks of gray in the wool, just like Hartley's eyes. When I hold it up, it looks like the right size.

"Did you make this?"

Like she's embarrassed, she nods, and my chest strains. Why is she making sweaters if she left? Why is she inviting me over for Christmas parties with her friends and meeting my girlfriend and asking about my dad?

"I made it last year. I wanted to give it to you then, but I lost my nerve."

I can feel the baffled expression on my face. "Last year?"

She winces. "I figured you already have everything you need and you wouldn't want it—"

This sweet ache in my chest, I think it's that worthy feeling Hazel talked about in yoga that one time. I set the box on the counter and hug my mom as hard as I can. Her warm, cinnamon scent wraps around us, and she hugs me back.

"Thank you," I tell her in a strange, thick voice. "I love it."

We pull apart, and she doesn't meet my eyes. "I wanted you to be warm enough. You're always traveling with the team to cold places."

The corner of my mouth tips up. Such a mom thing to say.

Back in the living room, I take my seat beside Hazel and slip my hand into hers.

"Everything okay?" she whispers, and I nod. She leans harder against me. "I'm not going anywhere," she adds, and I can breathe again.

LATE THAT EVENING, we lie on the couch in front of the fireplace, drinking hot cider again while snow falls outside and the Christmas tree glows. I'm wearing his hoodie, settled against him, covered with the warm blanket he bought for me, and his fingers toy absently with my hair.

"What did you decide about that studio space?" Rory asks.

Tension knots in my stomach. It's been two days since Laura texted, and I still haven't replied. I feel like a jerk for not answering her right away, but I've been talking myself in and out of it.

"I haven't decided anything."

Rory hums, still playing with my hair, and I know if I told him I didn't want to do it, he'd respect that and drop it.

I'm scared. There's so much at stake. If I fail, it'll be embarrassing and a huge waste of money, but more than anything, if I fail, what does that mean about me?

I can't stay in the same spot forever because I'm scared, though. And with the mentorship sessions Rory got me for Christmas, I'll have someone to answer my questions. My lungs expand with a big breath and I steel my spine.

"I want to go look at the space."

He lights up. "Yeah?"

I nod, smiling.

He tilts his chin to my phone on the coffee table. "Text her now."

"Now?"

"Yes." He nudges me. "So you don't lose your nerve."

He's right. I drag in a deep breath, grab my phone, and tap out a quick text to Laura.

"The place is probably gone by now," I mutter. "Which is fine."

She responds a moment later. *Great! Are you free the morning of New Year's Eve? You can take a look at the space then.*

Rory reads over my shoulder. We're supposed to be driving up to Whistler that morning for the League Classic game.

"We can make it work," he says, lifting an eyebrow.

I bite my lip.

"Come on, Hartley," he murmurs, smiling.

Reluctance surges through me because doing something big like this is scary, but Rory went over to his mom's place even though he was nervous.

Sounds great, I text Laura before letting out a whoosh of air.

"Good job," Rory says against my temple, and I flush, tossing my phone aside.

His eyes go to the framed photo of us sitting on his bookshelf before he glances down at me and smiles.

"Is this what you expected when you made that bet that we'd get together?" I ask. "Lying on the couch like an old married couple."

The piercing look he gives me makes my heart skip a beat. "It's even better."

I need to say something about how I'm feeling. I never expected any of this to happen, and I sure as hell never expected to feel emotions like *possessive* and *proud* and *sparkling, pinwheeling happiness* around Rory Miller. Anger knots in my stomach at my hesitation.

"Thank you for coming today," he says.

"Of course." This guy has no fucking clue what I'd do for him.

I think about Nicole and how happy she was to see him today. How she clearly threw the party together after she invited us because she wanted to see him so badly. When the downstairs washroom was occupied, she sent me upstairs, and I walked past her office.

"Your mom's office was filled with your hockey stuff," I tell him, and his brow creases.

"She hates hockey."

"She had the newspaper clipping from the day you were drafted, all your jerseys, and a bunch of Storm merch in there." An ache throbs in my chest for him *and* for her. "She misses you, Rory."

"I miss her, too," he says softly in my ear, and my throat tightens.

He's so honest with me, even when it's hard, so I push myself to give him more of myself.

"Connor said guys like him don't end up with girls like me," I rush out. I can't tell him the truth about how I feel, but I can give him this. I can take this tiny step forward with him.

His eyes sharpen, going hard at Connor's name. I cross my arms over my chest, frowning at the floor, and in my head, I'm back there, years ago at the party, feeling the burning shame of not being enough for someone.

"I wasn't enough for him." I can barely get the words out. They're slicing up my throat as I say them.

He shifts under me, moving so we face each other, hands framing my jaw while he wears the most urgent, earnest, furious expression. He tilts me up so he can look into my eyes.

"He's wrong, Hartley." Our eyes hold, emotion flickering in his gaze. "He's so fucking wrong."

My heart beats hard in my chest. I want to believe him. When we're sitting here, wrapped up in each other like nothing else exists, I want to believe he'll never grow sick of me or discard me.

I think I'd just die if that happened.

What have I gotten myself into? Panic spikes as I stare up into Rory's eyes. There's no way to extract myself from this without getting hurt.

"He's wrong." Rory looks down at me like I have to believe him. "He was never good enough for you, and he knew it. You're perfect, Hartley."

Something drums inside me, urgent, insistent, desperate to get out. This is agonizing, keeping the feelings inside like this.

"It's not fake anymore," I whisper. "Is it?"

Rory shakes his head. "No, Hartley. It isn't." His gaze moves over my face like he's trying to take in every detail about me, and he swallows like he's nervous. "It hasn't been fake for me for a long time."

There isn't enough air in the room, and I can't look away.

Connor said I wasn't enough, but maybe he's wrong. Rory sure looks at me like I'm enough. I want this, whatever we're doing. I want all of this.

"Can I tell you something?" he asks, tucking my hair behind my ear.

My pulse trips at his earnest and nervous expression, but I nod, biting my lip.

He searches my eyes, sucking in a breath. "I love you."

The world stops, fading away, and it's just me and Rory.

"What?" I suck a shaky breath in, like I'm scared, but I'm not.

"I love you." The long column of his throat works as he watches me, hand slipping back into my hair.

Two months ago, this would have been the last thing I wanted to hear. Now, I want to hear Rory say those words a thousand times.

"Don't look so surprised, Hartley." His smile is gentle and crooked. "How could I not fall for you? It was always only a matter of time."

My lips part, but I'm speechless. The girl from years ago who had her heart smashed can't believe how insanely lucky I am to have found Rory. And at the same time, I'm terrified it won't last.

"You don't need to say anything." He laughs quietly at my silence. "I know you'll say it back eventually."

He says it like he knows. He says it like he can see right through me, like he believes I'll catch up.

A glow expands through me. "So cocky," I murmur.

I've been avoiding the emotion, turning away from it, but I can't ignore it anymore.

I'm head over heels in love with Rory Miller. I've never said the words to a guy. With Connor, I always sensed they'd be unwelcome, so I kept them to myself.

That was a watered-down version of love, though, and Rory's nothing like Connor.

He's hurt someone before, an ugly voice whispers in my head. He didn't mean to, but he was careless with Ashley and broke her heart.

He could do the same to me, even if he does love me. Even if I love him back and we're wildly happy together. People fall out of love all the time.

My mind goes to yesterday, when Rory said that Jamie was

like his brother. They'll be in each other's lives forever, which means Rory will be in *my* life forever.

That would break me, if it didn't work out after I gave him everything and then had to see him all the time.

"It's okay," he says again, running a hand over my hair, and I see that he understands. He smiles like he can read my thoughts. It's just another reason my heart pounds for him— because he's endlessly patient and gentle. Because he knows I'm broken and trying to put myself back together for him.

"I'll wait," he says.

Oh god. Yeah. I really do love him. I think I might have loved him for a while. Longer than I'm ready to admit. I tried so hard not to but I think that might have been the dumbest thing I've ever done, trying not to fall for him.

I move to straddle him, our eyes locked the entire time. His hands settle on my waist, and I bring my mouth to his.

"How's your ankle?" he asks quietly.

"I don't care about my ankle right now."

Rory nods, eyelids falling halfway, and his throat works. He's probably going to say something about me resting it anyway, but instead, I kiss him.

WHILE WE KISS, Rory lifts me up and carries me to his bedroom, gently setting me down on the bed before kneeling on the floor in front of me. The air buzzes with electricity as his mouth moves over mine, pulling apart for a second at a time to remove each other's clothes, until finally, I'm sitting on the bed in a lavender bra and matching thong.

"I really needed you today," he whispers, throat working, and the look in his eyes is so heartbreakingly vulnerable that emotion pulses through me.

I know this. When it comes to his mom, he's lost, and I just want to hold his hand and make sure he's okay.

God, I want to be that person for him. So badly.

"Say those words again," I whisper. "From earlier."

He smiles, holding my face while he presses a kiss to my lips. "I love you."

I sigh, practically floating, and he climbs over me on the bed. Like every time we kiss, I forget everything else except the feel of his mouth, his hand slipping into the back of my hair, his knee nudging between mine. He settles between my legs, and the impressive length of his cock pressing against my clit sends sparks racing through me. My lips part and his tongue slips between them, and when I suck on it lightly, Rory's breath catches, and a low, pleasured noise comes from deep in his chest.

"Jesus," he murmurs before stroking back into my mouth, tasting me. I arch against him because something in that one word tells me exactly how much he needs me, how he might lose his mind if he can't have more. His hips tilt against me, fingers tightening in my hair, and shivers of delight and arousal dance down my spine. "I could come from just this, Hartley, I swear."

An aching throb starts low in my stomach, and I must make a noise of protest or need or both because he lets out a low chuckle that I want to lick off his smiling mouth.

"But I won't." Another slow, lazy kiss. My panties are damp. "And not before you get what you need."

Our kiss moves from slow and thoughtful to fast and urgent.

"Every time I jerk off, I think about the way your pussy tastes. I never fucking last, thinking about that."

I moan, arching against him again, chasing friction as I grind my hips into his. His cock hits the bundle of nerves between my legs and my whole body tightens.

He hovers over me, pressing himself into that spot again, making my eyes roll back. His mouth hooks into a smug, pleased smile, eyes hot and pinning me. He rewards me with a line of nipping kisses down my throat before he sucks a sensitive spot at the base of my neck, and I moan, tilting my hips toward him shamelessly.

"Are we doing this tonight?"

"Yes," I gasp as his tongue does small circles in the divot above my collarbones. "I fucking hope so."

"Good." His eyes darken and he rests his forehead on my

sternum as he takes a deep breath. His expression tells me this is the best thing that's ever happened to him.

Me, too, I think.

I want him. I don't care about the consequences, and I don't care if I get hurt.

His hand slides between my legs and he presses a firm circle against the front of my panties. My back arches as pleasure loops through me.

"Oh my god," I murmur, looking up at Rory's dark, lazy grin.

"You get so wet for me." A flush spreads over his cheekbones. "I fucking love that, Hazel."

I jerk a nod, running my hands over his chest while his hand works between my legs, winding me higher, but when I reach for his stiff cock pressing against my stomach, he shakes his head.

"Not yet."

"Please."

He lets out a low laugh and lifts his eyebrows, still rubbing intoxicating, pleasurable strokes against that bud of nerves. "I'm not going to last if I give you what you want."

His gaze drops to my breasts and his expression turns tight. A moment later, he's on his knees, reaching around to unhook my bra and yank my panties down.

"That's better," he says before his hand returns to my pussy and I arch into him.

His lips find my nipple, and the feel of his tongue on the pinched peak sends electricity rippling through me.

I reach for his cock again, but he grasps my wrist and pins it to the bed above my head.

"Give me your other hand," he says, still massaging my clit, and I desperately want him to keep going, so I do what he says.

He binds my wrists together with his big hand, and a slow smile spreads over his mouth.

"I don't know why I like this with you," he says, gaze flicking up to where his hand holds my wrists down, "but I do." His throat works and he's breathing hard, studying my face between glances at where his hand moves between my thighs. "I just want you all to myself."

Pressure builds low in my belly, around the base of my spine, and behind my clit. "I want that, too," I admit. "I like when you do this."

He smiles that dark, pleased smile again like it was the perfect thing to say, and I get another hit of pleasure from giving him what he needs. Whatever Rory wants, I want to give it to him.

His jaw tightens as his fingers slide through my wetness. "You know you're mine, right?"

I nod again, eyelids drooping at the increasing ache behind my clit.

"Mine and only mine."

My toes curl. I never thought I'd love hearing those possessive words out of Rory's mouth, but here I am, soaking them up with delight.

"Say it." His amused voice is cut with possession, and his gaze pins me.

"Yours and only yours," I breathe. "I need to come."

He sucks in a sharp breath and releases my wrists. "Get on your stomach."

"What?" I lift my head as he kneels, waiting. His cock juts out, begging for my attention, moisture beading on the tip. I lean forward and lick it off, and his hand sinks into my hair, gripping tight. "Hazel." His tone is dark and teasing as he pulls me back from his cock by the hair. "What did I just say?"

Even though I'm wound tight, swirling with heat and pressure and the desperate need to come, I'm laughing silently.

"I can't remember," I lie, grinning at him, and he shakes his head, eyes bright and mouth curling into something wicked.

Wicked and fucking hot.

"I was going to fuck you," he says in that playfully threatening voice, still holding the back of my hair in his fist. "But now I've changed my mind because you're a fucking brat."

CHAPTER 67

HAZEL

EXCITEMENT SWOOPS IN MY STOMACH. This is it, isn't it? This is exactly what I've always needed in a guy. What Rory and I have trickles into everything. *He* is what I've always needed in a guy. My pulse picks up in anticipation.

"Get on all fours."

I've barely turned over when his hands come to my hips and he hauls me to my knees, wet and bared for him. Hesitation streaks through me—I haven't been in this position for years. It's submissive and vulnerable, and I usually don't like it.

Like he senses my skittish thoughts, his big hand smooths over my lower back. "You okay, baby?"

I focus on the warmth of his hand on my skin and nod, dragging in a deep breath. "Uh-huh."

He'd never push me too far. He's always watching me, gauging my reaction.

Behind me, he shifts, and his lips are on my back, kissing a trail down my spine. "Do you trust me, Hazel?"

"Yes."

"You sure?"

"Yes." I'm wet and aching, waiting for him to get me off, and my frustration slips through in my tone. "I trust you."

He makes that low, pleased noise I love. "Good."

His tongue circles my asshole and my eyes go wide at the warm, wet sensation. A hoarse noise of pleasure chokes out of me and his fingers tense on my hip.

"Have you done this before?" he murmurs as he strokes back and forth.

I'm blinking at nothing, my full attention on where his tongue touches me as heat moves through my body. "No."

"Do you like it?"

"*Yes*," I gasp. I'm getting wetter. "Rory," I moan. "I need to come. I need more."

"I know you do." Still, his tongue draws those lazy, slick circles against the tight pucker. "How badly do you want to come?"

My hands clench into fists. "I'm going to fucking kill you later."

"I have no doubt." His tongue delves inside me and I moan, high and needy. My spine is tingling. "Oh, fuck, Hazel," he groans. "You just clenched on my tongue. That's so good, baby. You're doing so good."

I grit my teeth, breathing hard. I'm about to burst out of my skin.

"If you want more, you need to earn it."

I whimper, teetering on the edge of insanity. This is torture, but I love it. "What do you want?"

"Stay with me here until the League Classic."

"What?" I can't think straight when he's touching me like that. "Until New Year's?"

He pauses before pressing a kiss to my lower back, exhaling against my skin. "I like you being here. It feels right."

His words and the way he says them, soft and sincere, settle right into my heart. "Okay. Yes. I'll stay here."

I'd probably say anything right now, with the way he has

me worked up, but the past few days have been a dream, us in our own little snow globe.

"Say that it feels right."

"It feels right."

"Say that if we do this, it's not the last time."

My rule. My stupid rule that was supposed to keep me from catching feelings. "It's not the last time."

"Good girl." Is that relief in his tone? "Alright, Hartley." His hand returns between my legs, rubbing my clit in firm, wide circles with the flat of his fingers, fast and light, exactly the way I need, and goosebumps scatter across my skin. "You've pumped up my ego enough for tonight."

My head sinks to the bed as I tip closer to the edge. The orgasm stirs and builds inside me as he slides his hand over me, his tongue stroking into my back entrance, claiming me, coaxing me closer. Need arcs through me, firing through my blood, and my body seizes up with pleasure as the pressure between my legs reaches a climax.

"I'm coming," I moan into the mattress as Rory plays with my body, making my toes curl. The muscles in my core tighten, spasming around nothing as his hand works faster. I can hear how wet I am against his hand but I don't care, I'm just spinning out, gasping and clenching and tightening on his tongue.

Dirty and depraved, I think to myself, but I don't care. If Rory wants it, I want it.

My pulse roars in my ears as my release subsides and I sink forward onto the bed, but Rory climbs on top of me, straining erection pressing into my lower back as he kisses my shoulder.

"How're you doing, Hartley?"

"Good," I moan through the aftershocks, and he chuckles.

"Are you tapped out for tonight?"

I lift up on my elbows with a start and shake my head.

"No." His face is flushed and his eyes are bright. Hair messy and fucked up, just the way I love. "We're not done."

His mouth crooks, throat working like he's holding on to his control. "Good."

Rory reaches into his nightstand, rips open the box of condoms, and rolls one on.

"Turn over," he says quietly, and I roll onto my back.

He settles between my knees, cock pressing against my clit, and my breath catches. Rory's mouth is on my neck, on my shoulder, pressing soft, nipping kisses, and I sink my hand into his hair.

"Don't be gentle," I whisper, dragging myself against his length. "Take what you want, Rory. I like it."

He groans like it's exactly what he wanted to hear, and then he's there at my entrance, nudging into me. With a ticking jaw and heavy, labored breaths, he pushes into me, watching my expression. I can feel the second release starting as my body stretches for him. He's too big for me, but the burn is incredible, sending sparks up and down my spine at how full and tight it feels. When his hips press into mine and he's inside to the hilt, my eyes roll back.

"Rory," I moan, gazing up at him.

I could come from his expression alone. Tense jaw like he's barely holding on, eyelids drooping with a clouded, unfocused gaze. Seeing his desire all over his face like this adds to the pressure building inside me again.

"You are so fucking tight," he rasps. "I knew I wouldn't fucking last."

He pulls out and thrusts back in, and we both moan. I'm going to be sore tomorrow but I don't care, I need more. My hands are everywhere on Rory—in his hair, on his arms, raking up his back.

"Can I—" He thrusts back in, faster and rougher this time, and a ragged noise rumbles in his chest.

"Can you what?" I'm breathless as he fucks me, pinning me down, using me to come. "What is it?"

His hand comes to the base of my throat and he meets my gaze with a question in his eyes. "Like this?"

He's not squeezing, not hurting me, just resting his hand there, keeping me under him. I nod hard. There's something about Rory wanting to pin me down and fuck me that sends me into outer space. "Yes. Like that."

"Good."

His hips move faster, finding a punishing rhythm, and my body begins to tighten again.

CHAPTER 68
RORY

BEING inside the woman I love is the most intense experience of my life.

Hazel looks up at me like I'm everything to her. Finally, she trusts me. Finally, we're doing this. I know she loves me back, and until she's ready to tell me, I'll wait. I've had plenty of practice with her.

She bites her lip, frowning with need. "Harder."

"You sure?" I'm barely holding on, my control fraying at the edges. Around the base of her throat, my fingers flex.

Fucking hell, I love her letting go for me, letting me in. Trusting me to use her like this.

She nods hard, and her fingernails dig into my back. The pinpricks are another layer to this moment—her scent in my nose, the wet slip of her arousal against my cock, the way she looks under me, so pliant and soft and open.

Jesus Christ, I won't survive this. I'm going to come so hard it'll kill me. The heavy tug in my groin pulls harder, driving my hips faster, and the sparks start.

Around my cock, Hazel begins to flutter, and my eyes widen. "Again? You're going to come again?"

Her lip curls and she jerks a nod. "You're hitting my clit," she gasps. "And everything inside me."

Smug male satisfaction has me by the throat. Her perfect round tits bounce as I fuck her up the bed, the pressure inside me boiling over. She clenches, searching my eyes, arching, and her delicate lips part. My pulse pounds in my ears, my balls draw close to my body, and my release slams into me.

My mind splinters into a thousand pieces. I spill into her, burying my head in her neck as I groan her name, coming deep inside her.

My Hazel. Mine. With each thrust, her name beats through my blood. I love her, and she's mine, and now that I have her, I'm never letting her go.

As our releases fade and we catch our breaths, I settle against her, kissing her forehead, stroking her hair. I'm still inside her, but I'm not ready to pull out yet.

"You okay?" I ask. "I wasn't too rough?"

She shakes her head. "No. It was perfect." Her lashes flutter as she looks up at me, sighing with a small, sated smile, and my thoughts still at how beautiful she is.

"If you don't actually want to stay here until the League Classic—"

"I want to."

Stay forever, I think.

She brings her hand to my chest, over my hammering heart. "I like it here."

I wonder if she can feel my heart skip a beat at that.

"Your heart's beating so fast still," she whispers.

"It's so fucking good with you, Hazel." It's not sex; it's bliss.

Her eyes widen, and the moment before she speaks lasts an eternity. "I'm falling for you, too." She's so quiet, barely above a whisper as her eyes search mine. "I'm scared."

My fucking *heart*.

"I know." I trail my fingers over her forehead, pushing a lock of her hair back. "I think it's supposed to be scary, and I'll be right here with you the whole time." Our eyes meet. "Okay?"

She nods. "Okay."

She loves me, and one day? I'm going to marry Hazel Hartley.

IT'S BOXING DAY, the day after Christmas, and I'm sitting in the Filthy Flamingo with Owens, Volkov, and a few other guys when my phone buzzes with a photo from Hazel.

She's in the bathtub, covered in bubbles, face flushed with heat and eyes filled with mischief. My fire-breathing dragon.

Thinking about me? I text. My knee bounces as I grin at my phone.

Maybe.

That's it, I respond. *I'm coming straight home.*

Don't you dare. Stay out with the guys and have some fun for once.

For once. It's laughable. Every moment I'm with Hazel feels like fun.

"Thanks for bringing me to that pickup game," Owens says. The other players—both professional and pickup league—are debating whether the Storm will make it to the playoffs this season. "Streicher couldn't make it?"

I shake my head. "Their flight just got in. He said he'd meet us for a drink, though."

Owens fit right in with the guys on the pickup league, but that's no surprise. Hayden Owens could be abducted by bloodthirsty aliens, and within an hour, he would have everyone laughing and hanging out and having a great time. The second he stepped on the ice tonight, he understood the team dynamic and played accordingly. Guys passed to him but he didn't take any shots for himself. To make it more fair on the pickup guys, they made us professional guys play one-handed and in different positions. Volkov made for a terrible goalie, letting shot after shot slip past him while the rest of us howled with laughter, but on offense, Owens was a natural.

My eyes narrow, thinking about a Storm game last week. "You've got a hell of a wrist-shot for a D-man," I tell him.

He shrugs, looking around the bar. "Yeah, well, it was just for fun."

"It's a good thing." Games move so fast, and players need to be ready for anything. "You're a well-rounded player and an important part of the team."

Wow. I feel like Ward, saying that. A spark of pride ignites in my chest, rippling through me.

He gives me a close-lipped smile, ducking his head like he's pleased. "Thanks, Captain." He clears his throat. "Everything go okay with the stuff I dropped off?"

"Yeah." I grin, thinking about the gifts Hazel got me. "Thanks for doing that for her. I appreciate it."

He waves me off. "I owe her for putting up with my lazy ass during physio." He lifts an eyebrow, teasing me. "She staying at your place tonight?"

I think about Hazel smiling at me from the stands while we played the pickup game tonight, and then the photo she sent me a few minutes ago of her in the bathtub. In a few short days, it's begun to feel like *our* place.

My thoughts flip to last night, sinking into her, and how fucking *right* it felt. And again this morning. The way she moans my name. The way she looks waking up in my bed, tucked against my chest.

Owens crows at whatever my expression is, and a few of the players glance over. "So that's a yes," he says, grinning over the rim of his glass.

"She stayed with me the entire break. I'm not going to let her stay alone at her place with a sprained ankle."

Owens watches me with an expression I can't name. "Hazel's the best," he finally says.

My heart beats harder. "I know."

"And she deserves the best."

My gaze turns sharp, and I picture the face my mom made when her friend said I looked like my dad. "I know."

Owens just gives me that kind, open smile. "So it's a good thing she has you, buddy."

He gives me a playful shove. Something in my chest eases.

"You stayed here for the holidays?"

"Yep. Kit's parents moved to Toronto to be closer to his sister, so I mostly hung out with Darcy."

Right. Kit's girlfriend. The one he's always looking at. My eyes narrow, and guilt flashes in his gaze.

"Nothing's going on," he says quickly, clearing his throat and looking away. "I don't mess around with girls who are taken." Around his beer glass, his knuckles are white.

"And Darcy's taken."

"Yep."

"You guys went to university together, right?"

He nods. "Kit and I were friends in high school and we met Darcy in our first year. We all lived in the same dorm and Darcy and I had a bunch of classes together."

"Isn't she an actuary?" That's what Hazel mentioned the other day. "Why would you be in math classes?"

"She was in my English classes."

I sit back and fold my arms over my chest. "You like her."

"We're friends." His mouth tightens. "Best friends. And now Kit's making comments about them getting married." He downs the rest of his beer. "I don't want to make things weird with her." His throat works. "And I'd never do that to Kit," he says, like that's the end of it. His expression turns wry. "Maybe I'll do what you did and find a girl to play my fake girlfriend to make her jealous."

I nearly choke on my beer, coughing.

"Come on." He shoots me a grin. "Hazel fucking *hated* you, and then McKinnon shows up and you're together? You don't have to be a genius to figure that one out."

I start laughing. "Does everyone know?"

He shakes his head, still grinning. "Nah. I didn't say anything." Jordan drops off another beer and he thanks her.

"You're a good guy, Owens."

"And you're a good captain." He clinks his glass against mine. "Cheers, asshole."

I finish my beer, and because it's still the break, I catch Jordan's eye, silently requesting another.

It's the holiday, and I'm having fun with my friend. Hazel would say I deserve good things in my life.

"The question is," Owens says with another playful grin, "does Hazel know it's not fake?'

My smile stretches from ear to ear as I think about her whispering *say it again*. "Yep. Told her last night." Excitement races through me. I can't wait to get home to her.

"Ah, shit." Owens stands and moves to my side of the booth, engulfing me in a back-slapping bear hug while I laugh. "Happy for you, man."

Streicher walks in the door and waves hello to Jordan before making his way over to us.

"Hey," Owens calls, lifting his glass as Streicher slides into the booth. "There he is. Get a drink. We're celebrating."

———

After saying goodnight to Jordan, we pour out of the bar and into the cold, crisp night.

My head's spinning, so I take a deep breath, closing my eyes. "You guys. The air smells so good."

I think about waking up this morning with my face buried in Hazel's neck, inhaling her.

My Hazel.

I grab the front of Streicher's jacket as we walk. "Hazel smells incredible. Does Pippa smell good? Why do girls smell so good?"

He shakes his head at me, smiling, and behind him, Owens and Volkov laugh.

"You're drunk," Streicher says.

"I'm drunk," I admit to them. "I haven't been drunk in years."

"Don't worry, Miller," Owens says. "We'll get you home safe to Hazel."

I hum to myself, thoughts floating. "She's so pretty." I dig into my pocket and yank my keys out, holding up the plastic dragon key chain she got me. "Did I show you this? She bought it for me. She made me a *stocking*." My words smear together.

Owens groans. "You showed us. You showed everyone in the bar."

I smile at the little dragon, glinting from the streetlights above. It's so cute. I love it.

"I love Hazel. I love her a lot." I tuck the key chain back in my pocket and grin stupidly at Streicher. "We're going to get married."

Streicher cracks another grin, Volkov rolls his eyes, and Owens is laughing so hard he can't breathe.

"Does she know that?" Owens asks.

I pull out my phone to look at the picture of her in high school, smiling reluctantly. "Not yet. But one day."

She went with me to my mom's house. She *knows* me. She sees who I really am, and yet she's still sleeping in my bed, telling me she's not going anywhere.

A sign in a tattoo parlor window catches my eye—*OPEN*.

"Wait." I grab Owens's shirt to stop him, staring up at the glowing letters, and behind me, Volkov swears.

I grin big. "Let's go inside."

CHAPTER 70
HAZEL

A JINGLING sound wakes me in the middle of the night, followed by a thundering boom. I sit up in Rory's bed, half-asleep.

My phone's ringing. I squint at the screen. Hayden's contact photo lights it up, and I answer.

"Hayden?" I rasp, confused. "What's going on?"

"Can you open the door?"

"*Don't wake her up*," Rory says in the background, and my head clears a little more.

"I'm at Rory's." The booming noise sounds again. Someone's pounding on the door.

"I know." Hayden chuckles. "I have a surprise for you."

A moment later, I open Rory's front door. His arm is around Hayden's shoulder and he takes one look at me, wearing his t-shirt with bare legs, and his eyes light up.

"Hi, baby." His words slur and his grin stretches wider.

Hayden gives me an entertained, expectant look as he ushers Rory into the apartment. "This belongs to you. He couldn't figure out which key to use."

"Hazel." Rory grins down at me, unsteady on his feet.

I take one look at his red, bleary eyes, and burst out laughing. "Oh, wow. You have fun tonight, honey?"

The endearment slips out, but it feels right.

"Yep." His grin broadens as he wraps his arm around my waist.

"You get into any trouble?" I pat his stomach and he flinches.

Hayden snorts, and Rory slides a glance at me, still grinning. Mischief sparks in his eyes.

"Alright," Hayden says, lifting a hand and backing toward the elevator. "I'm off."

"Thanks for getting him home safe," I call as I close the door, laughing because Rory's snuffling my neck, kissing me. "Let's get you to bed, and then I'll grab you some water and electrolytes—"

He bends down and hauls me over his shoulder.

"Rory," I laugh, upside down. "Put me down."

He slaps me on the ass before his teeth scrape my hip. "No."

I deliver my own smack to his butt, still laughing and hanging upside down as he walks.

"You're so pretty," he murmurs, hand smoothing over the back of my thigh as he carries me down the hall. "I like you so much and you smell so good and I like it when you're mean to me."

I roll my eyes at him but my heart feels like it's sparkling. "You're drunk."

"Uh-huh." In the bedroom, he sets me on my feet before pressing a line of kisses down my neck. "And I also like you so much. More than anyone." His hands come to my jaw, framing my face, and he gazes down at me with his full attention, looking adorably serious. "I like you *and* I love you."

God dammit, he's so lovely to look at. It's not just that he's handsome. It's that he took care of me and decorated the apartment for Christmas and makes me laugh, and that I actually enjoy every moment with him.

He's also really fucking handsome.

"I like you more than anyone, too," I whisper. And I love him. "You should get into bed."

He wrenches his shirt off and my eyes go wide. I'm suddenly very, very awake.

"Rory," I warn, staring at the fresh tattoo covered in clear plastic wrap on his ribcage. "What the fuck is that?"

He sighs happily, smiling down at me. "It's you."

It's a dragon. I blink at the black lines stretching over his ridged muscles and swallow. Alarm bells ring in my head but he takes my face in his hands, smiling down at me.

"Because you're my tiny fire-breathing dragon," he murmurs. "Mine."

I clap my hands over my mouth, still staring at it in shock. The tattoo stretches up the length of his side. Emotions swirl inside me—disbelief and panic, and cutting through those like a hot knife, elation. Hopefulness.

Fuck.

I love that Rory likes me so much that he drunkenly got a tattoo for me, and that is so, so fucked up.

Mine. That's what he said about me. That I'm his. My heart stumbles. "You need to get it removed. This is unhinged."

His grin is back. "That's how I feel about you, Hartley. Unhinged. I'm not getting it removed."

Oh god. This is real. This is so fucking real. "Everyone's going to see."

His laugh is high and amused as he tucks a lock of my hair behind my ear. "So let them see."

It's not the *worst* tattoo I've ever seen, but it's not the best, either. It looks like a drunken middle-of-the-night tattoo.

"Hazel." My eyes lift to his, and worry rises in his gaze. "Do you hate it?"

"No," I breathe.

I'm falling for him and he got a dragon tattoo for me. I'm so in over my head it's not even funny, but a laugh bubbles out of me anyway. Rory arches an eyebrow, flipping between confusion and amusement at my reaction.

I shake my head at him. "You're insane. Why did you do this?"

"You know why."

My heart races, and all the feelings growing inside me thrash for attention as he watches me with that velvet-soft gaze.

He's drunk, and maybe tomorrow, he'll regret all of this, but even I can't ignore the evidence of the past few weeks. Holding these walls up all the time is exhausting.

I think back to Pippa's engagement party, where I wondered what it was like to be everything to someone.

It's not as scary as I thought it would be.

I want to tell him I love him. He's given me everything, and I don't want to hold it in anymore.

"I'm not scared," he whispers, "and I'm not going anywhere."

"I don't know what to do with you."

A tattoo. A fucking tattoo.

His fingers come beneath my chin and he tips my face up. "Keep me."

How could I not, knowing how kind and funny and sweet and special he is? I kept him at arm's length for as long as I could, but he never gave up.

He's my safe place to land, and when the time is right and he's sober enough to remember, I'll tell him.

CHAPTER 71
HAZEL

ON THE MORNING of the League Classic, New Year's Eve, Rory and I meet with the owner of the studio space.

Laura's family friend, Nadir, leads us on a tour, and I can barely talk, I'm so excited and nervous.

It's perfect.

"Wiring looks good," Rory murmurs in my ear, and I stifle a snort. I'm sure he's never looked at wiring in his life, but last night, I spotted him googling what to look for when renting yoga and dance spaces.

"I'll give you two a few minutes," Nadir says. "Take your time. I'll be outside if you have any questions."

"And lots of room in the foyer for people to store their stuff," Rory adds, gesturing at the lobby. "Do you think you'd need to do a lot of renos?"

Until the end of January, this space is a yoga studio. "Maybe a new coat of paint. Adding the ballet barre to one of the studios." My mouth twists, and an urgent excitement hums in my chest. "The smaller rooms would need shelving and equipment." I meet Rory's curious gaze. "I like it," I admit.

"Yeah?"

"A lot." My teeth sink into my bottom lip as I bounce on the balls of my feet. Is this happening? It feels too good to be true.

It would be available as of February first, Nadir told us. On my first mentoring session with the woman from the states, we talked through how the next few months would work if I rented a space. I'd probably need a month for small renovations, and in the meantime, I could prepare the admin side of the business, like creating a schedule, doing the marketing, building a website, and hiring staff.

Until we're ready to open, I could continue working with the Storm. I'd still have my other teaching gigs to bring in money. It would be incredibly busy, but I could make it happen.

My heart flutters as I gaze through the windows at the mountains. For this place? I could make it happen.

The situation with my mom wafts back into my mind, and I remember the phone call we had before Christmas. Can I do this? I want it to be so much more than a fitness studio, but what if I'm not ready?

What if I am, though? Bright, sparkling excitement bursts through me. What if it works out and it's everything I want it to be?

Rory's hands land on my shoulders, kneading the tight muscles, and I relax under his touch while my mind whirs.

If it was Pippa hesitating, I'd tell her to give the middle finger to imposter syndrome and get out of her own way. I rub my palm over my sternum, glancing around the space.

It really is perfect. Rent's a little high, but manageable.

Rory believes in me, and his encouraging smile is the nudge I need. My hand slips into his and he gives me a squeeze.

"Hey, Nadir?" I call, leading Rory out of the rental space. "I'll take it."

Early that afternoon in Whistler, Ward sits across from us in the hotel meeting room wearing a curious frown. The team's warm-up skate starts in half an hour, but I sent him an urgent meeting request.

This thing with Connor has gone on long enough. If it was happening to a colleague or friend, I'd urge them to talk to someone and put a stop to it. Between this and signing the lease, I'm doing all the hard things today.

"Thanks for meeting with me on short notice," I tell him before taking a deep breath.

My heart pounds, but I remind myself that Connor *kissed* me. It was unprofessional and gross and went against everything the team promotes. I don't know why this is nerve-racking.

Maybe because we egged Connor on all season. We purposefully made him jealous. A tiny part of me whispers *this is your fault*, but I squash that voice like a bug.

It wasn't okay, even if Connor was jealous.

Rory's hand slips into my lap, squeezing my fingers, and my nerves settle.

"The night of the charity event," I tell Ward, "Connor McKinnon got very drunk and kissed me. I told him to back off and he wouldn't."

Revulsion climbs up my throat, putting a bad taste in my mouth. Alarm flashes in Ward's eyes as he listens.

"I don't want to be his physio anymore."

Ward's jaw tightens. "You're definitely not his physio anymore." His eyes meet mine, and I see fury and regret. "I'm so sorry, Hazel. McKinnon is benched until this is resolved. I need to think more about his future with the team." His throat works. "What can we do to support you? Whatever resources you need, they're available."

I shake my head, letting a breath out of my tight lungs. Ward's concerned reaction is already calming me. "I'm okay. Thank you for taking it seriously."

"Of course. If you change your mind, you know where to find me. I'll back you up." His brow furrows harder and he shakes his head. "I'm so sorry, again."

"I know." I give Ward a tight smile, squeezing Rory's hand. "Thanks."

———

In the hall outside, Rory puts his hands on my shoulders to stop me and searches my eyes.

"You okay?"

I nod, mouth twisting. "I wish the whole thing hadn't happened, and talking to Ward wasn't fun, but I'm glad we did."

"Me, too." He pulls me into his chest and gives me a tight, warm hug, pressing his mouth to my temple. "I'm proud of you."

"Why?" I lean my head against his sculpted chest, listening to his heartbeat.

"You did the hard thing."

I hum. "Thank you for coming with me."

He makes a scoffing noise. "That's what we do for each other, Hartley."

The warm-up skate starts soon, so Rory heads down to the arena and I return to our suite, thinking about another hard thing I've been putting off. I flick the fireplace on in the living room and sink onto the couch, staring out the windows at the snow-covered mountains surrounding the ski resort.

My mom and I haven't addressed things since we spoke before the charity event and I lost my cool with her. My parents phoned on Christmas, but Rory and I were on speakerphone with them, Pippa, and Jamie, so the conversation was about easy topics.

Before I change my mind, I'm dialing.

"Hi, honey," my mom answers.

"Hey."

"You must be at the League Classic by now."

"Yeah." On the suite's patio, a bird hops around before flying off.

Keep being a safe place for her to land, Pippa said.

Everyone's journey moves at a different pace, my mentor said during our first meeting.

"I'm really sorry about what I said," I tell my mom, my throat feeling tight. "I shouldn't have pushed you so hard, and you're right. You can feel however you want about yourself."

"No, Hazel—" She cuts herself off, pausing. I can practically see her pained, uncomfortable expression on the other end. "I didn't realize it had that effect on you. I forget, you know, that just because you aren't little anymore doesn't mean you don't absorb what I say like a sponge." She sighs. "I never want you to feel bad about yourself or think you're anything less than beautiful."

"I don't," I say quickly. "I really don't feel that way."

"Good."

There's a beat of silence between us, and for the first time, I feel like I haven't failed her. I left space for her to feel what she's feeling and I'm not making her feel like shit about it.

"If someone wanted to feel differently about themselves," she starts, a note of reluctance in her voice. "What, um, or where would they start?"

Emotion rises in me and I blink it away. "Well," I say,

clearing my throat, "an easy way to start would be to only say positive things about myself. When I think I look good, I say it out loud." I laugh to myself. "Even if I'm alone in my apartment."

My mom chuckles.

"And maybe I'd keep a journal, and every time a negative feeling about myself or my body comes up, I'd tell my journal about it. I'd write down what triggered that feeling—what I was watching on TV, what I was reading or thinking about that made me feel like I wasn't enough, so I can find a pattern."

She listens in silence.

"And maybe after a month or two of that, I'd make a list of all the things I secretly want to do but feel like I can't, and why. Clothes I want to wear, places I want to visit, activities I want to try."

I picture my mom dancing. Not at twenty, but now, in her fifties. Strong and tall and happy and beautiful.

"And when I felt strong enough, I'd list the reasons I can't do those things and ask myself if they're really true."

I hit the brakes because I don't want to overwhelm her.

"And I would remind that person," I add, "they can go at whatever pace they want, and they're not expected to be perfect, because no one is."

"Well, I'll let her know what you said," my mom says lightly, and we both chuckle. "I love you, honey."

"I love you, too."

"THIS GAME IS FOR THE FANS," Ward says in the dressing room that evening, moments before the game, "but it's also for us." His eyes land on me. "Remind yourselves of what matters and have fun out there tonight."

He crooks a smile at me, and I grin back. The players head to the ice, and I'm the last one out of the dressing room when McKinnon calls my name from behind.

"Miller."

He's in street clothes. Players sent wary glances at him the entire time Ward spoke. By now, even the guys who weren't at the bar that night know what he did.

"Your fucking *girlfriend* got me benched," he snaps, stalking toward me. "Thanks a lot."

"You got yourself benched." I bring myself to my full height, staring him down.

He shakes his head, seething. "You know what my fucking problem is?" He shoves a finger in my face. "You. You've always been my fucking problem, Miller."

He wants to fight. I take in the way he looks at me with hate in his eyes. Last year, or even two months ago, I'd take this opportunity to scrap.

What matters, Ward said.

Hazel matters. Streicher and Pippa and the team and hockey matter, but McKinnon? He's nothing. He's angry and selfish and bitter. I feel bad for him.

McKinnon doesn't matter, and I don't want to be anything like him.

Hazel would want me to walk away, and more than anything, I want to be the right guy for Hazel, and I want to be the captain the team needs.

"I hope you figure things out," I tell McKinnon as I walk away. "Good luck."

This is the captain and the guy I want to be.

———

The other team scores another goal in the third period, tying the game, and Ward calls for a time out.

We skate toward the bench. Above the outdoor rink, stars twinkle in the dark sky. It's below zero in the mountain ski town, and the fans are bundled up in hats and gloves and thick winter coats. The pickup league is here, watching the game from the front-row seats I snagged for them. Under a plaid blanket, Hazel and Pippa huddle together, sipping hot cider.

And now the strategy I've been using on the ice with assists isn't working anymore. A weight settles in my gut.

"Calgary sees what we're doing," Ward says, eyes lingering on me. "They watched enough games this season to know you're the decoy."

I give him a terse nod. This game doesn't count toward our season, but we're still competitive, and we still want to win. I need to step into my old role and be the star.

Stars score goals. My dad's watching, I'm sure.

"What's the plan, Captain?" Ward asks.

I glance over my shoulder to Hazel, and she gives me a small smile.

You're unhinged, she said, laughing, when she saw my tattoo that night after the pickup game.

The pickup game. *You've got a hell of a wrist-shot,* I remember saying to Owens that night.

Something clicks in my head, and I look to him.

"I think you should play offense again," I tell him, and his face goes blank. "Center forward."

He gestures at Volkov. "We always play together."

"I know."

Maybe it won't work, but Ward watches with a curious spark in his eyes, and that night Owens played offense against the pickup league? He was so fucking happy, and good at it, too. I think about how his face lit up when he scored and how he might be in the wrong position. He's probably been trained as a defenseman since he was a kid, just like I've been a forward since I was a kid.

"Let's just try it this once and see how it goes," I urge. "I'll play defense."

Volkov nods. "Worth a shot."

"I've always played defense." Owens looks reluctant. "I don't know if this is a good idea."

"If it doesn't work, we move on. But this is our shot to try something new. What matters?" I ask him before looking around at the rest of the team. Everyone is quiet. "This isn't just a job, and we aren't machines. It needs to be more than that."

Owens looks uneasy, but he nods. "Alright. Let's do it."

Ward runs through the play again, and as the guys skate off to take formation, Ward grips my shoulder.

"I knew you'd figure it out, Miller."

I smile, feeling that weight in my gut dissolve into something light before skating to my position.

"Here we go, boys," I call as the puck drops.

Owens steals it, and we run the play so fast the other team doesn't know what's happening. He passes between the other forwards and sinks it in the net, all within twenty seconds.

The fans are on their feet, cheering and screaming. The look of relief and pride on Owens's face makes my heart soar, and this time, it's me putting him in a headlock while he laughs and pushes me off.

"Knew you could do it," I tell him, and he grins wider.

———

At the end of the third period, we're up two points. It's a matter of running out the clock at this point. They don't need me to score, they don't need me to be the star I used to be. I've done my job as captain.

When play stops, I look over to Hazel behind the glass, who winks at me. I pretend to yawn, rolling my eyes, and she laughs, light spilling out of her.

You deserve good things in your life, she said when we ran around Stanley Park.

I want to score a goal tonight. It's not about the attention or the glory of winning the game; I just want the satisfaction of the play working out, of doing what I love.

"Let's run an old play," I tell Ward and the team. I swallow. I don't want to come off as selfish. "I want to score one for myself."

Owens flashes me a shit-eating grin. "Jealous of all the attention I'm getting, Miller?"

I shove him off as he jostles me, but Ward nods. "Run it."

We line up for the face-off, me playing center forward again, and when the puck drops, I'm flying, skating hard toward the net before I slide it in. The stands erupt with noise and my heart lifts, but it's Hazel I look to. She's on her feet, clapping and grinning at me with a proud smile.

CHAPTER 73

RORY

"YOU'RE sure you don't mind spending your New Year's Eve out here instead of with the guys?" Hazel asks as we glide around the ice that night, hand in hand. Her hair flies behind her, fluttering in the wind, and the tip of her nose is red from the cold. Under the stars in the sky, her eyes glow bright and mesmerizing.

"You're sure your ankle feels okay?"

Her laugh is a puff of air in the cold night. "Alright. Point taken."

I move so I'm facing her, skating backward, holding both her hands, and she tilts her head at me with narrowed eyes. "Something changed during the game tonight."

"Caught that, did you?"

She smiles, waiting, and I'm quiet as we circle the rink.

"Everyone compares me to my dad. I look like him, I play like him." I catch myself. "Or, I used to."

Her hand squeezes mine.

"And I believed it, that I wasn't just like him but that my life would be the same as his. I'd be old and miserable and alone and obsessed with hockey, and any woman who got to know me would see whatever ugly thing women see in my dad and walk away."

My heart beats with urgency, blood whooshing in my ears. I've never said these things out loud.

Hazel gives me a soft, kind smile, though, and I think maybe she knew all these things. We never talked about them, but somehow she knew, and instead of being scared that she can see right through me, I'm relieved and grateful.

"But I'm not that guy. I just let myself think that." My throat feels thick. "I never thought I would be a good captain, but I want to be, and I think part of being a good leader might be seeing what people want and who they are, instead of who they're told to be."

Hazel hums. "You're a good captain."

Affection and pride flood my chest. "Because of you, I am."

She looks down, smiling to herself, and I wonder if her heart's exploding with this feeling, too.

"It's New Year's Eve," she says quietly.

"I know."

She sends me a side-long glance, and not for the first time, I wish I could read her mind. "Our deal was supposed to end tomorrow."

My heart stops. We said it wasn't fake anymore, but maybe she's changed her mind. "Do you want it to?"

"No." Her answer is immediate as she turns to me, eyes roaming my face, searching my gaze. "I don't want it to be over." Her lips part and she looks like she wants to say more, but she just bites her lip again. "I don't want it to end."

A possessive ache fills me. I'm so happy with her that it hurts, so I put my hands on her waist and skate us to a stop, holding on tight to her because she isn't great at braking.

"I don't want it to end, either," I tell her, brushing her hair back, looking down into her eyes. "Let's keep it going."

"For how long?" She looks so hopeful but uncertain that my heart breaks all over again.

"For as long as you want, Hartley, I'm yours. Even longer, probably."

Forever, I hope.

"I need to tell you something," she whispers, and her eyes flash with worry and nerves.

When I take her hands, they're shaking.

"I love you," she says quietly, searching my gaze.

All I can hear is my pulse beating in my ears; all I can see is Hazel.

"I was scared to say it. I'm still scared, but—" She cuts herself off, biting her lip, studying me as my heart does somersaults. "I always want you to know you're loved."

Christ, my heart. My sweet, terrified Hazel is handing me her fragile trust to hold in the palm of my hand. I'll do anything to protect it.

"I do." Emotion surges through me, so strong it hurts. "I've known for a long time."

"You have?" Her brows lift.

I nod. My hand slips to her cheek, and her skin is cold under my touch. "I was waiting until you were ready."

She holds my eyes, swallowing. "You're so patient."

"You're worth the wait."

The furrow in her brow eases, and she lets out a long breath. "Aren't you going to tell me you love me, too?"

My mouth tips into a smile. "You know I do."

She nods. "Yeah. I know you do."

I lean down to kiss her, hands in her hair.

"I love you," I say anyway, and she smiles against my lips.

This must be what it feels like to have everything I've ever wanted.

"I love you, too. Happy New Year, Rory."

"Happy New Year, Hazel."

TELLING Rory I loved him unleashes something in him, because the second we're in the elevator ascending to our suite, his hands are all over me.

"I thought about this all day," he says as he rubs slick circles on my clit, hand down the front of my pants with a strong arm locked across my front to hold me close.

In the mirror, I watch my lips part, arching against him. His erection pushes against my ass while he strokes me higher and higher. My body responds to him, thrumming and tightening.

The elevator stops at a floor that isn't ours, and Rory takes his hand back, straightening up. The doors open, someone steps on, and the three of us stand there in silence while my heart hammers and my clit aches for more attention.

Rory meets my eyes in our reflection and he gives me a tiny smirk. I press down on my laugh.

He's wild, and he makes me wild, and I can't imagine the trajectory of my life if we hadn't gotten together. Life would be so dull without him.

When I'm a hundred years old and thinking back on my life, I'll think about being in love with Rory Miller.

The person steps off and before the door is fully closed, his mouth crushes mine, claiming me. On our floor, we stumble to the door of our suite, kissing and laughing and fumbling for the keycard.

"We're not even inside yet," I laugh as he pulls my jacket off.

"Hurry up, then," he says.

My sweater is off the second we step in the door. His follows. The path to the bedroom is a trail of discarded clothes. Rory's hands are everywhere on me. His mouth is urgent, pressing kisses down my neck before returning to my mouth, coaxing me open. He slips an arm around my waist to hold me upright while he yanks my leggings off before his gaze drifts over the cream lace set I'm wearing.

His eyes glaze and he lets out a heavy breath before he hooks the bra cups down and flicks his tongue over my nipple, fingers toying with the other. My pulse thrums between my legs, and I sigh as his mouth works, sinking my fingers into his hair and tugging lightly, pulling a deep moan from him.

It's not sex with Rory; it's so much more.

His pants and boxers disappear, and he removes my bra and underwear in a distracted way that makes me smile. He's already hard, cock jutting out at an angle as he hands me my jersey.

"Put this on," he says in a rough voice, eyes going dark, and a shiver runs through me.

I'm independent and strong and self-sufficient, but I'm powerless against Rory's possessive, demanding side.

I slip the jersey over my head, the fabric brushing against my peaked nipples as I pull my hair out of the neckline, and Rory's gaze roams me with territorial heat. I lean up on my tiptoes to kiss him, savoring the feel of his mouth on mine, the light scrape of his stubble on my chin, the feel of his sculpted chest under my palms.

We kiss for maybe ten seconds before his hands are on my hips and he's turning me around. We've bumped up against the dresser, and above it sits a large mirror.

I meet Rory's hot gaze in the reflection, just like in the elevator, and his mouth hooks up.

"I love seeing you in my jersey, Hartley." His teeth nip my neck and I press back into his arousal. His hand drifts between my legs, drawing those same slick circles from the elevator, and more heat blooms inside me while I watch his hand work in the reflection.

"I love when you play nice for me." His eyes sear me, watching with satisfaction, and I get wetter.

"Rory." His circles become tighter, firmer, and my eyebrows pull together. "I don't want to wait."

"Greedy," he murmurs. "So fucking greedy for me, aren't you?"

Every stubborn cell in my body claws at me to argue but I nod, sighing with frustration and impatience. "I want you."

Something pleased and smug lifts in his expression, and he starts toward his bag for the condom, but I stop him with a hand on his arm. "Wait." My heart hammers. "I don't want to use a condom tonight."

Rory's breathing turns shallow. "I've never done that before."

"Me neither."

I've never trusted anyone to do this, but I trust Rory. I've never loved anyone like I love Rory.

"You sure?" His eyebrow goes up, and his gaze locks with mine, so full of concern.

"I want to. Do you want to?"

He gives me that dark, knowing smile. "Oh, Hartley. I want to."

His mouth returns to mine, kissing me so sweetly. Rory's

the perfect mix—cocky and competitive and playful, but with a sweet openness that makes me melt into him. His tongue glides against mine, sucking lightly, and I breathe in his masculine scent that's forever imprinted on me.

He pulls back, turning me to face the mirror, his hand heavy on my shoulder for leverage as he lines himself up at my entrance. I flatten my hands on the dresser, bracing myself.

My thoughts stop as he nudges into me, stretching me, and in the mirror, I see my parted lips. His slack jaw and pinning gaze. His big hand on my shoulder, tightening against my jersey.

"Fuck," he chokes out as he fills me with his thick length. "This changes things. Holy fuck, Hazel." He leans closer, seating himself to the hilt inside me while a shudder rolls through me.

"You feel so *good*," he groans in my ear, and I could come from hearing Rory's pleasure alone.

He pulls out and pushes back in, hitting a spot inside me that scatters sparks up my spine.

"It's so deep this way," I moan.

"I know." His hand tightens on my shoulder, holding me steady while he thrusts in and out, finding his rhythm, and my nerves start to fray. "So fucking good with you, Hazel. You're exactly what I need."

Rory taking his pleasure sends another ripple of heat through me. I clench around his thick length, and a groan rumbles out of him. In the mirror, his eyes burn hotter.

"You like hearing that?" His voice is a low tease in my ear, watching my reflection. "You like hearing that you were exactly what my life was missing and that every moment is better with you?"

My gaze drops to the tattoo over the chiseled muscle of his torso, and I nod.

"Good." He hits a particularly sensitive spot, making me whimper. "Because you're so fucking perfect, Hazel." His hips move faster, and a lock of hair falls into his eyes as he watches me in the mirror with a hungry look.

I moan again, pressing back into him. The way Rory's hitting my G-spot is making my blood heat and thicken, and I can feel the release building low in my stomach.

"Yes, baby, just like that. Keep taking it." His eyes are feverish, and the heavy ache between my legs tightens. His gaze drops to the jersey I'm wearing, and his nostrils flare with pride. "As deep as you can."

My arousal soaks my thighs, and the feel of him inside me with nothing between us? It's like nothing I've ever experienced.

His eyes clench tight like he's grappling for control. "I'm so fucking close, Hazel."

"Not yet," I moan.

He shakes his head, gaze returning to me with a drugged, desperate look in his eyes. "Not yet," he repeats to himself. "Not yet." He curses. "You're so fucking *tight*."

I clench my muscles on purpose and his eyes widen.

"Don't you fucking dare, Hartley," he says with a laugh. He delivers a sharp slap to my ass before he palms it, squeezing. "I'm obsessed with your ass," he growls. "Always have been."

I tighten again, wearing my own smirk as his jaw ticks.

"You want to play?" He leans forward, surrounding me, bringing his hand between my legs, drawing wet circles on my clit in a way he *knows* is going to make me come.

Fucking antagonist. I hold his eyes in the mirror, clenching tighter, and he shakes his head, wearing that lazy smile, circling faster. A sweet ache of affection takes up all the space in my chest, expanding through me, because knowing Rory and getting to see all the sides of him, it's the best gift I've ever gotten.

Love bursts in my chest, and the tremors start.

"Rory," I moan, dropping my head. It's too much, the feel of him inside me, pushing against all the spots that make me lose my mind. The competitive focus in his eyes only makes it hotter.

"I hate to lose, Hartley," he grits out.

My release closes in on me and I see stars, muscles spasming around his arousal. Wave after wave of pleasure ripples through me but I anchor to the feeling of him inside me, his hand gripping my shoulder, and the desperate, possessive look in his eyes as I spin out, shuddering. Again and again, my pussy clamps down on him, and a moment later, I feel him stiffen.

BEING INSIDE HAZEL, watching her face in the mirror as she falls apart for me, it snaps me in half.

My hips jerk against her, rhythm turning erratic as I slide toward my release. There's no holding off, not when she's wearing my name on her back so enthusiastically, not when her pussy is still squeezing and gripping my cock like a fist, and sure as fuck not when there's nothing between us and I can feel every slip and slick inside her perfect pussy. The heavy ache in my balls surges and I'm pounding against her, coming inside her, losing my fucking mind with pleasure and need as I groan her name.

It's always been Hazel.

I give everything I have to give, spilling into her, eyes locked with hers in the mirror as her pussy flutters around me, and when our orgasms subside, I'm pulling her to me, burying my face in her neck and huffing in her scent.

"You're mine," I rasp, chest heaving for air, and she nods.

Running on pure instinct, pure desire to claim her in every way, my hand drops to between her legs. I pull out of her, dipping my fingers inside her, watching as her eyes flare with surprise and desire.

"Like that?" I ask, stroking in and out of her, my fingers slipping against the wetness of my release.

She nods, eyes going hazy.

I drag my fingers up between her cheeks, circling the pucker of her ass, drawing my release over her. My heart pounds and possessive instincts roar through me as I push my wet finger inside.

She gasps. The way she's positioned, braced against the dresser, bent over and open for me, it both satisfies me and makes me want more. As much as she's willing to give me.

My perfect, trusting Hazel.

"I'm addicted to that look on your face," I tell her.

My finger pumps in and out, working my cum back into her, and she tightens around me, meeting my gaze in the mirror, lip curling with need. Blood rushes to my cock, and within seconds, I'm stiff again, aching and ready to go.

With my finger still buried inside her tight asshole, I lift my gaze to hers with a question in my eyes, and she jerks a nod like she can't wait.

I sink back into her tight pussy, groaning at how wet and hot she feels. Around my finger, she tightens again. My other hand drifts to her clit, and within a minute, her eyes go wide and she starts to flutter around my cock.

"Rory," she says, gasping for air. "I'm coming again."

I slam in and out of her, stroking my finger deep inside her ass as she clenches, and a moment later, my release follows.

"This doesn't happen," I choke out as I spill into her, heat rushing through my blood and pressure expanding through me. In my hazy thoughts, I remember her saying that to me once. We've had a hundred firsts together, and when I think forward to the future, I beg the universe that we'll have a hundred more.

After, in the shower, I kiss Hazel on every inch of her body while the hot water trickles down her skin.

She once asked me what made me feel worthy and I came up with nothing, but as I wrap her in a towel and carry her to bed, my answer glows bright like the stars outside our window.

CHAPTER 76

RORY

TWO DAYS LATER, I sit in my car outside my mom's place, staring up at the house with a tight, nervous feeling in my chest. It's late afternoon, and the January sky is already dim.

"Freaking out yet?" I asked Hazel this morning when we woke up.

She gave me a soft, sleepy smile and shook her head. "Nope."

After driving home from the League Classic yesterday, we stopped at her place to pick up more of her stuff. Her hair products clutter my shower, the bathroom drawer is now filled with her makeup, and her clothes hang in the closet.

My life is so full with Hazel in it, and now I need to make sure I don't fuck it all up. I should be at home taking it easy before my game tonight, but after Hazel took the leap and told me how she felt this weekend, I need to address things with my mom so I don't repeat the pattern. It can't wait.

And a part of me is addicted to this happy, full feeling. Hazel said my mom misses me. Maybe there's a chance for us.

Headlights flare behind me as my mom pulls into the driveway, parking beside me. She gets out of the car with a grocery bag in each hand, dipping down to peer in my passenger window.

"Rory?"

I climb out of the car. "Hi, Mom."

"Don't you have a game tonight?"

"Yeah." My eyebrows lift in surprise that she knew that. "Can I talk to you?"

"Of course." Her expression turns wary. "It's cold out. Let's go inside."

In the foyer, I kick my shoes off and set my jacket over the back of the couch while she zips around, flicking lights on with nervous energy, darting glances at me.

"What can I get you?" she asks. "All I have is water and almond milk, unfortunately. I didn't know you'd be dropping by." Her eyebrows shoot up. "Tea. I can make tea."

I shake my head. "I'm fine. I don't need anything. We can just talk here." I take a seat on the couch.

"How's Hazel?" she asks when she takes the seat across from me, crossing her legs.

"Good. She's subbing for another teacher tonight at a studio so she won't be at my game." She offered to come here with me, but this is something I need to do on my own.

It feels weird, talking with my mom so casually like this. My gaze lands on a framed photo on the side table, and my heart jumps into my throat.

It's me and my mom on a hike when I was a kid. Joffre Lakes outside Whistler, with the turquoise lake behind us. Her arm around me, both of us wearing big smiles.

"That wasn't there for the Christmas party," I tell her, frowning at the photo. My phone buzzes with a text in my back pocket but I ignore it.

She shifts with embarrassment. "I put it away because I didn't want you to feel uncomfortable."

She thinks me knowing she cherishes those memories of us would make me uncomfortable? "Why would it make me uncomfortable?"

Her mouth tightens. "We don't have the strongest relationship."

"You're my mom."

The words hang in the air between us, and the embarrassment fades from her eyes, leaving pain. "I know." Her throat works. "What did you want to talk about?"

There's no gentle or easy way to say this, so I blurt out the question that's been sitting in my head for years as my phone buzzes again.

"Why did you leave me?"

She freezes, staring at me a long moment before her gaze drops to her hands clasped in her lap.

"What was it about me and Dad that made you want to leave? What did I do?"

"Nothing." She gives me a shocked look. "You did nothing wrong, Rory."

"Then why did you leave us?" The words are strained, and I feel sick. "Why don't we *know* each other anymore?"

"At the time, I thought I was doing the right thing." The living room is silent except for the ticking clock in the kitchen. "Your father was *obsessed* with making you into a better version of himself, but you were a kid. You were going to five a.m. practices and working on your slapshots out in the driveway for fourteen hours a day on weekends, but I didn't want every hour of your day to be about hockey and getting drafted when you were twelve." Her eyes move over my face like she's wading through memories, and she shakes her head. "It was all you cared about, though. You and your dad?" She crosses her fingers. "You were like this. All you talked about was hockey this, hockey that, and then there was me on the periphery, trying and failing to be a part of your life. I didn't want to sour something you loved so much. And by that time, my relationship with Rick was in pieces. I loved your father, I still love him, but he was always just waiting for me to leave."

I think about Hazel, and my skin prickles at the similarity—how, for a long time, I was waiting for her to realize she didn't want me. My phone buzzes again and again. And then it starts ringing. I haul it out—it's my dad calling, fucking perfect timing—and turn it on airplane mode to block the rest of the world out before I set it face down on a side table.

"And I told myself that when I asked if you wanted to come with me, I gave you a choice—"

"I was twelve!" The words come out sharper and louder than I meant, and my mom flinches. "I was twelve years old. And you wanted me to choose between you and Dad? That's really fucked up."

"I know." She nods, taking a deep breath. "I hate myself for that, Rory. I think about it every day." She glances at the photo of us with a sad smile, throat working. "When you stayed with me, you wanted nothing to do with me. I thought you didn't need me. Your dad told me the both of you didn't need me, and I believed him because I wanted the best for you. But now I realize you were just being a preteen. I should have fought back. I shouldn't have given up custody."

"You gave up so easily." My chest aches. "Like you didn't care."

"I thought it was the right thing to do." She swallows, staring at her hands again. "If I could do it all again, I'd do it differently. I know that doesn't erase anything, though."

"I did need you. I still do."

Hope rises in her gaze. "I think about you every day, honey. I have Google alerts on my phone. I watch all your games."

I shake my head. "I thought you hated hockey."

"I hated that hockey was becoming the only thing in your life. Your dad put hockey above all else—above me, especially—because he told himself it was the only thing he was good at."

Like me. If only I'd talked to my mom months ago, maybe she would have told me what it took me so long to figure out. All these things we should have said years ago, but instead, we kept them to ourselves and lived our lies.

"I'm sorry I acted like a little shit," I tell her.

She shakes her head. "I'm sorry I didn't fight harder for us."

She gets to her feet and when I stand, she wraps her arms around my stomach, squeezing me tight. Relief and elation and acceptance and love course through me, expanding into every corner of my chest. That worthy feeling floods me.

"I love you," she says, squeezing me, and her familiar scent washes over me, making my chest tighten with affection.

"I love you, too," I say into her hair.

"I want to come to your games and sit in the front row beside Hazel and Jamie's fiancée. I see Jamie's mom sitting with them, and I want to be there, too."

Warmth radiates through me. "I'll get you tickets."

"And I want to have monthly dinners with you and Hazel."

"Done."

It's the future I want—talking and laughing with my mom and Hazel over the dinner table.

"Honey." My mom glances with worry at the clock in the kitchen. "The traffic gets really bad on the bridge to downtown on game nights."

She's right. Attendance at pregame team meetings is nonnegotiable, especially for the captain, and even if I leave right now, I'll barely make it.

"I love you," I say again at the door, and the smile she gives me warms me.

"I love you, too." She gives me another quick hug. "Now, go. I'll be watching on TV."

I hurry to my car. On the merge lane to the bridge, traffic comes to a standstill, and my anxiety spikes.

The bridge is an endless line of red taillights. There must have been an accident. I suck in a deep breath and go to call Streicher through my car's Bluetooth, but it isn't connected. My hand slips into my back pocket for my phone, but it isn't there.

Fuck. I left it at my mom's place, on the side table.

Traffic inches along, not fucking fast enough. I groan, gritting my teeth in frustration and impatience. Ward hates players being late—it's the ultimate disrespect to the team, the fans, and him.

I'm stuck in the line of cars on the bridge, so all I can do is wait.

CHAPTER 77

RORY

I BURST into the dressing room.

"Defense is their weakness, so play accordingly," Ward is saying, lifting his eyebrows in disapproval while everyone stares.

"Sorry." I'm breathing hard, gut in knots. I think I left my car door open.

He turns to the rest of the team. "Alright, get out there for the last warm-up and let's win this."

The team disperses and I rush to my stall, yanking my clothes off and dressing in my equipment as fast as I can.

"Miller." Ward's still frowning. "You're in pregame press tonight."

I nod again, and he's gone.

On the ice, I do a few laps before I head to the press station at the side of the rink.

The reporter gives me a friendly nod. "Good evening. As of this afternoon, an insider with the Vancouver Storm said the team is entertaining trade offers for you from various organizations."

My pulse stops. I stare at the reporter, not sure if I heard right.

"And your father and agent, Rick Miller," she adds, "confirmed the presence of these offers."

The missed call from him. The texts blowing up my phone.

"We've seen a different playing style from you this season, and you're no longer the top scorer in the league," she continues, but I'm half listening. "How does the Storm organization feel about this when you have the highest salary in professional hockey?"

She tips the microphone to me while my world collapses.

I'm getting traded. I thought Ward was proud and all the pieces were falling into place, but now I'm being traded. I'm getting sent away from the woman I love.

She signed a studio lease; she needs to stay in Vancouver. She's going to need me over the next year as she opens her studio. I can't leave her.

Before our life together can truly start, it's over. I say the first thing that comes to mind.

"I'm not leaving."

The reporter gives me a strange frown. The decision is up to the coach and owners, not me. "Is there another organization you're favoring?"

"No." I shake my head, pulse hammering. "I'm not going." My words are sharp. "I love this team, I love playing for Tate Ward, and I love my girlfriend. Her job and life are here and I'm not moving away from her." I can feel the stubborn set of my jaw as I glare at the reporter. "I'm not leaving."

CHAPTER 78

HAZEL

I FINISH TEACHING SHORTLY after nine that evening, but instead of walking home to my apartment, I head to Rory's.

Maybe I'll take some photos for him, I think with a coy grin. Ward has a no-phones policy in the dressing room, but Rory will see them after the game.

The night is chilly as I walk, and I'm overcome with the urge to text him. When I pull my phone out, though, a slew of messages and missed calls light up the screen.

Three from Pippa. A few from my dad. Texts from Hayden and a handful of other players and staff.

Call me, Pippa says.

"Finally," she answers when I call.

"Tell me what the fuck is happening."

She hesitates.

"Tell me." People on the sidewalk flinch away from my sharp tone.

"Rory might get traded."

I stop walking, and every muscle in my body tenses. "What?" I ask softly.

No. I heard wrong.

"Rory might get traded," she repeats, quieter. "I'm sorry."

But—no. He loves playing for Ward, and he's worked so hard to earn his spot on the team. Rory's finally playing in a way that makes him happy. His teammates are like his brothers, and he's developed into an incredible captain. He's talking to his mom again.

I love him. He can't leave Vancouver.

A weird noise comes out of my throat, but no words form.

"Rumors started online this afternoon," Pippa adds.

I've been teaching all afternoon, and my phone has been in my bag on silent.

"His dad confirmed the Storm have offers from other teams."

I've seen this happen before. The trade rumors start and teams throw in their offers for a player in case there's any legitimacy to them.

We love each other. I finally gathered the courage to say it to him, and now this? Our relationship is so new and fragile, and now that I've signed a studio lease, my dream is happening *here*. I can't move. I can't go with him unless I back out of the lease.

"I'm sorry," she whispers.

We say a tense goodbye, and I open Google. The top search result is a video, and I open it right there on the sidewalk.

It's Rory being interviewed in pregame press, wearing the same stricken look he wore during yoga that time, like he's been blindsided. My eyes sting. He doesn't want to leave the Storm, and my heart's breaking for him.

"And your father and agent, Rick Miller," the reporter says, "confirmed the presence of these offers."

His jaw ticks. "I'm not leaving."

My eyes go wide. What is he doing?

"I love this team," he continues, staring daggers at the reporter like it's her fault he might get traded. "I love playing for Tate Ward, and I love my girlfriend. Her job and life are here and I'm not moving away from her."

"Oh my god," I murmur, heart pounding. "What did he just do?"

My eyes go to the time—the second period just ended. If I hurry, I can get to the arena and talk to Rory before the third period starts.

My unhinged, impulsive, heart-on-his-sleeve hockey player needs me.

CHAPTER 79

HAZEL

"I'M SORRY," the security guard says when I try to get into the hall that leads to the dressing room. "If you don't have your employee pass, I can't let you in."

I'm breathing hard. The third period's going to start any second. I need to get back there before Rory gets on the ice. He must be freaking out.

I growl with frustration. "My photo is on the team website. I can show ID."

The security guard shakes his head. "Employee pass only. Those are the rules."

He's new and he's just doing his job, so I clamp my mouth shut, even as every cell in my body vibrates with impatience.

Five minutes later, ticket in hand, I'm hurrying down the steps in the stands toward the tunnel where the players will come out of. I take a spot along the railing, shaking with anticipation. People stare at me, but I don't care. They probably think I'm an obsessed fan, or maybe they recognize me as Rory's girlfriend and wonder what the hell I'm doing, but all I can think about is how devastated Rory must be.

Finally, the team files out. Hayden gives me a questioning

look, but my attention's on the player with a C on his jersey right behind him.

"Rory."

He does a double take at me, shock all over his face, and I lean over the railing, grab the front of his jersey, and pull him to me.

Security guards rush at us from all sides.

"Ma'am," one says, "take your hands off him."

"Back off," I snap.

I am the unhinged, impulsive one with her heart on her sleeve.

Rory starts to smile, eyes wide like he's afraid of me, but he shakes his head at the employee behind me. "It's okay." His eyes meet mine. "What—"

"I love you." I pull him closer, and his hands come to my shoulders so I don't fall over the railing.

He huffs a laugh, relief flooding his eyes. "I love you, too."

"I know. I'm not letting you go."

"I'm not letting *you* go."

I see it in his eyes—he means it. Rory's all in, but so am I.

The players are either on the ice or the bench, and Ward glances over at us, wondering what's holding up the captain. My gaze lifts to the Jumbotron, and my pulse jumps. The camera's on me and Rory. Great.

"If you get traded," I tell Rory, "we'll figure it out. We'll figure it all out. I'm not scared."

His expression is so earnest it breaks my heart. "I'm not leaving you."

"I know." I pull him closer, leaning down to kiss him. Our lips crash together and cheering breaks out in the arena. My feet are in the air, and a moment later, Rory's pulling me over the railing, setting me down, kissing me harder.

The applause turns into a roar, people hooting and

hollering as Rory's hand comes to the back of my head and he kisses me deeper. I feel his kiss all the way to my toes, warming every nerve and cell in my body. When we break apart to sneak a glance at the Jumbotron, our faces are still up there for everyone to see.

"I can't leave this team, Hazel," he whispers, worry in his eyes.

"I know."

"After the game," he says, holding my face, "we'll go talk to Ward about the trade, okay?"

I nod, and he presses another kiss to my mouth. God, I hope Ward keeps him. The idea of Rory playing for another team after everything this season feels so wrong.

"Miller, let's go," Ward calls.

Rory presses one, two, three more kisses to my mouth before pulling away, and I watch him skate to center ice for the puck drop.

For the rest of the game, my stomach is in knots while the fans murmur around us about the trade.

OUTSIDE WARD'S OFFICE, we can hear him talking on the phone, probably fielding calls from other organizations. Nausea rolls through me, but Hazel slips her hand into mine.

"Freaking out yet?" I ask.

She shakes her head, eyes steady on me. "Nope. I meant what I said about us figuring it out."

"Your studio—" I start, but she covers my mouth with her hand.

"I said we'll figure it out."

I sigh, nodding, and she replaces her hand with her mouth on mine. I think about her snapping at the security guard to back off while telling me she loved me and I feel like laughing, but then I remember that I might get sent away and leave everything good I've collected this season, and the ugly feeling in my chest hardens.

At our side, someone clears their throat, and we break apart.

My blood runs cold at the sight of the man in front of us. "Dad."

I didn't even know he was in town. He's the last person I want to see right now.

"Rory." He shifts, glancing between me and Hazel, and for the first time, he doesn't look like the stern man who raised me.

He looks worried.

Hazel stiffens, removing her hand from mine before sticking a finger in my dad's face.

"You," she says in a demonic voice. "I have a bone to pick with you."

My dad's eyes go wide.

"You're the fucking worst," Hazel spits out, stabbing her finger in the middle of his chest.

"Can I—" he starts.

"No." She pokes him again. "*I'm* talking. Your only job was to love Rory, and you fucked up, Rick. You fucked up big time."

She's terrifying.

My dad turns to me with a strange expression, eyebrows at his hairline and eyes flashing with pain. It's the expression he wore when my mom walked out, I realize, and my chest aches.

"Is that what you think?" he asks in a low voice. "That I don't love you?"

My exhale is shaky, and I swallow. "I think you love hockey."

He takes a step toward me, but Hazel moves between us. My territorial dragon, ready to strike. My hand comes to her shoulder.

"It's okay," I tell her. Nerves are spilling over inside me, but after the conversation I had with my mom today, I know I need to be more up-front with my parents. I can't run from this with him.

"I'll never be enough for you," I tell my dad, "and now you're trying to trade me away from the only team I've ever loved playing for? The only coach I've looked up to?" My heart races. "I don't want you to be my agent anymore. We want different things for me."

He looks crushed. "I thought this was what you wanted." He shakes his head, confused. "You're not playing your best anymore. When we started getting offers, I figured a new team would get you back to where you were last year."

"What, fucking miserable?" A cold laugh scrapes out of me. "I *am* playing my best, but all you care about is the points on the board."

He shakes his head again, not getting it. "I just wanted you to be at the top of the league so you'd be happy."

Something in my chest deflates with exhaustion. "That doesn't make me happy anymore. I don't know if it ever did. You want me to be you, but I'm not. I don't want to be the star anymore. It's..." I swallow. "It's lonely."

"Life is lonely," my dad says in a flat tone, like it's a fact.

Our lives are about hockey first, he said on the phone a couple months ago.

"No, it's not." My gaze goes to Hazel, and she gives me a small, supportive smile. "It doesn't have to be." Emotion hitches in my throat. "I'll never be enough for you, but I don't need your approval anymore."

I have Hazel's, and I have my own. Even if I get traded, I like the player I've become this season.

"Not enough for me?" My dad blinks at me. "You're *every-thing* to me."

"Every game, every pass, you're watching and making notes so you can call and tell me everything I've done wrong. We're done with that, though." I fold my arms over my chest. It hurts saying this.

He stares at me before he looks away. Defeat pulls tight in his features. "My dad never gave a shit about me playing hockey. It didn't matter that I played professionally or broke records."

My grandfather on his side passed when I was a baby; I

never met him, and my dad never spoke about him. My mom once mentioned that he was a professor, a workaholic, and an alcoholic. My dad runs his hand over his hair, and it's like looking in a mirror.

"I didn't want you to think I didn't care," he says quietly.

He shows it the only way he knows how. Through his eyes, I see his calls and emails in a different light. I see him wanting what *he* thinks will make me happy. "That's what Mom said."

He stills. "You talked to Nicole?"

"We're trying to patch things up." Vulnerable honesty flows out of me like water from a faucet. It's addictive, telling the truth like this.

He stares at me for a long time, frowning, regret flashing in his eyes.

"She asked about you."

"She did?"

"Yep."

A long pause. "I think about her every day."

His honesty shocks me. Rick Miller doesn't care about anything but hockey, or so I thought. "Maybe you should call her."

He shakes his head, glancing down with a hard set to his jaw. "She left me."

The corner of my mouth tilts in a sad smile because for years, I told myself she left *me*, but my dad has his own lies he tells himself.

"I compare everyone to her," he says quietly. "That's why all my relationships fall apart. No one's Nicole, and it's only a matter of time before they realize that."

My chest aches, and even though he's made me feel like I wasn't good enough for years, made me think hockey was my only value, he's still my dad.

"Call her," I tell him, "because I think she thinks about you, too."

He grunts, acknowledging but not agreeing, and the three of us stand in silence.

"Hockey's the only thing we have in common," he finally says, looking lost. "I don't know what else to talk to you about."

"Maybe we should change that."

At my side, Hazel watches, guarding me. My dad's gaze swings to her and he clears his throat.

"Hi." He sticks his hand out to her. "Rick."

"Hazel."

My dad is an intimidating guy—tall, broad, with an intense, commanding presence—but Hazel can be intimidating right back. She holds his eyes, and in her gaze, the message is clear. *Don't fuck with Rory.*

I hide a smile. I love her so fucking much.

"The physio and yoga teacher," he says with a nod. "Good to finally meet you, Hazel." He clears his throat, glancing at me. "I love you, Rory. I don't say it enough."

"You don't say it at all."

Shame passes over his features. "I want to, it's just..." His Adam's apple bobs. "Hard."

I can't imagine a guy like my grandpa told my dad he loved him.

I think about the things I've done this season—going back to the pickup league after I failed miserably, taking risks in games with the team, telling Hazel I love her.

"Hard things get easier with practice." The knot in my chest begins to loosen, and I follow my own advice. "I love you, too."

He pulls me into a hug, and while we embrace, whatever I've been missing all these years opens in my chest, taking up every inch of space.

We break apart, and he clears his throat. "I'm in town for a couple days," he says. "Maybe I can take you two for dinner." He nods to her with a serious expression that I think might be nervousness. "I'd like to get to know you better, Hazel, if that's alright."

"Of course." She smiles, any trace of anger from before gone. "Rory plays in a pickup league on Tuesday nights," she adds lightly. "I'm sure they'd love for you to drop in."

He gives me a sidelong look, arching an eyebrow. "Pickup league?"

"Mhm. It's fun."

"Fun," my dad repeats, like he isn't used to saying the word.

"You gotta pass the puck, though. No hogging the shots."

His expression turns bemused, and I snort, because watching him try to be a team player after fifty-five years of being the star is going to be a trip.

"Passing the puck," my dad murmurs. "Okay, then."

Stars score goals, but there's so much more to life than being the star.

Ward's office door opens, and my coach looks us over.

"Come on, Miller." He tilts his head into his office. "Let's talk." My dad steps forward, but Ward levels him with a hard look. "Just Rory."

My dad opens his mouth to protest, alarm in his eyes as he looks at me.

"We're not negotiating," Ward says. "He doesn't need an agent for this. I just want to talk to my player."

"It's okay," I tell my dad. "I take back what I said about you not being my agent anymore, but I want to talk to Ward alone."

He looks between me and Ward before he nods. "Okay."

I follow Ward into his office, close the door, and pray I can convince him to keep me.

BEHIND HIS DESK, Ward lets out a long sigh, closing his eyes and rubbing the bridge of his nose.

"What a fucking mess," he mutters, and I'm grateful he didn't send me to postgame press.

All the questions would have been about the trade, and my answers wouldn't have been professional.

"Alright." He folds his arms over his chest. "Let's get some things clear. I think I know the answer based on your pregame interview that's being broadcast on every sports network, but do you want to leave?"

"No." I swallow past the rock in my throat, looking Ward dead on. "I love this team. It's the first place I've ever felt like I belonged. I know I'm not playing like I did last year, I know I'm not the superstar you signed, and I'm probably not even the captain you wanted—"

"You are." He pauses. "I didn't make it easy on you this year, Miller, but I wanted to see what being captain meant to you, and who you really are." His eyes glint. "You've shown incredible progress. What you've done so far this season? It wasn't easy. I know that. I see Rick commentating, I see the headlines about you." He looks out the window at the city.

"Part of this job is learning to block out what doesn't matter and hold on to what does."

A flash of memories hits me: running up the stairs with Hazel while she shrieks with laughter, passing to the guys at the pickup league, celebrating with my team when a play worked. Telling my parents I loved them, even though it was hard.

Those are the things that matter.

"And even tonight," he goes on, "when the pressure was higher than ever to revert to your old ways, you didn't."

I considered it—ignoring the plays and taking the puck for myself, sinking it in the net to get my numbers up and show management I can be whoever they want me to be.

I can't, though. Now that I've had a taste of winning as a team, I don't want to go back.

"That being said," Ward adds, "there are three offers on the owner's desk."

My lungs feel tight, and there isn't enough air in the room. None of it matters if the owner wants to sell me. I'm either an asset or a liability. It's all money, in the end.

"Here's what I'm going to do." Ward leans forward, interlacing his fingers. "I'm going to call in a favor the owner owes me and ask to keep you, and you're going to keep up whatever you've been doing this season."

I'm hit with a tsunami of relief. I'm not leaving. It wasn't all for nothing.

"It was Hazel. She changed my life."

"You made quite a spectacle earlier." Through his exhaustion, his eyes dance with amusement.

I wince. "Sorry."

He shakes his head, smiling to himself. "It's okay. I'm happy for you, Miller. It's not every day that you find that."

"I know." I pull a deep breath in, letting the anxiety drain from me. "Thank you, coach. You don't know what this means to me."

"You have my jersey hanging in your home." He shrugs, eyes twinkling. "I can't trade a fan."

He shoots me a good-natured grin and I chuckle.

"It's not actually up yet. It's propped on the floor because I haven't had a chance to hang it."

"You put me on the floor?" He shakes his head, still smiling. "Deal's off."

We share a laugh and I think about his jersey, and his career. "Do you miss playing?"

He stills, looking down before shooting me a tight smile. "Every day, Miller. But developing players, seeing who someone can be before they realize it themselves and then *being right*? It's just as rewarding, maybe more. What you did at the League Classic, putting Owens on offense, was very interesting. Got me thinking about a few things."

Something snags in my thoughts. "Did a team make an offer because of what I did?"

His mouth flattens. "No. The offers came after the rumors started." He glances at the door. "Call Hazel in, would you?"

When I open Ward's door, Hazel jumps to her feet. My dad paces beside her, waiting.

"What did he say?" Hazel asks.

"That he's going to call in a favor to keep me."

She wraps me in a tight hug, and I relax into her as it hits me that I won't have to leave her.

"Thank god," she whispers, and I nod, rubbing her back.

"Miller, Hartley," Ward calls from his office. "Let's go."

Hazel shoots me a confused look and I take her hand, pulling her into the office. Once we're seated, Ward clears his throat.

"McKinnon has been sent back to the minors."

Hazel stiffens. That's why he wasn't there tonight. I figured he was still benched.

"Because he tried to kiss me?" she asks.

Ward lets out a heavy sigh. "No, but I should have made the call when that happened." He glances between us. "This doesn't leave this room, but he was the inside source who started the rumors. There were no offers until the rumors started."

"Shit," I murmur.

"Yeah," he says, unimpressed. "Shit. He wasn't the right fit for the team from day one but I thought," he gestures at me, "with the progress you were making, maybe he would, too. I wanted to give him the benefit of the doubt, and I thought a new group of guys he could learn from would push him to change." He rubs his jaw. "But no. My gut said he wasn't a good fit but I ignored it." He shakes his head in regret and frustration. "I'm sorry to both of you."

"It's okay." Hazel's mouth twists. "It's behind us."

He gives her a terse nod, and I wonder how long this is going to weigh on him. Hazel's hand slips into mine, and we smile at each other.

"It's late," Ward says, glancing at our joined hands. "Go home."

We say goodnight and I pull Hazel out of his office. We walk my dad to his car, and he gives me a quick, uncertain hug before climbing into the driver's side.

Hazel and I watch as he drives away, and she looks up at me with all the love and affection I've been searching for my whole life.

"Rory. I'm so proud of you."

"Thanks, baby." My chest beats with pride and elation. "Let's go home."

I'm exhausted, she's exhausted, and I intend to keep her in bed for at least twelve hours straight.

She nods, smiling, leaning on me. "Let's go home."

CHAPTER 82

HAZEL

THE NEXT MORNING, weak winter sun filters in through the windows of Rory's bedroom while we lie in bed. I'm lying on him, listening to his heartbeat as his chest rises and falls with his steady breathing.

"Move in with me," he murmurs as I trail my fingers up and down his flat stomach. The dragon tattoo on his ribs is mostly healed.

I lift my head and look into his crushing blue eyes, a knot of emotion in my throat. "You think?"

He nods.

"It's soon." I bite my lip.

"Is it?" A smile quirks up on his mouth. "It doesn't feel too soon to me."

I picture myself living here, waking up beside Rory every day. The images are seamless and filled with joy.

"Yeah." My brow wrinkles. "I guess you're right."

Excitement whistles through me as I let my imagination run wild: hosting dinners with our friends and family, curling up on the couch together, sitting in the hot tub on the patio overlooking the city and telling each other about our day.

My gaze comes to him, and I smile. "Okay."

"Just like that?" His eyes spark with teasing surprise. "Okay? I don't even need to convince you?"

"Nope." I grin wider. "I'm in. I'm all in."

His eyes warm with affection. "Finally."

My heart squeezes, and I give him a soft kiss.

"Are you sore from yesterday's game?" I ask.

"A little."

"Turn over."

Rory groans as he rolls onto his stomach, and I sit on top of him, kneading up and down his spine, searching for muscle tightness. Between his shoulder blades, the muscles are tense and knotted.

"There." I dig my thumb into the tight muscle.

His low, tortured groan is muffled by the pillow. "You're evil."

"Shut up and take it," I say, laughing, and I can see him grinning.

"I love it when you're mean to me, Hartley."

I bring my lips to his back and give him another soft, affectionate kiss. "I know."

He lets me rub his back for about sixty seconds before he flips over with a mischievous look. I straddle his hips, running my hands up and down his hard chest, and beneath me, he's fully erect.

"Bet I can make you come without touching your clit."

I let out a high laugh of disbelief. "Your ego is ridiculous, Miller."

His brows go up, and that teasing spark in his eyes sends heat racing through me. "Aren't you a little curious? Where's that competitive spirit, Hartley?"

He pulls my t-shirt off, leaving me in just my panties. His eyes heat as his hands cover my breasts, callouses scraping over my skin and making me shiver in delight.

"Perfect tits," he murmurs, staring at me with hunger.

The way he toys with my nipples goes straight to my clit. Arousal stirs, dampening my panties.

"What's the bet?" I ask, trailing my finger over his ridged chest and stomach. "Anything you want?"

He shakes his head and pulls me to him, kissing my neck.

"I already have everything I want. This one's just to prove you wrong."

Holding me against him, he pulls my panties aside and drags his fingers over my seam. Pleasure arcs through me, and I moan against his strong shoulder.

"I already have everything I want, too." My voice is thin as heat gathers between my legs.

"I know, baby." He pushes a big finger inside me and my muscles clench on him. "Hazel," he says like a curse. "You're so wet."

His lips find mine and our kiss is frantic, desperate, consuming. I'm overwhelmed with sensations—with his stubble against my face, his tongue stroking mine, his second finger pushing inside me, making my head spin, and his hard, strong body beneath mine. His cock pressing against me with urgency.

"Need you," I mutter, and my hands move clumsily as I reach for his cock, pushing his boxers down.

He nods, and my panties disappear. He lines himself up, and my heart jumps at the look in his eyes—so full of love and need and awe.

I sink down onto him and we moan together. The sharp stretch around his thick length sends fire through my body.

"You're everything to me," I sigh as I sink farther, until he's in to the hilt. The first burst of sparks goes off at the base of my spine, and I drag my teeth over his chest as my pulse whooshes in my ears.

"I love you so fucking much," he grits out, jaw tight, and

with his hands spanning my waist, he begins to move me back and forth on his cock.

Not up and down. Back and forth, and—

"Oh, *fuck*." Desire surges through me, tightening and spiraling. "Rory."

He crooks a wicked, lazy grin up at me, watching in fascination as he moves me on him. It's like he knows his cock is hitting the exact right spot.

"Lean forward a bit," he whispers.

I do, and when my clit slides against his base, my jaw goes slack.

His mouth hitches. "There we go."

"You're the evil one," I gasp as a wave of heat sweeps through me.

Rory moves me faster, biceps flexing. I never stood a chance. The flutters start, and his eyes flare hot like he feels them.

"Let go," he rasps, eyes bright. "Let go for me and let me win."

The noise that slips out of me is half-frustration, half-defeat because I'm already tightening up. The pressure rises and I bite my lip to hold in the moan, but the way he's hitting my G-spot is too good, the way he's rubbing my clit with his body is too perfect. I can't hold off.

"Oh god." I pitch forward, shaking and tensing on Rory as my release hits me. I'm mindless as stark pleasure hurtles through me, nails digging into his muscles. Wave after wave radiates through me and my teeth sink into his shoulder while I hold on tight.

"I need to come," he grits out and I nod feverishly.

"Come with me," I beg.

Inside me, he swells, and his hips jerk upward, pounding into me, before he groans my name and stiffens. Through the last tremors of my orgasm, I memorize how his lips part, how he looks at me with desperation and love, how he holds me tight like he'll never let me go.

We drift back down to earth with our hearts pounding, me pressing kisses to his neck, his cheeks, his lips.

"Told you," he murmurs, and I laugh against his mouth.

"I guess we both won."

He sighs happily before he takes a deep breath and sits up. "Okay, Hartley. No more lazing around. We've got a big day ahead of us."

I roll onto my back and kick him away when he tries to pull me out of bed. "You don't have practice today."

He tilts a grin down at me. "We need to move you in."

"Today?"

He nods. "Today, Hartley. I finally got you to say yes, and I'm not waiting a second longer."

My heart explodes with love, and I shriek with laughter as he lifts me out of bed, hauls me over his shoulder, and carries me to the shower.

"Unless you've changed your mind."

"Never."

I'm still laughing, still squirming over his shoulder as he turns the water on. He sets me on my feet and I loop my arms around his neck, gazing up at my handsome, unhinged hockey player.

"I'm keeping you, Rory Miller."

EPILOGUE
RORY

ONE MONTH *later*

"This studio will be used for dance classes," Hazel says, leading the party into the second room.

Hazel got possession of her studio yesterday, and today we're having a party in the space to celebrate. The sign isn't finished yet but her website and social media is up, and gaining momentum and interest.

Ember Studios. Spark your love of movement.

Everyone is here—her family, my family, the Storm players, the team staff, and her yoga students. Someone turns the music up, champagne is popped, and people wander over to the big windows overlooking the North Shore Mountains, talking and laughing.

At my side, Hazel smiles with a wistful look, like she can't believe it's real.

I know exactly how she feels. I'm still pinching myself that Hazel Hartley fell for me.

"I'm so proud of you, Hartley." I press one, two, three kisses against her mouth. "So proud."

"Thanks." Her palms flatten on my chest and she gazes up at me, biting her lip. "I love you."

I would have thought the thrill of hearing it so often would wear off, but no. Every fucking time Hazel Hartley tells me she loves me is the best moment of my life. "I love you, too. So fucking much, Hazel. You have no idea."

Her smile turns teasing. "I have *some* idea."

The grin I give her is pure arrogance. This morning, we played the *how many times can Hazel come before begging for mercy* game, and I've been thinking about it all day. Especially the part where she got on her knees and sucked my cock so well I'm pretty sure my soul left my body.

"You sure?" My lips brush her neck, and she shudders. "Because just say the word and I'll remind you."

"Cocky." She smiles. "So fucking cocky."

I press another kiss to her neck, addicted to her. "You know it."

My parents appear in front of us, and we straighten up.

"Congratulations, honey," my mom says, wrapping Hazel in a big hug, and when she pulls away, my dad gives Hazel a firm handshake.

"Great job, Hazel."

She grins. "Thanks, Rick."

He steps back beside my mom and takes her hand, holding on like she might get away again. My mom meets my eye before smiling down at their joined hands.

Seeing my parents holding hands is still a little weird. They never did it before, but they never went to couples' therapy either, or went on date nights or smiled at each other the way they do now.

I've gone a few times with them to therapy. Slowly, we're putting our family back together in a better way than before.

"Hazel said you're a dancer," my mom says to Hazel's mom. They all met last night when Hazel and I took our families out for dinner.

"Oh." She blanches but recovers, laughing a little. "I'm not the dancer I used to be." Her throat works and Hazel gives her an encouraging smile. "But it's just for fun, even if I don't look like I used to."

Hazel beams, eyes shining bright. "Exactly."

Our moms make plans to have lunch later in the week while Ken and my dad pull Streicher into a conversation and Pippa and Owens wander over from the group of players.

"Look at this place!" Pippa practically jumps on Hazel, hugging her. "It looks so good."

Hazel sighs as they pull apart, looking around the space with that sparkling, wistful expression again. Over the past month, she's put every spare moment into her studio plans.

"Thanks." Her mouth twists and she glances at me and Owens. "I'm glad I made the decision to stay on with the team part time, though, even if it's busy."

When Hazel put in her resignation so she could start studio renovations, Ward must have seen her reluctance to leave a position she loved, so he made her an offer. Part time, as many or as few players to work with as she wants, and flexible hours. Streicher, Owens, and Volkov all volunteered to come to her studio for physio sessions, which made her decision easy.

"Aw." Owens gives her a bear hug, lifting her off her feet. "We're going to miss you at the arena."

She chuckles. "You'll see me at games. I'll be the one wearing Miller's jersey."

We smile at each other, and my heart beats with pride and affection.

Owens's phone rings and he pulls it out, frowning. "Darce?" He steps away, still frowning as he listens.

Hazel and I exchange a look. Owens has been uncharacteristically quiet in the past month, and I know it's because Kit and Darcy got engaged on New Year's.

When he returns, worry is written all over his face.

"Everything okay?" I ask.

"I don't know." He blinks, shell-shocked. "Darcy and Kit broke up."

Hazel, Pippa, and I fall silent. Owens stares at the floor, distracted, before he shakes himself.

"I need to go," he tells Hazel. "Congrats on the studio."

He gives her a quick hug before hurrying out the door, and the three of us watch him leave.

"Where's he going?" Pippa asks.

Hazel shrugs. "I'm not sure."

My conversation with Owens back at the bar the night I got my dragon tattoo is hazy, but I remember the basics, so I clamp my mouth shut and don't say a fucking word. Like they smell blood in the water, Hazel and Pippa whirl on me, cornering me.

"What do you know?" Hazel asks, gaze boring into me.

I put my hands up like I'm innocent. "Nothing."

"He's lying." Pippa's eyes narrow, but she's smiling.

"He's absolutely lying." Hazel runs her tongue along her bottom lip like she's thinking of all the ways she can use her mouth to torture the information out of me later.

I don't know whether it's a good or bad thing that I have plans for us after this.

"Streicher," I call. He looks over, mouth twitching in amusement when he spots the Hartley sisters interrogating me. "Your fiancée needs another drink," I say, testing the word out.

I like the way it sounds. I think I might start using it myself soon.

Streicher pulls Pippa away. She mouths *I will find you* while Hazel and I laugh, and I slip my arm around Hazel's shoulder while we take in the party—our families, our friends, our people.

"Is it everything you expected so far, Hartley?"

She smiles, looking so happy and at peace. "Miller, it is everything and more."

―――――

"We're going to get in trouble," Hazel hisses late that night as we sneak into the dim outdoor rink near our apartment, lit only by the moon and the stars.

"We're not going to get in trouble." I sit her down on a nearby bench and start lacing up her skates.

The staff know we're here because I arranged for this months ago. They know to stay out of sight, though, because that would blow the surprise.

I move to my own skates, and Hazel gazes at the stars with a wistful smile. "Every time I look up at the stars on a cold night like this, I think about skating outside after the League Classic."

When she turns to me, holding her hand out with that searing look of adoration, I think my heart might burst.

I press a quick kiss to her mouth but pull away. "Hold on a second," I murmur before heading to the control box the staff showed me and flicking the switch labeled RORY.

Around the boards, twinkle lights illuminate, bathing the rink in warm, sparkling light.

Hazel stills, a tiny smile curling up on her mouth. "Rory."

"Hazel." I make my way back to her, holding a hand out.

With my heart beating up into my throat, I help her onto the ice and we glide, hand in hand. My focus is torn between the way her hair flutters in the wind, how her eyes glitter in this lighting, and the velvet box in my jacket pocket.

I spin her and she laughs, clutching my hands.

"I've been thinking," I start, pulse beating hard in my ears.

She sends me a curious glance.

"You have your studio now, I'm with the team for probably the rest of my career,"—I signed a seven-year contract a few days after the trade rumor fiasco—"and we share a home."

Curiosity and amusement rise in her expression.

"What's next, Hartley?"

I wait for her response, listening to the sound of our skates hitting the ice.

"I love your smile," she says on a happy sigh. "I love it so much, I think about it all the time."

A chuckle slips out of me. "You didn't answer me."

"You're going to ask me to marry you," she says, lifting her chin and looking me in the eye.

Butterflies burst into motion in my stomach and I suck in a deep breath, narrowing my eyes at her, teasing her. "Yeah?"

"Mhm." She looks so confident, so certain. "Rory, I saw the ring. And now this?" She smiles wider.

"You saw the ring?" My eyebrows shoot up, but I'm grinning.

"I didn't mean to find it. Honestly."

"Did you like it?" I dragged Pippa and Streicher to the jeweler about ten times to make sure the white gold band with a cluster of rare blue-gray diamonds was perfect, but if she doesn't like it, I'll toss it out the window and get her whatever she likes.

"Yes," she says quietly, throat working as she glances at me. "I loved it."

"It isn't too flashy?"

She rolls her eyes. "It is, but—" She laughs, shrugging. "It reminds me of you."

A sly, arrogant grin hitches on my mouth. "Huge, expensive, and gorgeous?"

She shakes her head, smiling ear to ear, and my heart lifts up into the starry sky. "Yes. All those things. Also," her smile softens and she swallows, "one in a million. Perfect for me. Everything I didn't realize I wanted."

"It isn't too soon?"

I know I'm reckless and impulsive and we should probably date for at least a year before getting engaged, but Hazel's it for me.

Again, she smiles to herself, shaking her head. "Not for us."

I hum, nodding with a casual air like I'm not brimming with emotion. "So, say I ask you to marry me. Then what?"

Her eyes soften. "Then I'll say yes."

I move so I'm facing her, skating backward, and when my hands come to her hips, I slow us to a stop, gazing down into her stunning blue-gray eyes. "You sure about that?"

"Never been more sure of anything in my life."

"You can change your mind."

She smiles. "I won't."

"I won't, either."

"I know."

She tracks my hand as I slip the box from my pocket, and when I kneel, her eyes shine.

"Hazel Hartley, will you make my goddamned life and marry me?"

Her smile? It's everything, and I'll remember this moment forever.

"Yes, Rory Miller, I will."

I take her left hand and slip the outrageous sparkling ring onto her finger before I stand and kiss the woman I love. The woman who made me into the best version of myself. The woman I fell head over heels for years ago, and who's finally caught up.

The woman I can't wait to live the rest of my life with. Get married to. Have kids with. Grandkids.

"I love you," she whispers against my lips.

"I love you, too, Hartley, and I'll never let you forget it."

———

To read the bonus scene of Rory and Hazel's wedding (and wedding night!) and get hints about future characters, sign up for Stephanie's newsletter at www.stephaniearcherauthor. com/rory or scan the QR code below:

Hayden and Darcy's book is next, but in the meantime, check out the Queen's Cove series, a small town series with four hot brothers, loads of tension, big laughs, and some serious spicy praise. Keep reading for an excerpt of **The Wrong Mr. Right**, a spice-coaching She's All That style rom-com with a hot surfer and shy bookstore owner.

THE WRONG MR. RIGHT EXCERPT

"So you kissed him and there was no chemistry." Wyatt raked his hand through his hair, mouth in a hard line.

"Kissed him? No." I made a noise of frustration. "We never got that far. I spent the entire date talking about—" I broke off before I said something embarrassing.

"Talking about what, bookworm?" His dark gaze was back on me.

I shook my head, pressing my mouth closed.

He took another step toward me and I backed up, the backs of my knees hitting the bed. "Talking. About. What."

I threw my hands up. "You. Talking about you. Oh my god. You're so pushy." I rolled my eyes, when really, my heart raced, my skin tingled, and nipples pinched hard. I had all this energy and nowhere for it to go.

I put my hands on his chest to push him back a step but he grabbed my wrists. A smug grin grew on his features. Paired with his dark gaze, the effect was hypnotic.

"Me?" He raised his eyebrows, cocking his head. His hands scorched my wrists. It was like he ran hotter than normal people. Maybe that was why he was never cold in the water.

I rolled my eyes again. "You came up in conversation because of the surf lessons."

"Right. Because of the surf lessons." His gaze stayed glued on me, still heated. "So you didn't kiss him because it didn't feel right?"

I gave him another tiny nod.

"Interesting." His thumb brushed my wrist as if he didn't realize he was doing it. It sent tingles up and down my arm, making it hard to breathe. That could have been from his proximity, too. Or how he smelled freaking incredible.

He exhaled through his nose, and a muscle in his jaw ticked. "Are you disappointed?" His chest rumbled against my hands as he spoke.

I chewed my lip. "No. Beck's nice—" His hands clenched my wrists at the mention of his name. "—but he's just a friend." I swallowed and met his gaze. "I was looking forward to making out with someone tonight, but I don't want to do it with the wrong person."

Well, *that* sounded suggestive. Wyatt's eyebrow ticked up, still watching me with that dark gaze, and a shiver rolled down my spine. His warm hands seared my wrists. My heart hammered in my chest. I inhaled a shaky breath but it caught in my throat when Wyatt pressed his fingers into my wrist.

"Your pulse," he murmured.

I nodded again. Another flutter through my core, another clench around nothing.

He watched my face with heavy-lidded eyes. "It's been a long time since you've kissed someone, bookworm."

Another nod from me.

"I don't want you to be out of practice." His gaze dropped to my mouth and he cleared his throat. "You know, for when you meet the right person."

"Right. I don't want to be out of practice either."

I swallowed again, watching the curve of Wyatt's mouth, noticing the rise and fall of his chest against my hands. My hands tensed, my nails dug into him, and his breath caught.

"So we should practice." I lifted a shoulder in a half-shrug. Casual, so casual. Like Wyatt.

He frowned like he was torn. He glanced from me to the window, then back to me, then to the bed behind me. My core clenched hard again and I almost whimpered. My underwear was wet. That *never* happened, and definitely not from standing beside a guy for a few minutes.

I watched his mouth again. I wanted a taste of him. Just one. That would be enough.

You know what? Screw this.

I raised up on my tip toes and kissed Wyatt.

Read The Wrong Mr. Right in KU, paperback, or audio!

AUTHOR'S NOTE

Thank you for reading *The Fake Out*! If you enjoyed, I'd love if you could write me a review. Reviews help readers find books they love.

I feel a little sad letting these two go. Rory and Hazel have probably been my favorite characters to date. There's a quote on The Office that I love: "I wish there was a way to know you're in the good old days before you've actually left them." I'm already excited to write Hayden and Darcy's book, but Rory and Hazel will forever own a piece of my heart.

The inspiration behind Hazel's dream of a body-positive fitness studio is one of my best friends, Helen Camisa, the owner of Fat and Happy Yoga. Helen's one of those people you immediately fall in love with, because she's hilarious, wise, and compassionate. When Hazel says things like "you deserve to feel good in your body" and "it's okay to enjoy food," that's Helen telling me every body is beautiful, and fuck what our media tells us. Helen, I'm so fucking lucky to know you. This book is a love letter to you and the work you do.

My author friends, Grace Reilly, Brittany Kelley, Olivia Hayle, and Lily Gold, and Maggie North. Thank you for helping to shape this story into the best it can be and for providing guidance and laughs in this incredible career path.

My real life friends (lol), Sarah, Alanna, Anthea, Bryan: thank you for holding my hand, championing me, and letting me be my weird self.

Many thanks to my hilarious beta readers, Maggie, Esther, Wren, Jess, Marcie, Brett, Callan, and Nicole, who cracked me up with their comments and made this story so much better.

Thank you to Becca Hensley Mysoor for your wise and enthusiastic guidance on Rory and Hazel, and for the genius idea of the wildly overpriced crystal dragon.

And for my husband, the most gentle, kind, patient human I've ever met who makes me laugh harder than anyone. My books are filled with love because I write them thinking about you.

And lastly, my beloved readers! Thank you for reading my books, for telling your friends and your sisters and your moms, for posting about them on social media, for your lovely emails and DMs, and for letting me live my dream!

Until next time,

Steph

ALSO BY STEPHANIE ARCHER

Vancouver Storm Series

Behind the Net (Jamie and Pippa)

The Fake Out (Rory and Hazel)

Queen's Cove Series

That Kind of Guy (Emmett and Avery)

The Wrong Mr. Right (Wyatt and Hannah)

In Your Dreams, Holden Rhodes (Holden and Sadie)

Finn Rhodes Forever (Finn and Olivia)

Standalone Romantic Comedies

The Heartbreak Rule

ABOUT THE AUTHOR

Stephanie Archer writes spicy, laugh-out-loud romance. She believes in the power of best friends, stubborn women, a fresh haircut, and love. She lives in Vancouver with a man and a dog.

instagram.com/stephaniearcherauthor
tiktok.com/@stephaniearcherbooks